Cat in a
Leopard Spot

By Carole Nelson Douglas from Tom Doherty Associates

MYSTERY

MIDNIGHT LOUIE MYSTERIES
Catnap
Pussyfoot
Cat on a Blue Monday
Cat in a Crimson Haze
Cat in a Diamond Dazzle
Cat with an Emerald Eye
Cat in a Flamingo Fedora
Cat in a Golden Garland
Cat on a Hyacinth Hunt
Cat in an Indigo Mood
Cat in a Jeweled Jumpsuit
Cat in a Kiwi Con
Cat in a Leopard Spot

Midnight Louie's Pet Detectives (anthology)

IRENE ADLER ADVENTURES
Good Night, Mr. Holmes
Good Morning, Irene
Irene at Large
Irene's Last Waltz
Marilyn: Shades of Blonde (anthology)

HISTORICAL ROMANCE
*Amberleigh**
*Lady Rogue**
Fair Wind, Fiery Star

SCIENCE FICTION
*Probe**
*Counterprobe**

FANTASY

TALISWOMAN
Cup of Clay
Seed upon the Wind

SWORD AND CIRCLET
Keepers of Edanvant
Heir of Rengarth
Seven of Swords

*also mystery

Cat in a Leopard Spot

A MIDNIGHT LOUIE MYSTERY

Carole Nelson Douglas

FORGE®

A Tom Doherty Associates Book
New York

CAT IN A LEOPARD SPOT

This book is printed on acid-free paper.

A Forge Book
Published by Tom Doherty Associates, LLC
175 Fifth Avenue
New York, NY 10010

www.tor.com

Forge® is a registered trademark of Tom Doherty Associates, LLC.

Library of Congress Cataloging-in-Publication Data

Douglas, Carole Nelson.
    Cat in a leopard spot : a Midnight Louie mystery / Carole Nelson Douglas.—1st ed.
        p.cm.
    "A Tom Doherty Associates book."
    ISBN 0-312-85370-X (acid-free paper)
    1. Midnight Louie (Fictitious character)—fiction. 2. Barr, Temple (Fictitious character)—Fiction. 3. Public relations consultants—Fiction. 4. Women cat owners—Fiction. 5. Las Vegas (Nev.)—Fiction. 6. Cats—Fiction. I. Title.

PS3554.O8237 C2765 2001
813'.54—dc21

                                                    00-047711

First Edition: April 2001

Printed in the United States of America

0 9 8 7 6 5 4 3 2 1

For all defenders and rescuers of creatures great and small.
You know who you are, and you know what you do,
and why it matters so much.
And the animals know it too.

Contents

Previously in Midnight Louie's Lives and Times . . .   13

Prologue: Caged Heat   16

Chapter 1:   Caged   18

Chapter 2:   Bad News Breakfast   25

Chapter 3:   News Flush   34

Chapter 4:   A Wolf in Sheep's Clothing   37

Chapter 5:   Magic Act   47

Chapter 6:   Sister Act   54

Chapter 7:   A PR in PI Clothing   58

Chapter 8:   Portrait   70

Chapter 9:   Heads or Tails?   77

Chapter 10:   Animal Instincts   79

Chapter 11:   Portrait of a Shady Lady   101

Chapter 12:   Caged Meat   115

Chapter 13:   Trial and Error   117

Chapter 14:   Heaven Scent   122

Chapter 15:   Hussy Fit   124

Chapter 16:   Hissy Fit   134

Chapter 17:   Judgment Day   140

Chapter 18:   Day of the Jekyll   143

Chapter 19:   Sketched in Suspicion   149

Chapter 20:   Feast   156

Chapter 21: Taxidermy Eyes 161

Chapter 22: Likely Suspects 170

Chapter 23: Déjà Vu 179

Chapter 24: Chuck Wagon 184

Chapter 25: Guilt-Edged Invitation 189

Chapter 26: Polishing Off the Past 194

Chapter 27: Cousins Under the Skin 204

Chapter 28: K as in Karrot Stick 207

Chapter 29: Damage Control 217

Chapter 30: Ringed In 230

Chapter 31: Elvis Leaves the Building 232

Chapter 32: Animal Wrongs 234

Chapter 33: Track of the Cat 247

Chapter 34: Calling on Agatha 254

Chapter 35: Tiger Paws 268

Chapter 36: Synth You Went Away . . . 278

Chapter 37: Human Error 290

Chapter 38: Murder Wears a New Face 294

Chapter 39: Collusion Course 297

Chapter 40: Calling the Cops 312

Chapter 41: Hunt Club 314

Chapter 42: Secret Witness, Silent Witness 318

Chapter 43: The Black and Blue Max 324

Chapter 44: Pretty Please Don't! 327

Chapter 45: The Most Dangerous Dame 331

Chapter 46: Stalemate 334

Chapter 47:   Dead Ahead   337

Chapter 48:   Men in Beige   339

Chapter 49:   Bless Me, Mother   344

Chapter 50:   Action Traction   355

Chapter 51:   Cops in Khaki   359

Chapter 52:   AnticliMax   364

Chapter 53:   Cat Burglar   372

Tailpiece: Midnight Louie Enjoys Being a Pussycat   376

              Carole Nelson Douglas Considers Louie's Future   379

Cat in a Leopard Spot

Midnight Louie's Lives and Times . . .

As a serial killer–finder in a multivolume mystery series (not to mention a primo mouthpiece), I want to update my readers old and new on past crimes and present tensions.

None can deny that the Las Vegas crime scene is a pretty busy place, and I have been treading these mean neon streets for thirteen books now. When I call myself an "alphacat," some think I am merely asserting my natural feline male dominance. But no, I refer to the fact that since I debuted in *Catnap* and *Pussyfoot*, I then commenced to a title sequence that is as sweet and simple as B to Z.

That is when I begin *my* alphabet, with the *B* in *Cat on a Blue Monday*. From then on, the color word in the title is in alphabetical order up to the current volume, *Cat in a Leopard Spot*.

Since I associate with a multifarious and nefarious crew of human beings, and since Las Vegas is littered with guidebooks as well as bodies, I wish to provide a guide to the local landmarks on my particular map of the world. A cast of characters, so to speak:

To wit, my lovely roommate and high-heel devotee, freelance PR ace Miss Temple Barr, who has reunited with her only love . . .

the once missing-in-action magician Mr. Max Kinsella, who has good reason for invisibility: years of international counterterrorism work after his cousin Sean died in a bomb attack in Ireland during a post-high-school jaunt to the Old Sod . . .

but Mr. Max is sought by another dame, homicide lieutenant C. R. Molina, who is the mother of preteen Mariah . . .

and the good friend of Miss Temple's recent good friend, Mr. Matt Devine, a radio talk-show shrink who not long ago was a Roman Catholic priest and has tracked down his abusive stepfather, Mr. Cliff Effinger . . .

which did not delight Matt's mother in Chicago, who is emerging from her unhappy past and desperately seeking Matt's real father, purportedly long dead in Vietnam.

Speaking of untimely pasts, Lieutenant Carmen Molina is not thrilled that her former flame, Mr. Rafi Nadir, the unsuspecting father of Mariah, is in Las Vegas taking on shady muscle jobs after blowing his career on the LAPD . . .

or that Mr. Max Kinsella is hunting Rafi himself because the lieutenant blackmailed him into tailing her ex. While so engaged, Mr. Max's attempted rescue of a pathetic young stripper soon found her dead . . . and Mr. Rafi Nadir looks like the prime suspect.

Meanwhile, Mr. Matt has drawn a stalker, the local girl that young Max and his cousin Sean boyishly competed for in that long-ago Ireland . . .

one Kathleen O'Connor, for years an IRA operative who seduced rich men for guns and roses for the cause. She is deservedly christened by Temple as Kitty the Cutter . . .

and—finding Max impossible to trace—has settled for harassing with tooth and claw the nearest innocent bystander, Mr. Matt Devine . . .

while he tries to recover from his crush on Miss Temple, his neighbor at the Circle Ritz condominiums, when Mr. Max was

AWOL by not very boldly seeking new women, all of whom are now in danger from said Kitty the Cutter.

This human stuff is all very complex, but luckily my life is much simpler, revolving around a quest for union with . . .

the Divine Yvette, a shaded silver Persian beauty I filmed some cat food commercials with before being wrongfully named in a paternity suit by her airhead actress mistress . . .

Miss Savannah Ashleigh, whose brutal measures against me resulted in a lawsuit filed by my dear roommate Miss Temple . . .

who is unaware that my unacknowledged daughter . . .

Miss Midnight Louise, has been insinuating herself into my cases, along with the professional drug- and bomb-sniffing Maltese dog, Nose E., or—when he is not available—most unsuitable substitutes . . .

or that I have had a running battle of wits with the evil Siamese Hyacinth, first met as the onstage assistant to the mysterious lady magician . . .

Shangri-La, who made off with Miss Temple's semiengagement ring from Mr. Max during an onstage trick and who has not been seen since except in sinister glimpses . . .

just like the Synth, an ancient cabal of magicians that may take contemporary credit for the ambiguous death of Mr. Max's mentor in magic, the Great Gandolph, and the GG's former lady assistant, not to mention a professor of the metaphysical killed in cultlike surroundings among strange symbols, Jefferson Mangel.

Well, there you have it. The usual human stew, all mixed up and at odds with each other and within themselves. Obviously, it is up to me to solve all their mysteries and nail a few crooks along the way. Like Las Vegas, the City That Never Sleeps, Midnight Louie, private eye, also has a sobriquet: the Kitty That Never Sleeps.

With this crew, who could?

Caged Heat

The big cat kneaded, kneaded, kneaded its clipped claws into a huge pillow covered in plush leopard print.

Its long, spotted body lay in leafy shadow, blending with the dried mesquite leaves beneath its splayed hind legs.

Distant security lights cast urine yellow puddles on the varying terrain the big cat called home. Like walls, sheer slick stucco cliffs enclosed areas of thick, glossy tropical greenery, rocks where mini-waterfalls plashed into deep and drinkable pools, and desert scrub with ready-made dirt wallows where the sun would heat earth and fur into one harmonious purring, simmering mass.

He lived alone, the big cat, except for the birds of passage that paused in the higher branches of his compound, but he answered to the name of Osiris. It was called by those who fed him and played with him and took him away every nightfall to a vast, confusing place where he performed tricks in other, cooler pools of light.

Osiris's sharp shoulder blades shifted as he bent to groom one massive paw, huge canine teeth gnawing matted tufts of hair between the pads. He knew this life and accepted it. Sometimes he would meet others of his kind who performed the same rituals he did. They understood each other and walked softly around their scents and space, except for an occasional growling match. They too had clipped or even missing claws on their forepaws, and were more likely to hit than slash.

The big cat rolled over, stretching long and lithe. His neat ears flicked backward. Did he hear the brush of a footfall on a dry leaf, a rustle in the night? He turned, his expanded pupils studying shades of gray, most of them familiar.

He twisted and vaulted to his feet. Something came.

A warning growl warmed his throat, soft but escalating.

Something moved. He moved as swiftly.

And felt a sting in his shoulder, sharp as a cactus thorn, but with a burn that didn't ease after first prick. No, this pain dug in deeper and wider, until his whole big frame felt as soft as the pillow he had been pummeling. He collapsed bonelessly beside it like a litter mate, lost to the night and his own senses. Dead to the world.

Chapter 1

Caged

At 2:00 A.M. Matt Devine stepped outside the radio station, glad to find the parking lot deserted for once. What a guilty, if rare, pleasure. Staying an hour after his radio show ended meant that the loyal fans who gathered to greet him at 1:00 A.M. had given up and gone away.

He took a deep, liberating breath. Signing photos for fans in the wee hours was not a favorite part of his radio-shrink job.

Only four vehicles squatted on the otherwise empty parking lot. Each hugged a light pole, parked by staff members who knew they'd be the last to leave and wanted as much light as possible against the dangers of the lonely night.

Wanting as much light as possible against the dangers of the lonely night. Sounded just like what his call-in clients craved.

Matt grimaced. Life was a metaphor, especially when you earned your living as a radio shrink. Still, he glanced carefully around. There was one particular "fan" he hoped never to see again. She made a habit of jumping him after he got off work in the wee hours, both here at WCOO and before that at ConTact, the hot line counseling service where he'd honed his phone advice technique.

Each parked vehicle reminded Matt of its owner: the producer/radio personality known as Ambrosia's late '70s red Cadillac convertible; Dwight the technician's beat-up minivan; Keith's decidedly downscale aging Toyota hatchback with its spindly tires about as wide as a '60s necktie and that's all.

Then there was his transportation.

Locked and tilted toward one of the sentinel parking lot lights the Hesketh Vampire's convoluted silver silhouette looked like it belonged in a movie. The British custom motorcycle was borrowed wheels, but it could make a faster escape than the Volkswagen Beetle that was recently his, courtesy of Elvis. Or Elvis's ghost. Or one of Elvis's whacked-out impersonators. Or fans.

After his most recent unscheduled encounter with the woman Temple had nicknamed—*Ouch!* "nick" was the name of her game, all right—Kitty the Cutter, Matt felt safer with the 'cycle's speed and agility, although more exposed on the bike than in a car. He still wasn't sure that the phantom biker he glimpsed now and again wasn't Miss Kitty. Then again, it might not be. If not, who was it? How about a ghost?

Matt smiled at his own fears. Monsters and ghosts. He was acting like a kid scaring himself with the dark. Except that it was indeed dark at this hour, and getting darker. Another metaphor.

He stopped thinking, an occupational hazard in both the radio talk-show game and his old vocation of priest, and went over to the streetlight-turned spotlight to unlock the bike, don his helmet and gloves, then spur the metal steed into the dull roar that would soon become a whine as it hit the streets and cruising speed.

Like any performer coming down from a late-night show, Matt was in no hurry to head home to the Circle Ritz.

He found himself pondering the mysteries of human, and more often inhuman, behavior after an hour of hearing everybody's miseries. Now he had his own lethal mysteries to ponder. The current crop made his recent search for his lost stepfather look like a cakewalk. Poor Effinger, the ultimate loser; outclassed by an uppity hit-woman.

At least he assumed that was what Kitty O'Connor was. An odd, sadistically seductive hit woman, with a modus operandi of introducing herself to her victims. And, in his case, she had an even odder price. Or was it only his case? Was he part of a longtime pattern with her?

She had been Max Kinsella's Waterloo years ago, when he was still a teenage tourist propelled into the lethal jig that politics, bombs, and the IRA had played for decades in Ireland. Now Kinsella, all grown up, was Matt's personal bane, ever since he'd come back and taken Temple back, not that Matt had ever had her. It was easy to blame Max for Kitty's brutal entrance into his own life. And wrong.

Wanting to resent Kinsella for every loss in his life, Matt tended to overlook one key fact: Kathleen O'Connor had first approached him during his hunt for Effinger. To this day, she still didn't seem to know that Matt had become infatuated with Temple while Kinsella was among the missing. So Kitty was stalking him long before she could suspect any connection between him and Max, via Temple. She still seemed blind to the faint outlines of a former romantic triangle, and Matt would do anything to keep it that way. Temple must be protected at all costs. That was probably the only issue he and Kinsella would agree on.

The howl of the Vampire's famously loud motor mimicked the chaos of his thoughts. The bike almost took its head like a willful steed. Soon the powerful motor was idling in another parking lot, this one utterly empty, except for the cold puddles of blue-green night lights.

A large, low building huddled like a bunker in the moonlight.

Matt locked the bike, hung the silver moon of his helmet on one handlebar, where it reflected its twin sister in the sky. Then he ambled across soundless asphalt to the sidewalks leading into the man-made Garden of Eden beyond the building.

Well, part Garden of Eden, he corrected himself. The other part of the Ethel M candy company's famous cactus collection was Garden of Gethsemane. Garden of thorns. Where Jesus had spent his last hours before submitting to the mockery of trial, torture, and death.

Naturally, an ex-priest in Las Vegas needed to find someplace lone, harsh, and absolutely natural for contemplation. The area was meant for self-guided tours, kind of like life itself, and was a no-man's-land at this hour, even in around-the-clock Las Vegas: 24/7, like they said.

Everywhere was getting onto Las Vegas time nowadays: twenty-four hours a day, seven days a week. Somewhere in that blur of time, Sunday had been swallowed up. Were God interested in creating Las Vegas, which Matt was pretty sure He would pass on, as He had on Sodom and Gomorrah, He'd probably skip taking the seventh day of rest off. Las Vegas and the Internet never slept.

Matt's footsteps ground slightly against the paved walks someone had slipped into his Garden of Woe when he wasn't looking.

When he'd first moved to Las Vegas, straight from leaving the priesthood, Matt had come here often, especially in the punishing summer heat. It reminded him of Jesus' forty days in the wilderness before he began his ministry, and struck him as fitting that he should tarry in a cactus garden at the end of his own ministry.

Tonight, though, Matt found that someone had paved purgatory (if not put up a parking lot, as the song said) since his last visit. Instead of raw sandy footpaths, broad sidewalks meandered among the cactus specimens. He couldn't read the small identifying markers impaled in the ground by moonlight, but the plants' bristling forms were somehow even more satisfying half-shrouded, their exact identities hidden.

A handsome wooden bench was now the centerpiece of an artistic break in the gently hilly layout. Matt sat on it, surrounded by shadow and silence.

He didn't know if he sat in a paradise about to be lost forever, or a garden of thorns, of the uncertain angst that precedes the final agony.

He knew he was at a crossroads. Someone actually wanted his soul besides God. That's what a religious vocation was, giving your soul to God. What happened when you walked away from that path? Did God return your soul, slightly used? Was it now up for grabs? Not that many people aspired to soul robbing these days.

That made Kitty O'Connor unique.

Was she the Devil then? Or just his private edition? He had to take her at her word. She wanted to force him to do the thing he least wanted to do. With her, anyway. Her weapon was to threaten those he cared about, anyone around him, really. Even a mere acquaintance like Sheila had been injured at the New Millennium Hotel only a few days ago. So Temple, Lieutenant Molina's preteen daughter, Mariah, anyone he associated with, was in danger.

Therefore . . . he would associate with no one.

And she had won.

Or . . . he lived his life as before, took his chances. And gambled with the lives of everyone who touched his.

Temple. Sheila. Mariah. Electra Lark, his motherly landlady at the Circle Ritz. Another name joined the roster. Janice. He'd forgotten about her telephoned invitation to dinner Monday night. Tomorrow.

Who else would be coming to dinner?

Sitting there, alone in the dark, he heard the occasional hiss of tires on a nearby thoroughfare. When he'd first come here, the world had seemed so remote. Now it crowded in, smelling and sounding like city.

Or was he just now hearing the civilization that had always hemmed in his private piece of wilderness?

The civilization, and the corruption.

Okay. What did Miss Kitty want? Nothing any teenage boy wouldn't gladly give in a Las Vegas twenty-four-hour second. His body. His virginity. The unblemished record of his priestly chastity. Since coming to Las Vegas, Matt had actually come to consider his sexual inexperience an encumbrance in dealing with a secular world. Kitty O'Connor wasn't, as she pointed out, ugly, so why agonize over it? She probably wouldn't kill him anyway, because once having forced him to do what he didn't want to do, she'd want him to live with the aftertaste. Why not? The answer in his gut was simple: because it didn't matter the issue or the history or even whether it was him or some other guy or girl: forcing someone against his will was coercion, and in the sexual arena, it was assault, molestation, rape.

So was that any worse suffering than the Passion of Christ and Way of the Cross? Identifying with Jesus was hubris, or delusion, but the issue Matt faced was simple self-sacrifice. What made his innocence so precious that one hair on one other person's head should be harmed by it?

Kitty the Cutter had sliced right to the heart of the matter: pride. He was proud that he had left the priesthood not a fallen priest but a mistaken one. Why not be proud that he'd honored his promise of chastity, along with obedience and poverty? Maybe because—although any kid knows what being obedient and poor meant, being powerless—Matt had never really understood what chastity meant. Or, rather, what not being chaste promised.

His Achilles heel. Achilles was another of mythology's indestructible demigods with one small, nagging vulnerability. No wonder the world had embraced the notion of a destructible God who chose to share human frailty, if not fallibility. Although even Jesus had hesitated in the Garden of Gethsemane. If this cup . . .

But . . . blasphemy! He wasn't Jesus. He wasn't here to prove he was either godlike or frail. He was here to . . . what? Do the best he could. Be the best he could be. Be in the army? Army of God.

Dying for the Cause was an honored act for both messiahs and martyrs. Living for a cause was sometimes trickier.

Matt had often thought that the old-time religion had emphasized too much self-abnegation. The Good Friday psalm came to mind, Jesus intoning as he walked meek as a lamb toward the Cross, "for I am a worm and no man." Such self-abasement would not go over well with the human potential movement today.

It wasn't going over with him now that he'd encountered someone who truly wished him ill. Ill in the sense of making him sick to his soul.

What did he most lose from caving in to Kitty the Cutter's demands?

He wouldn't respect himself in the morning?

No: the idea of being ignorant and vulnerable in the hands of his worst enemy. Pride again.

And worse. Since he had started admitting his sexuality, he had discovered it was a headstrong force. Could a man will his body not to respond when stimulated even by someone he hated and feared? Wasn't that what torture victims attempted so valiantly? Is that why the line between love and abuse was so narrow in certain warped fringes of human behavior, including torture, including, sometimes, intimacy?

And last, but so very far from least, was something he had pretended was past, and wasn't. That was his love, passion, hope for Temple. No matter how much he had forced his rational mind to move on, he had never lost hope that she would be his manna in the desert, she would be the one and only to lead him beyond his past and into a fully sexual future. To think of experiencing his first sexual act with someone as much the opposite of her as Kitty the Cutter . . . that was blasphemy. Better he should have succumbed to the strange, lazy moment on the threshold of Janice's bedroom the first time he met her. Better some careless, but so very human, hormonal tango than deliberate surrender to a woman who was antilove, antilife, antisex if she used it as a weapon. An anti-Christ, in fact.

And yet, she could kill. And if she killed anyone because of him, then any innocence he kept was lost beyond redemption.

A foot scraped the walkway.

Matt looked up into the dim light of a distant lamp.

A dog stood there, big and dark. Great Dane maybe.

He swallowed, aware of how isolated he was, how isolated he had made himself. This could have been Kitty herself.

Before he could think, the dog turned and trotted off.

Probably it was as surprised to see him there as he was to see it.

Anytime. Anywhere. Anything. Anyone.

That was the lesson of the Garden.

The Judas kiss was always waiting somewhere.

Chapter 2

Bad News Breakfast

Dreams are only in your head.

Max woke up slowly, his dead cousin's face and voice fading too fast.

Dreams are only in your head.

His cousin Sean hadn't said that. Bob Dylan had said that in a long-ago song, using the wrong verb tense, is. Mock ignorant. Mock wise. Mockingly.

That was the mantra adults crooned at kids with nightmares, dreams are only in your head. True, but a true lie, also. And even scarier when you think about it, because when you grow up you find out that the only reality that matters is what's in your head. Or what everyone else put there.

A lot scared Max, who had lived a mostly dreamless life of deception and danger, but Sean in his dreams didn't scare him. Sean in his dreams was eternally seventeen, his features still blurred by baby fat, but the bones starting to push through to make a statement . . . until they had pushed through on a blast of explosive to make a final statement no one had expected, least of all Sean.

Sean in his dreams was whole and as precise as a class photo. Senior-high grin, polished mahogany-colored hair and the freckles that went with it. All-American boy via a Celtic pedigree. A middle-class, modern Huck Finn. Or Opie from Mayberry with size twelve feet treading on the brink of manhood. Full of pranks and daring. Class clown. Aching to kiss the girls and make them reveal the sweet mystery of sex. Adolescence personified.

And still that way in dreams.

Much as Max blamed himself for Sean's death, Sean in his dreams never haunted him. Never showed the bombed-out fracture of a face he might have flaunted. Max always awoke in calm nostalgia, almost as if he had received a benediction.

But then other remnants of his dreams began paying court to his dawning consciousness. A nameless man in a leopard-spotted mask. The Cloaked Conjurer, obviously, seen far more recently than Sean Patrick Donnell Kelly.

Max found the Cloaked Conjuror's memory erasing the pleasant tension of his smile as Sean's never had. In the dream the Cloaked Conjuror had transformed into Gandolph, Max's dead mentor in the art and illusion of magic. Gandolph had been all the family Max had allowed himself to have. Since Sean. He wished the old man were still here, in this house that Max rattled around in alone like a single die on an empty baize-covered table.

He wished Temple were here. He never had dreams like this when he slept with Temple.

But he hadn't slept with Temple—routinely, all night, with nowhere to go before and/or after—for months. Sean had died too young to understand why "sleeping with" was a euphemism for having sex, for making love. Sleep and the satisfying security that came afterward made having sex into making love.

Max's memory jolted him with another unpleasant dream image from the motherland, that long-ago Ireland that he and Sean had visited as naive returning sons.

A memory of having sex. First sex. With an Irish colleen named Kathleen O'Connor.

And then, with a dream shift that was only in his head, he finally remembered the dream's parting illusion. Peace dissolved. He had awakened not seeing Sean but copulating with a corpse.

Max left the coffeemaker clucking and drooling under the kitchen fluorescent lights and went into the dark yard to retrieve the newspaper.

Only 4:00 A.M., but the newspaper lay there like a dirty leg bone, a pale oblong encased in clear plastic that reflected the distant streetlight.

Max never ventured outside without scanning for lurkers. Sometimes he wished he owned a dog that could fetch. Leaving the house in the predawn dark was the most dangerous thing he did all day. A man on his front lawn in the wee hours was like an astronaut on a space walk: isolated, vulnerable, cut off from shelter and safety, so near and yet so far.

Millions of suburbanites did it every morning, but they didn't have Max's past.

Inside the house, he poured the black coffee into a white mug, then sat on a stool at the huge island counter and spread the paper wide as he skipped the usual front-page headlines—endless foreign talks and sports results—and paged through the rest.

Las Vegas papers always sizzled with entertainment news. Max found himself perusing small items on openings and closings and newly contracted acts, the longer features on the old standbys, as if he were still an up-and-coming performer with a professional interest in these constant comings and goings. As if he still harbored the unsinkable illusion of a career.

He missed the intense physical, mental, and social stimulus of doing his magic act, almost as much as he missed sleeping nightly with Temple. For the year they had lived together at the Circle Ritz apartment building while Max performed nightly at the Goliath Hotel, his life had seemed real for the first time since Sean. Imagine . . . the surreal atmosphere of Las Vegas making him feel so normal.

The next steps, and he had seen them clearly then, marriage. With children? A house, he could afford a nice one. A long-term contract with one of the spectacular megahotels always rising from the Vegas sands these days like the new Atlantis exchanging a watery mythological grave for a gravy train run on the glittering sandbox of the Strip here and now. What a magic show he could dream up for a place called the Atlantis! More than a magic show, a post–Cirque du Soleil and Eau mélange of sophisticated circus acts with a futuristic accent. . . .

Max sipped a fragrant distillation of the other, legal, and less lethal export of Colombia: the innocuous bean. His career had always been a cover, not his real job. He was dreaming to think he could resurrect it. Dreams are only in your head. With Sean.

Still, he felt a bit . . . wistful? Envious? Professionally curious? He reread a veteran columnist's spiel about the latest hot Strip magician, who happened to be someone Max had introduced himself to only recently in the line of his other work. And had dreamed about only minutes before. According to Gene Igo, the Cloaked Conjuror's brand of now-you-see-it, now-you-know-how-it's-done magic show violated every unspoken tenet of the magician's code but was packing them in at the New Millennium Hotel and Casino.

Max read about the multimillion-dollar, multiyear contract, the CC's desert retreat/fortress and dedication to "unmasking the mystery of magic" in a "thrilling, dramatic fashion."

The next paragraph outlined the other magicians' wrath at the CC flaunting trade secrets for fun and profit.

And then Max read his own name. The familiar letters exploded in his mind like Fourth of July rockets. The Mystifying Max Kinsella. Stage name and real name in one marquee-spanning phrase.

The bloody fool! It was true, CC said in Igo's column, as was now being reported, that the Cloaked Conjuror's act was literally death-defying, that he'd received many death threats. The columnist suggested that surely these couldn't be serious.

"Of course they're serious," the CC had "snapped," wrote the columnist, who had greater latitude in description than a fact-tied, objective-voiced news reporter. "The Mystifying Max Kinsella retired from magic a year ago because of death threats. Just vanished."

At this point the magician who appears everywhere in what amounted to almost armor snapped his leather-gloved fingers. "Like that. Gone. No magic involved. The Synth had caught up with him."

At first we thought he'd said "the Syndicate," as in old-time crime organizations, but the CC explained that the word was "Synth," and even spelled it for us: an ancient secret society of magicians formed to protect trade secrets.

This is why he uses no name and wears a leopard-spotted mask with a built-in voice modifier that hides his head completely. The gloves he wears constantly prevent leaving even fingerprints as a trail. The effect is a cross between Darth Vader and a protected witness, if you ask us.

"What about baths?" this reporter joked.

"I dry-clean," he said wryly. And seriously.

The Cloaked Conjuror also said he isn't married, for which the ladies must be very grateful.

Max shook his head and rattled the open pages, as if to shake sense into what he was reading. "The fool!"

Like most fools, the Cloaked Conjuror had managed to pull a boatload of others into the dangerous currents of his folly with this one interview. Not only Max but Temple and God knew who else. Never name an enemy. You warn him. Or her. Or it.

" 'The Mystifying Max Kinsella.' Well, well, well."

Lieutenant C. R. Molina wasn't prone to gloating over her high-fiber breakfast cereal. She wasn't even used, at that early hour, to being anyone more than Carmen Molina, working single mom, until she donned her clip-on leather paddle holster and left the house for police headquarters. But the morning paper had snapped her from domestic to professional mode in the crunch of a bran nugget.

"Is it a show?" her daughter Mariah asked, eyes still glued to the comics page. "This 'Max' thing?"

"Was a show. Mostly a no-show now." Molina, muttering, stared at the newsprint until it went out of focus. "Death threats. That's something Little Miss Red didn't mention."

"Mom! You're talking to yourself again. I was supposed to remind you not to do that."

"Oh. Right. Sorry." Molina eyed her daughter over the crinkle-cut edge of the newsprint. "Are you supposed to be wearing that to school?"

"That" was an assembly of beads and fishline that hung over the top of one twelve-year-old ear.

"I'm giving a report on TitaniCon."

"With visual aids?"

"Yeah." Mariah liked that idea. "Right."

Carmen saw that she had inadvertently given her daughter an excuse instead of an objection, so she just dropped the discussion. "You walking to school with Yolanda?"

"Like always."

"Watch out for bogeymen. There were two cases of guys trying to grab school kids last week."

"Those were little kids, Ma. Do I have to hear about every creep on the streets? I know what to do."

"So do police officers, and sometimes even they get caught sleeping."

"Anyway, I gotta get going if I'm not gonna be late."

Carmen nodded, her eyes back on the newsprint. She heard Mariah's dishes slide into the sink, and tap water rinsing them. Then a hasty " 'Bye," and the slam of the front door before her maternal mouth could open to forestall the bang.

Molina was still shaking her head as the frown she'd kept Mariah from seeing settled into her features like an old friend into a favorite rocking chair.

Death threats. First motive for Kinsella's disappearance she'd heard. And what was this "Synth"? Magical nonsense, she'd bet. A catchword that meant nothing, like "presto."

But she was familiar with the man quoted. At least she'd seen the Cloaked Conjuror up close at TitaniCon. Speaking of creepy guys who weren't out on the street . . . that animalistic mask, the mechanically altered voice . . . at least the Mystifying Max had performed bare-faced, which she supposed suited a congenital liar like him.

What did the Cloaked Conjuror know about Max Kinsella? She'd just have to find out someday.

Whatever this Synth was, she could well understand why it would issue death threats to the irritatingly mysterious Max Kinsella.

The clock hadn't even touched 8:00 A.M., but Temple's doorbell rang as if suffering a knockout punch. The mellow '50s melody continued through its changes as if it had ODed on caffeine. She swam her way through morning grogginess to the door.

"Electra!" Temple was shocked to find that her friendly neighborhood sixty-something landlady owned the right jab behind the doorbell abuse. "What's happened?"

Electra's floor-length cotton chintz muumuu, apparently a nightgown, rustled as she hurried in. "Now I know why that black-haired rascal hasn't been sleeping here nights."

"Louie likes to go out on the town, but he's home now." Temple nodded to her living room loveseat, on which the midnight black cat in question lounged like a sphinx who had been tarred, if not feathered, his forelegs stretched out magisterially.

"Midnight Louie nothing," Electra said, sitting beside the large cat with a nod of greeting. "No offense, Your Highness." She eyed Temple fiercely. "You know I meant Max."

Temple crossed her arms over her chest, a gesture meant to lend stern authority to her five-foot frame, which looked particularly lacking with stuffed bunny-head slippers on her feet. "No, I don't know any such thing. And why are you keeping track of where Max sleeps?"

"You two used to share the unit, remember?" But Electra's good-humored face was looking sheepish. She patted the confetti-colored ringlets that matched the flora fluorescing against the muumuu's black background. "Anyway, now I understand why he didn't move back in when he came back from, from wherever he disappeared to. Death threats! Why didn't you tell me?"

"Maybe it was none of your business."

Electra's ovine expression grew owlish.

"And maybe I don't know what you're talking about," Temple added, "so I can't tell you."

The landlady flourished the rolled-up news section in her hand as if jousting with a fly.

Beside her, Louie's ears came to attention as his green eyes began searching the room's upper air.

"Well, all Las Vegas knows about it now," Electra said.

Temple went to take the paper and unroll it, turning to avoid Louie's big black paw batting it as if begging for a look-see.

She studied the inside feature-section page. The text in question was some show biz interview continued from the section front. Words like "audience" and "popular" leaped up at her. And then, "Max" and "Kinsella," preceded by the oft-repeated phrase "death threats."

Temple sat on the sofa arm, eyes still glued to the Roman type, her rear almost mashing the end of Louie's now twitching tail.

Before she could make much sense of the context, a knock sounded on her door.

"You must have jammed the bell pounding it," Temple accused her landlady as she went to answer the summons.

If she hadn't been concentrating so hard on the article, she would have figured out who it was. The blond man who stood in the private hallway, reading his folded copy of the morning paper by the faint glow of Temple's entry wall lamp, always knocked, not rang.

"Did you know about—?" He stopped as he saw past her to Paula Revere on the couch.

"I do now," Temple said. "Come in and join the pajama party."

That seemed to be his first clue that Temple was indeed attired in something skimpy and cotton knit.

"I should have called," Matt said, hesitating on the threshold.

"Why? Electra didn't. I can't believe you two got to the morning paper ahead of me. I'm an absolute news junkie. Oh, wait! Don't tell me it was on the early TV news."

"Well—" Matt looked sheepish, just as Electra had only minutes earlier.

Temple closed the door after him, wondering why Matt seemed a little punch-drunk this morning, and why a professional night owl was up so early anyway. Wondering also what full frontal news coverage would do to Max's cover.

While Electra leaped up to greet her favorite tenant, Temple took a side trip into her tiny black-and-white kitchen to see what she could offer her surprise guests.

"Coffee, tea, or cranapple juice?" she asked, sticking her head around the barrier wall.

"Coffee," they caroled obligingly. If Temple could cook anything, it was coffee. She filled the coffeemaker higher than she had since Max had inadvertently moved out a year ago by vanishing from the Goliath Hotel, and pulled a trio of mugs down from the cupboard.

"Does it say anything else?" she yelled into the other room. Cooks were always kept busy in the kitchen and had to miss all the good conversation, another thing she had against the culinary art.

"Just that," Electra yodeled back in the fruity register of late middle age.

"Isn't that enough?" Matt put in.

"You've got it." Temple shuffled out on her cozy but Disneyesque bunny slides. Her mother had sent them one Christmas, and they were too small to pass along to anybody else along the bunny trail on the gift chain. Temple wondered what Freud would make of the mother of a thirty-year-old daughter who still shopped in children's and junior departments for her daughter. Probably that the daughter was a shrimp.

"You two rip that article to shreds while I go change," Temple suggested. "And if the coffeemaker makes strange choking noises, go to its aid."

They nodded, the blond and multicolored heads lowered over Max's first ink in over a year.

Louie nosed his way between them as if to join the confab.

In five minutes Temple's cherry-amber waves of chin-length hair resembled a style and she was dressed in a two-piece knit outfit. The bunny slippers had been replaced by svelte Onyx platform sandals with clear plastic uppers embellished by silver studs.

Donning the right shoes was as magical for her as Dorothy's red sequin numbers. She returned to the main room, her mood upbeat, to find the coffeemaker docile and her guests still rapt over the story.

In two more minutes the ritual mugs were steaming on the coffee table and Temple had retrieved her own copy of the morning paper from the hall to study the story for herself.

A silence broken only by sipping noises finally cried for a major interruption.

Matt went first. "Do you think Max Kinsella knows about this?"

The phone rang.

"He does now."

Chapter 3

News Flush

There is nothing more boring than old news. Unless it is a group of people going gaga over old news as if it were new news.

Now I am subjected to the old "three's a crowd" situation in my own living room.

Not only am I crowded on my sofa by Miss Electra Lark's encroaching muumuu, but they nose me out of my morning peek at the paper too.

Much ado about *nada*. Nothing. Like they did not know (or could not guess in Miss Electra Lark's instance) that the Mystifying Max had probably gone AWOL all those months ago because of death threats.

My Miss Temple surely knows that, as certainly as her name is Temple Barr and she is the most devoted roommate a guy of my propensities could have, except for a troubling tendency for getting involved with dudes of her own species when she should be concentrating on dudes of my species, specifically me.

It is true that, like fickle people everywhere, this threesome soon bustles off on their daily duties: Miss Electra Lark to tend to affairs at the Circle Ritz condominium and apartments, Mr. Matt Devine to do the sensible thing and go back to bed, as his evening shift did not end until early in the morning; Miss Temple to race over to the Crystal Phoenix Hotel and Casino to ready every last detail for the grand opening of its newest attractions. One of its less advertised attractions is likely to be the Mystifying Max, whom I suspect she will meet en route in hopes no one will be any the wiser. Except me, of course, who is the original Wise Guy.

So there I am left alone in the wink of an eyeball, with the newspaper to myself, not to mention three mugs with congealing coffee rings in their bottoms, and not a drop of cream, or even skim milk, in sight.

I do not even have to stretch too far to pull the disheveled pages toward me. I do so hate to be the last to get to the morning paper and find it shopworn.

I use my built-in clippers to scratch out the desired article, the column in which the fateful mention of death threats was made.

Are any of my erstwhile companions aware that I have been drugged, caged, and transported against my will time and again? That I have so many death threats hanging over my head they would weigh as much as a showgirl's headdress at the Rio?

No, no one worries about Midnight Louie except Midnight Louie.

So. The Cloaked Conjuror is working with a new cat. That is the part of the article that perked my ear, naturally, since it had to do with matters closer to home. Could the sinister Hyacinth be moving her act to another magician? That Siamese siren has a habit of showing up on the scene of the crime, including the murder at TitaniCon only a few days ago.

Time for me to find out. And this time I am not going to beard this lioness in her den alone. This time I am going to bring some muscle. To catch a thief, use a thief. To trap a tricky dame, use a tricky dame.

Now, let me see . . . where would a wise-guy PI like me find one of those?

Chapter 4

A Wolf in Sheep's Clothing

Molina felt like the wolf at the three little pigs's door.

She was still huffing and puffing, at least, from hoofing it up three flights of stairs. Needed more time at the gym than behind a desk.

The faded stucco apartment building had no elevator, and the cheapest units were at the top. A scuffed plastic trike sat abandoned by the door. Who would let a three-year-old ride a trike on this narrow concrete balcony that ended in a corkscrew of stairs downward?

The dusty windows along the wall of the unit were covered with miniblinds, the thin metal slats crushed askew, as if the inhabitants were always peeking out.

Her outfit was more a costume than clothes, so she took quick inventory before she knocked: scuffed moccasins missing beadwork, worn jeans, a cotton-polyester shirt, and a fringed suede jacket the color of diarrhea, all courtesy of the Goodwill.

The cheap watch she had found there too read 10:00 A.M., a bit early to be rousting ladies of the night, but she wanted to find them home. Finding them sleepy and hungover as well would be a bonus.

Her fist hesitated above the door's scratched surface. She hadn't gone undercover in years; she felt like an ingenue about to make her first entrance on stage.

And she wasn't undercover at all, officially.

She ran a hand through her hair, mussing it. This wasn't a situation where pounding and badge flashing was going to get her anything.

She knocked.

Waited. Waited some more.

Knocked again.

No shouts of "Police! Open up!"

Just knock and wait, like the pizza delivery guy.

And hope you don't get mugged while doing it.

No one was stirring yet in the complex, though. And vehicles born to be towed away littered the parking lot three stories below like a kid's battered and scattered toys.

Through the door, she heard a child fussing, the whining, accelerating cry that sounds eerily like a siren.

The door shook and opened the length of a scratched safety chain.

"Yeah?" The face could have sold cold cream, so bleary, morningafter it looked.

Molina tried for a tone as jaded, and fell short. "Name's Gina Diaz. I'm looking into what happened to Mandy."

She had been summed up while she spoke. "Why?"

"I've been hired to do it." True, in a way.

"You some female PI?"

"You could say that. Look. I just want to know some personal details, so I have a prayer of helping these folks out."

"Her parents?"

Molina shrugged. "Sometimes they like to know what happened to dead daughters."

A crinkle of curiosity crossed the swollen features. Behind her, the kid's whine rose to a screech.

"Oh, God. Okay, come on in, lady. We don't know anything, though."

Once in, the door was locked behind her. "Good idea," Molina noted. Cripes, had to forget being Cop Lady for a day.

"Sometimes good ideas aren't enough, though. Sit down. Name's Reno."

Sure, Molina thought. Name was anything but Reno. As for sitting down . . . well, on what junk pile?

She chose a sofa end that was stacked with washed department-store-quality kiddie clothes, clean but wrinkled.

A moment later a sprite of two with tear-slicked cheeks was lifted atop the kitchen counter. Molina heard a toaster thump and soon the child was gnawing on a Pop-Tart.

Mom was a spare, attractive brunette somewhere in her late twenties, wearing lime green capri pants and a white-lint-strewn black sports bra.

Molina guessed they were the easiest clothes to grab when she had come knocking.

"You live alone here with the little girl?"

"No, but Ginger slept right through your pounding on the door. God, Trifari, don't gobble! You're getting raspberry on your new Gap top."

Reno swiped the kid's chin and set her on the carpet cluttered with plastic toys and dolls.

She noticed Molina folding the clean clothes and suddenly grinned. "Thanks. Just stack 'em on the end table. On top of the magazines. So you're really a detective?"

"Really."

"Say, do you want some coffee?"

"Why not? You look like you could use some anyway."

Reno returned to the kitchen to fuss with a coffeemaker. "You probably figured out I work the clubs too, like Mandy did. Her real name was Cher." She poked her face through the pass-through over the snack counter. "How long you been a detective?"

"About twelve years. How long have you been a stripper?"

"Forever." Reno came back into the living room and plopped down on the floor beside the little girl. "I bet they don't mess with you much, not at your size."

"It helps. But they mess with me if they think they can get away with it. And they always do. You?"

"Let's just say I hope Trifari grows up a little bigger than her mother. But I manage." She smoothed the blond hair off the child's brow. Raspberry jam smeared her lips like gloss, for a painful instant reminding Molina of photos she'd seen of Jon-Benet Ramsey. "She will, too," Reno said softly, more to the kid than to Molina. "I'm gonna see she gets a much better deal than I did."

"What kind of deal did Mandy/Cher get?" Molina had pulled out a stenographer's notebook from which she'd torn half the pages before coming.

"You've seen the parents?"

"Well, the mother."

Reno's mouth soured. "Yeah. It's interesting she's coming around now. I mean, that stepfather . . . the usual scum."

Molina nodded. "Maybe she learned too late that the kids have to come first. It's a long shot, finding someone who killed a stripper."

"Don't we know that. Just paint a target on us. The cops could care less."

"*Not* care less."

"Huh?"

"Sorry. My, ah, aunt was a grammarian. It's 'could not' care less."

"What-ev-er. You make much money at this?"

"No. It's just how the movies show the old-time PIs. You know, the borderline guys with the junker cars living alone and suddenly they get this one case that all the bigwigs care about and they save the day. It's like that, except for the big case and saving the day."

"I probably make more dough than you do."

Molina nodded. It was likely even true in terms of her real job. "Probably. Did Cher?"

"Cher?" Reno laughed, a bit pensively. "Not Cher. She was new, but she was worse off than that. She was . . . raw, you know? Didn't have a clue how to take care of herself. She hated stripping, but pretended she didn't. Drank like a fish. Drank like a whale. Just a mess."

"An easy victim, then?"

"Listen. We're all easy victims. That's why we're there, pretending we're somebody, that we're pulling the strings. But we're not. We get paid good, though." She glanced at the child, content with her dreadful breakfast and her upscale toys. "I'll be able to send her to college. If I manage to hang on to my money. Sometimes it's hard."

"Boyfriends? Drugs?"

"I stay off the stuff." Her face deadened. "My boyfriend, though . . ." She sighed. Looked at the child. Sighed again.

Reno laughed uneasily and jumped up, as fluid as a teenager. Stripping kept a girl in tip top condition, oh, yes. Molina was surprised no enterprising media queen had put out an exercise video based on stripping moves.

"Coffee's ready," Reno called from the kitchen. "Man, I could use a hit of caffeine."

She brought two steaming, if water-spotted, mugs into the living room. Molina eyed the magazine-covered end table wondering where she would balance the hot mug.

"Just put it on the magazines. We don't worry about coffee rings around here." Reno settled cross-legged on the floor, while Molina felt a twinge of envy. She felt a lot older than Reno. Why had a woman this street savvy been caught with a pregnancy? Maybe she'd just wanted a kid.

"So. Any suspicious characters around that strip club? Secrets."

" 'Suspicious characters.' That is so *NYPD*. You crack me up."

"Sorry. Why'd Cher leave the last club she appeared at?"

Reno shrugged, her face buried in the child's hair, then looked up. "She didn't say. I only saw her for a few minutes the day she died. She was all high on some guy she met named Vince. Said he might look out for her. I guess he played white knight when the bouncer got overeager."

"The bouncer?"

"Guy named Raf. Likes to throw his weight around. Most of us don't take guys like that seriously. All show and no go, but Cher was a scaredy-cat."

"Maybe she was right." Molina made a point of writing down the names of the men. Vince was new; Raf, of course, was not.

"This Raf been at the club long? What does he look like?"

"We called him our man from the Iranian secret police. Iranian *Secrets* police in our case, I guess."

"What do you mean 'Iranian secret police'?"

"Oh, Raf, our bouncer, just has that dark and dangerous look. Kinda foreign, but I don't think he is. Kinda dominating. Then there was this Vince guy that came in. He was dark and dangerous looking too, but Cher was jazzed on him, oh, boy. He gave her money for nothing, after all. No dancing, no sex. Got her thinking about hairdressing school, my gawd, can you believe it? Standing all day and no money in it? At least hookers get *paid* for standing around. And their blow jobs are over a lot faster. And then this guy tried to talk her into calling some counselor. For someone who looked like sleaze on a skateboard he sure acted like Mr. Goody Two-shoes."

Molina nodded. Straight arrows, even cops, could fixate on reforming hookers and strippers. Probably unconscious libido.

"She say what this Vince looked like, anything identifying?"

"Tall, dark . . . you fill in the blanks. She offered to sleep with him for nothing, but he wasn't interested. Gay, you think?"

"Maybe. Maybe just a do-gooder, like you say. Or a do-badder setting her up. No address, no way to get in touch with him again?"

"She didn't say. She did say he tangled with Rafi. Raf. That's short for Rafi. I ask you, what kind of name is that?"

Molina held back a smile in answering a woman who'd named her daughter Trifari. Trif? "Foreign maybe, like you say. Middle-Eastern, I'd bet."

"Oh! Don't tell me about those guys! Control freaks, and it's all okayed by their religion or whatever. Anyway, that's why Cher was switching clubs that next night. That she . . . died. Didn't want to run into Rafi again at Secrets."

"You're free to do that?"

"Yeah. Not at the hoity-toity clubs, but at places like Secrets, it's just who shows up. We move around. Get a wider clientele that way. More bucks. Poor Mandy. She coulda used more bucks. I hate to say it, but she was born to be somebody's victim. Was it a nut case, do you think? Or that guy Vince?"

"Murder like this? Night. A woman alone in a strip club parking lot. It could be anybody."

Molina read between the ancient lines. Despite Reno's hard-nosed survival attitude and her genuine desire for a better life for her daughter, she would be putty in the hands of any controlling guy who threw a little money, time, and attention her way before taking over her life. Like the late, mostly unlamented Cher, little Trifari was in a race for her future with her mother's abusive background. Would conditioning or maternal instinct win?

Molina hoped Reno was one of those women who, even if she couldn't stop being a victim in her own life, at least could draw the line at that happening to her kids.

Some did it, and they deserved a medal. Most didn't, and they deserved what they got: another generation reared for heartbreak.

Molina nodded at the little girl. "Why did you name her Trifari?"

"Don't you like it?"

"I do. Much better than Tiffany."

"Yeah. That sucks. Like anyone from where I came from would ever have anything from Tiffany's. But they might have some Trifari, huh?" She leaned back against the sofa, grabbed her knees, grinned like a teenager.

"I had this aunt, too, only she didn't care about grammar. But she let me try on her jewelry when I was a kid. And some of it, the glittery stuff, had this little tag that read 'Trifari.' I always swore I would get me some of that someday."

"And you did." Molina nodded at the child.

"Yes, I did." Reno slid into a kiddish singsong. "Mommy sure did, precious baby." She hugged and rocked the little girl, stealing raspberry kisses while the child giggled.

Molina could have felt a lot of things at witnessing this mother-with-child scene: skepticism, anger, sorrow. Instead she just felt helpless. It was a feeling she hadn't indulged for years. Not until Rafi Nadir had recently turned up in Las Vegas.

Belated rage literally straightened her spine. Reno wasn't just a struggling single mother from a rotten background, she was a link in safeguarding Molina's own daughter from the past, and the future.

"So Cher was a basket case. Why would anyone strangle her?"

"She was there? She was easy? Maybe that's what it comes down to." Reno's grip on Trifari tightened until the child fussed in protest. "That's why I don't let any man live with us. Too many of them try things with little girls."

Molina nodded. No argument. Every woman these days knew a woman whose child had been molested, and most molestations happen within the charmed circle of family and acquaintances. Those just were the odds, plain and simple. The only certain odds in Las Vegas related to domestic abuse.

"About this new guy, Vince. New at the club?"

"I've never seen him, but Rick had. He's one of the bartenders."

"How about this theory? Say someone Cher knew or met at Secrets got big ideas, or was mad at her. Suppose that person followed her to the new place and killed her there to keep everyone from thinking about any suspects from Secrets?"

"*You* suppose. That's your job. Me, I don't know. Could be someone from Secrets."

"Who?"

"What guy, you mean?"

"Strangling isn't the average woman's choice of attack. It helps to be taller than your victim. Was Cher a tall girl?"

"Yeah, as a matter of fact. Here. I've got a photo." Reno rooted in the drawer of the end table that seemed more useful for holding the stuffing in the couch side than putting things on. "One of the club photographers took this."

Molina took it in turn, a five-by-seven horizontal group shot of whatever girls at Secrets happened to be around. They stood in a ragged line, arms around each other like cheerleaders, most of them wearing only G-strings and the grinning expressions of the happily smashed.

"It was Senegal's birthday. We all hung around after and broke balloons and sang 'Happy You-Know.' That's Cher there."

Molina stared at a face slightly blurred by booze and movement. "She looks pretty tall. Five eight, nine maybe."

"You got a great eye." Reno nodded, both impressed and suddenly sad. "Cher was about that. I know because she was always bitching about having to wear high-heeled boots. Said men like women who weren't as tall as they were. What do you think?"

"From the photo, five nine."

"No." Reno was grinning like a girlfriend at Molina. "I mean, do men like tall women? You oughta know."

Molina, surprised, said, "I doubt it. Too many guys are nervous about women anyway. I'd say short girls have it all over us tall ones."

"Kinda what I thought. That was Cher's problem. She felt like a horse and acted that way. Turned guys off. And, she was drunk as a skunk most of the time. She wasn't stripper material. Had to drink to do it. Probably had to drink to do sex too. I think there was, you know, in her family."

Molina nodded, making aimless marks in her notebook. Scratch a stripper and find a depressing life story. "What other guys hung out at the club?"

Reno curled up in the couch's slightly soiled corner. "Too bad you can't interview the police. They went over all this with me."

"Did they?"

"Oh, yeah. Two of 'em. Over and over, everything."

Molina felt a rare, secret satisfaction. "You remember their names?"

"No, just detectives. Like you. Notebook, the whole deal. Only with IDs."

"So what'd you tell them?"

"Just about the usual suspects. They were interested in the photo guy. I noticed you wrote his name and address down from the stamp on the back of the picture. And there's the deejay, Tyler. Just a kid, underage, but I didn't tell the cops that. Loves music, likes to watch naked girls dancing. All pimple-faces do. And he doesn't have to pay for it."

"He ever bother any of the girls?"

"All he knows how to bother people yet is by playing his tapes too loud, although you can't possibly do that at a strip club. Naw, he's a good kid, and the bartenders and bouncers, they're just regular guys. You'd be amazed how boring it is to be around women shedding their clothes after the shock wears off. That's why we move so much from club to club. I just don't see any of these guys going berserk and offing a girl. Why?"

"You like the idea of an outside stalker better?"

"Yeah. Maybe it was her old man. Stepdad. Those are the kind who can diddle their own kids and then get mad when the kid grows up and goes off and lets someone outside the family do it. Maybe it's that Hannibal freak, huh? Most of the guys who come to strip clubs are pussycats. That's why we love doing it, putting a smile on their pussycat faces while they stuff our G-strings with cash money."

Trifari started banging a plastic assembly toy on the floor, and Reno jumped down to take it away. "Come on, honey. Save that toy for next time."

Molina had noted down the names of Secrets' male workers. The detectives' reports would cover all of them.

"Only one guy from Secrets came anywhere near Cher away from the club," Reno said as she straightened up. "That guy she met her last night there."

"The day before she was murdered."

"Right." Reno shivered as she sat again to sip strong, cooling coffee. "I think I know how to take care of myself. I've been at this a long time. Too long. But the money's good and I come and go when I want, and I'll be free days to go to my little girl's school stuff when she's older. When she's in the school play, right, little star? If I hold up." She laughed. "I look pretty good for my age, don't I?"

Molina smiled. "I don't know. What's your age?"

"Guess."

"Twenty-eight or nine?"

Reno preened. You could almost see a spotlight on her. "Add ten, honey."

"Really?" Molina was honestly surprised. Reno was in great condition.

"I get in another ten years, I'll have this kid in junior high and a nest egg for college. Then I can do nails at the Goliath or something."

If, Molina thought, shutting her notebook, nobody ever caught her in a parking lot alone.

Chapter 5

Magic Act

The widening vee of seats unfurled like a fan. The audience filled the seats, a hydra-headed monster in miniature. Tiny pale faces glimmered beyond the spotlights like pearlescent fingernails.

From the front-row red-velvet chairs that curved into a smile to match the stage's dark, grinning lip, the seating section lifted and expanded, making the faces dim into distant painted figures on a Chinese vase.

Most of the audience could never know that, to the performer, the seating section of a theater resembled a chasm, in time as well as in space. The spectators themselves became ignored attractions, mere curiosities, creatures trapped beyond the invisible "fourth wall" that every stage possessed: a cellophane curtain, a psychic force field.

The audience, by virtue of its assembly and its conspiracy of silence, its expectation of witnessing something, was not a mass of individuals anymore, but that ancient Greek-chorus embodiment of society at large. It was also the same thumbs-up, thumbs-down monster that had circled the gladiators in a Roman coliseum.

That ancient Roman audience had expected blood.

This contemporary Las Vegas one merely thirsted after amazement.

But even modern times were quickly reaching the point where blood was the only amazement left. At least in live performance.

And this performance was designed to amaze. The man who moved in the laser shafts of spotlights that raked the dark stage like dueling light sabers was tall, dark, and masked in sinister spots that resembled arcane tattoos in the theatrical lighting.

Unlike an actor, he could shatter the fourth wall to speak directly to the audience. That didn't mean they were any more intimate to him, that ocean of whitecap faces bobbing gently now and then to cough or address a seat partner.

Such signs of inattention were not encouraged.

The man stepped into the upright coffin behind him, a carved and polished box fit for a vampire. A red velvet curtain lowered over it.

The masked man stepped through a breakaway back panel just as the curtain whisked up again to reveal an empty box.

He stepped through to confront an eerily similar figure to himself, a man in black everything, except for the mask. This man's face was painted black. The smell of greasepaint hovered like a halo over the almost mirror images.

"Pay no attention to the man behind the curtain," the intruder murmured.

"My God, what are you doing here?" The magician's mechanical voice sounded even hoarser than normal. "My bodyguards—"

"You have fifteen seconds." The other man flashed his wrist to show the sickly green luminescent dial beneath his pushed-up matte-black sleeve. "Where can we meet privately?"

"Here? Now?"

"Eleven seconds."

"Damn you . . . my dressing room. Go now! I'll keep the bodyguards out. If anyone sees you—"

"They won't. Six seconds."

"This whole stage section turns. How will you—?"

"Not your problem."

The mechanism beneath them jerked into action.

"My act—"

The magician turned to face his audience as his simple hiding place spun into view. He was literally beside himself. He glanced at his unwanted doppelgänger. Gone!

Underneath the mask, his jaw tightened. This interlude had been the real magic trick.

His pulse still staccato, he stepped aside, swept a dark arm to indicate the false wall, bowed as applause hit him like a tidal wave.

Sweat trickled under the spandex false face he wore.

Below the stage, Max amused himself after he had wiped off the camouflage paint by trying on the Cloaked Conjuror's spare mask. He spoke softly through the tiny built-in microphone. "Elementary, my dear Watson."

He sounded like a robot gargling tinfoil. He contemplated resuming his performing career in some exotic disguise. But he liked performing magic with a bare face. A magician deceived to the degree that he was able to seem sincere. Since the Cloaked Conjuror's whole shtick was revealing the devices behind magical illusions, he didn't need to show his face. He wasn't there to convince but to debunk.

It was magical deconstructionism, like an artistic or literary movement. What had the art of legerdemain come to, feeding on its own destruction? Entropy as entertainment.

Or was he just jealous? Max regarded his masked, expressionless feline face in the mirror. His own cover was blown, his career lost. Magic had been his first passion; revenge his second. Temple his third. The first was history now. The second was strangely dormant after eighteen years. Eighteen years, longer than Sean had lived . . . As for Temple, their passion was bound and gagged by the fallout from the second.

Through a tinny speaker mounted under the ceiling, he could hear the music, the Cloaked Conjuror's disguised vocal croakings, the applause that sounded as mechanical and distorted as the magician's voice.

It was like eavesdropping on another, unreal world. One he had once lived in intimately.

Was he just jealous? Not if dreams are only in your head.

He wasn't used to being confined alone with his own thoughts. It felt like being penned in a well-lit confessional, waiting eternally for some unknown person in the other confessional to finish his business and the small window beyond the pleated white linen to slide open so the man hidden behind the curtain could wait for Max to say "Bless me, Father, for I have sinned."

Lord! He was going back to his earliest childhood at his grandmother's church. The Catholic Church did open-air confessions now, in large, well-lighted rooms with no hint of claustrophobia.

Max had to wonder if his childish hunger to escape the small dark room where he enumerated his failings to the hidden listener had first interested him in escapology and magic tricks. Yet the king of escapology, Houdini, hadn't been Catholic but Jewish. Escape that fact.

The dressing room door creaked. Max leaped up to confront his visitor with his borrowed face.

"I'm fine," the husky computer-disguised voice of the Cloaked Conjuror rasped from outside the open door. "Just keep anyone from entering, okay?"

The door opened only enough to admit his muscular form. He was a bit too thickset to perform the most agile illusions, one reason he'd turned to unmasking unreality, probably.

He knew what the magical community said of the debunkers: failed magicians. Those who can, do; those who can't, criticize.

The Cloaked Conjuror turned on Max the moment the door was shut and dead-bolted.

"I can't believe you! Right onstage. You could have ruined my act. Are you crazy? My bodyguards could have thought you were an assassin. Are you suicidal?"

"I can't believe you," Max charged back in an eerie, altered, amplified tone of voice. "Right in the public print. Telling the world that death threats forced my retirement. That's not true. Why in the name of Harry Houdini would you mention me at all in that interview? Are you crazy? Suicidal?"

Their masks glared at each other, then Max pulled his off.

"How did you get offstage so fast?"

"Jumped up and was assumed into the wings on the curtain pulleys."

"My bodyguards—"

"Never look up. They watch you, and you stay with your feet on the ground."

"That was a nervy thing to do."

"It was a nervy thing to drag me into your interview. I vanished for a reason, and I'd prefer the public, and everybody else, to forget about me entirely. You've just blown a year's worth of invisibility."

The Cloaked Conjuror lifted his arms and dropped them to indicate helpless regret. The mechanical voice forced him to rely on gesture rather than speech even in private. He resembled a mute Phantom of the Opera.

Max stopped being envious, if he ever had been.

The magician sat at his dressing table, where Max had warmed the seat only moments before. He didn't remove his mask.

"I didn't know how to get in touch with you." Even the mechanical voice sounded weary. "I figured if I mentioned your name you might contact me. But not onstage in the middle of my act! My bodyguards are all over that backstage. Man, you are crazy."

"No. I just know that the safest place to be when a man is under constant guard is right next to him. Even if they had noticed my brief visit, they weren't about to shoot until they knew which man in black was who."

The Cloaked Conjuror shook his head. "Whatever you are, you're the only one who tumbled to the fact that my assistant was killed at the TitaniCon weekend. I've got a new problem, but it might be from an old source."

Max pulled a chair closer to the mirror and sat beside the magician. "The Synth?"

"Maybe. I've been working with a new cat. Going to reveal the old cat into woman trick. Add a little femme pheromones to the act, you know? Somebody's swiped the animal."

"Big cat? Leopard, I suppose?"

The leopard-spotted mask nodded. "Cost a bundle. And a fine, mature animal. Worth . . . a bundle."

"You blew my cover over a cat-napping?"

"A note was left, signed 'the Synth.' "

"You've contacted the police?"

"Would you?"

"No. What's the ransom?"

"The note didn't mention a ransom."

"Any calls?"

"Not for money. Not about the leopard."

Max pondered the sense of announcing you're the kidnapper without demanding ransom. "Do you think they'll ask for money after you sweat a little, or do they really want the animal? Or is this a nuisance attack? Harassment."

"I don't know. I do know my security force is pretty teed off about someone breaching the perimeter and taking the cat. Either way, it's a message."

Max nodded again. "A major message. So the leopard was taken from your residence. I suppose you're not about to share the location of that with me."

"Not unless you convince me that you absolutely need it."

"It's near Las Vegas, though?"

"Yeah. Near enough."

"Obviously, there are several messages here: one, they know where you are. Two, you aren't as secure as you think. Three, they know what you're planning for the act. Four, they can extort your money from you, or maybe they think they deserve it and you don't, since you're an antimagician. So why do you think I can do anything for you? Especially after you've irritated the hell out of me."

The Cloaked Conjuror kept silent for a good minute, his masked face as still as a corpse's. "I've seen tapes of your show. You're the real thing. Man, you nearly gave me a heart attack when you showed up backstage. See, no one's supposed to be able to do that. I figure if anyone can go up against the Synth, you can. I'll pay you whatever you need to get the cat back and find out the who, what, and why behind this whole thing."

Max stood, shoved his chair under the dressing table, glanced at the empty mask he had abandoned on the tabletop.

"I may need to produce money for the cat, and I may need that in advance."

"Just ask."

"Who was the woman?"

"What woman?"

"The woman you were going to change into a cat, and vice versa. One of your lissome assistants in the leopard catsuits?"

"No. I found someone a little more exotic, but she's out of the picture for now. She wasn't going to join the act until after the cat was trained."

"How exotic?"

"Hot."

"Like that's a rarity in Las Vegas?"

The Cloaked Conjuror chuckled. "She does her own act, but it's small-time. You may have heard of her. Shangri-La."

"Shangri-La. I guess she's used to working with a cat, or a house cat anyway. What is its name?"

"Her house cat?"

"No, your missing leopard."

"Osiris."

"The Egyptian god of death. Not a nice omen. Let's hope that the real cat has as posh an afterlife as a pharaoh is granted."

"Listen, if this big cat just has the regulation feline nine lives, I'll be happy."

"If I have them, I'll be happier."

Chapter 6

Sister Act

If there is anything I hate more than an overzealous bodyguard, it is two of them.

These particular two bracket the Cloaked Conjuror's dressing room door as if they were guarding Pharaoh.

I know a thing or two about Pharaoh from a past life—
Pharaoh's past life, not mine—and I know that the Royal
Bearded One takes it most unkindly when the hired help clings
to the doorjamb like a couple of caryatids. Okay, caryatids
were these naked ladies from a little later era, but the ladies
along the Nile were not big on overdressing either. Anyway,
these statuesque broads would have done well in a late-night
topless chorus line at the Stardust, and it is a downright shame
to find these two overgrown musclemen making like doorposts
on the Cloaked Conjuror's doorstep, thereby interfering with
my eavesdropping.

So I am forced to cosy up to them and rub on their cowboy

boots until I could have polished the varnish off a whole herd of ostriches.

Above my head there is much speculating about how I got in here (with my hands and feet just like you did, numbskull, although with a lot more finesse, as my kind is not normally welcomed or allowed on the premises). And about if I am hungry. (Do I look hungry? I weigh about as much as your favorite pit bull, pal.) And some idle chatter about how the Cloaked Conjuror is in a bad mood tonight. (You think your *boss* is a bit peeved! How about me, who has managed to spy the Mystifying Max in the dark onstage, trail him through the flies and the wings, which are stage parts and not insectoid in the slightest, track him below-stage, and now here I am balked on the threshold of revelation by a couple of oversize klutzes who would rather feed the kitty than protect their boss's fake leopard-skin mask.)

Luckily, I have a trick up my sleeve.

Okay, I do not have a sleeve to speak of, but the trick does put in a sudden appearance.

It is the old Lassie shtick, and I must say it is the prettiest enactment of a dumb blond of the canine kind that I have ever seen.

I notice her first, leaning against the wall twenty feet away and panting.

Immediately, I stop my boot-black work so the idiots I have been forced to associate with can notice something under their noses down the hall.

She stutters forward on her little black feet, but soon sinks against the wall again, this time giving a little cry.

The dolts stop, look, and listen. By now they have graduated into making good crossing guard material.

She sighs, staggers upright, and begins limping away.

'Atta girl, Lassie! Timmie and the well he's fallen into must be down that dark hall somewhere. Or a pony. Maybe these guys will be useful enough to stumble into it.

By now her tail is lifting, then jerking down, then perking a bit, then dragging behind her heels. It is a sort of epilepsy of the anterior and it gets the guards running down the hall to tend to the poor thing.

I rub up tight against the door, pressing my left ear to the eighth-inch of air beneath it.

That is how I learn that Miss Shangri-La, the ooh-la-la lady magician who is one nice plate of chop suey in the looks department, is waiting in the wings to join Mr. Cloaked Conjuror's act. And I learn that a cat is the crux of the matter (of course).

A sharp hissing sound like acid boiling over down the hall tells me that my assistant's good nature has expired like an underfed parking meter downtown.

The pair of lummoxes heading my way are muttering about "damn cats" and scuffing their pointy-toed boots on the concrete floor as if entered in a roach-kicking contest.

I decide I do not wish to be mistaken for same, and rocket through their ranks, joining my compatriot on the dark end of the hallway.

"What a bum assignment," she greets me, still fussing and spitting. "I nearly broke a nail on the dumb guy's jean's leg. Who ever heard of starched denim?"

"Calm down, sister."

"Oho. You will not acknowledge me as your daughter, but I am good enough to be your sister when you need a little undercover work done. No go, bro!"

There is no doubt that Miss Midnight Louise needs handling with kid gloves, but there are no convenient kids in the vicinity, and besides, who would want gloves made from their sticky-fingered little hands anyway?

So I resort to my velvet tongue, which I stroke a few times over Midnight Louise's twitching shoulder blades. Ooh, sharp!

"Cut out the velvet glove treatment," she snarls, shrugging away. But her shoulders stop twitching. "So what did you learn while I was attracting the attention of those doorstops?"

"That one of our kind is in trouble. The Cloaked Conjuror told Mr. Max Kinsella that a big cat he was training has been kidnapped. There was also some talk about an associate of that lady killer I told you about."

"I know. The knockout showgirl with the lavender-gray shoulder-length gloves and thigh-high hose. I think she is a figment of your pheromones, Daddy Dude. Her type of femme fatale went out with cigarette holders."

"Anyway, it behooves us to track Mr. Max Kinsella as he investigates."

"And hooves is what we will need if we try to keep up with that gentleman."

Midnight Louise sits down on the cushion of her fluffy tail and begins one of those obnoxious, discouraging lists that dames are always going on about.

"We are not going to hot-foot our way through this case on pedal power this time. From what you have told me of your Mr. Max, he would be impossible for a bloodhound to trail. You do not even have a clue as to where he hangs his brass knuckles. Also, from what you tell me, he is not some amiable associate like your wire-haired so-called roommate, who will let us tag along in her motorcar. Hell's bells, Daddio, he does not even use the same car from day to day. Nor would he be an easy dude to let us hitch a ride unnoticed, as we did in Mr. Matt Devine's motorcycle pouches. And even that vehicle was originally owned by Mr. Max Kinsella, so I do not see how we are going to get anywhere trying to follow the likes of him."

"I suppose I could call Nose E. in on the case. There must be plenty of essence de Max Kinsella lingering around my roomie's domicile. And she is not 'wire-haired' like a terrier, but blessed with soft, flowing waves like an Irish setter."

"Please spare me your paeans to human hair. It holds all the attractions of the lint trap in a clothes dryer for me. And speaking of hairy little individuals, I am not going to baby-sit the inside of an Oreo cookie again. Nose E. indeed! The Maltese flatfoot. I thought it was *my* assistance you required. Now you are inviting everybody but the kidnappers in on the investigation."

"I suppose," I say meekly, "you have a suggestion?"

"Why must we follow the human investigators? I say we forge our own trail and get there first."

Midnight Louise nods as she strips the excess hairs from between her long and razor-sharp shivs.

And I am worried about a mythological beast named Hyacinth.

Chapter 7

A PR *in* PI Clothing

"I need," Max said, gazing deeply into Temple's eyes through his green contact lenses, "a clever shill who doesn't know too much."

"Great. What part of that is supposed to win me over? Not 'shill.' Not 'not knowing too much.'"

"Clever," Max pointed out.

"If I were really clever, I couldn't be talked into being a shill."

"I meant a convincing shill."

"Clever and convincing. I suppose I could live with that."

Max had arrived that morning by one of his literal second-story-man entrances to her, formerly their, condominium. He had entered, attired as usual in cat-burglar black from head to foot, by the patio French doors like a missing husband in a French farce, just in time for breakfast.

Temple had reciprocated this act of home invasion by popping two frozen waffles in the toaster. She and Max were now cosied up to the kitchen eating island on bar stools, applying bits of waffle to their blackberry preserves, pools of butter pockmarking the waffle grids amid the surrounding moats of maple syrup.

"Nutritionally, this is the pits," Temple noted.

"I don't come here for good nutrition," Max commented.

"So now I'm empty calories."

He shrugged, and ate.

"What do you want me to do?"

"Nothing much. Just buy a big cat."

Temple stopped sopping up waffle long enough to look pointedly at Midnight Louie lounging on the adjacent kitchen countertop, managing to look both bored and hopeful. "Got one."

"Bigger."

Temple was too busy chewing to speak with more than her raised eyebrows.

"That new attraction at the Crystal Phoenix is on the verge of opening, isn't it?" Max asked, switching from syrup to coffee. "I've been hearing and reading nothing in the local media lately but squibs about the new Action Jackson subterranean virtual-reality mine ride and the Domingo flamingo farango–whatever performance-art installation and the children's petting zoo."

"Mmphhank ouuu!" Temple got out before she could finish mashing waffle.

Nothing paid tribute to a public relations person's expertise more than a host of well-planted news items. You had to nibble the public to death to make an impression: repeated, needling mentions, rather like piranha love bites.

"So you're perfect for the job," Max went on.

"Of buying a big cat."

"I don't expect you to tote one home in your U-Haul. Just to . . . go shopping."

"You can shop for lions, and tigers, and bears?"

"Unfortunately, yes. Of course it's highly illegal."

"Illegal." Temple polished off the last swipe of waffle and reached for her morning multivitamin pill, which was almost bigger than she was. "I love to do illegal."

Max grinned. "Yes, you do. I had no idea when I ran into you in Minnesota—"

"You ran into a ficus tree while looking at me."

"You ran into a drinking fountain while looking at me."

"At least we didn't damage the greenery and the water supply."

"No, they damaged us."

"Then did *we* damage us?"

He sobered instantly. "No, fate and the past damaged us. Not too badly, I hope." She shrugged it off good-naturedly, but he went on. "I often wonder if you would have been better off, safer and saner anyway, if I'd just stayed lost."

"You would have never come back? Why did you?"

"I told myself that it was safe, for me, but especially for you. Sometimes magicians get so good at deceiving audiences they even fool themselves." He pushed the plate of waffles and syrup away as if sickened by sweetness when his thoughts had turned so sour. "If I hadn't come back, you'd probably be married to Devine by now."

"No! There wasn't anything that serious between us."

"He sure hates me enough for there to have been."

"Matt doesn't hate you, he just thinks—"

"That I had no business coming back and getting you into trouble. He's right."

"Max. Those thugs were going to waylay me whether you came back or not. Molina was going to hassle me whether you came back or not. Better you're here. Now when I'm hounded, I've got a secret weapon."

"Too secret. This isn't the way I wanted us to live. I don't think you're happy with it either."

"No," Temple admitted, "but I don't see how we can change things."

"I keep telling myself that it wasn't ego, my coming back and winning you back. That seeing you'd met Devine didn't make me territorial. But I'm so used to everything going my way, by hook or by crook. And now look—the ring I gave you in New York, missing. Stolen, onstage, yet, in front of Devine and Molina and everybody. The future I promised you in New York—no bogeymen or women, me free of my undercover past and us living like a normal couple, married with . . . cat. Enter Kathleen O'Connor, stage left-wing. Or is she right-wing? Either way, she's no angel. Domesticity is history."

"That's not your fault, Max."

"You've changed. And that is my fault." He frowned down at the countertop tile, his long fingers moving over it like it was a chessboard mysteriously vacant of kings, queens, bishops, knights, and pawns that he could move.

Max did not do angst, but he was perilously close now.

"Maybe it's for the better," Temple said.

He glanced up, startled.

"Maybe I've changed for the better. Gotten stronger. And what shape would I have been in if you'd never come back? Do you know how everybody pities and despises a woman whose guy has walked out on her? It's nasty. Everybody thought I was crazy for believing in you, but you did come back. You proved me right."

"Even if they think you're still crazy for sticking with an invisible man."

"You manage to show up when it matters. So. Have you figured out why you really came back?"

"I always knew, Temple. I love you."

"That simple?"

"That complicated."

She put her hands around his, smiled. "I always knew that you love me and I love you. And at least we're together again, in a way. Barr and Kinsella, undercover detectives. I think we make a good team, even if it's not onstage."

He finally smiled back. "I admit I underestimated your capacity for the lurid and the offbeat during our Minneapolis honeymoon."

"See. That's what was wrong. Most people honeymoon in Las Vegas. We came to Las Vegas, and suddenly the honeymoon was over."

"Not completely over."

"No," she admitted, looking down at their empty plates. "I wish you still lived here with me."

"I can't, Temple. It would blow my cover and make you a target."

She looked up. "At least you ask me to help out now and then."

"Like I said, I underestimated you. Doing PR for a regional repertory theater looked like such a respectable position. Maybe it was your previous life as a TV news reporter, but you really have a heck of a need to know. Tell you that you can't go somewhere, and you'll scratch, kick, and burrow—or con—your way in. And look as innocent as Shirley Temple all the while. No wonder you drive Molina nuts."

Temple basked in Max's regard. She had developed her serious snooping instincts during the long year he'd been missing in action, and was glad to hear the professional spook admit that the amateur sleuth was effective, even useful. In limited ways, at least. It was more than Molina would ever do.

"So what's the story on the big cat?" she asked, using a caffeine chaser to wash down starches and sugars.

"I don't know yet. The Cloaked Conjuror's leopard has been kidnapped. It could be by a ring of illegal animal dealers. It could be by some disgruntled local magicians who don't like him squealing on how stage illusions are done. It could be—"

"The Synth."

Max nodded, staring into the dark depths of his coffee as if expecting an image to appear there. "CC has heard from them. It. Supposedly. The note could have been a misleading hoax."

"Cee-cee?"

"I can't keep repeating that corny title. The Cloaked Conjuror. Ye gods, what the public will buy."

Temple squinted at her kitchen wall clock, a rhinestoned Felix the Cat model with twitching tail for a pendulum that Electra had given her after her most recent brush with death.

"The CC seemed nervous at the TitaniCon judges' table even before all hell broke loose. Once the action started, he and his bodyguards got out of there fast."

"He's a nervous man. The media aren't kidding about death threats. He makes enough money to live behind the security measures of a drug lord, but I don't think that would help him against a cabal of rogue magicians."

"They make bad enemies?"

"The worst." Max was dead serious. Then he lightened up. "But I don't know that this leopard snatching has anything to do with the Synth, if there is such an entity. No ransom demand has turned up yet, which is a little disturbing. So I'm going on the first premise: the cat was taken by someone who wanted a 'tame' wild animal to peddle for big dough to a drug lord or a vanity collector."

"Isn't it dangerous to abduct a leopard?"

"Osiris's front nails were clipped, and he was probably shot with a tranquilizer gun."

Temple looked at Louie and winced. "Please, no gory details in front of the c-a-t. Louie's ears are flat back; it's like he knows you're discussing an attack on a cat."

"He knows he's not going to get any leftovers," Max said. "That's *his* problem."

"But he's scowling. Can't you see the little vertical wrinkles in his forehead fur?"

"Yes, and they're always there. With all the bad actors I have on my tail, I refuse to get worried about being eavesdropped on by a cat."

Temple exchanged a glance with Louie. He blinked in what she could choose to regard as complicity, or as the usual feline boredom with messy human affairs.

"So you need me to pose as a woman desperately seeking a leopard for . . . oh, I get it! For the new Crystal Phoenix animal attraction. But we have a consultant doing that. I have nothing to do with it."

"You don't have to tell anyone that."

"Of course not. When do you want to do this?"

"Starting today? Osiris is a pampered performing animal. I'd like to get him back home with as little trauma as possible."

"Then you think the snatchers, and the sellers, are around here?"

"No sense transporting an animal when there are plenty of buyers in Las Vegas. This town attracts people who like to live big and break rules."

"You don't think they'd hurt the leopard?"

"Not intentionally, I hope, but for all the animal compounds around Vegas, the biggest being Siegfried and Roy's, there are also some sleazy, questionable operations."

Temple, who longed to visit Siegfried and Roy's white stucco wonderland especially designed for their rare white tigers and other big cats, recalled the sleek black panther that Max had borrowed for his unsettling Houdini "haunting" illusion at the Halloween haunted house attraction the previous fall.

"I'd hate to think of Kahlúa in bad hands," she said.

"A lot of love and training go into a performing animal," Max agreed. "They're a special breed. Every animal is a partner in the act. Stealing one is more than nipping an investment."

"You never worked with big cats."

Max glanced to the countertop. "Maybe that's why Louie and I have never gotten along."

"Oh, I wouldn't say you two don't get along. It's just that you're both too overprotective of the same person."

"Yeah, you can take care of yourself," he mocked. "Seriously, you've got the gumption of a pit bull when someone is trying to keep you from knowing what you think you should. Where did that come from? Besides the news biz."

"I suppose that didn't hurt." Temple hadn't thought about it much. "Maybe mostly from being the youngest and littlest and femalest in the family. Everybody was always beating me up by sheltering me from something. It got tiresome. The more they whispered or concealed, wouldn't show me or tell me, or wouldn't let me tag along, the more I wanted and needed to know, to hear, to go there. That's all."

"Picked on with love," Max said, almost nostalgically.

"Picked on is picked on, whatever the motive." She pulled her own coffee mug near, nursed it between her slightly cool fingertips. "So what did your birth order do for you? You've mentioned your cousin, but even I don't know about your immediate family. I never thought to ask, because you always seemed so . . . solo."

"That was my act. The Mystifying Max. I deliberately avoided using the usual assistants. No nubile girls. Just me."

"Even Zorro had a henchman."

"Only on TV. But in the family, I was the oldest, with younger sisters and one very little brother. That's why my cousin Sean and I bonded. Brothers more than buddies. A guy your own age to do everything with, with none of the little everyday family tensions to drive us apart, or make us fight over stupid things. Until Ireland."

Temple nodded, not mentioning the disastrous fight over a woman in the end. "A soulmate. I grew up alone in a large family."

"So did I," Max said.

"We're absolutely unique, and two of a kind."

"Yup. Now, will you be my shill?"

It wasn't a proposal of marriage, but when he put it that way, how could she refuse?

Max was still driving the Maxima dropped off for him a couple weeks before by some anonymous contact. Such edgy manipulations were the only proof Temple had that Max led an undercover life for a shadowy international antiterrorism organization.

He seemed to relish the black car's nondescript profile, and its play upon his name. It was as if his life always had to be so anonymous that brand names became extensions of his personality.

Today he drove the Maxima out Highway 95 into the desert that surrounded Las Vegas like a white paper doily surrounds a glazed fruit tart, Las Vegas being the tart, of course, and a gaudy little number she was, too.

Temple adored going places with Max and doing things together again, even if they were clandestine. Their "honeymoon" period was symbolic; intimations of marriage had been scuttled by the realities of Max's antiterrorist past when it rose up like a deep-sea monster.

Today, there were no monsters, and there never would be any sea here, just desert. The blue sky was cloudless, yet grew misty at the horizon where the distant mountains shimmered like the mauve and lavender glints in an opal.

Much as Temple loved to drive herself, a bit faster than the law allowed, she loved letting Max drive her somewhere, somewhere surprising. He was a magician by profession, after all, even if he was now forcibly retired.

When the car finally turned onto a rutted sandy road, it drove into the encroaching desert for a quarter mile. Then she saw a big wooden sign with white-painted lettering carved into its wind-weathered surface.

" 'Animal Oasis,' " she declaimed and asked at the same time.

"No shills needed here," Max reassured. "This is where we'll research your upcoming role. Ever wonder where I got that cloud of cockatoos for the finale of my act?"

"You kept them in that wonderful mesh aviary at the Goliath theater. They looked so gorgeous flitting around that tropical greenery. I'd never seen plants backstage before, unless it was for a production of *Little Shop of Horrors.*"

"Audrey Junior was hardly a plant," Max objected, referring to the domineering carnivorous growth that had starred in the cult film and the later musical play and film. He was as much a theater and film buff as Temple was, another reason they had clicked like the opening tumblers of a bank safe.

"I'm just in a gruesome mood," Temple admitted. "Did you know your cockatoo retreat inspired my idea for an elegant petting zoo at the Crystal Phoenix?"

"That Goliath setup was only for the length of my contract. The birds came from here. And they came back here when I went."

"Do you miss them? I mean, did you like working with animals?"

"Sometimes better than with people. Well-trained birds are easy to work with. Except for the occasional dropping. A real drawback when wearing black is your trademark."

"Kind of like really large, gooey dandruff."

Max grimaced at her comparison. "Luckily, the distance between stage and audience hides a multitude of flaws."

Temple didn't mention that sometimes the distance between magician and mate could also hide a multitude of flaws.

She thrust aside past issues, leaning forward to see their destination, intrigued to encounter a place that housed performing animals. Animal Oasis. It sounded like a shelter, but was there really any true shelter for creatures that could be bought and sold like household plants?

They parked behind a low beige-stucco building set into the brown bezel of the usual desert scrub. Beyond it, Temple glimpsed higher stucco walls fringed by exotic greenery. As they left the car, she could hear water trickling in the distance. A lush, damp smell tinged the dry wind that riffled across the sand.

"It does look like an oasis in there," she told Max, pushing up on her toes to see over the wall. "No! I know. It looks like the wall that kept in King Kong on Skull Island."

Max laughed so hard that the man coming out of the building to greet them froze in his tracks and looked back to see if a clown car was following him.

"You're not a bloodhound on the track of crime," Max told her, "you're an unlicensed imagination in search of a Stephen King storyline."

They approached the bewildered man, a typical outdoors guy for these arid parts. Time and the desert had impressed a road map of wrinkles onto his features like a tooling die biting into leather. His teeth gleamed bone white in his weathered face, and his eyes were Lake Mead blue.

"Max Kinsella," he was saying, with wonder. And warmth. He strode forward to grab Max's right hand and wring it as much as shake it. "I thought you'd left us for good. Damn, but you look fine."

Then he turned the weathered charm on Temple, grinning expectantly.

"Temple Barr, PR." She extended a hand before Max had a chance to explain her. "I'm helping Max out on a project."

"Kirby Grange." He didn't offend her by shaking hands any more delicately, but the grip wasn't punishing, just firm and brief. "This here's my outfit."

"Any great apes in there, Kirb?" Max asked, removing his sunglasses, and glancing at Temple.

"Only some of my crew. But come in outa the sun, folks. It's already fixin' to turn into summer on us." Kirby turned to Temple with a grin. "Not that I haven't housed an ape or two. Terrific fellas and gals."

Inside, the building was functional with a capital S as in Spare: Concrete floor, discount office furniture, battered file cabinets and a lot of metal folding chairs sitting around.

Temple got the impression that not a lot of sitting around was done at the Animal Oasis.

"Have a seat."

They took the only ones available, two folding chairs raked into a rough conversational angle. Kirby Grange leaned against a desk edge. Beer belly, jeans, and rolled-up faded denim shirtsleeves made him look like a ranch hand, and Temple supposed that was what he did.

"Why'd you rush off like that, Max? Not a word. And not that you weren't paid up, but the birds just left downstairs at the Goliath."

Max did something Temple had never seen him do before. He fidgeted with guilt.

"I had to leave town fast, Kirby. Personal matter."

Kirby nodded, craggy face impassive but his blue eyes sparkling with speculation. "It was all right. Got a crew to disassemble the aviary and we moved the whole shooting match out here. You need the birds again?"

"No." Max took a deep breath. "I'm out of the magic game."

"Glad to hear it, because I'm out of the performing parrot game too."

"They were cockatoos, and they didn't really have to perform that much."

For a moment tension hung between the two men like an invisible curtain, like the heat giving the desert air a permanent wave right before your eyes.

"For now," Max went on, "I'm helping out a friend. Not her," he added as Kirby automatically glanced at Temple.

"No." Kirby grinned. "You don't look like jest a friend, miss. Leastways I wouldn't want it that way if I was twenty years younger."

It was the kind of gallantry older men felt entitled to make to much younger women. Temple ignored it because it was so harmless in this instance, and because Max might need reminding.

He looked on benignly, as avuncular as Kirby now, as if he had somehow taken on the older man's coloring like a chameleon.

Temple was shocked to realize that this was what Max did: he presented himself to people and fell into their patterns so completely and naturally that he could blend into any environment, any situation, any persona.

"What can I do for you?" Kirby asked, pleasantries over and business beginning.

"I'm looking into something for a magician friend," Max said smoothly, seriously.

He was only half lying, Temple noted. The Cloaked Conjuror wasn't a friend.

"His big cat's gone missing. We're thinking it might have been taken by someone who deals in illegal wildlife sales."

Kirby's friendly face hardened. "Got a few of those around. Worse varmints than anything on four feet or no feet. How can I help you?"

"First, let me take a stroll through your records. I know you keep tabs on some of the shady operations for the authorities. Then show my friend—" Max grinned and corrected himself. "My *not*-friend around your compound. And tell her how to spot a big cat that's not at home."

Kirby's eyes played ping-pong between Max and Temple, their expression bouncing from surprise to worry before he fixed his attention on Temple. "Well, now, miss, showing you the Oasis would be a fine break for me."

He went over to a file cabinet, jerked open a drawer, and eyed Max with much less pleasure. "You'll find what you want under *V*. As in 'vermin.' "

His boot heels clacked the concrete as he came to Temple. "Follow me. I hope you got shoes that can stand a cleaning. These animals don't always use the bidet."

She laughed and accompanied him out into the searing sunlight.

Behind them, Max was already shuffling papers. She saw him pull a small object from his jacket pocket and lift it to a page. Too big to be his mascara-size camera. What?

But Kirby Granger was drawling out a guidebook spiel to his animal kingdom. Temple trotted alongside him to the inner gates, to the animal Shangri-la beyond: big, looming wooden stockade gates, now that they had penetrated the electrified cyclone fence that defined the fringes.

Uh-oh. Maybe King Kong was on the menu after all. Or she was.

Chapter 8

Portrait

Molina thought Janice Flanders sounded oddly flustered on the phone.

"You have a job for me?"

"I know. The computer has made you obsolete," Molina said, "but not in this case. I don't trust eyewitness descriptions, particularly when they come from a bartender. I'm betting your fine Italian hand will get a better translation. Besides, he's not exactly Mr. Cooperative."

"A challenge?" Janice's voice had perked up.

"And he works nights, and the only place he'll consent to be debriefed is on the job."

"Which is where?"

"Secrets strip club, on Paradise."

"Oooh, Lieutenant, you do know how to appeal to the artistic soul. What do you suspect this unidentifiable guy of? I assume the suspect is a guy."

"Oh, yes. Well, anything from loitering to public intoxication to murder."

"You wouldn't need a portrait of a suspected loiterer. Or a drunk."

"No. Are you willing to do it? 'Rick' works Monday through Saturday."

"Even the bartender works under a nom de guerre? I can't resist. Sleaze factor wins every time. Besides, I'm sure we'll always have Paris. The regular rate?"

"A thirty percent sleaze bonus."

"All right."

Molina eyed the detectives' reports again as she hung up. Although they had thoroughly grilled Secrets habitués and tracked Cher Smith's ragged family background, her death still had unsolved written all over it. The cold facts: 78 percent of strippers are stalked by customers; 61 percent are assaulted by them. Add the usual late-night muggings in bad neighborhoods, and the odds grew longer than a lying Pinocchio's nose in favor of whoever had killed Cher getting away clean as a wolf whistle.

This Vince character was the only missing piece in the puzzle. She hoped Janice—wry, solid, talented Janice—would piece enough of Vince together to give her detectives a face to find. A face that wasn't Rafi Nadir's. Ironic, how much she needed him to be not guilty this time.

Matt was surprised when his phone rang again so soon after he'd hung up. He jumped as if guilty of something, but the only possible offense was still feeling guilty about the call he'd made on that phone only half an hour ago. Guilt only goes around to come back and give the owners a good hard kick.

"Matt?" Her voice came breathless, unusual for Janice, and not at all like it had sounded a half hour ago when he had called. Before he could acknowledge that she had indeed reached him, she rushed on. "Listen, I don't blame you for canceling our dinner tonight. That was pushing it. Inviting you here for dinner, I mean. Kiddies off. Home alone. Actually, you didn't cancel it, you just didn't accept it. I don't blame you."

"Janice, that isn't it at all."

"No? What else could it be? I feel like the Venus fly trap that failed."

While Matt pondered an answer to that, she rushed on. Her anxiety to smooth over an apparent snag in their tentative relationship both aggravated his guilt and intrigued him. He was glad his late-life entry into the dating game was rattling someone else besides him.

"Just listen," she was saying. "Right after you called, an identification job came up. Just now. I could do it tonight. But. The neighborhood's not the best. Want to come along? I could use a bodyguard."

"You don't know how much. But it's not me—"

"It could be fun. Well, okay. Interesting. Secrets. It's a strip joint. I've got an uncooperative bartender to deal with. I feel like a gunfighter strutting into a new saloon. Draw, partner, draw!"

Matt laughed. "Janice, where on earth did you get this assignment?"

"From your friend the homicide dick."

"Molina sent you into that kind of a situation?"

"Why not? She'd go into it. Why shouldn't a sensitive artist type like me soak up the scintillating ambiance too? Besides, she's paying extra and I could use the money."

"It's not an environment I'd visit in a million years."

A long pause. "I know. I'm asking too much. It might freak you out."

He was feeling too guilty about saying no to dinner, at home alone, to let her go unescorted into a seedy situation like a strip club. He was already figuring a strategy to make sure that Kitty O'Connor knew nothing about it, or about Janice.

"Janice. Why'd you say yes?"

"I need the money. I could use something weird in my life. I'm trying my damnedest not to drive you away."

Matt shook his head at the phone, where the gesture didn't do any good. As Janice had caved in to Molina, he was about to cave in to her. Maybe life's everyday plotline was constructed by a daisy chain of cowards. He couldn't let her face a strip club alone. For the moment, Secrets sounded a lot more hazardous than Miss Kitty.

"I said yes to the job," Janice admitted, "before I really thought about what it would mean." Another pause. "And . . . you wouldn't be trapped with me. Plenty of other female competition to think about." She was still coaxing. "A dozen topless dancers will be our chaperons, honest."

"I don't feel trapped. At least not by you. I can see I'm going to have to explain myself, and I'd better do it in person. All right. I'm off work tonight. When do you want to do the dirty deed?"

They settled on what seemed a reasonable time, if there ever was a reasonable time for going to a strip joint. Matt hung up finally, pondering how to completely rearrange his life in a few short hours.

Living alone meant that the apartment was utterly silent when he was. He wasn't used to solitary living. Rectory life bristled with people always coming and going, both residents and visitors.

He sat on the red sofa savoring the silence. And then he wondered if the place was bugged. He couldn't underestimate Kitty O'Connor. Her uncanny way of knowing where he was, and when, was probably based on years of undercover experience.

His skin crawled at how easily the most innocuous life could be compromised. One determined monomaniac could weasel her way into every crevice of his routine.

Matt stood.

He left and locked the apartment, for whatever good it might do, and took the elevator to the building's main floor.

The Circle Ritz lived up to its name both in its rotund construction and its aura of faded 1950s glory, when it had been architecturally reasonable to slather black marble on floors and exterior walls as if it were Russian caviar on Melba toast.

He passed through the modest lobby, his reflection on the black marble floor making him feel like he was walking on water, on very dark, deep water. At least the hall leading to the chapel was paved in step-softening walnut parquet.

A wedding was in progress.

Matt slipped into a white-painted pew as discreetly as he could. From much past experience of weddings and funerals, it was very discreetly indeed. He only glanced at his seatmate once his settling rustles had quieted.

Oh. Of course. Elvis.

Elvis sat as still as a corpse. Matt couldn't see beyond the dark, silver-framed aviator shades to anything resembling eyes. Electric candelabra stationed at the pew ends threw dancing lights on the colored stones studding Elvis's wedding-white jumpsuit. His pompadour and sideburns were angel-hair white too.

Platinum Elvis took up a lot of space. Matt squeezed against the pew end. Wouldn't want to crowd the King. He put his respectful attention on the ceremony. He had, after all, crashed this wedding.

Electra, looking like a late-life girl graduate in her black JP's robe, officiated. In a few minutes she released the fortyish couple to a slow walk back down the aisle between a smattering of friends and the host of soft-sculpture figures with which Electra populated the pews so every couple would have a full house.

Taped music—Hawaiian Wedding Song—played until everyone involved had hula-ed down the aisle and out, except Electra and himself.

Matt stood as she noticed him. "Got a few minutes?"

"Got scads of minutes," she said. "Las Vegas weddings are much less impromptu now. Everything's scheduled. Like real life. Kinda boring."

"I see the organ is a stage prop these days."

"Oh, yes." She shrugged out of the robe. "It's easier not arranging for Euphonia to come to play it. Besides, couples want a high-tech ceremony today: their favorite songs; videotapes-to-go; balloons released; all the wedding bells and whistles."

Matt moved to the silent organ, his fingertips pausing on the pale keys. "Kind of a shame."

"You're welcome to come and play any time the chapel's dead."

"Dead?"

"Not hosting a wedding."

"Speaking of dead—" He looked questioningly toward Elvis.

"My newest." Electra fondly regarded the figure. "He just didn't want to be left out. And, you know, I met this neat Today Elvis guy at the big Kingdome Hotel opening with all the impersonators present, and have never seen hide nor snow-white hair of him since. I thought we had something special. So this is a memorial to Izzy."

"Izzy?"

"Too complicated to explain, Matt. Aren't there some things in your life too complicated to explain?"

"How about everything?"

"Such ambition," Electra joshed. "You're too young to be that mysterious."

"Not mysterious, just mystified. Anyway, I want to offer you a deal you can't refuse. I'm hoping that Elvis in the pew is on my side."

"Really?" Electra's thinning gray eyebrows lifted as high as they were capable of.

"I want to make a trade."

"Trade?"

"My Millennium Volkswagen Beetle for your Ford Probe."

"Your silver Elvismobile for my old faded pink Probe?"

"Right."

"But . . . I've loved Elvis since 1955, and he gave that car to you."

"Exactly."

"To you, not to me."

"I don't believe in Elvis. I'm sorry, Electra, but I just don't. I believe in the Holy Ghost, but I don't believe in Elvis. Maybe he just isn't holy enough. So I can't accept a car from someone I don't believe in. It's fitting that you have the Beetle. It means something to you. And . . . I could use a less high-profile car."

"But your new VW is worth six times more than my old Probe."

"That's why I'd like you to throw in the Hesketh Vampire. You can keep occasional riding privileges, though. I'd hate to see you hang up your Speed Queen helmet for good."

"I thought you loathed that motorcycle."

"Did it show that much?"

"And how! This deal is saccharine sweet for me. But I hate taking advantage of you."

"You'd be doing me a favor, but I'd probably get the Probe repainted."

"Color it purple; see if I care."

"I was thinking . . . white."

"Oh."

"Practical in this hot climate."

"At my age, I don't want practical and white unless it's a private nurse. But suit yourself, dear boy. No doubt it'll be a tropical-weight white linen one."

"White may be practical in cars, but it's murder on suits. Besides, I got used to black."

Electra winked. "If you get too lonesome for black, you can slip on my justice of the peace robe and stand in for me."

"I'm not qualified to perform civil ceremonies. Besides, I always hated doing weddings."

"For goodness' sake, why?"

"So many of them end in shreddings and sheddings. A lot of them start from a position of insanity and go on from there."

"I guess I know that from experience." Electra, obviously recalling one or all of her vaunted five husbands, stared at the soft-sculpture audience as if searching for answers.

"And," Matt said quickly, before she was permanently lost on Moonlight Bay, "I need the Probe tonight, if that's all right. We can take care of the title changes any day this week after that."

"Borrow my car? Sure. I'll bring the keys down to you this afternoon about four."

"Great," Matt said, relieved.

The first part of his self-defense plan was going so well he was beginning to feel optimistic.

Chapter 9

Heads or Tails?

As soon as the denizens of the Circle Ritz have finished their chitchat in the chapel and departed, I remove myself from where I am curled up next to the Lady in Black and decamp to the side of my old friend Elvis.

He is looking a little pasty-faced today and quite unlike himself in the bleached hair with which Miss Electra Lark has saddled him. It makes me wonder in what state I will be represented after my demise. Bald or bleached is definitely not my style.

I curl up by the King and thoughtfully knead my front shivs into his overstuffed knee, occasionally scratching my chin on one of the prong-set stones bedewing his stretch polyester. Of course, the real Elvis's jumpsuits were fashioned from the finest Italian wool, but one cannot expect Miss Electra Lark to underwrite that level of authenticity.

I am quite pleased with myself, and for once that is for a

reason. I sicced . . . er, sent Miss Midnight Louise to tail Mr. Max Kinsella and find out what he is up to while on the trail of the missing leopard. No doubt Mr. Max is sympathetic to the Cloaked Conjuror's loss, as he himself worked with a black panther named Kahlúa during our Halloween caper. Actually, panther is a Miss Nomer. The beast in question is really a black leopard, so Kahlúa is a sister under the skin to Osiris.

Obviously, that is one big wild cat chase, as no one even knows where Mr. Max resides, except perhaps my Miss Temple, and she has been exceedingly canny about keeping even me in the dark as to his usual whereabouts.

Meanwhile, I have stuck to my base at the Circle Ritz, and have come up with a destination and a means of transportation without hardly batting a drowsing eye.

Of course, Mr. Matt is not on the trail of the cat, but he is up to something unsavory. I can tell by a certain air he wears when he feels guilty, which is frequently. I wish that they would bottle guilt and sell it as a unisex cologne. I can smell it from a hundred paces and following its trail never leads me astray.

So after lavishing my manicured attention on poor old Elvis for a while, I regretfully leave my cushy situation and hie out to the Circle Ritz parking lot to wait by Miss Electra Lark's pink Probe. I am hoping that Mr. Matt's appointment is after dark, so I can slip into the back seat as he enters the front without being detected.

Then we shall see where he goes and what happens there. I hope it is somewhere more exciting than an ex-priests' meeting at Maternity of Mary in Henderson.

I am not the churchy type, and especially not the maternal one.

Chapter 10

Animal Instincts

"What was that masked thing?" Temple asked as the Maxima jolted over the dusty road taking her and Max away from the Animal Oasis.

"This?"

Max pulled a small object from his pocket that looked like a tiny camera, but wasn't.

"It scans lines of type. Here. It's on. Scroll down with the arrow until you come to an address on Redrock Mountain Road."

"Wow. I'd never need a pen and notebook again. What's at this address?"

"Someplace you'd never want Midnight Louie to go."

"Really! What is it? The animal pound?"

"Worse. It's Rancho Exotica, owned by one of the area's biggest big game hunters. He's rumored to run an 'animal ranch' for breeding and sale. I've heard of his operation. Very hush-hush."

"What's so hush-hush about another Animal Oasis?"

"Word is he provides canned hunts and trophy heads for high rollers."

"Max! This is where you're going to send me? I like being independent, but that doesn't include suicide."

"Last time I looked, you were still two-legged. Relax. Cyrus Van Burkleo is untouchable in this town. He bankrolls all the right fundraisers. Very smooth operator. Rumors can't hurt him. If I went in there, he'd smell investigation. You . . . you're just an eager-beaver PR gal doing some background research. I took the liberty of setting up an appointment for you."

"Now, while I was wobbling around Animal Oasis with the gallant Mr. Granger? How?"

"I phoned." Max produced his cell phone from his other jacket pocket.

"But how did you get an appointment on such short notice?"

"I said I was Van von Rhine's personal assistant calling from the Crystal Phoenix. We were running up against deadline on opening our animal attraction and could Mr. Van Burkleo spare a few minutes with their ace project coordinator, who could use some expert tips for the Phoenix exotic petting zoo? Van Burkleo doesn't turn major hotel-casinos down, especially one with a manager whose name so neatly mirrors his own."

"The Phoenix isn't so major compared to some of the T rexes in this town now that MGM Grand has bought out Steve Wynn."

Max smiled tightly, never taking his eyes from the rutted road. "But Macho Mario Fontana *is* major muscle; this guy'd never irritate a Fontana operation."

"The Phoenix has nothing to do with Nicky's uncle Mario. I know that for a fact."

Max's terse smile widened into a grin. "But Cyrus Van Burkleo doesn't know that. And don't you tell him."

"So what is my mission at Rancho Van Burkleo?"

"Be on your toes"—Max glanced to the floorboard and at her platform wedge sandals—"which I don't have to tell you to do. Ask anything, see everything, and make mental notes on it all. If you happen to notice a leopard that isn't as happy a camper as the big cats you just saw at Animal Oasis . . . don't let on. Naive, nubile, and perky should do it."

"Max, that's sexist."

"So is Van Burkleo. I wouldn't send you in there if I didn't know he had a blind spot that's just your size. Think you can handle it?"

If Molina had asked her that question, she would have snarled "Sure" on a knee-jerk impulse. With Max, she was tempted to hedge. And that told her she was getting all too dependent on him.

Time to go face King Kong on her own, hopefully without her hands tied behind her back.

Rancho Van Burkleo was tucked even farther back from the highway than Animal Oasis.

It sported no workshop-lettered sign. Only a desert track that suddenly turned into asphalt running toward the end of the world.

"There's nothing out here, Max."

"That's the idea you're supposed to have. Slow down and drop me off here. I want to scout the perimeter."

"Dressed in black?"

"Left my camouflage clothes at home. It'll be all right. At this point, the security should be mostly to keep the animals in, rather than humans out.

"You seem to have scouted this place before," Temple observed as she slowed the car to a jolting stop on the rough road.

"No, but the data in Kirby's files was fairly specific, at least about the perimeter of this place. Van Burkleo is one of those quasi-legal operators every law enforcement unit—state police, DEA, INS, Initials R Us, ad nauseam—would love to catch with his fingers in some illegal cookie jar."

Temple said nothing more. Max was sending her into a serious danger zone. Either he honestly trusted her instincts or the umbrella of the Crystal Phoenix and the Fontana family was a larger, stronger defense than she realized. She was a little slow on the uptake, but half a lifetime of surviving on animal instincts had made Max a master at weighing danger.

Animal instincts. Number one was self-preservation. Temple had better dial hers up to maximum.

Max had told her to drive until she couldn't, so she continued along the road more cautiously than usual, in other words, slowly.

Thickets of scrub clustered on the flat land, obscuring what lay beyond. What lay beyond was rougher terrain, crisscrossed by dry washes that could fill up with water breathtakingly fast in a hard Nevada rain, which came seldom but devastatingly.

A lot of washes were damp in their rocky bottoms, despite a long lack of rain. She began to suspect that these washes could be filled mechanically to put off trespassers. Some moat!

Finally, a gate set into piled rocks loomed ahead like a minimountain. An iron fence extended in either direction as far as the eye could see. Must have cost as much as a Strip hotel-casino wet area, and almost nobody would see this. Except for Max's assumed high rollers. A modest sign read Rancho Exotica. She did a double-take when she read it, because the first time through she'd seen: Rancho Erotica. Las Vegas conditioning at work.

When she stopped at the gate, she noticed a speaker and camera set into the raw, red stone.

It squawked at her, so she squawked back after getting out of the car to get her mouth close enough to the speaker. The high-mounted camera recorded her most unflattering angle: from above she looked like a red-headed mop with no body.

"Temple Barr from the Crystal Phoenix Hotel and Casino. Mr. Van Burkleo's office is expecting me."

A voice so distorted it was genderless instructed her to proceed when the gates opened.

She tramped back into the car, irritated at being too short to lean out its open window and submit to this inspection with dignity.

The high, barred gates retracted into their red stone mountains with the slick mechanical ease of ancient tomb booby-traps springing on the wary hero of an Indiana Jones movie.

Another long drive—what was out on the perimeter all those miles back for Max to scout?—finally rewarded her with the sight of a low stone compound built along the base of the mountain.

The road took her to the center of a sprawling construction stabbed with walls of glass and redwood. A wooden door wide and high enough to befit a cathedral provided a focal point.

There the asphalt ended like a thermometer in a fat pool of parking lot-cum-turnaround.

Temple parked and got out of the car, wondering if she looked as dusty as its once-mirror-black surface.

She took off her sunglasses. The surrounding scene lost the vivid color the tinted lenses intensified. To the naked eye, the building seemed like a Bauhaus version of a '50s ranch-style motel: self-consciously low, long, and modern, a rugged man-made slash underlining the majesty of the mountain behind it.

The big doors entered the cathedral-ceiling main structure at the building's center. Call it Chapel Central. Temple headed for them.

By the time she got there, a normal-size door at the side of the impressive entrance had opened. A tall, slim woman stood waiting in it.

Tall, slim women always made Temple feel like a truant reporting to a principal, but definitely not p-r-i-n-c-i-p-a-l as in "pal."

Feeling as fraudulent as a delinquent seventh grader, Temple stomped to the low-profile door on her high-profile wedgies and gave her name and rank again.

In like a safe-cracker's lock pick.

In and face-to-face with a tiger.

Foot-to-paw, rather.

The quarry-tile floor before her was covered with the splayed hide of a magnificent Indian tiger, only its glassy-eyed head rising in repellant 3-D from the flatness of its glorious skin.

Max had mentioned moneyed scofflaws who would break the rules of God and man, but he hadn't warned her she was about to deal with people who needed to walk on wild animals to feel tall.

She shot a searing glance at Miss Tall and Slim, who was pausing casually on one flattened foreleg of the tiger.

After having so recently seen the magnificent live beasts prowling and lounging at the Animal Oasis, this scene was like going from a kindergarten slide show to a porno flick.

Luckily, the contrast rendered Temple speechless, or she would have blown her cover.

"I'll take you to Mr. Van Burkleo's den," the supermodel said. "If you'll follow me—" She moved on without looking back, expecting compliance.

Temple followed, but she walked around the animal skin.

It was a long walk. Like all rich men's residences, this one required a floor plan to get around in.

It was nice to walk this far indoors in Las Vegas without passing slot machines for once, though.

To take her mind off the tiger rug, she studied Miss T & S's tasteful sand-colored linen suit, which she accessorized with brown alligator pumps made from a hide so real that Temple expected the heels to start snapping at her if she got too close. Temple thought items like that were banned in Boston, and Austin, and all parts of the U.S.

But she wasn't current on what wildlife products were banned as imports. Maybe even the poor tiger rug was permitted.

But not permissible in her world. Imagine poor Louie hunted down for his hide and then slapped down on a cold terra-cotta tiled floor for eternity! Well, for a long time, anyway.

Temple's thoughts churned as she huffed and she puffed her way after Ms. T & S in her alligator shoes. Of course, Temple wore leather shoes, but that was a byproduct of cows that would have been killed anyway and she supposed she would have to reevaluate her whole footwear code shortly. Also fast food.

At least the Midnight Louie Austrian crystal shoes exploited no living thing. Except who had glued the crystals on? Oh, dear. Even Dorothy could hardly click her ruby slipper heels in good conscience nowadays if she *really* thought where everything came from. Temple supposed even Wicked Witches of the West had some rights. . . .

Speaking of which . . .

"Wait in here," the tall sylph announced in a tone so flat she sounded put upon by being forced to speak again. "Mr. Van Burkleo will be with you shortly."

"Thank you," Temple said, not mentioning that everyone was with her "shortly." She marched into the "den" and stopped abruptly just past the threshold.

The place was a jungle of stuffed animal life.

It was as if every animal she had seen live and glorious just an hour ago was now represented in its dead and stuffed state on every wall and floor of the massive room.

Amidst such a profusion of glassy-eyed accusation high and low any humans in the scene seemed pathetically lost, dwarfed by the dead beasts that surrounded them.

"Is there anything that you'd like?" her attenuated guide asked in a tone that devoutly hoped not.

Temple was a born redhead, and born to be contrary.

"Why, yes. I could use a little information."

"Information?" Repeated with distaste, like a dirty word.

"Yes." Wasn't that what the nameless secret agent had wanted in

The Prisoner, the cult '60s television show? She felt a bit like his rene-
gade spy character, suddenly inserted into a strange environment, not
knowing what was what, who was who.

"Information," Temple repeated, with gusto. "I usually deal with
much more mundane events than big game hunting."

"You must be new with the Crystal Phoenix," the woman suggested, not cordially.

"New at this position. Temple Barr." She extended her hand. Forcing people to shake hands was one way to break down even an icy
reserve.

"Courtney Fisher." The woman surrendered a long, thin, pale hand.

Temple pumped away like young Helen Keller at the family water-
ing trough learning the word "wat-er." "So nice to meet you, Courtney. How long have you worked for Mr. Van Burkleo?"

Temple made no move to sit down, no move indeed, to release the
limp mackerel (white and cold) in her custody.

"Two years. If you'd care to take a seat—"

Temple was not about to be unloaded that easily. "Gee, thanks, but
I sit all day at my job. And this room is so fascinating. Look at all
those animal eyes . . . it's almost like they're watching us. Of course,
they can't. They're only glass, aren't they? Not real."

Courtney glanced around with an expression of new distaste.

While the woman looked at the surrounding gazes with new eyes,
Temple studied her more carefully. Older than she first appeared. Perhaps thirty-eight. Skin wrinkling and tightening at the edges of her
eyes and jaw like a pantyhose mask. A lion's-head ring. A gold
charm bracelet full of lions and tigers and bears and giraffes and kan-
garoos and cheetahs, worth a lot more than a secretary earned if it
was eighteen-karat gold, as Temple suspected. Another gold animal
charm at her neck. A snake and something else, thin and geometric
unlike the sculptural animals, a shape that looked vaguely mystical and
somehow familiar.

Everything about her smelled of money. Did even secretaries here
bring down the big bucks? Temple remembered that this place was
probably a killing ground, and winced at the aptness of her metaphor.

She glanced at the lofty deer and antelope and mountain goat
heads bearing trees of antlers. They brought down the big bucks here,
all right.

"It must be fascinating to work for Mr. Van Burkleo. Do you shoot yourself?" Oops. She meant, do you shoot, yourself? In person.

Somehow it came out sounding as if Ms. Fisher should shoot herself, preferably in the foot.

The woman captured her lean wrist bone in the loose circle of the fingers of her other hand. "Shoot? No. Dusty, hot work. I prefer to stay under air-conditioning."

"I can't disagree," Temple said. "It really can get like darkest Africa out there. In the spring, summer, and fall, anyway. I guess Las Vegas has two climates: burning zone and some bad weather now and again, which is when it rains or gets below eighty degrees."

Courtney showed impeccable teeth. "Is there any refreshment you'd like? Soft or hard?"

"Dr Pepper," Temple suggested, assuming that would be a pain to get. She intended to study the room by herself.

Courtney did looked pained. "I'll see what I can do. Mr. Van Burkleo will be in as soon as he's finished with some international calls."

"Of course. We contacted him on very short notice. It's so kind of him to see me."

Courtney's composure cracked for an instant. Apparently "kind" was not an adjective that suited Mr. Van Burkleo.

She stalked out of the room like a gangly giraffe. For the first time Temple thought there might be some superiority in lack of height.

Once alone, Temple considered snooping, but it was hard to think about doing it under so many observing eyes. Talk about the "Eye in the Sky!" Las Vegas casino spy cameras had nothing on this phalanx of overhead animal heads. Temple was beginning to feel guilty just for being alive and able to move in their frozen presence.

I didn't do it! she wanted to shout, like some guy on his way to the death chamber in a '30s gangster movie. *I'm not the one who killed you all.* But she had a feeling that protest would ring as true in this room as Jimmy Cagney's had on celluloid.

Social attitudes had killed these magnificent beasts, not need.

And everyone in a society was guilty of those attitudes, one way or another, even if it was just taking them for granted.

Then a corner vignette caught her eye. A wall-mounted giraffe neck and head maybe, gosh, twelve feet long tilted down toward the floor. Giraffes really had such sweet faces. . . . Temple froze to realize that a baby giraffe stood on the floor and was stretching its slim, long neck up toward the "mother's" face.

They hadn't shot and stuffed a *baby* giraffe, had they?

It must be a fake baby giraffe, which was tasteless enough. Temple tiptoed over to check out the faux fur. It looked like authentic hide to her.

The baby stood taller than she and its big shiny glass eyes seemed almost to move as she stared at it in horror. Shooting a baby anything, and then setting up this Disneyesque mother-and-child vignette . . .

Dazed by disbelief, Temple tiptoed around a few other animal skin rugs, trying not to notice species. Zebra, she thought. Lovely, lithe zebra. Well, the hunters would say there were too many of them, or once had been, or would be if they weren't "harvested," as if living things could be harvested like onions or tomatoes. Which could be considered living things too, by some. What a slippery slope ethical consumption was!

She started at the sight of a huge gray elephant's foot . . . just a wastebasket by the massive wooden desk.

She tried to imagine someone cutting off her foot, hollowing it out, and keeping it to hold crumpled papers and broken rubber bands.

And where were the other three feet? At whose desk sides? In what attics and storerooms, antique shops? Imagine the places they'd been, far from the dusty and lush ground trod by the huge creatures when living.

There had been 100 million wild elephants in Africa once, she'd read recently. And now there were twenty.

Temple turned, looking for somewhere to sit before she got dizzy. Well.

Not the velvet-upholstered horn chair . . . or the zebra-hide direc-tor's chair. Maybe that ordinary black armchair . . . eek! Leather. How would she like to see her parents used as upholstery?

No wonder animal rightists got a tad agitated. Once you started thinking about how people used and abused animals, and animal "products," once you realized the human race was now launched into cloning and genetically designing animals to serve its every need or whimsy . . .

Temple turned as she heard the double doors into this chamber of horrors open.

A man stood framed by them, wearing a khaki jacket and pants bristling with pockets.

He was stockier than a stuffed laundry bag, his head sun-reddened between the spiderweb of thin gray hair strands still left to him. Huge freckles spread over his face and tops of his hands like fat rings in soup. Three large warts only emphasized his blunt, wind-burned features.

Beauty and the Beast had been given a cruel new twist, for the beauty was in the taxidermist's remnants of the animal kingdom, and the beast was the one puny man in their midst.

Oh, he wasn't so puny physically. In fact, Temple might ordinarily be intimidated, ever so slightly, by such a huge, hearty, and callous specimen of Homo sapiens.

But, buttressed by the wise artificial eyes of noble creatures from water buffalo to lion and tiger and bear to deer and the elephant foot standing at truncated attention as a wastebasket beside his massive mahogany desk . . .

Well, Temple had never been in the presence of a serial killer before.

Get the goods on this guy, she heard herself thinking, *and let Max take him down.*

She felt like just another bit of insignificant prey . . . and then like a tiger-in-disguise herself. Hidden by the jungle, moving silent and swift. Ready to pounce . . .

"Miss Barr, is it?"

He came forward, held out a callused hand (from holding an elephant rifle, no doubt), and shook hers in a relatively relaxed manner. "And how can I help the Crystal Phoenix today?"

All right, PR Woman, do your Clark Kent imitation. Or maybe Lois Lane.

"It's so kind of you to see me on such short notice, Mr. Van Burkleo. We're in a bit of a pickle at the Phoenix with our animal exhibit."

"I thought you were doing a petting zoo."

"We are, and we have a consultant handling that. But . . . at the last minute the owners—"

"The Fontanas."

Temple didn't correct him. The owner of the Crystal Phoenix was Nicky Fontana, singular. And Nicky had nothing to do with his family's mob background. But mentioning such a shocking desertion of his roots wouldn't serve Temple here.

"Yes," she said, smiling. "Such a nice family to work for."

Van Burkleo's sandy, hairy eyebrows raised. She didn't look like a mob soldier.

"We are not unaware," she went on, "that our best clients would very much like access to the services you provide. And we thought you might be willing to advise in our acquisition of one or two more . . . thrilling exhibits for our renovated areas."

"Have a seat."

She nearly threw up. The "seat" he indicated was that literal monstrosity, a Victorian chair constructed solely of deer horns upholstered in crimson velvet.

Temple arranged herself on it like Queen Victoria greeting a foreign dignitary (though her feet, even in three-inch-high wedge heels, didn't quite touch the floor).

"What an interesting . . . zoo you have here," she observed.

"A few of my personal trophies."

"Then you are a big-game hunter yourself."

He bowed.

"You have been to Africa many times?"

"Yes." He smiled. "But the best specimens were not bagged there."

Temple managed to look genuinely mystified.

"This," said Van Burkleo, "is what your Crystal Phoenix clients will be able to track, shoot, and bring home from here."

She nodded, slowly, absorbing the enormity.

In the desert outside of Las Vegas, if you paid enough, you could slaughter an endangered species and have it shipped home on ice for the taxidermist. But how?

"Surely there are laws—?"

'We fly meat all over the country. This is a working ranch. Cattle."

"Cattle." That made as much sense as raising llamas. The only head that did not gaze back at her from the crowded walls was that of the humble steer or cow. Too common. Too domesticated. Too doe-eyed. Too easy.

"Cattle," he repeated, pleased that she had so quickly learned their code. Their hypocrisies. "And what kind of 'stock' can I interest you in?"

"Nothing too exotic," she said apologetically. "A big cat or two.

I suppose white tigers are—"

"Very difficult. Not impossible, but very difficult. Luckily, we have some excellent breeders locally."

Temple sat still, shocked to her core. Was he implying that he could raid the breeding stock of the most public and protected big-cat programs in the country?

Such power—or nerve—was truly chilling.

"We really don't care to compete on that level," Temple said. "Something smaller would be fine. A panther. Or a leopard. Maybe both."

He nodded. "Excellent choice. You do understand that obtaining a prime specimen may be expensive?"

"What attraction in Las Vegas is not?"

At that moment the broad coffered door leading into this den of iniquity opened again.

"A guest, Cyrus?" asked the woman framed by the doorway.

Temple had expected the aloof Courtney. Instead, she found herself riveted by the most exotic-looking woman she had ever seen. In fact, she blinked hard a couple of times to make sure she hadn't been transported to the Island of Dr. Moreau.

The woman seemed to expect the unabashed wonderment of strangers. She slunk into the room, one leg crossing so markedly in front of the other that the gait underlined her resemblance to a jungle cat.

A tawny mane of painstakingly streaked hair haloed her face . . . or what was left of it.

Temple had seen TV reports on extreme plastic surgery: young adults having themselves tattooed, pierced, and cut-and-pasted into hybrid human/animals. The extremest example she recalled was a guy who was morphing into a lizard-man, surgically split tongue and all.

This woman's case wasn't as obvious, but it came close. Eyebrows plucked to a thin blond line were barely there. Her supplemented cheekbones jutted out so far they made her eyes look smaller and forced them into an unnatural tilt. Collagen-thickened lips went beyond starlet-swollen to misshapen, blending with her snubbed nose until together they made a . . . muzzle.

Worst of all, when she reached the desk, Temple saw she was wearing those patterned contact lenses. This amber-colored pair gave her pupils vertical slits, like a cat's eyes.

Add all that to the fact that everything she wore was bronze or hide patterned, and that costly gold charms shaped into the heads and bodies of big cats dangled from her neck, ears, and wrists, all winking with tasteless constellations of diamonds . . . Temple was speechless.

"Leonora," the woman said in a husky purr, extending a hand with nails so long they curved into claws. They were enameled a pale ocher color, which made them even creepier than if they'd been lacquered an obvious Carnivore Red. It was as if they were lying in wait for the real thing, like blood.

Temple had stood without thinking why. Maybe to be polite and shake hands. Maybe to be readier to run.

Leonora kept coming closer. She was wearing chamois suede capri pants, a tiger-striped silk-and-spandex top, cork-soled espadrilles.

One clawed hand, tanned pale mocha, reached for Temple.

Temple wasn't sure if her hand lifted to meet it, or to paw it aside.

Smooth, cool flesh grasped hers. The curved nails brushed the thin skin on the top of Temple's hand.

"Leonora Van Burkleo," the woman emphasized.

Temple glanced at Cyrus in dazed comprehension. This was his wife. From the marked age difference, his trophy wife. From Leonora's bizarre and deliberate resemblance to a beast, his *literal* trophy wife.

Leonora's smile revealed Hollywood-white teeth, quite emphatically pointed. Temple had met people with markedly pointed teeth before. But these were unnatural. They had been filed, just as Leonora's face had been reshaped.

Temple realized then that she had quite literally walked into the lion's den.

Max wasn't aware of being stalked until he was almost back to the drop-off point where he was to meet Temple.

He had sighted some of the ranch's security forces early during his ramble. These were camouflage-attired men with rifles, the kind of professionals that turned his blood cold: hirelings, not true believers.

Hard men who were used to doing unspeakable things. It was kill or be killed with their sort, and Max had always tried to stay well away from either role.

He flattened himself among some scattered rocks, a shadow among shadows, and waited until they were utterly gone before moving on.

And then he came on the trail.

He was an urban animal. Wilderness tracking wasn't his particular skill, but even a city slicker could see the random impress of a sneaker tread on the softer areas of sand.

Several sneaker treads.

The security forces wore desert boots. His own shoes always had smooth-soled leather. He had never left easily traceable tracks, like a tire, on carpeting or anywhere else.

Sagebrush was the only cover out here, but the three-foot-high growths pockmarked the flat desert floor as regularly as dotted Swiss. Max moved from bush to bush like a cartoon character, trying to figure out whether the sneaker set had been coming or going.

He had gotten close enough to the compound to not like what he'd found. Close enough to worry about Temple still inside. Now other trespassers were adding to the likelihood that either Temple or he might get into trouble.

Max checked his watch. Only an hour and forty minutes since he'd left Temple. Knowing her fondness for thorough jobs and her gift for talking her way into, and often out of, anything, she was probably still happily poking her nose into her host's business.

He glimpsed movement to his right, sensed a buzz on the air, possibly a distant Jeep.

He dove for the best cover, a small outcropping of rock thirty feet away, hitting the sand and rolling the last few feet. Before he could roll upright, a heavy weight jumped him from above.

Lord, one of the lions is loose, was his first thought. The weight squeezed the wind out of him, flailing buff-colored limbs blurred his vision.

A blow to the head reassured him. It was hard, but not clawed. A human pride had him in their grip.

Max promptly feigned unconsciousness to avoid any more cracks in the skull. No one could go as convincingly limp as a magician.

"Not a guard," someone whispered harshly.

"Then *what?*" demanded another whisperer.

"Shhh! The Jeep's coming this way."

The grips on Max tightened as the vehicle's motor and wheels ground, coughed, and spit sand through the sere desert air. It sounded like an eggbeater on the run.

The noise grew, hovered like a swarm of huge bees, then faded into a distant drone.

"Thank God." This whisper was raspy, but it was a woman's voice. "I hope we didn't kill him."

Max found that hope encouraging. Ranch security would have had no such scruples.

He played possum while they turned him over and poked at him like curious chimps.

"*Black?*"

Max, sweating, agreed. It was crazy to have gone a-hunting in city black out here, but he hadn't become really suspicious until he and Temple had arrived, and by then it was too late to send out for a safari suit.

Hands pawed at him. "He's not armed."

Not with obvious weapons anyway.

"What's a Joe Blow doing out here?"

Max stirred slightly, not wanting to start a ruckus. There were at least three of them, and while the odds didn't concern him, keeping the peace did. Guards with powerful binoculars would catch any dust-up in this terrain.

"What—?" he groaned, trying to sound like an innocent, head-whacked schmuck.

He blinked the sand out of his eyes, finally focusing on tanned, seamed faces. Two men and a woman. She was the party's senior member, a lean sixty-something with wiry strands of silver hair escaping a beige bandanna.

"What are you doing here?" she asked.

The men, a twenty-something and a forty-something with outdoor faces, kept what they thought was a good grip on him.

"Exploring," he answered.

"Alone? On foot? Dressed like that?"

"A friend dropped me off by car. I'd heard about this place. Wanted to look it over."

"Didn't you see the guards?" one of the guys asked.

"Yes. But they didn't see me." Max risked a grin. *You don't want to be seen by guards,* he implied. *I don't either. Maybe we're allies.*

The woman snorted contemptuously. "In that outfit, and they missed you?"

"I headed for shadow when I saw or heard them. Unfortunately, you were part of the shadow I was heading for here."

The woman's burnt sienna fingers curled into the fabric of Max's black turtleneck sweater. "Silk blend." Her eyes, so light a gray they seemed as silver as her hair, hardened. "What the hell is someone like you doing out here on foot?"

"I'm looking for a big cat."

"Going to take it down with your teeth, right?" asked one of the youngsters.

"Not going to take it down at all. Going to get it out of here."

That made them sit up and take notice. Literally. The hands loosened on his limbs.

"What is your scam?" asked a thin-faced man with a sand-grayed ponytail down his back.

"No scam. What I said. I'm looking for a stolen leopard."

The woman was unimpressed. "Alone. On foot. Out here. Unarmed. Dressed like that."

"My partner is inside, and I'd really appreciate it if you'd quit playing twenty questions and let me start worrying about when she's coming out, or if she's coming out."

Their custody eased even more. Max went on. "And you might mention who you are, and why you're out here. Together. On foot. On feet that leave quite visible tracks, by the way."

He looked around. Except for the walking stick that had beaned him, they carried nothing more obviously dangerous than water canteens and backpacks.

"She?" the woman asked.

Max nodded. "It was an impromptu mission, I admit. Not advisable in light of what I've found out here, including you."

"Mission?" The thin-faced guy still looked suspicious. "You some kind of . . . cop? Paramilitary?"

Max smiled. "No. Just trying to help out a friend."

"A friend who keeps leopards?" The man who asked this had freckles, a snub nose, earnest blue eyes. Must have been a cute kid, but his face and tone now were harder than the red rock in the Valley of Fire.

"A friend who works with a leopard. A magician."

"They'd steal a *performing* leopard?" Ponytail's voice shook with rage and surprise.

"Hard to come by unmarked heads." Blue Eyes flashed a meaningful look at the others.

"You don't know what you're getting into," the woman said to Max, having made up her mind about him. "We'll get you back to where you need to meet your partner, if we can, but we won't get caught to do it."

Max allowed himself to move into a crouching position that was still nonthreatening. "I know what I'm doing out here, and now I know what's going on out here, but why are you here?"

"What's going on out here?" Blue Eyes taunted him.

"Canned hunts. Trophies for rich men, culled from zoos, stocks of abandoned exotic felines, the old, the weak, and the domesticated, available to dress your mantel for the sum of several thousand dollars. Pretty ugly racket."

The woman let out an explosive breath, part relief, part unspoken expletive. "You got it. And that's why the security. They don't want anyone to know what's going on, and I'm not so sure they wouldn't shoot anyone who found out about it, especially someone out here on their own without witnesses."

"So. You're not government investigators?" Max eyed them all again. "You look like a college archeological expedition—sorry, no offense meant. And you don't have a handgun between you, much less a rifle. . . . So what are you?"

"Hunt breakers."

"And you think *I'm* a fool. You've seen the patrols, the weapons. Those men will kill you, whether you're alone or in a pack, if you interfere with their operation. That's what they're paid to do."

"But not in front of the hunters." The woman smiled grimly. "That's why we won't show ourselves until they've got a customer with a gun in his hand and some poor declawed retired circus lion cornered against an outbuilding so the coward can be a big-game hunter when he goes home with a dead head for the wall."

Max shook his own head, thankfully not yet dead, just aching. "You won't believe me, because I look like an amateur, but I'm not. If they'll steal a performing leopard from a Strip show just to get stock, they'll kill to protect their setup. . . ."

He let the sentence trail off because it didn't make sense, even as he said it, not even to him. He believed that these hunt breakers were in mortal danger, all right, but why would this illegal canned hunt operation risk drawing attention to itself by abducting a prized animal from a man as powerful as a multimillion-dollar-salaried magician?

Not just for kicks, but he couldn't see any other reason for the leopard's abduction. Maybe that walking stick had shaken up his brains more than he liked to think.

"Would you like to the see the operation up close and personal?" Van Burkleo asked, smiling genially at Temple.

"Of course," she said. "I'm already impressed. I had no idea such a sumptuous accommodation was out here."

"We like it that way," Leonora said. "But don't drag our guest— Cyrus, you haven't introduced her to me—"

"Temple Barr of the Crystal Phoenix."

"The Phoenix!" Leonora's virtually invisible brows rose with surprise. "We haven't had any clients from there yet. Of course we are pleased to accommodate a Fontana family enterprise. What is your position at the Phoenix?"

"Informal," Temple said, watching both Van Burkleo's eyes narrow suspiciously. She was by no means in like Flynn, which meant getting out might be dicey. Very dicey.

"I'm a humble publicist, but Nicky and Van have entrusted me with the concept and execution of their new virtual-reality Action Jackson ride and holographic experience, and also for a small animal area, with all the close-up and personal effect of a Vegas show, but strictly appropriate protection for the animals on display, of course."

"Of course." Leonora's frighteningly inhuman eyes regarded Temple with the same expressionless intensity she sometimes encountered in Midnight Louie's gaze. "We will have a drink while I explain our setup and rules. I'm sure Cyrus neglected the details. Would you like a golden lion?"

"Actually, I'm interested in something smaller. A panther or a leopard, possibly both."

Leonora's laugh was half a growl. "Silly. I meant a drink. A golden lion is my own invention. Lochan Ora with rum and Kahlúa."

"Sounds . . . delish," said Temple, who couldn't imagine combining coffee and scotch liqueurs with rum, but sensed that you didn't argue with a lioness.

Leonora opened a tall cabinet lined with mirrors and cut glass, quickly mixing the contents of two Waterford decanters in a pitcher. The amber-black concoction was poured into delicate liqueur glasses. Temple sipped at hers after Leonora brought it over. Maybe lion fangs weren't venom bearing, but Leonora's filed teeth looked fairly aspish.

During the social lull, Temple asked innocuous questions, which got innocuous answers.

"How long have you been here?" she tried.

"Long enough to develop the property, and our very quiet but solid reputation, as we wanted to," said Leonora.

"It's wonderful to have a nearby resource for the occasional animal," Temple soldiered on. "I don't know what I would have done if I hadn't heard of you."

"And how did you hear of us?" Van Burkleo asked, his voice as smooth as a rum sundae.

"Oh. A friend of Macho Mario's, of course. I mean, Mr. Fontana."

Leonora's eyes glittered as she looked significantly at her spouse.

Temple realized that her clumsy attempt to name-drop had gotten her pegged as the old man's girl Friday, Saturday, and Sunday night.

These people thought like *National Enquirer* reporters!

But the instant that false impression had been made, it was as if Temple had joined some secret sorority. Leonora came to take away the triple-power liqueur, favoring Temple with what passed for a wink from one of her beastly eyes.

"We better not keep you away from the Phoenix too long. Come along. I'll show you what we have available. Something, I'm sure, will suit."

Temple thanked Mr. Van Burkleo profusely, more from relief at leaving his presence and that of the surrounding animal heads than from gratitude, and trotted out after Leonora.

As she recalled, lionesses were the huntresses of the pride while the extravagantly maned males lay and sunned themselves like romance-novel cover models. So she had been handed over to the more dangerous of her hosts.

They left the house by the rear, after passing palatial rooms filled with animal memorabilia, that is to say, taxidermied body parts.

Temple began to imagine a wonderland filled with Van Burkleo parts to infinity. . . .

Behind the living quarters was a pathway and a deep moat, beyond which unnatural natural habitats for big cats and other exotic animals were established at the base of the mountain.

Temple was sure it was all impressive, but she was taken only to the big-cat area. She couldn't help thinking that the animals were on display like department store mannequins, only these were living. A lion roared from behind the scenes, causing her to jump and then come to a dead halt.

"Just old Leo," Leonora reassured her.

"Definitely not what we want at the Phoenix. The leopard and panther are . . . quieter, aren't they?"

"Of course."

"And, as I told your husband, we do have a wildlife consultant who will be in charge of the animals and exhibit. This is just a preliminary scouting expedition on my part, to decide whether we want to include a big cat or two. Or not."

"I understand. There we have two snow leopards. Very nice. Very expensive. Forty thousand apiece? Does that suit your budget."

"This is Las Vegas, Mrs. Van Burkleo. That is not exorbitant."

"A black leopard."

"Oh." Temple stopped. The panther was sunning himself on some rocks beside a narrow waterfall that trickled into the moat far below. His muscled black coat shone like fresh tar in the light, and his big blunt head was far more massive than Midnight Louie's. "He's gorgeous. Is he like a leopard?"

"The same thing, really, except for the coloration. Like golden retrievers and black Labrador retrievers. Black big cats used to be called pards, and the spotted big cat was named after the more golden lion—"

"Leo-pards!"

"Exactly. Yours for thirty, shall we say?"

"Oh!" Temple tried to sound pleased. "And a plain—that is, regular—spotted leopard? Van von Rhine is a blond, and more partial to spotted leopards than the black ones."

"I quite understand. People identify with beasts, don't they? I know I do. I am a lion person from start to finish. Besides the snow leopards, and it would be a shame to break up the pair, the only spotted leopard I have is still too new to be kept in an environment. You'd like to see it?"

"Of course."

Leonora headed for a low set of doors built into the mountain that Temple had overlooked while gawking at the animal habitats, which were as impressive as any modern zoo's.

They left the heat and sunlight behind them as they entered a metal door after Leonora clacked a code into a keypad with her overgrown fingernails.

Instantly, the air felt dank. Water pooled on the concrete floor.

Temple inhaled the stench of animal hair and waste and raw meat.

"The holding cages aren't as aesthetic as the environments. You will need similar facilities behind the scenes for your animals at the Phoenix."

"Luckily, we have plenty of room for that."

Temple followed her guide past empty cages. She saw huge water bowls, and pieces of half-devoured meat of some kind she chose not to speculate about.

Finally, she came to an occupied cage. A lithe leopard paced back and forth, its golden eyes burning in the eternal twilight of the cage area.

"This one is . . . fresh," Leonora said. "It's a bit nervous. Cats like stable environments and he was just brought in."

"How long ago?"

"I don't know. A few days?"

"Where is he from?"

Leonora turned to stare at Temple. "I don't keep the records. Cyrus's secretary does. I see he has plenty of water. He should be calming down."

She moved toward the bars. The leopard suddenly brushed against that side, then turned and screamed at her.

Temple jumped back three feet. The cry had been wild, furious, pained.

Even Leonora retreated. "I don't know what's got into him. Perhaps homesickness for his former environment. If he doesn't settle down, no one will want him and then what will we do with him, hmmm? Don't be a bad boy!" She shook a predatory claw at the animal.

It apparently read the same unspoken threat in her tone that Temple heard in her words, slinking to the opposite side of the cage, where it paced, back and forth, back and forth.

"It looks kind of skinny," Temple said.

Leonora whirled on her. "The big cats are in superb condition. Not an ounce of fat, all muscle. Lean, as nature meant them to be. We do not keep them to grow fat and lazy, like house cats."

"Of course not," Temple said hastily, wondering if she was overfeeding Louie on Free-to-Be-Feline. "He looks in peak condition. I'm sure we'd be interested in him. And the black one. But of course it is up to . . . Horst."

"Horst?"

"Our animal guy. Consultant. I'm the scout, as I said. Horst will want to make the final decision."

Leonora nodded.

Temple was already wondering if Max could do a believable Horst. Why had that name popped into her head? Van Burkleo would no doubt see right through a phony Horst. Who did they know who was German that they could trust? Maybe Max knew someone.

She looked at her watch. Galloping Guccis, she had been here for two and half hours. Max must be fricasseed by now.

"Oh, I must get back. Things to do. Thank you so much for such an informative meeting."

Leonora's face had become the lordly mask of a dozing lion. She turned without comment to lead Temple into the sunlight and the fresh air.

Behind them, the leopard screamed protest again.

This time Temple didn't jump. She just gritted her teeth and wished she had been a lion tamer in a previous life.

Chapter 11

Portrait of a Shady Lady

Janice lifted an eyebrow when she saw the Probe in her driveway, but didn't comment on Matt's "new" old car.

She looked like a schoolgirl with a sketch pad and a street-map guide to Las Vegas balanced on the crook of her right arm. She wore jeans for the first time since he had met her, and the arty earrings were gone. She noticed him noticing her outfit.

"What does the respectable self-employed woman wear to a strip club?" she mused, arranging herself and her gear in the Probe's front seat. "Something casual but nonconsensual? That's what I concluded. What do you think?"

"You don't look like a stripper, in civvies or out."

"That was the idea, but how would you know?"

"I've been backstage at some of the big hotel shows. I figure strippers don't dress, or undress, much differently from showgirls."

"Were these topless showgirls?"

"Ah, no."

"Well, the ones we see tonight will be. Maybe I should leave you in the car."

"I don't think so, Janice." Matt checked the rearview mirror for headlights. Nothing. Maybe Kitty the Cutter wasn't infallible, after all.

"What's with the car?" Janice asked at last.

"I'm trading my landlady for the Elvismobile."

"For this? Why?"

"I like a low profile."

In the strobelike flash of a passing streetlight, he could see her eyebrows lift skeptically.

"Okay," she said. "Who am I to cavil with low profile? I'm racing out to sketch felons in a strip bar." She squinted at the map under the rapid strafe of the next streetlight. "We need to turn left on Paradise."

He followed her directions religiously, trying to pretend he wasn't nervous about going ever nearer to a long-forbidden zone. Once Matt had parked the Probe in the brightest section of the flat, featureless parking lot that surrounded Secrets like an asphalt moat, a material black hole of night, they regarded the building through the windshield.

"Grim, isn't it?" Janice said.

"No windows, just that big winking neon sign and that little windowless door. It reminds me of an ugly mausoleum."

"Shabby. No advertising gimmicks outside. Like someplace you disappear into and never come out of."

"Apparently some woman did just that, or Molina wouldn't want a sketch of a killer."

"You always call her that?"

"Some woman?"

"The lieutenant. No title, no first name?"

"Almost always." Matt wasn't about to admit how deviously he used the lieutenant's despised first name. Knowing someone's secrets was definitely like holding a weapon. A weapon you didn't give away to anyone else.

"But not always." Janice waited for more.

"I guess always," Matt said firmly.

He recalled another secret he kept, and winced internally. Molina had custody of the opal-and-diamond ring Kinsella had given Temple in New York City. The elegant ring, instead of enhancing Temple's finger, reposed in a plastic evidence baggie: found at the scene of another death, of a woman killed in a church parking lot. Matt wondered where the woman whose killer they were tracking tonight had been killed. Here? Or somewhere else? She hadn't ever had an opal-and-diamond ring, Matt was willing to bet.

Was the victim even a woman? Molina hadn't said, and Matt had assumed stripper club meant dead stripper. He asked Janice, who shrugged her mystification. "I'm supposed to ask for a bartender named Rick to get a description of a guy named Vince. That's all we mere translators need to know."

"Translator. An interesting description of the art of suspect portraiture."

"All portraiture is suspect. It's filtered through the eyes of an artist. We make very unreliable witnesses."

"But you're good at drawing out witnesses."

She nodded. "Ready? To be honest, I've never been to a strip joint before either."

Although a few cars were scattered around the parking lot, no one was coming out or going in when Matt and Janice approached the graffiti-etched door.

"I don't suppose many women go to these things. As viewers, I mean," Janice said.

"I don't suppose many ex-priests do either." He pulled the heavy metal door open and waited for her to enter.

"On the other hand," Janice said hopefully, "maybe we're both wrong."

Sound blasted out at them like construction noise: raw and blind, teeth-rattlingly vicious. An aural attack. It was also a fortunate distraction for the terminally self-conscious.

Janice rummaged in her purse until she plucked out a couple of tissues, quickly tearing them to pieces and handing him shreds to jam in his ears.

Even buffered, the music was painful. After that sensual assault, any visual shocks were minor.

Both of them fastened on the long oblong of the bar as an island of safety. Except . . .

"There are two!" Janice shrieked.

"What?" Matt pointed at his stopped-up ears.

Janice's left hand raised, her first two fingers forked in a vee. Not V as in victory, but—

"Two bars," she mouthed now, more than shouted.

Matt turned to assess who passed for bartenders on each side of the room. En route, his eyes slid off mostly naked women writhing to the deafening beat they could feel through their feet and teeth.

A medieval vision of hell, that's all Matt could think of. Michelangelo's painting on the Sistine Chapel wall, where the artist pictured his enemies damned and writhing under torture. Matt, on the other hand, hoped not to see one familiar face in this nightmare vision. Or to have one familiar face see him here.

He pointed toward the farther bar. There the man behind the shiny expanse was a mustached thirty-something, instead of the beefy twenty-one-year-old who manned the nearest strip of shining bottles and background mirror reflecting long bare legs executing extreme variations on the splits.

Janice and Matt climbed onto the plastic-upholstered barstools like flood survivors finding purchase.

She laid her sketch pad atop the droplet-dappled counter.

The man noticed them, ostentatiously finished swiping down the far end of the bar, then ambled over.

It was early enough that the place wasn't crowded, Matt noted. Or maybe it never was crowded. There was something desultory about the atmosphere, despite the pumped-up music and sound system, the women bobbing and posing on the opposing bars, the one in the purple-white spotlight on the stage strutting to the beat. She was a hefty girl in a cheap version of the famous Marilyn Monroe white dress blown up by the subway grate.

Matt had to admit that he found photos of Marilyn Monroe engagingly earthy. She seemed to be mocking herself and the viewer even as she pouted and posed. From her to Jon-Benet Ramsey was one turn of the page backward. Sometimes all sexiness seemed an act the innocent put on to survive an anti-innocence world. That's what you thought, even as they died of being pinup girls. All girls under the skin.

"Rick?" Janice inquired. Shouted really.

"Who's asking?" Matt read the man's lips.

"Janice." She held out a hand.

He regarded it as a curiosity. "Yeah?"

"Lieutenant Molina sent me," she mouthed, putting her hands to better use at her mouth like a megaphone.

Rick reared back, as if bitten. "Molina?"

"I'm *here* to get your *description* of *Vince*."

Janice shouted every key word, punctuating the din, but the method seemed to work.

Rick nodded.

"Can we *go* somewhere *quiet?*"

Rick shook his shaggy head. "Can't leave my post."

Like he was a soldier, Matt thought. Like his was an honorable profession.

"Okay. *Tell* me about *Vince*—" Janice shouted.

The music, if it could be called that, ended as abruptly as an earth tremor, on a dissonant guitar twang drawn out to tortuous length.

Quiet hurt as much as cacophony. Maybe more.

Janice flipped back the cover of her sketch pad and held her pencil poised over the blank page. "I'm all ears, Rick."

"Okay, but you gotta buy drinks."

Matt was about to protest until he saw Janice's anxious look. "Two scotch on the rocks." He didn't expect to get much in the way of fancy mixes, and that was the fastest highball he could think of. Matt shrugged his disavowal of his order at Janice while Rick turned away to clatter ice cubes into thick, ugly glassware and to pour a thin drizzle of whiskey over them.

The silence reverberated in their abused ears, in waves and pulses, sounding like the ocean in a seashell.

Even as Matt's twenty-dollar bill was being scraped away, Janice was at work. "So. Coloring?

"Dark," Rick grunted.

"Foreign?"

"Just dark."

"Skin color?"

Rick shrugged. "Nothing unusual. I said not foreign."

"Face shape. Long? Broad? Prominent cheekbones?"

"Just . . . regular." Rick smirked at her busy pencil.

Matt slapped another twenty to the soggy bar top. "Molina said you'd cooperate. I bet if you don't she'll see no one wearing a badge cooperates with you or this place for a long time. Plus, there's a tip in it."

Rick tilted his head, droned rapidly. "Weird dude. Slouched over his drink. Looked like one of those guys who hands out private-dancer flyers on the sly on the Strip, except he was bigger. Narrow. Big but narrow. Not thick-necked muscle, if you know what I mean. Face was . . . angular, I guess you'd say. All sharp and asking things, you know? Eyebrows like question marks. Greasy hair. Moussed to death. Trendy clothes, if you're from 1975. Velour jogging suit, open at the chest. Cheesy gold necklace. Lots of chest hair. If he'd been broader you'd call him an ape, but he was . . . sleeker. Slippery. Yeah, that's it."

"Nose?"

"Long, like he was. Eyes slanted like a cat's. Eyebrows too, maybe. He looked like he was in a high wind all the time. That moussed-back hair just made him look more like he was running."

"Good-looking?"

"Mandy seemed to think so, the way she hung off him. 'Course, she was drunk six ways from Sunday, as usual."

"What on earth would make a girl get drunk in a place like this?" Janice muttered, her pencil flying, racing the deejay in the corner and his tape machine. She turned her pad to face Rick. "This close?"

He blinked. "Damn. You're good. But the face was broader, beneath the eyes."

"Broader cheekbones," she said as her pencil made it so. "And?"

"Younger. Guy couldn't have been much over thirty. I mean, he acted like the years of the world were on his back, but he wasn't that blown."

Janice's forefinger softened the bags under the eyes, strengthened the nose.

"Yeah." Rick nodded, getting interested despite himself. "And the mouth was more . . . mobile, not so tight. You take your fifties hood, and maybe put some, I don't know, early Sean Connery behind him—"

While Rick talked, Janice's pencil walked over the nubbly paper, changing, changing, changing. She presented the latest version silently.

Rick jabbed a stubby forefinger on the paper. "Eyes were funny. Out of it but in it, if you know what I mean."

Janice nodded, her mouth tightening as she worked and reworked the sketch.

Matt had never seen her sketch so fast. She had taken her time with him, teased every little detail out of him. Now she was sketching in lightning time, and the results were just as good. Matt wondered if she had needed to spend so much time with him, or had just wanted to.

She smudged, corrected, erased, kept flashing the sketch at Rick like a challenge. Each time he met the dare by mentioning another specific, another modification.

It was like watching a duel, thrust and retreat, revise and represent. Back and forth. So fast he couldn't keep track.

"That's it," Rick suddenly conceded. "It's him."

"Vince." Janice nodded satisfaction as she squinted her eyes at the sketch pad. "Wouldn't like to meet him in a dark pizza parlor."

Matt, who'd hardly glimpsed the results of the last ten minutes of rapid-fire exchanges, leaned close to see as Rick's hand swept the twenty under Matt's fingertips into his custody.

A blast of resumed music made Matt's heartbeat stop, then start again with great, galloping thuds. But it wasn't the music that unnerved him. Even done up as Marlon Brando on Prozac, Max Kinsella was recognizable to anyone who had reason to know and fear, or maybe even love him.

Thank God he was here with Janice, and not Temple.

"Think I've got it?" Janice said, shouted over the music, smiling. She leaned back to rub her neck.

Someone else leaned in to see the finished sketch.

"Wow. You're good," she oozed at Janice. "I don't see this guy here, though."

"Have you ever?" Matt felt obliged to ask, though he was trying to ignore the woman's presence.

From what he could tell, all the while trying *not* to see any better, she was attired in iridescent strings. A quartet of strips, and where they went, or didn't, he did not want to go, or know.

"Seen him?" Her face was bare naked too, but easier to take. Her full lower lip—collagen-enhanced?—swelled with doubt. "Don't think so. You ever seen me?" she asked provocatively.

Matt shook his head, glad Janice was supporting him with the same gesture.

"I'm the star attraction." She pointed toward the stage where the sleepwalking Marilyn wannabe was easing her halter-style straps off one shoulder, then the other. Even Matt knew this wasn't very seductive. "Aren't I the star, Rick?"

"Sure are, Redd."

Matt was glad of an excuse to look at her hair, a dramatic magenta-mahogany color found only in a chemist's lab. The color was nothing like Temple's natural coppery crimson mop. If the color was surreal, the way it was looped and piled on top of her head was even more artificial. At least, Matt thought, she had a greater mass of hair on her head than clothes on her entire body.

A long-nailed hand curled over his shoulder. "You're new here."

Janice was watching from what had become the sidelines with a distinctly chilly Mr. Spock distance. This was his show, and his problem.

"I intend to stay that way," Matt said. "New here."

"Aw, too bad. I was going to let you buy me a drink. I don't have to go on for a half hour. Onstage, that is."

She twined herself and her strings around him, in the process almost pushing Janice off the neighboring barstool.

Matt had never felt more embarrassed and less in the presence of a near occasion of sin. This B-movie seduction scene was so hokey it should be shown to the troops to turn them off, except he had a feeling not much would turn off troops.

He tried to pry off her invasive hands.

"What's your lady friend doing," she demanded, clinging more, "taking notes?" She looked over her shoulder at Janice.

Matt found a wave of relief turning into a churn of guilt.

"You need some ideas, honey?" the lady known as Redd said.

"I'm a staff artist for the *National Enquirer*," Janice answered coolly. "We're doing a piece on The Wacky Strippers of Las Vegas. Mind if I sketch you?"

"Yes. I do." Redd straightened. Her face was already painted as perfectly as Janice could ever do it: pencil-arched dark brows, bowed scarlet mouth, eyes so deeply shadowed their own color was neutralized by the shimmering smoky claret aura around them.

Redd's taloned hand struck out to capture the sketch pad, so swiftly that both Matt and Janice jumped, but did nothing. "This is no stripper." She eyed the portrait of Vince with an odd expression, part repulsion, part a hunger Matt couldn't name.

Janice reclaimed the pad just as swiftly. "I said The Wacky Strippers of Las Vegas, not just women strippers."

Redd's darkened eyes smoldered.

Matt smelled something really tacky brewing, like a catfight. He stood up, grabbed Redd's arm. "I thought you wanted me to buy you a drink?"

She whipped around to face him, eyes as feral as her mouth frozen in a half snarl.

"You ready to pony up?"

He shrugged. Anything to save the day, or night.

Rick spoke for the first time, like a member of an audience who suddenly finds his voice. "What'll it be, Reddy?"

"My usual." She undulated onto the empty stool next to Matt. He was glad to serve as a barrier between the two women.

Redd, or Reddy, threw a sultry smile at Rick. "A Bloody Mary."

Matt watched Rick mix the tomato juice and vodka over copious ice cubes, then stake the glass with a limp stalk of celery. He assumed the liquor content was about as limp, and as limp as the ten-dollar bill Rick extracted from his fingers. No change was forthcoming.

"So," said Redd, growing on him like kudzu, "you new in town?"

"Sure."

"You want to be sure to catch my act. In about twenty minutes. I'm the headliner."

He nodded noncommittally. He hoped he and Janice would be gone in ten.

Her arm twined his, her leg had stretched and then flexed over his thigh. He could feel her muscles, taut and as stringy as her costume. Stripping, he assumed, required both dexterity and strength.

It was like being embraced by a boa constrictor.

Matt had just about decided to be ungentlemanly and dump her, when Janice attracted her own variety of snake.

The guy who slithered up was as muscular as the voluptuous Redd. He and Janice must be wearing targets on their backs, Matt thought: newbies to the fleshpots.

Jaded must be the middle name around Secrets.

The man beside Janice was thick-set, obviously overbuilt and obviously flaunting it in a tight T-shirt advertising some heavy-metal band that looked like torturers on leave from Torquemada and the Inquisition. Torquemada and the Inquisition. Sounded like a rock band name. The guy's fleshy face sagged in all the wrong faces, just slightly enough to blur his strong features.

"You folks buying?" he asked. It sounded like a threat.

"So far," Matt said, just to divert the guy's slimy eyes from Janice. That merited a scowl and a glance at the entwined Reddy Foxx.

"Well, I know *you* must be a big spender, at least, if our star attraction is wasting her between-set time with you." He glanced back at Janice, who was trying to look cool but was doodling hard jagged lines on the corner of the overturned sketch.

Matt was so glad Vince was facedown for the moment that he barely noticed Miss Foxx's barely legal custody.

The bouncer smirked, glancing from one to another, all three.

Apparently everyone was too controlled for his taste.

He flicked Janice a glance. "We don't encourage dykes in here."

For an instant even Rick stopped nervously wiping down the bar. These were his private customers, and he didn't want the bouncer to find that out.

Matt was stunned, not knowing what was required in the way of defining his lady friend's honor.

After a few seconds' silence, Janice laughed easily. "Sorry to disappoint you, but I'm here on police business. You want to call someone a dyke, I suggest you call up the lieutenant who sent me here. I'm sure she'd be interested in the customer policies here at Secrets. Me, if I took your comment personally, I'd just call the ACLU."

His expression tightened, and he glanced suspiciously at Matt.

"What is this? Some gay door-busting setup?"

"Rafi." The voice of reason came most surprisingly from the entwining Miss Foxx. "Don't be a big bad bigot. It's bad for business."

His shoulders shifted uneasily, as if he knew he was in the wrong, but didn't know how to back down from it.

"We're leaving anyway," Matt said, standing up and automatically dislodging Miss Reddy Foxx.

Janice grabbed her sketch pad, uable to keep Raf from gawking at the image, and brushed past both the stripper and the bouncer.

"When I said I felt like a gunslinger here to 'draw,'" she muttered to Matt as they headed for the blackness that harbored the door out of there, "I didn't think I was speaking literally. Does everybody get harassed like that at these places?"

Matt glanced back at the unlikely couple—or maybe the perfect couple—their exit had marooned at the bar.

"Only if you're obviously out of place, I bet."

"And we are."

"Were," Matt said as they pushed through the big metal door and he took a deep breath of welcome smoke-free, sound-free night air.

He wished he could as easily leave behind the strange image of Max Kinsella that Janet had sketched tonight.

"Want to come in?" Janice asked on her threshold.

Matt hesitated, and watched her instantly regrouping for some face-saving comment.

He looked back to the pink Probe at the curb. Once. What serious whacko would tail a pink Probe, really?

"Since we're both gay, I'm sure it wouldn't do any harm."

Janice laughed in relief. "What a creep. Okay. Come on in." Now she was scrambling to appear unsurprised.

This dating dance was a version of the twist crossed with doing the hokeypokey.

She rattled the keys, while Matt savored his power at doing the unexpected. Janice was the soul of serenity, but now she wasn't sure of anything.

Matt was. Now was the time to face facts.

She walked in ahead of him, turning on lamps. Lamps, not overhead lighting. It gave her airy, ingratiating rooms by day a mysterious, shrouded look by night, suitable for seduction.

Except he didn't think either she or he was up to that.

"Coffee? Or wine?"

"Something in between?"

"Beer?"

He nodded, relieved when she left the living room. The clocks ticked down the hall and around the corner. Ticking clocks seemed old-fashioned for a woman with a modern style like Janice, but he liked their companionable predictability. If a grandfather clock could be heard around the corner, maybe a grandfather was lurking somewhere.

A stab of curiosity about his paternal grandfather crossed his mind. Forget it. Lost in space and time.

He sighed, relaxed. Janice's figure coming from the kitchen bearing two tall glasses could have been Betty Crocker's. Not Martha Stewart's. That was domesticity as de rigueur empire.

"It's odd," Janice commented as she sat beside him on the long, cushy sofa after setting the pilsner glass on the tile-inlaid coffee table. "But I got the impression both of our pickups recognized my sketch, but weren't saying anything."

Matt nodded, sipping the smoky, stinging beer.

"I got the impression that you did too. And you weren't talking either."

Matt swallowed more beer faster than he would have liked. "Me? Know this Vince guy?"

"Yeah. It's incredible that someone like you would know an obvious sleaze like him. Do they always do that?"

"Do what? And who?"

"Women. That stripper babe was wallpapering you. She could have come off one of those TV nighttime soaps. Bloody Mary! For gawd's sake. Reddy Foxx."

"It's the Mr. Midnight persona, not me."

"Did that broad know you were Mr. Midnight?"

"Broad?"

"Broad."

Matt realized that on some primal level, Janice—levelheaded, single-mom-to-the-core, earthy Janice—resented the heck out of some semi-naked woman messing with her escort.

"That was an excursion into a Mike Hammer novel," he said. "Too unreal. Vince. Rick. Reddy Foxx. And what was the muscle guy's name?"

"Raf. Gave me the creeps. The kind where you wish you were packing an Uzi."

"Janice!"

"Well, I did. Going there was a big mistake. No amount of money is worth getting slimed."

"I have to agree."

"So? Does it happen often?"

This was a perfect lead-in. "That's what I need to talk to you about."

She waited, never having sipped her beer. He felt like he was on trial.

"The reason I canceled coming over tonight for dinner in the first place is that I have a stalker."

"Stalker?"

"A stalker. Must have picked her up from the radio show. The downside of fame, such as it is. It became clear this weekend that she was obsessively jealous of any women I associated with. Which means it's dangerous for women to associate with me."

Janice sat forward. "So that's why you were so . . . distracted all night. Looking over your shoulder all the time. Made me think you were sorry you agreed to go along."

"No. I'm glad you weren't there alone. I was just . . . looking for a stalker."

"In the car too. Always checking your rearview and side mirrors?"

He nodded.

"You're not kidding. You're being stalked."

"What's worse is that people who have anything to do with me are being stalked by default."

"Isn't there anything you can do? The police?"

"First, it's considered funny when a woman stalks a man. The weaker sex, remember? Second, how many of those innumerable women who are stalked have to end up shot dead in a parking lot before the law can lift a finger against the stalker? Think it works any better for male victims?"

"Matt. That's terrible."

"I'm just beginning to guess how terrible it is."

"That's why you're driving the funky old car tonight?"

"Borrowed it from my landlady. Figured no self-respecting stalker would suspect a pink Probe."

"Matt. Is it that she-devil I sketched way back when?"

"Yeah. How—?"

"I just realized that was a face capable of extremes. How do you know her?"

"I don't. She used to know someone I hardly know years and years ago. I don't know what makes her tick. She just has it in for me, personally and generically."

"Generically?"

"She hates priests. Ex-priests. But I think she's mainly trying to get to someone else who's unreachable. So I'm the prime substitute. Plus, she knows I don't know how to handle this sort of thing."

"You seem to be doing all right. Going undercover in a pink Probe."

"That only works for a while. Believe me, I've seen anyone female around me, even a child, attacked by this woman."

"And that happened last weekend?"

"Last weekend. Lost weekend. The last weekend of my freedom, that's for sure. So I didn't cancel dinner because I'm afraid to be alone with you. That's what you thought, I know. I canceled because I'm afraid of what danger being seen alone with me will bring to you. Okay?"

"And tonight?"

"Tonight I'm taking a chance because I owe you an explanation. I did watch as best I could, and I don't think anyone followed us."

Janice sank her chin into her hand and contemplated the sour scenario. Suddenly she sat upright. "Well, that slut Reddy Foxx is in real trouble if your stalker somehow slipped into Secrets."

Matt laughed, enjoying the feeling. "Thanks. That's what I'll do. I'll associate only with fallen women from now on and let my stalker eliminate the femme fatales of the world."

"Well, I guess they shouldn't have to die for being cheap hustlers. I can't believe it. Matt, do you realize how constricting life could be?"

He nodded. "But maybe my stalker has underestimated me. I came from a constricted lifestyle, remember? Maybe I can outlast her."

"And in the meantime, your life is not your own."

"That's true. But isn't free will often an illusion?"

"I don't know. I'm just an artist, not a theologian. I'm going to miss you," she said, lifting her beer glass for a toast.

He touched glass rims with her. "Me too. I guess I'll find out a lot about free will in the next few weeks."

"I'm glad you told me."

"I'm glad too."

She smiled. He smiled. Maybe this evening could have ended differently, but not now.

Chapter 12

Caged Meat

The smell of blood and bone spewed all around him.

He paced back and forth, trying not to think about it, but the odor was too strong to ignore.

The night was panther dark. No lights except the vague overhead glimmer of most nights in this harsh land.

He had water at least. Not blood.

The smell was maddening! The smell of slaughter.

He couldn't understand why he was being tormented like this: caged and affronted with the stench of bleeding meat.

Or was it a dream? He had dreamed these dreams before.

How long in this prison?

How long since he had been stung into sleep and taken from his home?

No one knew where he was. He knew no one here. The blood wasn't the only smell. There was the reek of urine and dung. His grounds had always been cleared quickly.

In the hot sun flies buzzed around it all: filth, raw meat, his eyes and ears.

At night the smell was the overpowering assault.

He heard others move in the night. He heard a rhythmic scraping sound.

And sometimes he heard footsteps, as the keepers with the barking whips moved back and forth, as he did in his prison, only they were free.

He lurched up from a prone position on the cold concrete to the corner opposite the rancid hay that was his bed and marking place.

Water at least. He drank thirstily, satisfying no craving.

Without water he would have died in the day's heat. So they did not mean to kill him. Not yet. He knew that much, and no more.

But the smell, all around!

He lunged at the bars with a guttural cry of anguish.

He would go mad!

Why had they done this to him?

Chapter 13

Trial and Error

Louie lunged at the closing grille of the cat carrier, growling.

"I'm sorry, boy. This is lousy timing, but we have an appointment with the long arm of the law. Just think of it as stardom calling again," Temple told him.

She was still panting from the effort of cornering and corralling twenty pounds of reluctant feline. "We've got a media date. Tape will be rolling at ten A.M. sharp."

What a ham. As if hearing a magic formula, the big cat quieted down. Now apparently reconciled to the need for this odious means of transportation, Louie tucked his big black paws underneath him and settled into the folded Martha Stewart towels Temple had gotten for Christmas from her mother. There were bunnies on them, just as there were bunnies on her Christmas bedroom slippers.

Was her mother not-so-subtly trying to tell a thirty-year-old daughter that it was now time to breed like a rabbit?

First, to do the trick, Temple would need to find a jackrabbit.

Louie was her only live-in male of the moment, and he was the wrong species.

Temple sat beside the carrier to catch her breath and pull the back straps on her sandals into place on her heels again. She'd nearly dislocated an ankle wrestling with Louie.

He should be ashamed, the big lug, giving his ever-loving roommate such a fight when she was only enhancing his performing career.

She checked the address she had written on the margin of the neighborhood weekly shopper when the television producer had called with the good news. "Tomorrow at ten A.M., all right?"

Being a freelance PR specialist, Temple could always crowd this appointment into that day, or that bit of hooky into this schedule. That was the beauty of being self-employed; sometimes you were self-liberated.

"That's right, Louie, groom that foot, but not too much. You have to look abused for the camera."

He eyed her dubiously, whether in distaste at the redundancy of urging him to groom himself, or the impossibility of twenty well-fed pounds of glossy black fur looking abused.

"Helpless would be a huge help too," she added hopefully.

His yawn showed a maw of white fangs that would have done a rattlesnake about to be milked of its venom proud.

Temple shivered a little. Louie was big, but she'd hate to meet one of the real big cats face-to-fang. Unless they were the tamed variety provided to weekend warrior-hunters eager to bag a proud head for their office or home theater wall.

This sort of cowardly lion hunter was so common that Van Burkleo had called his pride of former pets and zoo residents MGM lions.

Mascots, in other words, ready to be pierced with bullets or arrows, hounded wounded against a wall and nibbled until dead with nonlethal hindquarter shots, all to preserve the handsome head for some creep's wall.

Temple was not surprised to find her fingernails dimpling her palms in pent-up fury.

Good. Fury was useful. All she had to do was think of Savannah Ashleigh as one of these canned-hunt impresarios, kidnapping a favorite pet, confining it to a cage, doing what she would with it.

From Louie's carrier came a low growl that climbed and descended a scale or two in a minor key before it was done. Was he trying to tell her something?

The *Judge Geraldine Jones* show was videotaped at a local sound studio. Temple and Louie saw not so much as an extension cord for the first two hours they spent there.

The green room, lovely term that smacked of theatrical tradition, although it was seldom green anymore, was a cavernous studio filled with folding chairs and people filling out forms on clipboards balanced on their knees.

Temple sat down, put Louie's carrier beside her on the cold concrete, and began doing likewise.

The forms, which released the producers from responsibility for every eventuality from act of God to hangnail, were duly signed and delivered to the perky teenage assistants who made the rounds of the plaintiffs and defendants, handing out paper cups of bad coffee and unbottled water when not collecting the signed sheets.

"Oh, who have we got in here?" one ponytailed assistant asked, crouching beside Louie's carrier and peering inside with little luck. "Oh. This must be the mutilated cat."

Temple was pleased that her spin on events had made its way into the backstage language, but she wasn't pleased to have Louie labeled so publicly. Not that the actual show wouldn't be a lot more public, but at least they got paid for the indignity. If they won the case.

"Yes," Temple said, sighing heavily. "Careful. He's a little people-shy now. As you can imagine."

"Oooh, the poor little boy," she cooed into the grille that was all she could see of the shadowy contents.

"Well, he's not a little boy in any sense now," Temple added direly.

"His name is"—the assistant frowned at the clipboard she had confiscated from Temple, along with the mostly nonfunctioning ball-point pen attached with a metal chain—"Louis."

"Louie," Temple corrected. "He's a very informal, friendly cat. Or was, before he was cruelly kidnapped."

"I don't want to get your hopes down," Miss Perkiness confided, her tender face softening with sadness, "but animal cases don't do too well here. They're only worth what the animal is, and that's not much."

"Maybe not in this case. Louie has made several national TV commercials for Á La Cat."

"Reelly!" She peeked and perked at the same time. "Oh, what a fam-ous little boy. Mr. Louis."

Temple held her tongue, also her tote bag close in her hands. That would keep her from strangling Ms. Perkiness.

A hustle and rustle across the cavern drew everyone's attention.

The clatter like hail on a tin roof announced the arrival of Savannah Ashleigh on stiletto Frederick's of Hollywood heels, a pink canvas bag bouncing against her lean hip: one word emblazoned in white embroidery on its side: Yvette.

Temple eyed her opponent with satisfaction. Savannah Ashleigh was wearing the usual overshrunk clingy top and the latest designer pants cut high on the calf and low on the torso, the better to show her belly button pierced by a tiny tinkling temple bell.

Egad, *temple bell* sounded almost like her own name.

Unlike Ms. Ashleigh, Temple's belly button's condition was kept secret behind an aqua linen suit whose skirt brushed her kneecaps and whose collar closed decorously at her throat.

Looking like the original Hollywood Barbie Tart certainly wouldn't help Ms. Ashleigh in Judge Geraldine Jones's court.

Savannah observed the stir her entrance had caused with satisfaction of her own and settled onto a folding chair. Yvette's carrier rested by her hyperarched insteps.

At Temple's feet, the hard-shelled plastic carrier containing Midnight Louie began to rock and roll as its tenant whiffed the pheromone-filled presence of his Persian co-star. Savannah Ashleigh's vengeful actions a few months ago may have rendered Louie sterile, but he was by no means "fixed."

Temple's blood began to percolate all over again when she remembered how the actress had jumped to the wrong conclusions about Louie and Yvette. How she had kidnapped the unsuspecting tomcat and delivered him into the hands of the surgeon. How she had returned him in sadly altered state to Temple's apartment door, wrapped like a mummy, just like poor Jimmy Cagney's body in that famous gangster-movie scene.

"This is one mummy that walks again," Temple muttered under her breath, completely caught up in 1930s film history.

While Savannah crossed her legs impossibly high on her bare, tan thighs and balanced her clipboard on her bony knees like a mortar-board poised on a pinhead, Temple slung her red canvas tote bag front and center. It was not embroidered with a prissy name like Yvette, but it bulged with incriminating evidence to help Temple make her case, including the—*ta-dah!*—sinister bloody satin pillow-case bearing the suggestively embroidered initials.

Chapter 14

Heaven Scent

I cannot believe that a day that started out so foul has turned
so fair.

From across the huge chamber naked of any amenities
wafts the sublime scent of my lost ladylove, the Divine Yvette.

I forgive Miss Temple for her cruel and unusual act of incar-
cerating me in a lowly cat carrier in an instant. No means of
transportation is too humiliating or humble when it whisks me
into the presence of such a unique and adorable example of
feline beauty and breeding.

What can I say that would do justice to the Divine Yvette?

How could a collar, a bone, and a halo of hair manage to
turn a cattle barn into a cow palace? Wait. Maybe I have not
put that right. What I mean is that this huge, brutal space has
suddenly been visited by a breath of spring, by the dainty
passing of a goddess, by a presence so ephemeral, yet strik-

ing, that it seems the surrounding humans, affected, should break out in joyous mews at the phenomenon.

But they are blind, deaf, dumb and—most important—scent-challenged at the way in which our very atmosphere has been honored. In fact, while there are words to describe a human bereft of sight, hearing, and speech, there are none to describe a human defrauded of the sense of smell. This just goes to show how low the species really is on the ladder of evolution.

Scent is truly the prime and primordial sense, and look at humans! Forced to douse themselves in aromas borrowed from the plant and animal kingdoms even to experience one good, uplifting whiff.

No wonder they have not noticed the advent of the Divine Yvette, although my Miss Temple, being a superior sort of human, has. That is why she is such a super sleuth. She is attuned to the animal world. I manage to peer through the air slots in the top of my loathed carrier. Even now Miss Temple is gazing toward the Divine Yvette hidden in her portable boudoir.

No doubt she is longing as much as I am to see the lovely form lifted from her temporary prison and shown to the whole wide world.

Then I notice that Miss Temple's expression is not the rhapsodic one I expect. It is quite something else indeed. In fact, it is rather deadly. And it is directed far above the Divine Yvette's carrier, directly at the puzzled profile of Miss Savannah Ashleigh, who is agonizing over some entry on a piece of paper she is filling out.

No doubt it is the line asking her age, or perhaps her name.

I hope this is not going to turn into a crime scene, or worse, a catfight of the human sort. That would be so upsetting to the Divine Yvette.

Chapter 15

Hussy Fit

Temple lumbered onto the courtroom set when the announcer called her name. She felt like a gunslinger toting a pair of howitzers. Louie's clumsy carrier bruised one hip, her overloaded tote bag banged into the other.

Savannah Ashleigh had been summoned first, so hers was among the craning faces screwed over their shoulders like Linda Blair's in *The Exorcist* to watch Temple's overburdened progress down the aisle.

It felt a little like a wedding day, only there was no groom looking expectantly for Temple's arrival.

There was only Judge Geraldine Jones, and she was looking annoyed. But then, she always did in court and on camera. No doubt that was why her ratings were so high.

She was the third wave of TV judges: first came Judge Wapner, a WOM (white old man). Then came Judge Judy, a JOW (Jewish old woman). Now it was open season for judges of both genders and every ethnic background, although they all tended to be in the sunset of their careers. Judge Geraldine Jones was half-black, half-Asian, and all cranky. Of course the number-one qualification for the job was disposition. TV judges had to be traffic cops of the personal relationship highways: ever ready to overtake, lecture, and punish offenders against common sense.

People watched live courtroom shows for the same reason they kept *The Jerry Springer Show* in the talk-show top three: they loved to see somebody else get chewed out.

The announcer had already blared out the opposing position:

"Temple Barr is a Las Vegas publicist who says her cat, Midnight Louie, was abducted and forcibly sterilized by Savannah Ashleigh, star of stage, screen, and a major cable shopping network, the owner of a female Persian cat named Yvette making a television cat food commercial with her tomcat. The Hollywood actress says that the Las Vegas publicist's cat got her cat pregnant against her will. The publicist says the actress "fixed" her cat against his and her will. Who will win *The Case of the Castrated Cat*?"

So many thumps came from inside Louie's carrier at the end of this public announcement that the container sounded like it was demon possessed, to carry the *Exorcist* analogy even further.

"This case is an exploration of the fine points of the civil law," the judge pronounced, staring over her reading glasses at Temple's hip-hugging luggage. "Not an expedition to the far Himalayas. Do you need help from the bailiff?"

"No, ma'am," Temple grunted, finally reaching the table, atop which she could heft both burdens like sacks of flour.

The judge blinked at the twin thuds. "I sincerely hope you don't have any bodies in there."

"Just bodies of evidence," Temple rejoined.

The judge flipped through the papers littering her desktop. "This case does indeed involve alleged rape, impregnation, abduction, and mutilation. My, my, my. These bodies have been busy enough for a soap opera, even though they seem to be feline.

"Since you, Miss Barr, are the complainant, you'll go first."

Temple whipped out a sheaf of papers from her tote bag and opened her mouth.

"But first, I advise you to keep it brief."

Temple shut her mouth. Just how brief was "brief"?

"My cat, Midnight Louie," she began.

"Wait a minute."

"Yes, Your Honor?"

"Does this Midnight Louie happen to be in one of those two pieces of baggage?"

"Yes, Your Honor."

"Well, bring him out to meet the people."

"He may not, uh, be feeling cooperative."

"Is he always hard to handle?"

"Well, he isn't called 'castrated' over a loudspeaker every day."

"I'm afraid you can't libel a cat, Miss Barr, so don't go trying to add to the charges against Miss Ashleigh."

Temple darted a glance at her opponent, forbearing to shoot back that you couldn't libel a Savannah Ashleigh, either, because anything bad you could say about the woman would be true.

But Temple's wrath was distracted by Louie, who actually bounded out of the carrier into the bright glare of the television lights like Milton Berle racing to a female impersonator session.

"Well," said Judge Jones. "He is one big, good-looking guy. I can see why a lady cat might be partial to him, even bowled over."

"Bowled over and assaulted," Savannah interrupted. "My little Yvette was defenseless."

"I will look at your 'little defenseless Yvette' in a moment," the judge said, "but first you will kindly keep your comments to yourself until it is your turn to complain. Oh, all right! Bring on your wronged cat and then we'll have a pair on the table."

Savannah tossed ashy bleached locks teased into something resembling burnt meringue over her bare shoulders. She unzipped Yvette's bag with the flair of a magician unveiling an illusion.

When Yvette's piquant Persian face, a symphony in silvery white fur, peeked over the pink rim, the courtroom *oohed* as one.

Temple felt like the owner of plain-marmalade Garfield, the comics cat, up against Nermal, the world's cutest kitten. Yvette was a sophisticated confection of wispy whiskers, perfectly round aquamarine eyes, and ears so delicately tinted pink they looked lavender through the thin down of silver fur that covered them.

Then Savannah, a ham actor who couldn't resist piling on the honey glaze, cooing adoringly and lifted little Yvette to her cheek, all the better for the judge and the audience to eyeball the petite charmer.

Yvette squalled like a demon infant. She flailed her dainty feet, lashed her plumy tail, and sank her tiny claws into Savannah's naked shoulder.

Savannah squealed.

Temple stroked Louie's back and tail as he paced and turned in front of her, a perfect gentleman.

At Yvette's uproar, he moved to the table's edge and directed a disapproving growl at Savannah.

"She's upset," Savannah said, whimpering as she tried to unhook each pearlescent curve of claw from her flawless, microdermabrasioned skin.

"I would be upset," Judge Jones said, "if I had been hoisted from my afternoon nap to have my manicure messed with. Put the cat down on the table and wait for Miss Barr to finish."

A dark, unyielding eye fixed on Temple. "And? What is your proof that Mr. Midnight there is innocent of all charges? That Yvette minx looks pretty irresistible to me. I can imagine what a dude of her own species would think."

"As you see, Your Honor, Yvette is more capable of self-defense than one would think. No one is contesting the fact that Yvette became pregnant during the commercial shoot. But I have photographic proof that all her offspring were yellow striped. Not a one was black. Or shaded-silver, for that matter."

"Wait a minute. Wait a minute!" The judge had grabbed her gavel at protesting sounds from Savannah. "What's this here 'shaded silver' stuff? Sounds like a designer drug."

"It's a designer cat," Temple explained. It was her turn to talk, after all. "A purebred Persian color."

"No doubt that is why Miss Ashleigh is upset over any unauthorized breeding. Just nod or shake, Miss Ashleigh, until it's your turn to present your case."

Miss Ashleigh nodded until her own particular Silicone Valley underwent an .8 on the Richter scale. No one could say she had disobeyed the judge's admonition to "nod or shake," having done both.

"That will do," the judge ordered. "I did not ask for break dancing. Now." Her gaze returned to Temple. "Where is this photograph?"

Temple whipped up a copy of a national tabloid.

The bailiff, a dignified man in police uniform, made a ponderous trip to collect the photo and convey the exhibit to the judge. He was like a not-very-good bit actor who had been given too many chances to execute long, silent stalks across stage.

Judge Jones was squinting at the telephoto-lens-blurred image. The paparazzi had caught Yvette in the act of nursing while her mistress sunbathed behind a privacy fence that wasn't quite private enough.

"These are definitely striped, every last one," was the judge's verdict. "Any similarly striped candidate for the office of father of the brood?" she asked Temple.

"As it happens, Your Honor, a yellow-striped male cat was on the set during the entire filming schedule. His name is Maurice, and he was the spokescat Midnight Louie replaced."

"*Hmmm.* Any expert evidence that Louie is not the father of the little convicts? Well, they *are* wearing stripes!" she told a protesting Savannah.

The audience tittered obediently at the judge's broad delivery of her own joke.

Temple, in the meantime, fished out another sheet of paper from her tote bag. "The veterinarian has written a statement about how unlikely it would be for a solid color black father not to produce any black offspring."

This too was brought to the judge's bench, which was really more of a high desk.

"Anything else?"

"Only that on the very flimsiest of suspicions, Miss Ashleigh had Midnight Louie abducted and taken to a facility where he was physically altered without my knowledge or participation, and obviously against his will."

"His will does not matter. He is a cat."

Louie stopped his contented sashaying back and forth against the grille of his carrier—such a nice side-scratching post—and regarded the judge balefully.

She seemed well aware of unfriendly fire when she saw it.

"An animal is property," she said, leaning forward to address Louie directly. "It does not have free will, and it has no more than demonstrable market value." Her glance skipped to Temple, but her tone remained stern. "I do hope, Miss Barr, that you are equipped to prove demonstrable market value. I can only award you damages in the amount of the animal's intrinsic value, and he is not even a purebred, like little Yvette there. Is he?"

"No, Your Honor, but he is a performing cat who earns a salary and residuals. I have here a videotape of his TV commercials."

The judge nodded, impressed for the first time. "Yes. I would indeed like to see this fellow performing. But you have not yet proven that Miss Ashleigh had anything to do with what you term 'permanent tampering.' I assume you mean that he was neutered without your permission."

"He was kidnapped, taken to a facility, altered, and then dumped on my apartment doorstep in a groggy condition inside a white satin pillowcase."

"White satin. That does sound like a Hollywood touch," the judge said, glancing Savannah's way.

Temple reached into her tote bag with grim satisfaction, soon flourishing a limp white article stained with small portions of red.

"The bloodstained pillowcase in which a drugged Midnight Louie was returned to me. It is embroidered with these initials: S. A."

A gasp filled the courtroom as the camera operator zoomed in on the lurid trophy.

"Bailiff."

Once again the kindly man clomped over to convey evidence from Temple's table to the judge's bench.

"S. A." The judge looked judicial. "This could stand for "South America, Miss Barr.""

Temple could hardly cite the most damning evidence: that only Savannah Ashleigh was dim enough to return an abducted cat in a Porthault pillowcase bearing her initials. That would sound like libel, even though it was the unvarnished, uncollagened, unteased and sprayed, and unlipo-ed truth.

The judge's eagle eye had rested on Savannah's table now. "Your complaint is that your cat was unwillingly impregnated."

"Well, we will never know how unwilling *she* was," Savannah said. "I cannot believe that a Persian of her breeding would run around with an alley cat like that Louie, or even that Maurice. But they are both big, nasty bruisers. Yvette is only seven pounds, and delicate. It would not take much to overpower her. As for the striped kittens, it so happens that tabby-striped cats were used to give white cats that faint silver-fox striping, so of course it might come out in the kittens. That tabloid photo proves nothing, except that I am a subject of such interest to the national press that even my cat cannot have kittens without an event being made of it."

Temple refrained from making gagging sounds, but Louie did not forbear from having a hairball attack.

"Must he do that?"

"I'm afraid so, Your Honor. Hairball attacks are unpredictable. And it is upsetting for the animals to come to court."

"You can't say they're not used to hot lights and attention. So. Louie was returned to you minus his, ah, hairballs."

The audience hooted.

"No."

"No! I thought this case was about unauthorized neutering."

"Not neutering. Louie was the victim of a vasectomy."

'Vasectomy. Honey, they do not do that to cats. They do that to dudes."

"Well, Louie must be a dude, then, because that's what he got."

"Now, wait a minute." The judge sat back against her chair, frowning. "You're saying that this cat had a *human* operation. What kind of vet would do that?"

"A veterinarian did not perform the procedure, which further points to Miss Ashleigh as the one behind it."

"This cat was vasectomized by an unlicensed individual? By some amateur? You may have a case here, after all."

"Not only that, I have a witness!"

"To the surgery?"

"Yes."

"Who is this witness?"

"The surgeon."

"But you just said the cat was not vasectomized by a vet."

"No. He was operated on by Miss Ashleigh's personal plastic surgeon."

"I object, I object," Savannah jiggled up and down in high-heeled indignation, one of her best camera angles.

"This may be a hostile witness, Your Honor," Temple warned.

The judge's gavel rapped the benchtop as Savannah jiggled, Yvette began hissing, and Louie yowled. "This is civil court, Miss Barr. We don't have hostile witnesses. Either you've got a witness who will support your story, or you don't. Where is this 'expert' who is not a veterinarian?"

A slow shuffling started from the back of the courtroom.

If this were a horror movie—and Temple was not sure that it was not—you would have heard the oncoming shuffling for a long time before any clue to the shuffler's identity came into camera range.

But this was court TV, and this audience was unwilling to wait.

A man in a two-hundred-dollar haircut and an antipasto of Italian designer clothing shuffled forward like an eleven-year-old truant.

"It is I, Your Honor," he said.

Savannah shrieked as if cut to the heart. "Dr. Mendel! *Et tu, Brut?*"

Temple didn't think Savannah's mangled Shakespeare had any relevance other than betrayed trust until Dr. Mendel sidled up beside her and she smelled his aftershave cologne. Brut. Unmistakably. Savannah was evidently astute in some very minor matters.

The doctor thrust his hands in his pockets until only a hint of his high-karat bracelet showed on the right wrist.

The judge leaned forward, glasses practically sliding off the tip of her nose. "Did you do this cat, Doctor?"

"I performed some procedures on him, yes." He directed a misery-filled glance at Savannah, whose toe was striking a furious beat on the courtroom floor.

"Procedures?" the judge demanded. "Is that what we call castrating nowadays?"

"I do not perform castration. Miss Ashleigh brought me the animal. I naturally refused to do anything, but she became quite hysterical."

"Ohhhh!" Savannah screeched.

He shrugged. "She insisted that I was to make sure this cat—"

"The black one here?"

"I'd have to examine the animal, Your Honor."

"Make it so," the judge barked, Captain Jean-Luc Picard style.

Both cats jumped and arched their backs.

Temple tried to hold and calm Louie, but he growled furiously as Dr. Mendel gingerly explored his hindsection.

"Yes, this is the cat. I see that my tummy tuck is holding up well. One of the best I've ever done, actually. The skin of cats is not attached to the underlying musculature, you know, so a tummy tuck can make a real difference. Especially in front of the camera, eh, boy?"

"A tummy tuck. So the dude got a free cosmetic procedure?"

"Unnecessary," Temple said. "You will see from the videotape that Midnight Louie's handsome coat of hair hides any presumed flaws."

The judge was uninterested in Temple's testimony. She was more interested in Dr. Mendel's.

"So you did not remove anything from the cat?"

"I merely snipped segments from his vas deferens and siphoned some ugly excess fat from the abdominal area. The incisions were so tiny they didn't require stitches."

"Impressive. I think you may have happened on a profitable two-fer for your human clients. I know more than a few gentlemen who would like to get fixed and lipo-ed at the same time. Why did you bother with the tummy tuck? That wasn't in Miss Ashleigh's instructions."

He shrugged. "I am a plastic surgeon, a perfectionist by nature. If I see something ungainly that's easy to fix, I do it."

Louie growled again and showed his fangs at Dr. Mendel's hand. The surgeon quickly moved both hands back to his pockets, out of Louie's snapping range.

"Some would say that Dr. Mendel, and Miss Ashleigh, had done you and Louie a favor, Miss Barr."

"Louie is a television star, Your Honor. Who is to say his breeding potential is not valuable? Not only that, the pain and suffering I underwent when he was missing, and then returned in such a savage manner, in a drugged and altered condition—"

"Pain and suffering are not awardable conditions, Miss Barr." The judge turned to Savannah. "All right. What's your defense? It appears you had no evidence but prejudice and contact to blame your cat's pregnancy on Midnight Louie. It also looks like you abducted the wrong Romeo. This Maurice fellow seems the far more likely suspect for Yvette's delicate condition."

"Well, later on, Your Honor, it did. But at the time . . . besides, I know my Yvette would never participate willingly in such an event."

"Wait a minute. We are talking cats here. Female cats who are not neutered—and the evidence is clear that Yvette was not and still is not neutered—do go into heat, don't they? You do know what heat is, don't you, Miss Ashleigh? Haven't you portrayed a human variation of that condition on film often enough?"

"Your Honor has seen my films?"

"Seen them? I've had them presented in evidence."

"Surely not as evidence of violating the ratings system? They are clearly marked 'R.' "

"No, Miss Ashleigh, I've seen them as evidence of fraudulent film-making. Some investors said the films were made with no intentions of being distributed, but merely to divest them of their money. But that was a while back, when I was a Hollywood judge, not a TV judge. Luckily"—the judge showed clean white teeth but did not smile—"I am not hearing that kind of case anymore."

Temple was trying to keep herself from jiggling up and down in triumph, even though it wouldn't have the gelatinous effect of Savannah Ashleigh's jiggles. Things didn't sound good for the Tinseltown floozy.

Judge Jones swept all the papers and Temple's videotape into a pile. "I'll adjourn to view all the evidence and then return with the verdict. "Ladies. Control your . . . cats."

The admonition was well deserved. Both Louie and Yvette, unobserved by their distracted human chaperons, had each come to their separate table edges and now leaned over the brink of space that kept them apart, sniffing futilely at the unkindly air that separated them.

"Get back in your carrier, you sssshaded ssssilver sssslut!" Savannah hissed. "Issssn't one mongrel litter enough?"

"He's fixxxxxed, thankssss to you," Temple hissed back. "And poor Yvette issssss only a victim in all thissss. She would have never chossssen Maurissse over Louie."

The kindly silver-haired bailiff stepped into the space between the cats.

"Ladiesssss, pleasssse," he hissed so that the microphones wouldn't pick up the catfight.

They each grabbed a peacefully purring cat and moved them back to the center of their tables, as if separating enemies.

The judge's "few moments" for the viewing audience was twenty foot-tapping, nail-nibbling, cat-herding minutes for the combatants.

The biggest problem, Temple found, was trying to keep the two cats apart. Louie and Yvette, that is.

Chapter 16

Hissy Fit

What an exercise in frustration.

Not allowed to testify on our own behalves.

Treated like nonpersons—okay, this is not new.

And kept apart like rabid monkeys.

I do not think much of human justice!

So I decide to take matters into my own mitts.

While Miss Savannah Ashleigh is busy inventing stage business for the camera, huffing and puffing and tapping her tiny toe and pushing her fat hair off her shoulders, she has neglected to fully zip shut the Divine Yvette's carrier.

I glance at my Miss Temple. She is fussing over her various papers, no doubt looking for the key piece of evidence she forgot to give the judge. She obviously is counting on me to be the little gentleman I have been for the past hour or so.

She should know that an hour is too long for the average cat to remain docile and obedient. As for an above-average dude like myself, I am ready to bust out of this low-rent trial-by-television.

In one graceful leap I am airborne and land on the opposition's tabletop.

With a swift flourish of my front fang, I hook it into the hole in the carrier zipper tag and rip the teeth apart, a maneuver I have performed before in less public circumstances.

My darling's adorable face pops into plain view, although nothing about the Divine Yvette could ever be called plain.

"Louie!" she mews with delight. The dames can never resist a swashbuckling kind of guy.

I assist her out of the collapsing pink canvas, ignore shrieks and admonitions from two sides, and urge my little pet into a leap to the floor. A quick flight through the onlookers creates a stir in our wake, but too late to impede our progress.

Then it is out the imposing double wooden doors (mostly painted plywood) and into the great concrete space that houses the technical set.

We speed over welts of black cables snaking across the floor and into the shadows behind the curtains used as room dividers in the massive space.

I can hear human footsteps and voices and consternation all over the place, but we snuggle down next to a cooler and are instantly alone on our own desert isle.

"Oh, Louie." Yvette sighs. "You are *très* unpredictable. Such a merry chase we have led them. I was feeling so cramped in my carrier." She catches her breath with a little gasp. "Oh! I am not used to such a sprightly romp since I first contracted my unfortunate condition."

"And how are the little stripe-heads?" I ask, feeling it necessary to bow to the maternal instinct.

"Gone to the neighbors, one by one. I cannot say that I cared to be reminded daily of the criminal proceedings that led to their birth."

I murmur sympathetically. I would not wish to be reminded of Maurice's ugly mug either, even if that likeness was now adorning the faces of my own offspring.

"I am glad that they have found good homes."

"Oh, yes. Unlike my mistress, her neighbors find having the

offspring of Yvette and Maurice, the cat food mascots, quite a plume in their tails. They do not care about pedigree, as my mistress does."

"And who are *her* blue-blooded antecedents, I would like to know?"

"Perhaps that is why she so prizes my own," the Divine Yvette notes in a flash of perception and loyalty that is especially touching coming from one born and bred to think only of her pedigreed self.

Perhaps I have been a good influence on her.

"Will we ever work together again, I wonder?" I say.

"Will you ever see my sister, Solange, again, you may be wondering too? Do not deny it, Louie! You are as weak as any of your gender when it comes to those brassy blonds."

"No, my sweet. You know that I prefer platinum blonds."

That remark permits me to rub cheeks with the Divine Yvette as a purr of satisfaction ripples through the luxurious fur ruffling her shoulders and chest.

"I am sorry, Louie," she says instantly. "I am in a bad mood because some foreign hussy is muscling in on my Á La Cat deal just as I was recovering from my . . . incapacitation and getting ready to resume my career. And the scandal had died down until your roommate gave it a kick-start again with this silly suit."

I grit my teeth. I cannot tolerate my Miss Temple being criticized, but neither can I condone any actions that put the Divine Yvette into a less than flattering spotlight.

"I am sorry also," I say. "There is no stopping these humans when they get a flea in their bonnet, or a bee in their ear, or whatever."

She nods sadly, biting her shiny little black lip with one pearly fang tip. "I cannot excuse my mistress. I had no idea how harshly you were handled by her. Kidnapped! Falsely imprisoned! Operated upon without permission. Altered inalterably! I am tempted to leave Pretty Paws litter all over my mistress's satin sheets the next time she is entertaining a gentleman friend."

"Ah, your commiseration is welcome, my dear, but I must

quibble about one point. I was not 'altered' in any crucial way. I am unable to sire kittens, but certainly am able to go through all the motions needed for that end. And then some."

"Then why do anything?" she asks with touching innocence. "I cannot say that the actual act is anything to write home about. And, on top of the painful unpleasantness, one is labeled a naughty girl for doing what one did not even wish to partake of in the first place."

There is no explaining to dames that they should like what guys like just because.

"But apparently your reviving good looks and the passage of time had restored you to favor with our sponsor, Allpetco."

"So I thought, and what is worse, so did my poor mistress. She finds film work scarce these days, and depends upon my income a good deal, so you can imagine how upsetting it would be if I lost my position. I would even accept my sister's replacing me if it would assist my mistress's finances."

"You are both beautiful and noble," I say, "but what makes you think this foreign interloper stands a chance of replacing you? I will refuse to work with her if they try anything!"

"Now you are being noble, but you may not have an opportunity to put your sit-down strike into action. I hear that this upstart's trainer favors Maurice as a partner. Not you."

"No! Obviously I miss a lot by not being near the scuttlebutt along Rodeo Drive. So we both are to be put out to pasture."

"They only put horses out to pasture, Louie. We will be put out to sleeping on sofas watching the Home Shopping Network."

"No!" Personally, I prefer QVC.

"It is true. I have seen it happen in my mistress's career. And now, with this hussy on the horizon—"

"You mean the foreign feline the Allpetco people are supposedly considering for the spokescat slot?"

"Precisely."

"Pardon me for being obtuse, but what does any alien female have that you do not have?"

The Divine Yvette shrugs wearily. "New face, new hair. Younger." She pauses to tidy her whiskers. "I have heard this upstart has some martial arts abilities. Apparently, underage females who can kick-box are the target media consumers these days. And she is the 'right' ethnic group."

My blood is beginning to thicken in my veins.

"This candidate is Asian, by some chance?"

The Divine Yvette's almost undetectable sneer draws her luxurious vibrissae, aka whiskers, into a dismissive arch of truly noble proportions.

"Siamese," she hisses in disdain. "One of the new breed that is so narrow it looks as if it has been run over and then peeled off the street."

I nod. I know the look, and I am afraid I may even know the dame in question.

"She is apparently appearing in some cheesy cable sci-fi series."

I gulp.

"Something about Khatlords," the Divine One continues, "although, despite their promising name, they are people, not felines."

"This Siamese is not called Hyacinth?"

"I do not know her name and do not wish to. All I know is that this kung fu feline is being pushed for the next set of Á La Cat commercials. My mistress is worried white. So white that she has purchased a plain white-cotton martial arts *gi* for me . . . for *me,* who has only worn satin and velvet before. I fear that the fashion in feline fatales has changed from sweet and fluffy to sour and stringy."

I am so horrified by what I have learned that I have neglected to soothe the Divine Yvette's injured ego promptly enough.

"Louie! Have you nothing to say of this interloper of inferior breed who threatens our livelihood, and that of our nearest and dearest?"

I shake myself free of unhappy thoughts.

"Only that the Allpetco people would be insane to replace you with an Oriental shorthair like a Siamese. Your aquamarine eyes are infinitely superior to their blue eyes, which are often crossed, I hear. As for coat color, your fiendishly subtle hues of white, silver, and black have a classic art deco sophistication that no other breed can match."

The Divine Yvette is not only purring by now, she is rubbing back and forth against me like I am a magic lamp with a genie inside. Ah, bliss. I sense a close encounter in the air. Then I have to go and talk a little bit too long. . . .

"Compared to your sublime tones, that common Siamese camel coat accented with the mouse-turd brown trim breeders elevate by the name of lilac points is something from the Goodwill. . . ."

"Louie!" The Divine Yvette has pulled away, something like lightning from Mount Olympus in her heavenly aquavit orbs. "How did you know that this usurper was a *lilac-point* Siamese?"

"Just a lucky guess?" I begin.

Before I can insert more of my feet into my mouth, and I have several—feet, that is, not mouths—the curtain behind which we shelter is jerked open, spilling a blast of light and noise into our hideaway.

"Yvette! Louie!" our significant others cry in tandem, united in the search for our missing selves. Their long-nailed hands reach for us.

We are between a concrete wall and a wail of people in full cry.

There is nothing to do but crouch down and allow ourselves to be plucked up from the floor and into our so-called owners' arms.

Miss Temple has a much harder time of it than Miss Savannah, who huffs off immediately with the Divine Yvette, muttering of genetic contamination.

"Louie, you bad boy!" Miss Temple pants. "I'm just glad the judge is still in chambers and didn't see you running away like a guilty party. You are the sinned against, not the perp. Act like it."

She stomps back to the set with me clasped to her bosom. It is not the triumph in court I had envisioned, but I know enough to act docile and maintain radio silence.

Chapter 17

Judgment Day

The judge's ill-tempered squint was more pronounced when she returned from viewing Temple's tape of Louie's and Yvette's commercials and reviewing the documents in the case, which were all Temple's.

She glared first at Savannah and Temple, and then at Louie and Yvette.

All four had the abstracted air of the blameless who had nothing to hide. The judge's glare deepened, then she rapped her gavel once to hush the hissing that had erupted among the onlookers at her reappearance.

"I don't know about you two ladies, but veteran viewers know that it is extremely unlikely for claimants to recover any monetary damages in cases involving animals or domestic pets. As we know, the law recognizes no intrinsic value other than as property."

Onlookers nodded, while Temple shrank and Savannah's posture puffed up, which wasn't hard to do in either case.

"We all know," the judge went on, "that however emotionally people may invest in their animals, the court cannot compensate them beyond the literal value of the cats in question.

"Besides, how much is an alley cat worth? For that is what Midnight Louie is." The judge stared into the black cat's green eyes. "About thirty-two dollars."

Temple gasped. The fee at stake for the winning party was twenty-five hundred dollars.

"Give or take a few dollars—or cents—more," Judge Jones added.

Temple, horrified, opened her mouth, but a searing glance from the judge stopped things then and there.

"Obviously," the judge added, "Yvette is worth considerably more, due to her pedigree. I have, in fact, the sole piece of evidence from Miss Ashleigh: Yvette's purchase price. "Twelve hundred and fifty dollars."

Savannah tossed her shaded silver locks.

Temple mentally kissed even half of the twenty-five hundred good-bye.

The judge looked down at the papers on her desk, then up at the camera.

"However, in this case, Midnight Louie is not just an alley cat. He is a performing alley cat. Thus, Miss Barr's argument that his offspring might have had value has credence. And although human pain and suffering is not a factor in this or any other case, no one can argue that being abducted and operated upon without the consent of his owner is a severe breach of the animal's welfare.

"So I am awarding Miss Barr and Midnight Louie the full damages of twenty-five hundred dollars. You should not jump the gun, Miss Ashleigh, and nail the wrong dude. It does not work with a smoking gun, and it does not work with a surgical scalpel.

"Case dismissed. Award to plaintiff of twenty-five hundred dollars."

The courtroom buzzed.

Or maybe the buzzing was just the sound of purring cats.

Temple thought perhaps she was purring. She had won. Made Savannah Ashleigh look stupid on dead (as opposed to live) TV. Got some shoe money! Well, some of it should go to Louie's Free-to-Be-Feline fund.

Justice was sweet.

"I'm not done with you, Miss Barr," the judge snarled.

Temple blinked.

"Whatever the outcome of this case," she went on, "the fact remains that you are a derelict cat owner. Why didn't you take care of your animal's irresponsible condition? Why has only Miss Ashleigh's wrongheaded intervention kept him from breeding irresponsibly? Only luck made him innocent of fathering a litter of unwanted kittens."

"It's—" Temple began. "He just ended up as my cat because no one else wanted him. I've never owned a cat before. I thought Louie was too old—"

"They are never too old, Miss Barr. You should remember that for your own personal protection as well. And what was Midnight Louie doing out where Miss Ashleigh or her minions could kidnap him?"

"Well, he's too big to keep in—"

"They are never too big to keep in, for their own good. Remember that. If pet owners like yourself would simply neuter your animals and keep them inside, millions of unwanted lives would not be sacrificed yearly. You owe, in fact, Miss Ashleigh thanks for unwittingly—and I do believe it was genuinely unwitting—putting your own house in order on this matter. From now on, if any suspicions of parentage come up, Midnight Louie will not be a likely suspect."

Temple nodded soberly. "He doesn't need a paternity suit. Not with his celebrity status."

Chapter 18

Day of the Jekyll

I am nursing my injured pride back at the Circle Ritz while Miss Temple is off gallivanting on matters that involve what she calls a job.

Actually, I am daydreaming. I was not able to get close enough to the Divine Yvette to discover which dive Miss Savannah Ashleigh was honoring with her presence this trip. My chances of finding the proper hostelry in this town of 60 zillion bedrooms are not good.

All in all, other than enriching my roommate by a fistful of dollars, this outing in search of justice was not a huge success. I get humiliated on national TV, as does my associate, and far too little money was paid for the privilege, if you ask me.

At least I glimpsed the Divine One, who appears to have fully recovered from the stresses of enforced motherhood. If anything, her limpid eyes are more blue-green than ever, and her coat is richer, longer, fuller. She could be doing shampoo commercials soon. And I have not heard a murmur of my services being requested for future film duties.

So I am in a pretty discouraged mood, when I hear someone tapping, gently rapping on one of my patio doors. 'Tis the wind, I tell myself, but eventually I force myself off the sofa and to the French doors.

Nope, not the wind. I spy a blobby black silhouette through the sheer curtains Miss Temple uses to keep unwanted eyes from peeking in at her at night when the interior lights are on.

Well, the blob is either Mr. Poe's raven or someone of an even more dire aspect.

I stick a mitt under the door to pull it slightly off-kilter, leap high up to swat the lever mechanism on the way down, and shoulder open the door against the now-sprung latch.

After all this athletic effort, I am more than somewhat disappointed when Miss Midnight Louise ankles in, rubbing her shoulder possessively against the doorjamb. I had been hoping for something svelte and lonesome in shaded silver fur.

"So this is where you hang your flamingo fedora," Miss Louise comments, moving right on in to deposit her proprietary scent all along the sofa side. Eeeeugh! Give a dame an inch and she will take eighteen square yards of upholstery every time.

"The peach chapeau was just a prop," I point out, tailing her. "Hmmm. You have picked up some exotic scents of late."

"That is what I get for following your roommate and her ex-roommate yesterday. Jungle rot."

"Did that assignment lead to the Mystifying Max?" I ask eagerly, for I am hungry to know what he has been up to while Miss Temple has been dallying with courtroom drama.

"Indeed it did, and also to a long drive into the desert, from which I returned only by the hair of my chinny-chin-chin."

I examine said article of anatomy. Miss Louise seems possessed of every possible hair that could grow there, and then some. Her coat is longer and fluffier than mine, as suits the female of the species, and is another argument in favor of the fact that I cannot possibly be her pater, as the Brits say.

"Your chinny-chin does not seem the worse for wear," I note.

She leaps atop my favorite lounging spot, sniffs, and moves to the loveseat's opposite end, where she turns around thrice and then settles into a classic meditation position.

"And what dangers have you been pursuing, Daddy Darnedest, since I was checking out the wild brown yonder?"

"Uh, I accompanied my Miss Temple while she had an unpleasant brush with the law. We barely got out of there with our skins intact."

Miss Louise merely grooms one airy eyebrow with the back of her mitt, a clear signal of disbelief. "I am sorry to say that Miss Temple and Mr. Max had a parting of the ways—"

"No!" I jump up to resume my accustomed spot, my heart beating with hope. "So they had a spat and are splitting up? I had wondered why I heard no aftermath from their expedition yesterday."

"Don't get excited, Pop. You are not sole king of the comforter yet. I mean that when I followed them yesterday he hopped out of the vehicle at the edge of nowhere and I had to decide who to stick with."

"And?"

"Where he got out was one big litter box. I decided against masquerading as a deposit for the next few hours and stayed with the car."

"Hmmm. A dedicated operative would have followed my instructions and stayed with Mr. Max. That was the one you were assigned to tail. You were not asked to take a cushy joy ride with Miss Temple."

"Yeah? Well, did you want me to find the missing leopard or not?"

Miss Louie spits on her fist and boxes away at her face as if wishing she were wiping me off the floor instead of knocking the desert dust off her cheekbones.

I am speechless, not to mention spitless. I send her out on one tailing operation and she nails the missing leopard. And all I have to show for today is having my undercarriage prodded by Dr. Mendel and my reproductive history filmed for posterity. Of which Miss Midnight Louise is not one. Any posterity. Of mine.

While I mull over the bitter fruits of fame and fortune, Miss Midnight Louise leans back and honors me with a report. Only it feels more like a lecture.

"My choice was clear. Did I follow the unreliable and unpredictable male, ruled more by hormones than by head, even though you had instructed me to? Or did I stick with the plucky and intuitive female? Did I have a choice?

"Your Miss Temple drove, fairly sedately for her, until the road ended at a mountain. I suppose most roads around here do.

"I smelled the spoor of many beasts, including those of the fortunate feline species, and also enough leavings to knock a sensitive nose to its knees, so it is a good thing I had not invited Nose E. along. This was far too crude a job for one of his connoisseur-level sniffing abilities. I mean, a blind human could have followed the ordure to its origins."

"Miss Temple noticed the obvious scent?"

"I fear not. Superior as she may be, in this case she was totally bedazzled by the structure built at the mountain's base, and getting into it. It was a modern, yet formidable sort of place, and I made my second momentous decision. I decided that I would sniff around on my own outside while she investigated inside. My greatest risk was that she and the vehicle would depart without me."

"From what you say, that would have been a disaster."

"Indeed. But as you see, that did not happen."

I look hard, but I do not detect the slightest trace of a callus on her dainty footpads. Drat! A long, dry, sandy walk would do her good.

"So what did you find?"

"A zoo," she says, working hard at the tufts of hair between her toes. "It will take me days to rinse off the scents of such a Babel of beasts. And interviewing them all was not a picnic either. I deserve hazardous duty pay."

"Cut to the chase," I growl.

"Strange you should mention that word. I do not know if you can scent the fear from where you sit, but I have spent the day dealing with animal sacrifices on the hoof. They are there not to be chased but to be easily caught. There are whole herds of horned beasts born and bred there and kept merely to be killed in their own pens by people who come in solely for this purpose. Fortunately, these herd-running creatures are far less intelligent than our breed, so they do not quite see the big picture, only that men come and lightning strikes, felling some of their numbers. Blessed are the dim of brain, who do not see the ax from the first."

I cannot help shuddering. I have never had any problems seeing the ax. I have been hunted in my homeless past by BB guns, handguns, arrows, and, on performance nights, shoes. It is never fun to be prey, and to be penned in for the kill is truly vicious.

"But the prize objects of these hunts," Miss Louise goes on, "I find in cages rather than herded into pens."

Miss Midnight Louise's voice has grown deep and ominous. She bites savagely at a matted foot tuft, then spits out a hank of fur.

"I regret to inform you that our larger brothers and sisters are the most prized victims of this coward's excuse for a hunt, and it is here that I found the leopard known as Osiris in his stage persona."

"He is to be hunted to death?"

"That may be the idea, but I do not think it will happen."

"He is safe?"

"I did not say that."

"Then speak up, girl, and quit beating around the bush!"

"There is very little bush out in the desert to beat around, and very little for the hooved ones to hide behind. But I doubt that Osiris will live long enough to be hunted and killed."

"Why?"

"When I found him, he was in a wrought and pitiful state. He had not been fed since his abduction."

"Not fed? Why not?"

"I cannot say. Even I could smell the raw meat in the other cages, but he had only a water bowl. A large water bowl, but only water nevertheless. I had no idea these big cats were quite so big. The lions and tigers seemed the size of Mr. Matt's new car."

"They have lions and tigers too?"

Louise gazes into the distance. "I was forced to, er, negotiate an abstraction of some undevoured meat from a black panther to give to poor Osiris."

"You took the food out of a panther's mouth?"

"Well, it was sleeping, so I slipped into its cage and wrestled a big nasty bone with lots of meat on it through the bars and dragged it into Osiris's cage. Then I was forced to wait while he devoured it so I could drag the evidence back into the tiger cage. I think it is best that the animals who run this death camp not know that I foiled their abuse of Osiris. In fact, if we cannot persuade your human friends to get Osiris out of there, one of us should return daily and feed him by the method I have devised."

This causes me to frown, and frown harder.

My so-called "friends" are not exactly at my behest. In fact, I am the most undercover of undercover artists, and work best in subtle and mysterious ways.

How I am to stage-manage daily jaunts to this distant desert hideaway to feed a kidnapped leopard, lead Mr. Max Kinsella to said leopard, and still tend to my hunt for the lilac Siamese while working for the good of my Miss Temple?

It is more than I can solve in the next few minutes, so I follow Miss Midnight Louise's example in berating my toe mats and chewing on both problems at once.

She, however, exhausted from her labors, has gone to sleep with her tail tip wrapped around the end of her little black chinny-chin-chin.

I foresee no such luxury for Midnight Louie.

Chapter 19

Sketched in Suspicion

"Sorry I couldn't see you sooner," Molina said.

She was rushing into her office where Janice Flanders had been waiting for—she checked her watch and stifled a word she wouldn't want her daughter Mariah to overhear—twenty minutes.

"Everything exploded this morning," she continued. "The case-load has been outrageous."

"I know, Lieutenant. Don't worry about me. I've been studying the portraits on your walls."

Molina glanced up at the familiar frieze of mug shots and most-wanted posters.

"Trophies?" Janice asked, "or just generic crooks?"

"Some we nailed. So. What did you get at . . . what's-its-name?"

"Secrets. Sounds more upscale than it is. I owe you thanks. I never would have visited a strip club otherwise. Neither would have Matt."

"You took a date?"

"I took muscle." Janice smiled. "Or thought I did. The star attraction ended up hitting on him."

Molina shook her head. "From rectory to raunchy. You and I have a lot to answer for in the education of Matt Devine."

"He did better with her than I did with the house muscle." Janice leaned forward, the pencil in her left hand tapping the glass atop Molina's desk. "I've made a find, I think. Remember the guy you had me sketch recently?" Janice glanced over the walls and frowned. "I don't see his handsome face on your Wall of Infamy."

"It's a pending case." She leaned down and reluctantly pulled the folder holding Janice's all-too-lifelike portrait of Rafi Nadir. "This guy?"

Seeing her sketch again, Janice grabbed her upper arms as if cold. "I could redo that for you, better now. This is what blew me away. I met him. Last night. At Secrets. I guess he's a bouncer there. Isn't that the guy you're looking into for something?"

"For something. So?"

"A stripper from the club was murdered. Not there, but she had worked at Secrets. And, listen, the hard time that guy gave me—"

"He came on to you?"

"Hardly! He implied I was a lesbian just for being in the club. I think he was going to call Matt gay, except that Reddy Foxx was all over him and usually her kind are pretty on target about gender preferences."

Molina was ready for a good primal scream: what hath subterfuge wrought? She could picture it all too clearly: Janice and Matt bellying up to the bar in a strip club to interrogate a gin-slinger named Rick on her request, while Rafi Nadir, the guy she most wanted to separate from any part of her life or anybody she knew or who knew her . . . and *Raf* hassling them both. With only a ridiculously named stripper putting the make on Matt to stand between them and his territorial temper.

If it didn't have the making of a first-class tragedy, it would be a surefire comedy.

"You had your hands full," Molina commented in the neutral tone of voice she was so expert at falling back on: the noncommittal neutrality that masqueraded for police politeness. It was really just a darker shade of doubt, but most civilians and good citizens didn't know that, though the bad actors knew it and didn't care.

"Lieutenant? You seem a little distracted."

Molina gazed into Janice's on-the-level eyes, now showing a shred of concern. "Just too many unclosed cases on my mind. So. You want another crack at the illustrated man." She pushed Janice's sketch toward her.

"Right. Now that I've seen and heard him, I just hope somebody gets him for something. I'll redo it gratis. Just for the lesbian crack."

"You can't believe anything you hear in a strip club. So that was it. A close encounter with the sketch subject. It must have been unnerving. Like seeing a ghost."

"Like seeing a nightmare. I'm not used to these hard customers. Matt didn't seem particularly worried, though."

"He's seen hard customers before."

"As a priest?"

Molina permitted herself a smile. "No. Here. In Vegas."

"That man I first sketched for him?"

Molina shrugged. "Unappetizing, but not particularly dangerous. Just mean."

"His stepfather. Matt says he . . . stalked him."

"Matt's being hard on himself, as usual. He found him. For me, frankly. For himself too. Looking for a criminal isn't stalking."

Janice nodded. Molina could tell she was unconvinced, that she was thinking of a subject that had not come up, and probably wouldn't. "That second sketch I did for him . . ."

"Second one?" Molina felt her nerve endings sit up and salute. Effinger was old news, an unsolved case that nobody really cared about. A minuscule serving of small potatoes at the biggest buffet in Las Vegas.

"The woman. The gorgeous woman."

"*Hmmm.*" Molina made it sound like she knew all about it and wasn't particularly interested. That's how you got troubled witnesses to talk: you overreacted to the trivial and tiptoed around the crucial.

Janice fell into easy compliance. "She didn't look like a criminal, but I suppose they don't all come from Central Casting, like that Raf character at Secrets."

Molina ached to shock Janice a little by revealing that Raf had been a cop. You couldn't take anything for granted in the law enforcement game. Nothing. Including gorgeous women that Matt

Devine wanted pretty pictures of. A self-indulgence? Someone he had a crush on?

"She wasn't a redhead?" Molina had never thought of Temple Barr as gorgeous, but Janice was one of those stolidly average-looking women, like Molina herself, who might confuse pretty cute with pretty.

"No. A cross between Snow White and the Wicked Queen. Skin as white as snow, hair as black as coal, lips as red as blood."

"Don't recall any Most Wanteds of that description." Molina's smile put a period on her dismissal of the subject. She would certainly have to find out what that was all about. Probably under the pretense of getting Matt's report on the outing at Secrets. Not here. Somewhere more social . . .

"Oh. I did get the other sketch you wanted," Janice was saying, reaching into the large flat tapestry bag she'd leaned against her chair. "The bartender, Rick, took a bit of coaxing, but I think I got a pretty dead-on likeness." She handed her sketch pad across the desk, opening to the top sheet.

Oh, my, yes. Max Kinsella as a dated lounge lizard. So "Vince" had been his cover persona when he charmed that doomed girl Mandy/Cher despite looking like yesterday's Spanish omelette. Where *did* he get that tacky '70s gold jewelry?

She wasn't surprised, of course. She had sent him there to snoop. She just hadn't anticipated that he'd snoop in such an odious guise. Greasy hair curling at the ends. Ugh. Sleaze personified. Would the real Max Kinsella please stand up? No, cancel that. Would the real Max Kinsella please put his hands up and assume the position?

Unfortunately, in this case the sketch only proved he was on the job, on her orders.

Molina suddenly realized that Janice was watching her study the artwork.

"Almost too perfect as the very model of a modern lowlife, isn't he?" Janice said. "I think that guy's just playing at being a big man. If I were to say who would most likely have killed a woman, I'd pick him." Her blunt-nailed left forefinger came down hard on Raf Nadir's nose.

That was the last thing that Molina wanted to hear.

"So," Molina said a few hours later, carefully unwrapping her salsa–sour cream–green chili burger. "I hope you don't mind a quick meet at a fast-food place. I'm working late, and you go to work late, so . . ."

"Fine," Matt Devine said, looking nervous.

He was probably nervous about spilling something on the front seat of her Crown Victoria, which was in pretty good shape for a cop car.

The silver motorcycle he sometimes rode leaned against the single parking-lot light pole like a particularly out-of-place prostitute, all sleek and platinum-silver-blond in a black-dye neighborhood.

It was 9:00 P.M. and the parking lot light rinsed Matt's blindingly blond hair the albino shade of fiberglass-coifed Christmas-tree angels from a galaxy far away and long, long ago called East L.A.

She was a rat and no woman to use an unsuspecting schmuck (saint) like Matt for her larger purposes, but she had a daughter and a life to protect.

She found it uncanny that Matt had ordered the exact variety of Charley's Old-Fashion Burger that Max Kinsella had: lettuce, blue cheese, and sun-dried tomatoes.

Maybe all men were California cheeseburgers at heart.

"I suppose Janice told you—" he said, nervously.

"She did. She showed me."

"Vince."

Molina nodded.

"I don't know why he was there—"

"That's my job."

"—looking like that—"

"Maybe it's his natural coloration."

"—but I don't think he'd kill anyone. Not a woman, anyway."

Molina laughed. "Noble of you to defend him. You realize that if I put Kinsella away for murder one, our Miss Temple is one very unattached object."

He stopped negotiating a surrender with the four-inch-thick burger and eyed her in the twilight. Hard. "Temple is no object, attached or not. You realize that if you *did* put Kinsella in irons your Miss Temple would do anything to prove him innocent—including petitioning for a retrial before the ink was dry on the conviction? *If* you could get one in the first place."

"You *want* him out and about?"

"I want him paying for what he's done, not what you might wish he had done. I admit it looks bad that he was at Secrets before that stripper was killed, but I bet Temple can clear him of having anything to do with the earlier deaths. We know who killed the ex-nun and dumped her at the Blue Dahlia."

"But 'we' don't know who killed the woman in the church parking lot soon after. You remember, the former magician's assistant?" Molina kept her eyebrows raised in challenge.

"I understand what you're saying. An ex-magician's assistant could have been killed by an ex-magician like Kinsella. But he had no connection to her."

"That we know of. And he had a connection to the dead stripper, Matt, because I sent him into that club."

"*You* did? Why?"

She shook her head, ate a mouthful of bun and burger so she couldn't answer until she had come up with a good one.

"He seemed to fancy himself an undercover operator," she finally said. "I wanted him to tail somebody, and he ran into Mandy, actually born as Cher Smith, instead."

"Poor Max."

"Poor Max! Are we talking rival here or blood brother?"

"He's not my rival. You know that Temple and Max are . . . reunited. There are no rivals where there's no contest."

"Poor Matt."

But this time *he* had bitten off more than he could chew and was too busy to answer. Her comment lay as heavy as a cold French fry in a pool of congealed ketchup between them.

"Poor Carmen," he finally said when he had finished chewing, looking amused.

"I guess the only one of us who isn't 'poor' something is that blamed PR whiz."

"Temple's doing okay," Matt said. Serenely.

She tried not to grit her teeth. There wasn't a thing she could do with serene people.

"So." She started all over again. "It doesn't bother you that Kinsella was on the scene of the crime-to-be?"

"The scene where the victim of the crime-to-be had last been seen before dying. A lot of people must have been there that night."

Molina nodded. She had come here to disarm any suspicions Matt might have had. Instead, he was developing some of his own.

"I just wanted to warn you," she said.

"About what?"

"If it should turn out that Kinsella is as dirty as I think he is—"

"He's no murderer. Quite the contrary."

"If he were, he'd be out of your hair, Devine. Don't you care?"

"I do care. That's why I don't need to rise if someone else falls. You have chili on your chin."

"What!"

"Here's a napkin."

"I don't want a damn napkin, I want an understanding."

"You've said before that your nailing Kinsella would force Temple to turn to me, but you're wrong."

"About Kinsella being nailable?"

"I don't know. Maybe you *can* charge him with something serious. But that wouldn't force or free Temple to do or be anything other than she is. And she's committed to Max Kinsella. I've come to terms with that. Isn't it time that you did? You can't use her, and you can't use me.

"Poor Carmen."

He handed her a paper napkin.

Chapter 20

Feast

He lay sated.

Relieved.

The cub had come, playful, pushing its tiny paws between the bars of his lair.

All black, the same midnight color he had seen in some adults and fellow performers of his kind.

It was tiny, the cub, and for a moment his hunger was so sharp he had considered . . .

But it danced away before he could think any more about his hunger, his huge, black hole of hunger, gnawing at every thought and every instant like nothing he had felt before.

Where were the kind ones? Who brought food and water and reward?

Where were the two-legs he relied upon for everything?

Two-legs there were here. He had seen them shoveling food into the other cages, the aroma massaging his huge nostrils like his mother's tongue, creating a sense of want and fulfillment at the same time that he had not felt since his cub days.

Mother. She would feed him. Where was she, the constant presence, warm and purring as loud as a two-leg's machine?

But now he was not hungry. He heard an echo of his mother's purr within himself.

The cub he had spared, that he had been too hunger-dulled to threaten, had come back. Dragging meat! Food. Fresh.

It had struggled to push the trophy between the metal poles of his container with its tiny forefeet. Then it had sat and watched him eat. Asking nothing for itself. A very well-behaved cub! No pulling and fighting with it, small as it was.

He had eaten and eaten, and then gnawed bare bone. Eaten a great deal for a single sitting, as he had heard the Forepaws had done in the Far Place before meeting the two-legs. Feasting. You did not understand a feast until you had known want. Until you had known hunger gnawing at your innards like a predator, like a tiger or a lion at its meal.

But he didn't need to think of more meals yet. Now he was full. Sated. Lazy.

He dozed, his eyes shut, his purr an echo of his mother's crooning.

When the sharp bite nipped his shoulder again, his muscle twitched, that's all.

A fly. An irritating fly when life was so good.

Odd that the cub had come into his territory after he had eaten and was feeling drowsy. A brave cub. To enter his lair and wrest the naked bone away, through the tall shafts of iron grass.

A brave, strong cub. Where had it come from? He had heard no mewling of young here, just the snarls and cries of the old and forsaken. . . .

He felt himself slump over on his side. On the side where he had been bitten. Again. Perhaps he would wake up with the two-legs he knew and trusted. Perhaps the food would come often from now on, as before, and this last vision was just the uneasy milk-dream of a besotted cub. A small spotted cub. No. Black. Solid black. Of the kind they call panther. White teeth, red tongue like fresh meat, heart of lion.

If he saw the cub again, he would share some of his meat with it. His head felt as big as an elephant's. He tried to prick his ears, but they lay limp, dulled by the buzzing of a thousand tsetse flies.

* * *

The smell is odd. There is none.

No. There are traces of odor, but faint, like the scent the two-legs leave.

His head lifts. He now lies on grass.

No.

He lies on the short grass the two-legs line their lairs with.

It smells like the water in the pool in his home lair, pungent, sharp, not of blood and bone, but of nothingness. That smell had been all around his home lair, and his slowed heart begins to pound faster in the happy excitement of recognizing the familiar.

He is in his home lair again! Inside the two-legs' lair, as he had been allowed now and again. For flashes from their machines, when they praised him like purrs. Good boy. Handsome boy. Osiris. Yes.

He pushes himself upright on buckling paws. Gets to his legs, wobbles like a cub. Good cub. He is still full.

He had heard of the old days. Feast and famine, the elders called it. Wild days of hunt and hunger, one first, the other second. Always hunt or hunger. He had not known hunger until these last hours, these last three sunfalls and sunbeams.

Now it is dark.

No, not quite dark.

It is a dark filled with the balls of the two-legs' light. Warm when you sleep under it. Cool as sky-brights when it is far away.

He moves a step or two, feeling his pads sink into the shaven grass. He brushes a rock. One of the two-legs' rocks that sits on legs.

It shudders and shakes, as if oncoming hooves are thundering. He has heard hooves here. Like the great tall beasts in iron shoes he has seen from time to time, who also play for the two-legs.

The four-legged rock tumbles onto its side, as he had done not long ago, dropping some things that tinkle like stones and shatter.

He sees a long low shape in the night, much like his mother to his cub eyes. He goes to rub against it for warmth and purr and recognition. But it is cold and still, though somewhat soft. He stretches and feels a need to sharpen his dulled claws. Rip, rip, rip. They sink in as they have never done before, catching in the mother shape, making a sharp, shearing sound that both frightens and pleases him. Now there is a smell. Raw meat. Tangy juice.

He leaps back, his claws snagging as they never have before. The mother shape wobbles, then falls over on its side with a loud thud.

He leaps away, free, and skitters across the short grass, his amazingly long and sharp claws digging into polished wood, sending rags flying as he courses through the darkness shuddering into rocks and hummocks and toys, perhaps, like the huge smooth balls he has learned to perch on.

Noises follow this progress as they do in the dark lair lit by falling stars to which he is brought almost every night to perform his rituals that bring food.

Hunting, he calls it. He performs the rituals, and the food follows and he is full and happy and gets to sleep afterward for long, lazy hours.

He knows the rhythm of that life and those places, but all here is jangled and misplaced. He is clumsy and hurling into unseen, unsuspected barriers, all vaguely familiar, but all specifically strange.

His heart is pounding, as is his head. He is glad he has eaten, because the Hunger that was with him earlier was like a ravening ghost of himself and he could not say that he would be friend to any two-leg no matter how familiar because the Hunger said Eat, and the two-leg was to be Eaten. That is a terrible thought. Thank the Mother-cub that came to feed him. He is not driven by the alien Hunger. He is himself, though lost and confused and afraid.

A noise.

The startled sound of a two-leg.

A bright light sunshine all around him so he can see nothing through his narrowest slits of vision.

A two-leg, roaring with surprise or anger.

Osiris knows he is in the wrong place. He must return to where he is supposed to be.

He runs past the two-leg.

For a moment he scents flesh and running blood beneath it and his fangs and tongue yearn, as they had for so many unsatisfied hours. But he is fresh-free now. Good boy. Handsome boy. He runs past the flailing figure, butts it in passing, feels it overturn like the mother shape.

He senses for a moment that the Hunger is with him again, and says stop. Sniff. Lick. Bite.

But he is full. Good boy.

He runs until he is in the dark again, and feels safe.

Nothing smells like his home lair. Now that the Hunger is quieter he feels another yearning. Home lair. He wants to be in home lair. He is a good boy.

Chapter 21

Taxidermy Eyes

"I can't believe it," Molina says.

It is 5:00 A.M. and she stands in a living room as upscale as a high-roller suite at the Bellagio, staring down at a corpse.

The captured killer stares down at the corpse too, eyes dilated, whiskers visibly twitching.

Molina regards the full-grown leopard.

It stands in the cramped cage brought to the crime scene by three animal control people, who have retreated to the room's threshold to stare wide-eyed at the entire scene, as if they were sleepwalking.

The leopard roars plaintively and everybody jumps.

This is one perp who can plead diminished capacity and get away with it.

Molina turns to the other exotic animal in the room: the widow.

"It's a good thing you knew how to corral the creature," Molina comments.

She doesn't mean a word of it, she just wants to get the woman talking so she can figure out what happened here.

All she knows so far is that victim is moneyed, that his body bears the tracks of a big cat. And that he has fallen onto the stuffed head of an oryx (she thinks) whose unicornlike horn has performed a quadruple bypass on his major cardiac organs.

Which beast is the actual killer: the live one, or the dead one?

The widow might be dead too. She has said nothing, but sits staring at a huge square glass-topped cocktail table. Carved wooden elephants with upheld trunks support it at each corner. Even in a wooden form elephants have to work.

Molina blinks bleary eyes. She is surrounded by the glassy taxidermy eyes of a couple dozen trophy heads staring down from the two-tiered living room's walls. She can't name all the species, except that they run the gamut from hooved to clawed. The beastly atmosphere is so overwhelming that she is beginning to think the widow looks like a mountain lion.

"Mrs. Van Burkleo?"

The woman's oddly small eyes seem absent without leave in the overbearing frame of her massive facial bone structure. Her face looks like it has been trampled by an animal. She also has taxidermy eyes. Glassy amber eyes, bizarre somehow. From the age difference between the skewered corpse and the comatose widow, Mrs. Van Burkleo was a trophy wife. Fit right into the decor, especially with that lion's mane of thick tawny hair.

"Mrs. Van Burkleo, how did the leopard get into the house? Was it a . . . pet?"

"A leopard is a wild animal," the woman answers in a deep, low voice. "It's foolhardy to keep one as a pet."

"Did you and your husband—?"

"No. I don't know how the leopard got here. There was no cage, nothing. Just the leopard. And Cyrus."

Molina walks toward the body the widow regards with dazed indifference, as if he were now part of the trophyscape. Cyrus was a nondescript man in late middle age, thick of middle, thin of hair. Sixty-something.

The widow could be anywhere from twenty-nine to forty-nine, one of those high-fashion icons who freeze-frame into permanent limbo in the aging department.

Must take all of her spare time, and—Molina was finally believing the evidence of her own eyes—a lot of plastic surgery. Unsuccessful plastic surgery, or maybe too successful. The woman's face seemed kissing cousin to more than one head on the wall.

Van Burkleo, he was Homo sapiens at its most uninspiring, a figure of power for his money alone, surrounded by figurative reminders of what enough money and high-caliber equipment will buy the aging white hunter.

"Any children?" Molina asks.

The widow Van Burkleo shrugs lean and bony shoulders revealed by a tiger-print spandex halter top. "The usual two. Before my time. They're somewhere in the Midwest."

"School, or grown?"

She shrugs again. "We traveled so much. All over the world. Didn't see or hear much of them. Isn't that how children should be, not seen and not heard?"

"Seen and not heard."

"Oh. Well, Cyrus's were 'not' both. When we married—"

"Which was?"

"Six years ago, here in Vegas. At the Goliath chapel. A very nice place. I recommend it."

"I'll tell all my friends."

"I'm sorry. I still can't grasp it. Cyrus. The leopard. How, when . . ."

"The medical examiner will do his best to tell us when. And how. I understand the maid found the body. You only arrived here afterward."

"After the first police arrived, yes. I was at our suite in town."

"Did you and your husband often stay in different residences?"

Those razor-sharp shoulder bones shrugged again. Molina had the irritating impression she was showing off.

"Cyrus loved to gamble as much as he loved to hunt," the widow said. "So did I. But we didn't pursue both hobbies at the same time. They're a bit of the same thing, aren't they? People like to see the heads. He probably had clients to entertain out here."

"And a misplaced leopard," Molina said.

The woman stares at the big cat, now pacing in the small cage. It stops to stare back.

Molina has the oddest feeling that it knows her, it knows Leonora Van Burkleo.

"I don't know why or how the big cat got here. Cyrus admired them. He liked the fact that the big wild cats were so much more dangerous than any wild dog. The dog was a degenerate breed, he used to say. Only the domestic cat could claim a huge, savage ancestor still stalking the earth."

"However many are left," Molina said shortly. Dead bodies offended her sense of universal harmony. Even dead animal bodies.

The widow's feral glance froze on her with deadly intent.

"Hunting is the world's oldest profession. Oh, I know what they say it is, but they're wrong. It's not hustling. It's hunting. My husband was proud to put himself up against the wiles of a wild animal, and win."

Molina eyed the trophy heads. They were much more lordly-looking than the sorry lot of humans, alive and dead, gathered around the huge trophy suite in this trophy house so far from and yet so near to a city dedicated to the hunter and hunted, to the winner and loser. The hunted and the losers always outnumbered the others, even in the wild kingdom.

Is it poetic justice that a big cat has clawed the big game hunter into a corner? That the stab of a long-dead antelope's horn has finished him?

Or was the means of death not only a medium but a message?

She takes a last look at the leopard. It has stopped pacing and regards her with an expression she recognizes. Feline sagacity.

She wonders how many other people would be glad that this time the animal has won. Or has it?

By four that afternoon, Molina was alert and ready for a break in the case. She had heard from several highly placed men in city government and commerce that Cyrus Van Burkleo was a highly regarded member of the community. Translation: they owe him, she had better deliver a killer soon, and it had better be someone—or something—whose identity will not rattle anyone's cages. Enter the leopard.

Molina doesn't believe in worms turning, not even on fishermen. She certainly doesn't believe in leopards committing murder one.

Su and Alch think they have a prime suspect. In fact, they think they have three.

"Who found them?" Molina asked.

"Employees of the deceased," Alch said amiably.

" 'Animal keepers,' " Su put in, her china doll face wearing a mask of hard-edged suspicion that Molina reads like a child's book.

'You don't think Mr. Van Burkleo's employees are what they say they are."

"They're muscle," Su said contemptuously, as contemptuously as a four-foot-eleven black belt in karate can say of large lumbering musclemen.

"Why did Van Burkleo need muscle?"

"Because of these three people," Alch answers promptly, good Boy Scout that he was thirty-five years ago.

Alch and Su crack her up: such an unlikely team, and so effective for that very fact. The 180-degree difference in their ages, their sizes, their genders, their cultural background, Jewish and Chinese, makes them the perfect complement to any case, like sweet and sour sauce to pork loin. Except that, contrary to stereotypes, Alch is the sweet, and Su is the sour. Molina doesn't show her amusement, or her approval, of course. They would be insulted.

"You think these 'employees' were itching to have these people found?" Molina asked.

"Of course." Su stubbornly folded her arms, inadvertently displaying her Mandarin-long fingernails. Weapons, in her case.

Alch shifted in his chair, scratched his neck, put off an answer until Su's elderberry eyes flashed imperial impatience.

"Maybe," Alch conceded, with a wicked feint of a glance at his steaming partner. "But the fact is they were trespassers on private property. And they were armed."

Su spat out an unspoken comment. "Flare guns."

Molina nodded.

"They're animal-rights activists," Alch said.

"Interesting." Molina stood. "You've got their names, ranks, and serial numbers?"

Su nodded.

"Then I'll take a look at them." Molina checked the names and facts the detectives had recorded from their separate preliminary interviews, then led the way to the interrogation rooms, curious as a cat.

Three people might be just what it would take to stage-manage the Van Burkleo death scene to make it look like a wild animal had turned the tables on the hunter. Predator turned prey, turned predator.

Everybody liked a happy ending.

First Molina eyed the trio through three different two-way mirrors.

"The old woman's the leader," Su told her. "A retired professor from Davis, California."

"Late middle-aged," the thirty-something Molina corrected the twenty-something Su.

The fifty-something Alch just snickered to himself.

Su shrugged. Over thirty was one big Do-Not-Go-There Zone.

The twenties seem to last forever, Molina thought, remembering what it was to be kid-free . . . also as green as goat cheese that had been sitting out for three months. Don't-Go-Back-There Zone.

They marched off to eye the other suspects. Molina passed on the twenty-something surfer boy with the punk haircut.

At the late-forties tree hugger in the ponytail, she smiled nostalgically. "I'll try him first."

Su's sharply arched eyebrows rose. She plucked them in a dragon lady pattern that Molina had only seen in that old comic strip, *Terry and the Pirates*, drawn decades ago when the "Oriental menace" had been Fu Manchu instead of sweatshop labor.

Every generation reached back to find fodder for rebellion. With Mariah, it was ear decor so far. So good.

Alch was nodding approvingly, not that she sought it.

Molina left the two detectives behind the mirror and entered the room, sat down, turned on the tape recorder. "Lieutenant C. R. Molina," she began, adding date and time in a toneless official voice.

She flipped open a manila folder and appeared to study it.

"Evan Sprague." She repeated his name aloud without acknowledging him. "You don't have a criminal record."

"Of course I don't," he said, trying to sound indignant and merely sounding nervous.

Molina slapped the folder shut. "We're investigating a murder."

"I . . . I've been told that, Lieutenant."

"What were you doing on the deceased's property?"

"I told the other officers. Detectives. Whatever. We were . . . scouting."

"Just a bunch of Boy Scouts on a camp-out?"

"No, uh, we're green."

"I guess!"

"We're for animal rights."

"So."

"You must know what goes on at that ranch."

"We're just ignorant city police. You tell me."

"It's a head-hunting place." Mr. Limp Noodle was turning into Mr. Barbed Wire before her eyes. "They collect de-accessioned once-wild animals, like excess zoo stock, illegal exotic pets that have been confiscated from all over, anything that used to be wild and free and has a beautiful coat of fur or a handsome set of horns."

Molina nodded to show comprehension. He would never tell from her expression that she was also nodding agreement with his indignation.

"These animals are not wild in any sense of the word. They've become dependent on humans. They're domesticated, fed, watered like sheep or cattle. And then they bring in these wealthy weekend 'hunters' who don't have time to go to authorized hunting areas, these weekday lawyers and doctors who want heads for their office walls, and let them take potshots with bows and arrows and rifles and bullets at the animals until they kill them. It may take a while. These 'professional men' are lousy shots, and they don't want to mar the heads and shoulders before they're stuffed."

"I get the picture. So, if Van Burkleo was this . . . pimp for canned hunters"—Sprague's pale eyes glittered at the word she'd armed him with—"why couldn't your dedicated group have turned a leopard loose, thrown Van Burkleo on the antelope horn, and clawed him somehow, leaving a dead body with no suspect but a dumb animal, with which the community outrage is usually satisfied if it's put down for the sin of touching a human. Case closed. The leopard was doomed anyway."

Sprague practically leaped up from his chair at her throat.

"That's just it. We subdue, brutalize, imprison, abuse these wonderful beasts that nature has given us, and let one—one—raise a paw in protection or protest or plain animal instinct, and we kill the animal. We are the *animals* that deserve killing!"

"Exactly," Molina said coolly. "Which of your compatriots was the mastermind?"

"None! We didn't do it. We protest peacefully. We disrupt the hunt."

"You risk getting yourself skewered with an arrow or a bullet. Killed yourselves."

He took a deep breath. "If so, it shows what kind of 'recreation' this sort of hunting is."

"Then you don't object to sanctioned hunting on designated preserves in season?"

Another deep breath. "Those people observe the law, and at least give the prey a fighting chance. But I still wonder why they have to kill something when it's no longer necessary to survive."

"I hunt killers myself," Molina said suddenly, quietly, leaning closer. "There's nothing worse than someone who violates another creature's right to live. But I've never shot my firearm in tracking a killer. I let the laws levy justice. Did your group decide to levy justice for the law this time, in this case, for this man?"

"No! We protest. That's what we do."

"Who was to watch your protest, way out there? Those 'security forces' could have shot you all and buried your bodies hipbone-deep in sand for decades, eternity, and no one would have ever known. Just as no one would have ever known your group was out there to kill Van Burkleo if you hadn't been spotted."

"Who spotted us?" He was suddenly belligerent. "Not the security guys. They were looking for vehicles, and we hiked in. We're good at subterfuge; have to be to spring 'surprises' on the killers. Who was it? That guy who claimed to be on his own out there?"

"Guy?"

"He dove into the same wash with us to avoid being spotted by a patrol. Somebody else must have mentioned him. You want a suspicious character, he was it."

"I haven't talked to the other suspects yet," Molina said, "and I'm not interested in any lone wolf your imagination dreams up. I bet they don't mention any such person when I get to them."

"They will! He wasn't one of us. We have no reason to protect him."

"Glad to hear it. So tell me about this guy."

"Well, he dives right on top of us. Broad daylight. Doesn't want to be seen, all right, but he's wearing black from head to tail. Foot, rather."

"Black?"

"Yeah. Midday on the desert. Says there's always a shadow so it's a good cover. Black. He doesn't know at first what we're doing out there, but he figures it out real fast. Acted like he was sympathetic to the cause, but Alyce wasn't buying any of it. We didn't argue too much with him; any uproar would draw the patrols, but we never bought his lame story for being out there. And he got mad at us. Said we were fools and risking our lives. That the security forces would have us for barbecue. Well, they didn't catch us. Your people did."

"City slickers," Molina said, pleased.

"That's what this guy was. A city slicker. He had a lot of nerve to be out there with us."

Molina was struck by the last sentence. A city slicker with a lot of nerve. All in black.

"What did he look like?" she asked blandly.

Sprague rolled his eyes as if the gesture would jump-start his memory. "Tall guy. I think. Lean as a whipsnake. Dark hair. Eyes . . . not sure. Thirty-four or-five maybe. Maybe younger. Acted . . . seasoned. We were kind of dazzled when he was there, and when he took off, we wondered what kind of line he was handing us."

Molina leaned her head on her hand. Turned off the tape recorder. "Can you just sit here for a minute?'

Sprague looked startled to death at her question. What the heck else could he do until someone told him he could leave or bailed him out?

She left the room, peeked in on the detectives. "Hang on," she told them. Then she did a straight-line dive back to her office and a certain manila folder in her bottom file drawer.

In four minutes she was back, sitting across from Evan Sprague and flipping open the folder.

"Look anything like this?" she wondered. Idly.

Sprague frowned at the single sheet of paper inside the open folder. "Bad hair. Worse jewelry."

"Can't argue with you."

"I guess it could be him. Yeah. The face structure is the same, but the effect is . . . way different."

"Can I call that a strong maybe?"

"Maybe." He frowned at Janice Flanders's sketch of Vince from Secrets. "Like the same person inside a way different skin, you know what I mean?"

"Oh, yes," Molina said, spinning the sketch to face her. "I do."

Snakes shed their skins all the time. . . . And at last one of them had done it on the scene of a crime in her jurisdiction.

Chapter 22

Likely Suspects

Max was waiting in Temple's living room when she schlepped Midnight Louie up from the car in his carrier.

"Just in time," she announced, not a bit startled to find Max arranged like an art deco print (Big Black Panther on Big White Sofa in a Big White Hollywood Set from the '30s) in her locked condo. "Let the revels begin! Louie and I have triumphed in the courts of justice."

Max sat up to watch Temple liberate the cat from his grille-front carrier. "I thought Louie the Wonder Cat was such a good traveler that he didn't need a carrier."

"*He* doesn't. But courts of law require animals to be 'contained,' unlike even the worst human criminal, even just to show up to collect a judgment. It makes me boil. Did you know that animals are legal nonentities? Mere property! Like they didn't have feelings, and we humans didn't have feelings for them. Would you believe this magnificent cat has a courtroom value of thirty-two dollars?"

By now Louie had emerged from durance vile and was regarding the Max-occupied sofa with loathing, but definitely not fear.

Max regarded Louie in turn. "Thirty-two dollars seems generous."

"Oh, come on, guys! Get over it! Louie, sit on the other end of the sofa, there's plenty of room, even for you. Max, just sit. Don't move a muscle. If you stir, Louie may not go up on the sofa."

"This is mentioned to *encourage* me to play statue?"

"It's my sofa and if either of you want to sit on it you'll just have to get along."

Even Louie seemed to understand this last threat. After giving Temple a long green stare over his black shoulder, he stretched to pointedly sharpen his claws on the nubbly fabric. Then he leaped atop the arm farthest from Max and began smoothing the saw-toothed dishevelment of the hairs along his spine. Presumably the presence of the Mystifying Max had turned his usually sleek coiffure into an instant Afro.

"Okay," Max told Temple, "now that we're friends"—the two were five feet apart—"I'll let you tell me about your court date before I tell you about the court date I've just avoided. So far."

"Really." Temple regarded the two black figures on her sofa with the satisfaction Roy might take in a pair of white tigers' going to their proper stools. "Well, first I'm going to get a glass of wine, then I'm going to take my shoes off, and then I'm going to sit down."

She headed briskly to the kitchen while Max took belated stock of her shoes, a beige suede pair of pumps apparently judged sober enough for a court of law.

He checked the cat, which was glaring at him while whipping its tongue over its muscular shoulders and showing its teeth in the process. At the moment, Louie reminded Max of the disapproving father of a teenaged daughter.

Not that Louie could possibly know what fatherhood was all about, having the morals of an alley cat.

Temple had not offered Max any refreshment, alcoholic or non, which meant that she was in a ruffled mood. Despite her air of cele-bration—zip-a-dee-doo-dah—not everything was going her way.

Temple always tended to micromanage when she was under stress, even cats and lovers. Nobody had ever said she wasn't a brave woman, and her recent excursions into crime-solving proved the point.

So Max sat back, and waited. Once Temple had settled down, he would get his chance to astound and amaze. He always did.

Temple pulled a single, stemmed glass down from her cupboard—Max could wait on himself, he knew where everything was—and tried not to notice how pleased she was to see him here.

Pouring the red wine into the glass, she let her shoulders relax. Even getting her money today couldn't soften that judge's on-camera tongue-lashing yesterday, the sour topping to a very sweet day otherwise. Maybe they'd cut it for the actual broadcast. She couldn't even remember what she'd said during the parting interview, she'd been so stung by the charges Judge Geraldine Jones had hurled at the end.

She, an irresponsible person? A bad pet owner? She hadn't asked for a cat, gone out looking for one, or for a dead body, over which she and Louie had met so propitiously almost a year ago.

When neither one of them had panicked, she knew that they were made for each other. And did Judge Geraldine Jones have any idea of Louie's remarkable intelligence and enterprise? He was not an ordinary cat. You couldn't keep him penned up inside. She knew you—*she*—should. Everybody else should with every other cat. Except Louie. Who would annoy Lieutenant Molina and contaminate her crime scenes if he were confined to the condo? Who would bail Temple out of hot water, in which she was so frequently immersed, through no fault of her own but nosiness?

The fact was that Louie was not an ordinary cat, and he could not abide by ordinary rules. And Temple had never expected to be a cat owner. Hah! What a contradiction in terms that was. One did not own a cat, one cohabited with a cat. On its terms.

Rather like Max.

Why did anyone put up with either one of them?

Buttressed, she came back out into the living room. Why? Well, they were handsome devils, no doubt about it, and so much alike they should be blood brothers.

Temple sat on Louie's half of the sofa. Actually, it was the only vacant human half, since Louie was still holding himself aloof on the sofa arm. Nothing can be more uppity than a cat with a point to prove.

"So how was your day in court yesterday" Max said genially.

"Do you want to get yourself a glass of wine first?"

"No, thanks. If we're going out to celebrate I'll save it for later."

"We can go out? In public? Together? Really?"

"If Louie lets us. He looks exceptionally disapproving at the moment."

"I mean, you don't have to . . . lurk?"

"I always have to lurk, Temple, but I think we can risk the occasional public foray."

"Gosh, we haven't eaten out in a real restaurant since . . ."

"Since Michael's in New York." Max took her hand, her bare left hand. "When I gave you the ill-fated ring. You did say that opals were unlucky."

"You did say that was just superstition. I'll get that ring back someday. I know I will."

Max only smiled and lifted her fingers to his lips. "Your day. Remember?"

Temple had almost forgotten, but she kicked off her pumps . . . had to dig out something snazzier for dinner tonight . . . and kicked off her tale of indignities.

She stopped just short of the judge's searing lecture.

"No wonder Louie's so pleased with himself," Max commented. "He earns you twenty-five hundred bucks and manages to squeeze in some quality time with the foxy lady."

"Honestly, the way those two cats were behaving, you'd think Louie *was* the father of those kittens."

At that the cat thumped resoundingly to the floor and disappeared.

"Alone at last," said Max, who had never released her fingers. "Apparently fatherhood is a tender subject for Louie just now. He can never be one now, you know."

"You'd think he'd thank me! Look at the grief those striped kittens have caused. Besides, Louie isn't the paternal sort."

"How do you know?"

She looked after him, or where he'd disappeared to, probably her bedroom. He knew how to pick his theater of operations. Lose one beachhead, take over the next most likely contested spot.

"I don't," she admitted. "And I never will. Anyway, it was so delicious to see Savannah Ashleigh wailing and screaming. Such a baaaad loser."

Temple decided not to ruin the celebration by mentioning the judge's lecture. "Where are we going for dinner?"

"How about the Rio?"

"Oh, great! I love that blue-and-magenta free-form neon all over the new high-rise building in the complex. It has more ooomph for being off the Strip. Did you ever notice how the swoopy wings and plinth look like that ultramodern statue, the Christ of the Andes?"

"No." Max laughed. "And don't point that out to anyone else. Las Vegas is supposed to be godless."

"More churches here per capita than any city in the U.S."

"Thank you, fountainhead of PR information. Now, are you going to change into something celebratory? You do sort of resemble Allie McBeal."

"Ick! Lawyer power suit. At least *my* skirts cover my bony... knees."

Temple hied to the bedroom, where Louie was sprawled diagonally across the zebra-print comforter, managing, with his forelegs and luxurious tail extended, to pretty much make the surface unfit for human habitation.

Since the Rio cultivated a Mardi Gras air, and since Fat Tuesday was coming soon, Temple pulled out the Midnight Louie heels in all their Austrian crystal glory. With her feet shod in Stuart Weitzman's, she was up to anything, including rummaging through her jumbled closet to find something suitable to wear. What did you wear with your Cinderella shoes? She paged past a simple black dress with buttons all down the front, quickly, and settled on—aha!—that exquisite vintage '60s silver-knit suit with short swirly skirt and tailored jacket.

Grabbing a small black purse, she was ready for a night out.

She did pause in the living room to grab Max, not literally.

He stood when she entered the room. No matter what she wore, Max had the gift of looking perfectly attired to complement it. His wardrobe of magician's black was just casual enough, and just expensive enough, to suit any occasion. A shawl-collared Italian blazer over his black turtle neck made him look fresh from the Concorde, and before that Paris and Milan.

"Aren't we a couple of quick-change artists?" Temple asked rhetorically. "You still driving the Maxima?"

"Afraid so."

"It's actually nice to know what our transportation is, for a change."

He opened the door to the hallway just like a regular date, and they were off.

Within thirty minutes they were seated at a window table in the VooDoo Café, on the fiftieth story, just a story below the rooftop VooDoo Lounge. The restaurant was dim, the better for diners to eat up the view. Tables lit by candles in colored glass holders were standard, but the view of Las Vegas as the Bloody-Mary sun slid down behind the mountains and the Strip's neon landing lights gassed up for the night ahead was spectacular.

Temple didn't ask how Max had managed to get a good table so fast. She suspected it had something to do with a cell phone and his invisible but potent brand of "pull."

Their before-dinner drinks were tall, exotically colored, and expensive, but uniquely flavored.

"To twenty-five hundred dollars in a day's work." Max tipped the sickle moon of orange slice hung on his glass lip to her lime-slice-hung glass lip.

"Peanuts compared to what you used to make," Temple noted.

"At least brazil nuts. And I didn't make it from upgrading a thirty-two-dollar cat to a twenty-five-hundred-dollar one."

"They don't usually award much of anything for crimes against animals. Luckily, Louie's high-profile performance history played a role."

"I imagine you're still enjoying seeing the Great Satan, Savannah Ashleigh, properly fried."

Temple nodded, sipped, then thought. "You know, she was really disappointed. I had the funny feeling she could have used the money."

"Now, don't ruin your victory by worrying about the loser."

"Worry? Me? About Savannah? *I* can really use the money. I've been so busy putting the finishing touches on the Crystal Phoenix campaign that I haven't taken another job in weeks."

"If you need any money—"

"I know. You've got it. Or is that *It*?" She smiled wickedly as she put the capital *I* in her inflection. "I'm fine. It's nice to know I have a chump to fall back on, but I'd really rather do it myself."

Their waitress came to take their orders and by the time she had gone their cocktails were at half-mast.

"So," Temple said, feeling really relaxed for the first time in ages. "That was my day in court. How was your day?"

He told her.

Temple's jaw dropped about two minutes into the recital, and stayed that way until she finally could round up a question or three hundred.

"You've been back out in the desert with a pack of wild animal-rights people?"

"Just three."

"And . . . hit patrols?"

" 'Security' is the formal term."

"Why didn't you mention it earlier? So where I was snooping a couple days ago really is a top-secret, high-dollar canned-hunt ranch?"

"Not so secret now."

"And the owner got killed last night? That man I met? Van Burkleo?"

"The medical examiner's report hasn't said homicide yet."

"Like you know all this stuff! Out of the mouths of the police and into Max Kinsella's ear?"

"The worst part is the nature of the killing."

"A killing of nature, what with the leopard on the scene, I bet. Do you think the animal did it?"

Max shook his head. "Too . . . pat. Especially when you know who the leopard is."

"You're sure the Rancho Exotica leopard is CC's? Do leopards have identities?"

"Doesn't Midnight Louie?"

Temple nodded. She was starving, but the information download at the table was far more taste-tempting than anything she had ordered, as good as it sounded.

"But I know Louie. Big cats I only glimpse. I've seen Kahlúa, the black panther you borrowed for a special effect once, but I never knew who owned it. Gandolph didn't ever work with a big cat—?"

Max shook his head at mention of his mentor. "No."

"There are probably lots of leopards in Vegas. A dozen magicians around town must use leopards. They love to change them into human vixens. You once said maybe I could be your assistant. I suppose I could change into a snarling, sensuous leopard lady."

"Maybe you could, but get your mind back on who might use a leopard as an accessory. In the criminal sense. You already were in a position to see who would use a leopard as an accessory in the magical sense, even if I hadn't told you who the kidnapped leopard belonged to."

"I was in a position? To see? When? Oh." Temple nodded sagely, finally getting his reference. "TitaniCon was crawling in Khatlords from *Space Trooper Bazaar* wearing spotted masks like the Cloaked Conjuror's. And then I saw CC in person at the judges's table in his leopard facial appliance . . . but, Max! How would you *know* that I saw the Cloaked Conjuror at TitaniCon? You weren't there, except on the outside."

For a moment he seemed startled. "Elementary, my dear. Titani-Con was held at the New Millennium, which is where the CC does his act, so you might have seen him. You managed to keep Molina Junior from evil influences, remember?"

"That was the strangest thing. Her mother, particularly—"

"What about the esteemed lieutenant?"

"Oh, nothing." Temple wasn't about to describe TitaniCon's dramatic denouement to Max, particularly since it put her archenemy Molina in a favorable light. If you considered personally tackling the perp a favorable light . . . and Temple did. At least she did when she or Louie managed it.

"Whoever the leopard is, the police think it killed the guy," she concluded. "And you?"

"I think that there are loads of likely suspects, all of them able to walk on two legs. What I want to know is who you saw inside the place."

"Oh. Oh! The wife. The widow now. Wow. What a weird woman. I think she was having herself surgically altered to look like a big cat."

"This is a motive for murder?"

"Maybe her husband made her do it? Or maybe she wanted the ranch and the money?"

"Anyone else around the place?"

Temple grimaced. "It's so hackneyed. The comely secretary. Thin and tall enough to pose as a straw. Snooty too. Let's have her do it."

"You don't know anything about her?"

Temple shook her head. "I imagine Molina's people are assembling dossiers on the dramatis personae."

"If they haven't been dazzled by the leopard at center stage."

"Molina wouldn't fall for that, would she?"

"From what I gather, the murder scene looked enough like an accident to confuse the issue. And most people have no idea of what performing leopards are about, or what they can and cannot do."

"Which means?"

"The leopard was a pro. He was people-friendly. True, you can never fully trust a wild animal, especially one big enough to hurt or eat you, but he wouldn't just go berserk and attack a person. Unless he'd been goaded into it."

"Teased, you mean?"

Max nodded. "Animal instinct is powerful and rapid. These foolish people who keep big cats as pets always underestimate that a second's worth of sheer instinct taking over could gravely harm a human."

"Sounds like murder in the human kingdom too. You obviously think that Molina and company won't investigate the leopard angle, or won't investigate it well enough. Why not?"

Max grinned and drained the dregs of his long, potent drink. Rum and everything.

"Because my friends in camouflage, the animal-rights protesters, are going to tell all about the man in black they saw lurking in the desert before Van Burkleo died."

"You! That's right. You were out there. And you were on the scene. You're a likely suspect."

"And wait until the widow and the snooty secretary tell the police that *you* were there."

"Oh, no!"

"Worried?"

"Only that Molina will have a nervous breakdown trying to decide which of us she'd most like to nail with murder."

Déjà Vu

Reno, as she called herself, was too short to be a stripper. Maybe five four on a good day and the right high heels.

She was in superb shape, though, especially for a relatively recent mother. And she made the most of it. Even at two in the morning.

He watched her from the smattering of audience: bored guys trying to decide how many dollar bills it was worth stuffing down her G-string to give them some reflexive kick, some nervous system surge that could be identified as erotic through the smoke and the sound and the booze and the damn emptiness of life itself.

Strip clubs were the most depressing places in the world when you stripped away the jacked-up sound, the rote sexy motions, the scent of money and sweat.

Max had donned Vince with the same professional dispassion and distaste that cops pull on latex gloves these days: it was a habit, it was useful, it was a protective device from the unnameable stains of life in the sleaze lane. One hoped.

Onstage, Reno grabbed her ankles in their four-inch-high heels, bent over, back arched, and showed where life began. And sometimes ended.

Max stared at Reno's splayed high heels, so different from the high-fashion form Temple wore.

High heels were supposed to be sexy, and he supposed they were. The culture had seen to that. Yet there was a world of difference between Reno's spikes and Temple's high heels, and he'd have to be somewhere else to explain it to himself.

He glanced at the bar. Rick was there, waiting for Godot, or Ilsa, or Claude Rains. Rick was looking at Max . . . Vince . . . when he looked Rick's way.

A bad sign.

Max slid off the armless chair, built for lap dancing.

Out of the corner of his eye, he saw the rolling gait of an overmuscled man heading his way.

He didn't even look to see if it was Rafi Nadir.

He was out the door, in the still of the night. Around a corner. Another corner. Back in Dumpster Row, where the neon didn't shine.

He had seen Reno arrive in a banged-up Toyota. His luminous watch dial, pure '50s, told him it was only 1:40 A.M. How much longer could Reno shake it for the dollar-bill fools?

He'd wait.

He heard the front door wheeze open, then hold the position. The bouncer looking for him.

After a while the muffled sound of music softened, then cut off.

Door closed.

Max edged around the building to the end of the parking lot that hosted Reno's Toyota.

He moved into the scraggly brush edging the asphalt. Looming over it was a two-headed streetlight as sleek and sinister looking as the Martian ship probes in *The War of the Worlds*. But both lamps were dead, blind, only faint moonlight reflecting from their burned-out reflectors. They made an odd but apropos metaphor for the stripper club called Secrets and everybody in it. He settled into the shadows to wait.

* * *

She came clicking across the parking lot on her four-inch hooker heels. Swaggering.

Apparently a good night.

Halfway to the car, a pursuing shadow bolted from the dark hulk of Secrets and caught up with her, hard.

It spun her around.

"Reno."

Max heard the name, heard everything, as the words hissed across the dry asphalt like a sidewinder snake.

"You want?"

"Had a good night."

"Okay."

"Not over yet."

"It is for me."

"You haven't shared."

She shook off the man's arm. "You work here, like I do. You don't get a cut."

"I can take it any way you like."

"Nothing!"

He reached for something: her, or where he thought the money was.

Reno's arm struck out.

He backed up. "You—"

"You work here, just like I do. You don't own anything about me."

Max was easing over on silent shoes, but they were facing off and didn't notice anything but their own anger.

"Your roommate thought the same thing, and look what happened to her."

"Mandy? That mouse? She was dumb and sweet, but I ain't. Let me be!"

By then Max was there.

"Trouble?" he asked.

They both rounded on him.

Maybe he had sounded too much like a cop.

"Get outa here!" the man warned.

The woman said nothing, especially not thank you.

Something hissed besides footsteps on dry asphalt. Something high and shrill.

A pop like a gun made everyone jerk, but nothing more happened.

Except that one of the dead streetlamps strobed into life again.

Thin blue light painted their faces a sickly color.

"You!" Rafi Nadir's hand dropped its viselike grip on Reno's elbow. "The cops sent someone in to get your mug down on paper. They must want you bad for something."

"Thanks for the warning," Max said, claiming Reno's released elbow. "Now I'll give you one. Call it a night before someone calls the vice squad. Do you want *your* face on the mug books?"

Nadir's mouth worked. He was the kind who was always spoiling for a fight. Max was ready, though he didn't look like it.

Nadir ignored him and addressed Reno. "This guy probably killed your roomie. Some white knight."

She was staring at Max as if Rafi Nadir didn't exist.

Before Nadir could get excited about being irrelevant, Max steered Reno to her car, took the fistful of keys from her hand, opened it and watched Nadir as she got in.

"I'll see you at home," he said affably.

In the slanted streetlight rays, her face looked hard, but curious. "You're Vince."

He shut the door on her, heard the oncoming scrape of shoes and turned to face Nadir, not so affably.

Reno started her car and drove away, leaving the two men plenty of room for . . . whatever.

"You're not leaving," Nadir said. "Not until that girl is long gone. I should call the police."

"But you won't."

"I don't need backup to deal with you."

"What's to deal with. I'm leaving, aren't I?"

Nadir stared down the street. Reno's beater was out of sight, out of hearing. He stepped back with an elaborate gesture of permission.

"Go ahead. But you gave me trouble with another stripper, and she ended up dead the next day. If anything happens to this one, it would look bad for you."

"That works both ways, doesn't it?"

Nadir stared sharply into Max's face, puzzled by his calm, unsettled by the implication.

"I don't ever want to see you at Secrets again," he said.

"You won't."

Max turned and crossed the parking lot to the street beyond, where he had parked the Maxima two blocks away.

At first he listened for Nadir following him. When he was in the dark between streetlights he finally looked for him.

Nothing.

Max was free to move on to the next low point of the evening.

Chapter 24

Chuck Wagon

You would think Miss Midnight Louise was a casino owner showing off a new armored truck.

There we are gathered in the delivery area behind a wholesale grocery establishment far from the shake, rock, rattle and roll of the Strip, our only audience a circle of Dumpsters and our only spotlight the sickle moon-on-the-half-shell, peeking over the rippled edge of a corrugated roofline.

There is just me and Miss Louise. Oh. And the two noses with fungus among us, name of Golda and Groucho.

I cannot believe that I am out here of a chilly March night with my dearly beloved not-daughter, Midnight Louise, and two pieces of dandelion fluff that have been foisted upon me by my erstwhile assistant, Nose E.

"What did you say these two are?" I hiss at Louise as we all hunker down near ground zero, eyeing the object of our expedition.

"Yorkshire terriers."

"Well, this is not Yorkshire anymore," I say, inhaling a bit of desert sagebrush on the wind and exhaling it with an untimely sneeze.

"*Shhhh!*" Louise hisses back at me. "And you say *they* are noisy."

I eye our objective: the truck.

It is big, white, and nondescript, in fact a refrigerator on wheels.

Miss Louise is trying to sell this anemic pumpkin on ice as our coach to the palace. Or our buckboard to the ranch.

"Think of it as a chuck wagon," she urges. "Meals on wheels. You can snack on the way."

"And freeze our tails off," I growl. Then I look at Golda and Groucho. I realize that I am not sure if they *have* tails. "Ears off." Do they have ears? "*Noses* off." I *know* they have noses. Those I can see, those shiny wet-asphalt blobs dead center under the perky little red bows on their noggins. I think there are matching eyes behind the waterfall of silky gold and gray hair dangling from the bows.

"These two will be frozen Vienna sausages before we even get out of Vegas," I say. "Noses on ice are worth nothing."

"The unit is not fully refrigerated. They do not wish to deliver ice cubes, merely keep the fresh meat from spoiling."

"This is my aim exactly. I wish to keep the fresh meat from spoiling, namely us."

Midnight Louise shakes her head as if to dislodge a flea in her ear: me.

"Look, Pops. Do not tell me it cannot be done, because I have already done it and anything I can do you can do better."

"Darn tootin'," say I before I can think. I am about to head out to the ranch on a chuck wagon with climate control with one setting: chilly.

"And," Midnight Louise adds with a glance at our two canine partners, "I did not even have earmuffs for my trip to and fro."

So it transpires that we all hunker down behind a Dumpster and wait until men pushing carts of raw meat come out of the building. They open the double doors at the truck's rear and start loading. It is interesting that this delivery van only operates under dark of night. Miss Midnight Louise has scouted the delivery service for Rancho Exotica, decided that we need trackers, no matter how minute, and that we can rescue the leopard and clear it of murder with the mere use of our wits and the Yorkie's miniature noses. I am not convinced of any of it.

"How do we get in the truck undetected?" I wonder in a soft growl.

"I will distract the men just before they finish loading. You three hop in and hide. I will come in last. On arrival they will unload and then take each cartful away. That is when we debark."

"These two will never debark." I jerk my head over my shoulder at the twins, who have been mum as ordered, but not without as much fidgeting as a human two-year-old would do.

It goes just like she wrote. Well, almost that way, not counting hitches. And there are plenty of hitches. When the last cart is almost unloaded, Midnight Louise creeps around to the front of the truck and there emits an unearthly scream. In other words, she sounds like a puma in heat. I thought she had been surgically prevented from engaging in such tasteless displays. So much for modern birth control methods.

The two men hesitate, scratch their heads, look around the side of the truck.

Miss Louise leaps atop the truck's hood and we hear the sweet sounds of claws scratching painted metal.

The men run around to the front of the truck.

"Come on!" I order the twins. "Eats ahoy."

I hear their tiny nails making mouse tracks behind me as we race to the truck's gaping back doors.

I am ready to leap up into the icy heart of darkness when I hear an objecting squeak behind me.

"Mr. Midnight!"

I pause to regard the speaker: Golda. Or Groucho. They all look alike to me. "What?"

"We cannot leap that high."

"Oh, for Bast's sake . . . that is what you get for having push-pins for legs."

Meanwhile, there is screaming and cursing coming from the front of the vehicle. Louise is doing the screaming. She is a strong girl, but I do not know how long she can hold the attention of two cursing teamsters without incurring severe bodily harm.

Nothing for it but lowering myself to their level.

I bend down, bare my incisors and canines, squint my eyes shut in distaste, and bite down on dog hair until I have pincered a scrawny bit of loose skin along with it.

I leap into the truck, one Yorkie dangling from my mouth like a mouse wearing a Brigitte Bardot wig. I deposit it behind a huge slab of meat.

I bound down, get another mouthful of Yorkie toupee and vault upward again, my pads kissing chill aluminum flooring. This one I hide behind a stack of semifrozen mackerels.

Then I lay me down to sleep behind what would be a standing rib roast, were it cooked, and prepare for a cold, bumpy ride, also waiting for Midnight Louise to pounce down beside me.

The sound of a few last items being tossed into the truck makes me cringe. It is dim enough in here that a few extra carcasses aren't going to show much, but I do not want post-flattened Yorkie when we arrive at the ranch.

Suddenly it is as black as midnight. The double doors slam shut; the latches fall to.

Trapped until arrival.

And where is Louise?

Could something have happened to her?

Naw.

I am not going to worry about it.

I have enough to worry about.

A yip from one side of the area is echoed by a sneeze from the other.

Oh, great. Nasal congestion. Just what a sniffing-nose dog needs.

I may be riding on one nostril and a prayer tonight.

The truck jerks into gear. I try to sense if we roll over any impediments.

Naw.

Midnight Louise is one tough kitty-cat. She will be fine.

She will be high, dry, and dogless, safe in the city, while I roll toward the Great Nothing in the company of two toy terriers and a truckload of fresh meat designated for the gullets of seven-hundred-pound Big Cats.

The only thing that is going to eat Midnight Louise is knowing that she missed the boat to fun and adventure in greater Las Vegas.

Who has chosen the better part, I ask you?

I, ah, I ah . . . ask . . . ah . . . you . . . ask . . . as . . . ah *CHOO!*

Chapter 25

Guilt-Edged Invitation

When Max knocked on the scuffed apartment door he wasn't surprised to hear a muffled radio or television blare through the hollow-core wood.

It was 3:00 A.M. and strippers would be just winding down, counting the night's take, getting out of their thongs and tassels.

She opened the door the length of a gold safety chain, also scuffed.

"I'm not going to ask how you managed to ditch Raf and still follow me home," Reno said. "You're just like the horse to grandmother's house, Vince. You know the way."

"I've been here before," he admitted.

"How do I know you didn't kill Mandy?"

"Pretty dumb of me to come back."

"Maybe."

Her one eye that was visible though the door slit tilted to match the cynical slant of her head.

She shut the door, hard.

A moment later the chain latch slid and the door opened enough to admit him.

Max dove into the stuffy atmosphere of food, cosmetics, and kid odors.

"How'd you and Raf end up?"

"We had words."

She nodded and went to the shabby upholstered sofa, sitting on the corner near a tilting end table.

Max followed. "You were worried about one of us?"

Reno shook her head. She slumped into the corner of the couch and lit a cigarette from a matchbook on the end table.

"Moxie's," the cover read. Max had never heard of it.

"So you're Vince," she said, narrowing her eyes through the veil of smoke she puffed out on her first draw.

He shrugged.

"I suppose that Mandy never noticed you were too bad to be true."

"Mandy was too drunk to notice much." Max looked around, removed a stack of folded kid's clothing from an armchair seat, and sat there. "That's why I ended up getting her home."

Reno took another deep drag on her cigarette.

"Why am I too bad to be true?" Max asked.

She laughed. "Disappointed? Listen, I've been studying sleazy guys since I started stripping when I was fifteen. You're just too perfect."

Max tugged at his stretch velour V-neck shirt. "I shop in all the worst places."

"That's just it. To me, you're a little too sleazy. But I'm an expert on sleazy guys, believe me. What are you? I don't smell undercover cop."

He shook his head. "I'm nobody official, even unofficially."

She nodded, no longer interested in any particular label now that she'd pegged him. "So why'd you take Mandy home?"

"Nadir was hassling her, and she wasn't as good as you at handling him back."

"He's all bark."

"You don't think he killed her?"

"Why?"

"I interrupted him. He doesn't like to be interrupted. And . . . I had to knock him down. It was too dark for him to ID me, but he wouldn't like that. He didn't know who I was or where I was from, but Cher—"

"You remind me of that PI that saw me yesterday."

"PI?"

She nodded. "Now that she's dead, everybody's interested in Mandy. Or Cher. That was her real name. You know why strippers take stage names?"

"Privacy. It keeps the customers at a distance."

"Yeah, sure. But for another reason. Most of us, we hate our real names. We heard them yelled at us since we could crawl. Maybe a slap came with it, or just more yelling, or . . . if we were real lucky, daddy or stepdaddy with a little game to play."

Max nodded. "Makes sense."

"So Mandy didn't like to admit to the name Cher. But she told you. Why?"

"My honest face?"

Reno laughed with him. "No, you got to her. She acted like she'd been visited by the angel Gabriel the next day. And she did exactly what you said and went to a different club the next night. She was even going to call that radio shrink you mentioned when she got time. She was real happy when she died."

Max closed his eyes.

He heard Reno inhale on her cigarette like a sigh.

"So it was mutual," she said.

When he opened his eyes she was snuffing the cigarette in an empty Gerber glass jar.

"Okay," she said, "I'll tell you what I told the PI. No one would want to kill Mandy but a freak. She was so harmless. That's why we took her in here, same reason you brought her home. You aren't the only softie left in Las Vegas, Vince. Ginger and I were real fond of Mandy."

Reno teared up and looked away. "She was like a kid, still hoping things would turn out all right, just because. I guess she died quick."

He nodded. "The police had a couple other women strangled about the same time, but there were markers at those scenes that weren't there in Mandy's case."

"You do sound like a cop sometimes."

"This PI. Who put him on the case?"

"Mandy's family, I guess. That's what she said."

"She?"

"Yeah. There are lady PIs. I gotta say, the ones I've seen before were these little old dames all curlicued and mascaraed. You know, fifty-something types with bleached hair. This one was plain and simple, looked like she knew her stuff."

"You get a name?"

"Sure, but I'm not sure I believe it. Vince. *Vince?*"

"It does have a certain sleaze factor, Reno."

She laughed and reached for another cigarette. "That it does. Serious lady. Not like you."

"How not?"

"You're relaxed. She was edgy. Didn't really show it, but I know edgy. I think she knows her stuff, though, that's why I talked to her. I want the creep who did Mandy to pay."

Max nodded. "What did she look like?"

"Mandy?" Reno asked with exaggerated innocence.

He waited.

"Tall, real tall. If I were that tall I'd make twelve thousand more a year. But like I said, plain vanilla. See, that's what's wrong with you, Vince, you stand out. She didn't. Except for those Bausch and Lomb eyes."

"Eyes?"

"Seriously blue. Unreal."

Max nodded again. "A handicap for a PI if you don't want to be remembered."

"Now, your eyes are—" Reno leaned forward through her own halo of cigarette smoke to study Max's face. "Now, yours are blue, but nice quiet sky blue. If you toned down the rest of your image, you'd be pretty forgettable."

"Thanks."

"How do you know about these other women who were strangled? The PI didn't mention that. You got an in with the cops?"

"Yeah. I cheat."

"I believe you do."

"You have any letters of Mandy's? Any information on her friends, where she came from?"

"They never come from here, do they? Me neither. And I didn't come from Reno, that's for sure. No. The PI went through her things. You can too."

Max stood. "Did she take anything?"

"Only notes. I see you don't."

"I'm looking for things that aren't worth noting."

Reno stood, sighed. "Well, that was Mandy, alive or dead."

"Not true," Max said.

"I guess we tried, huh?"

He didn't say anything more.

"Not enough." Reno turned and led him down the cramped hall.

Polishing Off the Past

Matt pulled off his gloves and stuffed them into the pockets of his down jacket. He felt like he had alighted from a time machine instead of a taxicab. The scene before him proved his problems were half a continent away. He savored the view: a snow-whited sepulcher of night in a city that counted wind chill factors instead of chips. Chi-ca-go. Safe at home. Kathleen O'Connor left behind in a lukewarm land of neon nightmares.

He dodged dirty mounds of slush, giant steps taking him from the cab to the restaurant's huge wooden double doors. His bare palm grasped icy wrought iron and pulled one door open. Outside, the weather was cold enough that the hot, rushed atmosphere inside Polandski's felt as welcome as a warming house on a January ice rink.

And it was already March in Chicago.

He watched waiters dressed in embroidered vests over white shirts careen to and fro, overloaded serving trays hoisted above their heads like little islands of pottery perched on the crack of a tectonic plate.

The constant balancing act was unnerving as the waitstaff sailed between tables crowded together, and crowded with customers. The noise level was a roar. To his chilled nostrils, the mingling scents of discreet sweat, hot sausage, and cold beer was narcotic.

"Sir?"

"I'm meeting someone." Matt's eyes panned the overpopulated room once more. It was embarrassing not to spot your own mother. "Mira—" *What last name was she using now?* He didn't have the vaguest idea, even more embarrassing. He'd have to ask sometime.

"Oh, you're Mira's son!" The woman hostess was as rosy cheeked as a grade-schooler in December, despite being in her sixties. "Right this way."

Her broad, embroidery-vested form tunneled a path through the chaos to a rear table for four.

His mother sat there fiddling with her silverware and keeping an eagle eye on the service transpiring at adjoining tables.

"Matt!" She leaped up when she belatedly saw him, smiling.

"Mom."

They hugged over an intervening wooden captain's chair.

"You look great," Matt told her, pulling a heavy chair over the rough-tiled floor to sit at right angles to her. She had posted herself to see the door, but the intervening traffic had made him invisible.

"It's these fancy clothes." She modestly touched her fingertips to the shoulders of the aqua blue blouse he had bought her for Christmas.

But it wasn't just the blouse, or the blue topaz earrings, also a gift from Matt. Her hair had been cut and fluffed into a cloud of blond intermixed with gray, a totally natural effect that somehow seemed expensively colored. God was still the best hair stylist around.

She looked at least ten years younger than her fifty-three years. Matt noticed that adjoining diners were still eyeing them speculatively after overhearing their greeting. He didn't look over thirty himself, so mental math was being frantically done at all the surrounding tables, much to Matt's amusement. If they only knew his history, and hers.

"You look," he said, sincerely amazed, "like a new woman. Is it the new job?"

"Partly." Her expression as she glanced around mixed caution and pride. Her voice lowered. "Serving as hostess at a famous place like this requires a little more maintenance than I needed at Thaddeus's Café in the old neighborhood. The Polandsky is a big tourist attraction. We even get movie stars in. Kevin Costner."

"Well, you look fit to escort a movie star, Mom."

She settled back to study him as only mothers can while a waiter brought menus and filled their heavy, stemmed water glasses.

"You look a little tired, Matt. Is it those late hours at that radio job of yours?"

"No, Mom, it's traveling for these speaking engagements. The luncheon address I did today was over at two P.M. but I was there until four answering questions and meeting underwriters."

"What group was it again?"

"The supporters of Wendy's Way, a group of national shelters for runaway girls."

She shook her head, which only improved her hair-do. "Poor girls. They don't have family support like in the old days. Now it has to be all out in the open."

Matt held himself back from pointing out that her family didn't support her much in the old days, other than making her feel ashamed. His mother might look like a modern woman, but a lot of old assumptions still lingered beneath the flashy renovation.

"A table for four?" he asked, changing the subject.

"Your cousin Krystyna is coming along later. I hope that's all right? She has a late class. Studio arts, she said." Mira sipped her water, then eyed him over the reading glasses, framed in indigo metallic, she had slipped on to skim the menu. "Boyfriend, too," she mouthed, rolling her eyes.

"You don't like Krys's boyfriend?"

"He's like all the young men these days. Odd." Then she took off the glasses and smiled. "I'll tell you what to order. I know the chef's best dishes. I like your jacket." She eyed him while he shrugged out of the bulky down jacket to reveal an amber velvet blazer.

"I wore it at Christmas at Uncle Stash's, remember? After living in a desert climate, this cold calls for clothes with a warm feeling."

"Cold! It's spring here."

"In Las Vegas, it's summer practically."

"Are you going to keep living in that awful city?"

"It's no more awful than Chicago."

"It's the Sodom and Gomorrah of the U.S."

Matt laughed. "The city's reputation is exaggerated. It's only like . . . Ninevah."

"So the speech went well."

He nodded. They always went well. "And I was well paid."

"Shouldn't you be donating your services, if it's for charity?"

"The point is these are fund-raisers. They expect to pay for a well-known speaker to get donors to contribute."

"A lot different from your last job."

"Not really. I just talk to a larger audience than I ever did at the crisis hotline, and I get paid a lot more."

"Hmmm."

Earning money for what looked like doing nothing was as suspect a notion as living in Las Vegas to his mother's generation and place.

"So what should I eat?" he asked, bewildered by creamed herring appetizers, kielbasa and borscht, varieties of *knedle*, or dumplings. He hadn't eaten "Polish" since he had entered the seminary.

She happily took him on a verbal tour of the menu before recommending the cucumber salad and chicken Polonaise. And she urged him to try the beer sampler, a specialty of the house for tourists. She would have a Stinger cocktail.

Matt supposed he was a tourist here with his own mother as much as any out-of-towner. His head began to spin from the noise and the heat and the long day, not to mention his mother's whip-lashing values: old-school Roman Catholic Polish Chicago with glittering bits of rez biz grafted on. She'd be ready for Sin City yet.

After they ordered, the waiter soon brought a tipsy tray of miniature glass beer steins filled with an array of ales colored like precious topaz from shades of palest yellow to dark amber. There were twelve in all, but each only offered about four swallows.

Matt decided to work his way from dark to light, picking up one of the silly steins. His mother looked sophisticated behind the sleek sculpture of her martini glass while Matt played with baby steins.

"To Chicago," he said, raising his Lilliputian lager.

"Chicago." She set down her glass after a genteel sip and rearranged her silverware. "I'm thinking of selling the two-flat."

Matt felt ambushed by a slap of raw emotion. He had a love-hate relationship with the old duplex he had grown up in, he realized in an instant of confused emotion. Its beloved, old-fashioned familiarity was forever married to his stepfather's brutality.

"Where would you live?" he wondered.

"A small apartment. Between the old neighborhood and here. There's plenty of public transportation, and Krys keeps pushing me to drive more in the city. It'd be easier to keep up, and I could use the retirement investment money."

"Makes sense to me."

Her lips tightened. "The family can't see it. But it's time to move on."

"I have," he pointed out.

She grinned shyly at him. "Have you ever! I hate to say it, but ever since you left the priesthood, your life seems to be on a magic carpet ride . . . speeches, radio shows. What about that girl you mentioned?"

"Girl?"

"You know. In Las Vegas. The one you liked a lot."

Matt downed a small stein of slightly red beer. "She's still there. We're still friends."

"Nothing more?"

"No."

"But when you were here at Christmas it sounded more serious than that."

"Did it? Maybe you just thought so. Or I did. I'm traveling too much to settle down now anyway." He hoped that didn't sound as much like an excuse to his mother as it did to him.

Her face had sobered, reading what he wasn't saying. "Well, she wasn't Catholic anyway."

As if that would make him feel better about losing Temple.

His mother was leaning over to one of the vacant chairs and lifted a smart new navy purse off it. Looked expensive. She unclasped the gilt catch and brought out an oversized business envelope stuffed with papers.

"These are copies of the legal papers on the purchase of the two-flat. You know, from your father's family's lawyers. It's got the firm name on it, and a lawyer signed for them. I thought if you had time to look into things—"

"You could do it more easily from here, Mom."

She hesitated. "But I'm a woman. They never take a woman as seriously as a man at these big law firms. And you're famous. Sort of. And . . . I can't do it, Matt." She looked away.

She meant that she was ashamed.

"It's fine. I'll do it." He put his hand over hers, was surprised when her other hand suddenly clasped it, as warm and dry as hot-water-bottle-heated sheets in winter. They had never been demonstrative at home under Cliff Effinger's despotic rule. Had never showed emotion so as not to trigger his rages.

Yet there had been comforts in that cold home, and Matt found himself wanting to go take final photographs of the old place before it was sold, even as part of him wanted to see it torn down board by shingle by rafter.

"You sure you want to find out who my real father was?" he asked. "He died in Vietnam, after all. The family lawyers made plain you would get that two-flat and that was all. There's no advantage in it."

"A photo maybe, huh? A name. I don't want money. Never did. I want a memory."

He looked away.

He was the product of a one-night stand between innocents on the brink of war. How many others like him lived in forgotten, bitter corners of the world? He was lucky he had been born in America of ethnically similar parents, that his mother's unwed status had only resulted in an abusive stepfather and social discomfort, not utter ostracization.

"You deserve to know," he told her at last. "I'll do what I can."

She nodded, and started asking him about the radio show, so he entertained her with anecdotes until the food came. He didn't mention Elvis. It wasn't nice to make fun of the dead, only of the living. But maybe Elvis was a little of both.

The food was hot, heavy, and delicious.

"I'm amazed that tourists eat up this old-style Polish stuff," Matt commented after sampling the beets and dumplings.

"Ethnic is in. Speaking Polish actually comes in handy here. Too bad you and your cousins never learned anything but silly phrases."

"We wanted to be mistaken for a more upscale group than the Poles," Matt said. "The Irish."

"Those Irish! They've got Chicago in their back pockets, that's for sure, but they had a rougher time than the Poles a couple generations earlier. I imagine you worked with a lot of Irish priests."

"That I did," Matt said in a faint brogue, "and nuns too."

"Now, that's another thing! The nuns are literally dying out. Sometimes I don't recognize this world."

"And sometimes," Matt reminded her gently, "we should be glad we don't."

She winced slightly as she nodded. They would never discuss her disastrous marriage with Cliff Effinger. Unlike the mixed feelings Matt still had about his childhood house, his feelings toward Effinger had evaporated after his successful search for the man. He had been like a devil who could be exorcized.

A house, though, being inanimate—being transcendent, as places always are—was an anonymous witness to the past with all its pain and survival. It was a shell you left behind as you moved on, and with it a record of how you'd grown.

He'd ask Krys, privately, to take some photos of the place.

Their plates were already cleared away when his mother looked up, beaming.

"Just in time for dessert! Krys!" She half stood to wave.

Matt felt a foreign pang, astounded to recognize it as a flutter of jealousy, a usually alien emotion.

Krys, his just-twenty cousin, came charging across the restaurant, booted to the knee, skirted to mid-thigh, her bare knees windburned in between, her spiky punk haircut grown out to shoulder-brushing Botticelli Venus tendrils, and her cheeks flushed with cold and probably a post-class beer or two.

Trailing her was loping young guy with hair half-shaved and half-moussed, wearing weathered jeans, a battered black leather jacket and a plaid flannel shirt so out it was in.

"Sit down," his mother half ordered, half invited, like the hostess she was. "Doesn't Matt look good?" So much for him looking tired.

"Yeah." Krys flashed him a nod of intense recognition. "This is Zeke. He's a sculpture major."

"What do you sculpt, Zeke?" his mother asked politely. "I've been doing some clay models and it's really fun."

"Body parts. Out of rusted automobile pieces. It's a statement."

"You mean . . . auto body parts?" She was trying to comprehend.

"Naw. Body parts. Like hands. Hips. Boobs."

Matt's mother glanced quickly at Krys. *Whose* body parts, she wanted to ask, but knew better not to.

Probably his girlfriend's, Mother, Matt wanted to answer the unspoken speculation. *It's a stage.*

Krys was rearranging *her* silverware after shrugging out of a heavy wool jacket. "Your mother's been taking some adult-ed art classes, and she's really good."

"I'm not surprised," Matt said.

"Are you taking the drawing-from-life class, Mira?" Krys asked.

"Not this semester," his mother answered blushing at the idea of sketching nude models. "I don't have time with the new job."

Zeke looked up at Matt from the menus a waiter had delivered to all four of them. "Krys says you used to be a priest. Like a Catholic priest. You sure don't look like it."

Matt detected a smidge of antagonism. "Sorry about that. Maybe I should get some bifocals or something."

"No, man. I mean, wasn't it heavy telling people what to do?"

"Priests don't tell anyone what to do. They just try to ask more pointed questions about life, God, the universe and all that than we ordinarily do."

Krys hissed her impatience. "Cruise for calories, Zeke. They have some wild desserts here. Matt wasn't that kind of know-it-all priest, anyway."

"How do you know?" he asked.

"I just do." Her eyes fell to the menu. "I'm going to have the plum dumplings. Anyone want to share?"

Zeke made a discreet retching sound. His mother raised her eyebrows, then frowned across the room. "One of my best customers just came in. I'd better seat him personally. Matt, order me a sherbet, please."

Stingers and sherbet? His mother was evolving all right.

Matt watched her rise and head for a steel-gray-haired man in a cashmere camel-hair coat.

Zeke announced, "I gotta split for the little boys's room," then lurched up and off.

"Have we been . . . deserted?," Matt asked Krys.

She looked at him, blinked, then laughed. " 'Deserted'? Did you say it! Zeke can be such a dork, but he's all right, really."

"Glad to hear it, but I didn't need to know it."

"Not interested in my boyfriends? I'm crushed."

"You don't look crushable."

In fact, Krys looked just like his mother. Like a new woman since Christmas. Only she was a new young woman.

He watched his mother guide her charge to a table for one against the wall. Was she flirting with the old geezer?

"She's doing fine," Krys said suddenly. "Took to the new job like Cinderella to a glass slipper. Mira was like some new kid at school, all awkward and apologizing, but I've got her thinking like a Chicago girl now."

"I bet you have." Matt put his attention where she wanted it: on her. "You seem a lot happier than at Christmas. Can I credit the avant-garde Zeke?"

"Oh, he's okay, really. Underneath it all. Young guys aren't worth much these days, but they're all I have at my age."

"They grow out of it."

"That's why I put in the time. Besides, I need an ally against my family, and you're not here."

"I was only here for a couple of days before."

"Seemed longer." She smiled at him, fairly tremulously for a Chicago girl. He glimpsed the pressured teenager from Christmas ready to commit crushes with an older cousin she'd never seen before. She'd been unhappy about her family not allowing her to go to art school in California, but settling for art school in Chicago had done her good, despite Zeke, and in Matt's absence, she'd taken his mother under her wing.

They were good for each other, the older and younger woman. Matt suddenly understood that spasm of jealousy. Krys was having the kind of almost-adult relationship with his mother that he never would have. Or maybe he would someday, thanks to Krys. So get over it.

"You've done so much for my mother, Krys. Thanks."

"Oh, she needed some prodding to get out of the old ruts. And it's not for charity. She backs me up with my folks about art school."

"And about Zeke?"

"No. Nobody would back me up about Zeke."

"Then I will."

"You that eager to get rid of me?"

"I don't think I ever had you."

"Oh, yes, you did." She tossed her tangled locks. "But I was an impressionable kid then. Thanks for being nice to me, though."

"Not hard. So do you think . . . Mira will go for the life drawing class?"

"Maybe. In a couple of years. She's got quite a flair for color and line. You should see if you've inherited an artistic streak."

"Not me."

She glanced at his jacket. "Maybe the girlfriend who picked out your jacket is the artist."

"Maybe."

Krys's fingers flicked across his sleeve. "Nice. She is still your girlfriend?"

"Friend."

"Still?"

"Still." He felt the hesitation flicker over his face. Dare he be friends with anyone, any woman, with Kitty O'Connor hovering in the wings? And was he right to feel safe here? What about Temple back in Vegas? Kitty the Cutter might be angry he'd slipped her leash. She might decide to teach him a lesson, and no one was nearer at hand for that than Temple. . . .

Krys's smile was probing, hopeful. "You don't look so sure."

He threw lame excuses, flailing to get back in the here and now. "I work midnights. I travel a lot. Hard to keep up friendships."

"Poor guy. If you're ever in Chicago on short notice—"

"I'll let my mother know. That new apartment your idea? Like the job?"

"She needed to escape the family thumb, like me. It's handy to have a chaperon sometimes, you know?"

He nodded.

"And sometimes not." Krys nodded toward the end of the room.

His mother and Zeke had intersected on their way back to the table. His mother was obviously asking Zeke a few too many questions.

"Looks like you two will look out for each other."

"Yeah. It's cool. She's not my mother, and she's not my generation. But in some ways, she's almost my age. It's like she didn't live twenty years of her life. I'm dragging her kicking and screaming back into her twenties."

Matt smiled. Mira and Zeke were bearing down on them, and Mira was dusting off the shoulders of Zeke's carefully battered jacket.

Chapter 27

Cousins Under the Skin

A long, long time later, the vehicle jolts its last jolt and comes to a stop.

This hurls us hitchhikers against assorted meat patties, but by then we are not feeling much.

I force myself to my feet (apparently my toes have chilled to the point of numbness) and stumble over to rouse the Yorkies.

"Up and at 'em, bowheads! We need to be lurking near the doors so we can scram when we have to."

"Scram?" cries Golda's faint, squeaky voice from behind a leg of lamb. "I can barely stagger."

"There will not be time enough for me to do another emergency airlift on you two. If we don't get out fast enough, we will either be smashed in the doors or tossed to the carnivores. Which route of doom you prefer depends on if you like your bones ground up fast or slow."

They shudder in tandem, making their silky hair shimmy like a go-go dancer's fringe. But they crawl gamely over the meat mountains and we all huddle behind a side of beef.

"When I say go, just go. Do not look down, do not look back. Just jump and run. Pretend Midnight Louise is on your tail."

"She is not so bad," Groucho objects in his best falsetto growl.

"Okay. Pretend . . . the Medellin cartel is on your tail." These are drug sniffers in training, after all.

"*We* are on their tail," Golda sniffs grandly.

For pipsqueaks, this pair must have nothing but nerve under that hair.

The latch squeaks and then turns.

Daylight tears a widening rent in the darkness that hides our presence.

The stack of steaks by the opposite door vanishes. We hear thumps and bangs, and men grousing.

"Now," I say, sticking the tip of a shiv into each little form.

Squealing like mice, the pair squirt out of the door. I am right behind them, but somehow I end up hitting terra firma first— oof!—and they land on me. Double oof.

We do not waste time discussing our exit order, but roll and scramble under the truck's welcome shadow, much as it stinks of gas and oil.

"Did you hear mice?" one man is asking the other, his work boots still for a moment.

While the other guy tells him he's crazy and hearing things, we belly-crawl to the truck's front. It is hard to see much but stretches of sand. I prod Golda out for a few seconds of recon. She reports a shaded area with a roof at three o'clock low.

Gee, that makes me miss my old man, Three O'Clock Louie, who is basking in the sun of Lake Mead while I am directing a raid on the ranch.

"Make for the shade," I tell the troops, then head off myself like a black bolt of cold lightning.

There is nothing but open ground in the desert, and a frontal assault is the best—heck, the only—approach.

Two gray bolts of lightning speed after me. Those canine shrimps can really move their pins when they have to.

We are reunited again in a dimness that gives us a cloak of invisibility.

"Looks like we made it unnoticed," Groucho notes, pausing to scratch at a sand flea that has managed to leap aboard despite our velocity. Some species are impervious to every trick and they are usually parasites.

I must agree. The two men are still unloading hunks of meat and any tracks our daring dash across the tundra may have left are being scrubbed away by a constant riffle of desert wind.

I pause to tidy my whiskers and straighten my cravat.

It is a good thing, because a long, low growl behind us that sets the floor beneath us vibrating announces that we do not have company, but that we *are* company. And maybe even dinner.

Chapter 28

K as in Karrot Stick

The Big Town felt a planet away.

Matt, hauling his down jacket over his arm, unlocked his apartment and breathed in the air-conditioned oxygen with relief.

Weather-clogged traffic, slush, raw winds, rain, bad memories.

Who needed it?

He dumped his duffel bag and the mail from the downstairs mailbox on a living-room cube table. First thing, he went to check his answering machine in the bedroom, his latest purchase before this out-of-town trip.

The next thing he knew, he'd own a cell phone and computer.

Well, he had the money for it now. Seven thousand dollars for a two-day trip, and a chance to get together with his mother. Sometimes life was too generous.

The machine's red light was blinking, but Matt didn't have the energy to sit down and take notes, which was what his schedule required nowadays.

Back in the living room, he noticed that one of his pieces of mail had somehow landed on the matching empty cube table.

This was a small padded mailer, exactly like the fateful one in which he had gotten the tape from what would become his on-air home, WCOO, "talk radio with heart."

He still didn't have a letter opener. Maybe he needed to get a small desk to sit by the door. Where to buy such a thing? Temple would know. He could call her, ask her.

The thought of contacting Temple always gave him a queasy push-pull in his gut, part guilty pleasure, part pure guilt. No. Be a big boy. He didn't need a spirit guide for every step of his life, even the small interior-decorating ones.

He fetched a table knife from the kitchen and opened the lone mailer first, out of sentimentality and weird expectation. What life-altering surprise would this one hold? He supposed lottery winners who still bought tickets often felt that way.

An irregular lump deformed this package, but too small to be a cassette. A single die, maybe? Key chain? Some Strip joint gambling promotion?

A small golden object tumbled into his palm. A sculpture? A snake biting its own tail. He recognized the motif. The worm Ouroboros, ancient symbol of eternity; destruction and renewal. A single potent image of the cycle of creation: it begets, weds, impregnates, and slays itself, like nature. Over and over.

In centuries past, worms, snakes, and dragons all intertwined into a quasi-fantastic, quasi-religious symbolism. You had St. George and the dragon. The worm Ouroboros. The serpent in the Garden of Eden. The new religion chasing the tail of established superstition and biting it. He took the object to the French doors. Now he needed—yes, needed!—a magnifying glass. *Who did he think he was, Sherlock Holmes?* Why be a piker? A whole brass desk set for his yet-unbought new desk: letter opener, magnifying glass, stamp holder . . .

He squinted at the bantam-size chicken scratchings inside the snake. A *K* as in karat. But was it a 12-, 14-, or 18-K item? All he could tell was that it was purportedly real gold. And some Greek letters:

Οὐροβόρος

He picked up the envelope to study its exterior. His name hand printed on the outside. No return address.

Finally, he pushed his fingers into the small envelop until he pulled out a plum. An ordinary Post-it note. Its adhesive edge had clung to the bubble-pack lining the envelope.

Green rollerball ink slanted across the pink rectangular surface.

"<u>Wear me!</u>" Underlined.

He lifted the snake to the light. Well crafted, but weird.

Wear? How? Why?

As he stared at it, his blood slowed, then chilled. The room's temperature hadn't budged, but he felt as reptilian as a hibernating rattler himself.

This was a worm Ouroboros, all right, but it was also a ring.

The last ring he had worn had been the simple gold wedding band of a Catholic priest, a symbol of his commitment to celibacy, of his marriage to the Church. He hesitated, but he had to know: he jammed the ring onto a finger—the middle finger on his right hand.

It fit perfectly.

Wear me.

An order from . . . he knew who.

Drink me.

And Alice had shrunk.

Matt stared at Kitty O'Connor's ring. At the order that came with it.

Wear me.

Or else.

And if he did, he'd shrink too.

Just like Alice.

He went to the bedroom to call Temple after all.

"You want Max?" she asked, incredulous, after two minutes of the usual banalities with which he had prefaced his request.

"I need to talk to him, or maybe vice versa. Can you ask him to get in touch with me?"

"Sure. I can ask."

"That's all that I ask."

"There's nothing you want to tell me?"

"I . . . had a good time in Chicago. Saw my mother."

"Oh. I didn't know you were gone."

"Speaking engagement." The word "engagement" suddenly took on a sinister new resonance. "Temple. Call him right away."

"You got it." She hesitated, didn't want to say good-bye, wanted to ask a few questions. He didn't want to answer any.

"Thanks," he said quickly. " 'Bye."

It was ironic that he was rushing to hang up on Temple. Usually it was the other way around. A nasty thought had surfaced. Maybe his phone was tapped. He should have called Temple and made his unprecedented request from somewhere else.

Kitty O'Connor was the last person in the world he wanted to know that he was calling in Max Kinsella.

Matt tried to watch TV, then to listen to his new stereo. He went to the bedroom and looked for a book he hadn't read before, or one he had and that he could count on to distract him.

Nothing worked.

The gold snake ring lay coiled on the otherwise empty gray cube table. All he needed was an apple to make an apropos still life. And maybe a naked woman. God knew there were a few in Las Vegas.

Probably his mother had been right. It was a godless town.

It takes a thief to catch a thief. To catch a stalker, did it take . . . Max Kinsella?

No. To catch a stalker, stalk the stalker's past.

He ought to know that by now.

At 8:10 P.M., his doorbell rang.

Matt approached the coffered door with uncustomary caution.

When he opened it, Max Kinsella was leaning against the opposite wall, the illumination from Matt's doorbell-level lamp uplighting his face into a Boris Karloff mask.

"I thought you'd call first." Matt almost stuttered.

Max Kinsella, tall, dark, and all in black, including a long Western duster, on your doorstep was not a reassuring sight. Especially in eerie lamplight.

"I'm not a vampire." His mocking, deep voice sounded very much like Bela Lugosi without the accent. "You don't have to invite me in. But it would be nice."

Matt stepped out into the small hall separating his unit from the building's circling arterial hallway. He left the apartment door ajar.

"Maybe it's better you turned up out here," Matt said. "The place may be bugged. I thought of that after I called Temple."

"Calling Temple seems to be a knee-jerk reaction with you."

"It was the only way I knew to reach you."

"Bugged. Curiouser and curiouser." Kinsella pushed himself away from the wall in a motion as fluid as India ink. "Say nothing until I'm done."

Matt let Kinsella precede him into the apartment, then sat on the red Kagan sofa that Temple had spied at a thrift shop and insisted he buy.

Spotting it stopped Kinsella cold, but then he moved to the bedroom, not making a sound.

Gumshoe, Matt thought, noticing his leather-soled shoes that resembled costly Italian loafers, but were probably a knockoff chosen for their quiet, downscale soles.

Kinsella was back in the main room like an apparition, passing through en route to the spare bedroom that Matt kept practically nothing in. Matt glimpsed an ebony ghost standing on a chair seat to check the ceiling light fixture.

Then Kinsella visited the kitchen and inspected all of the cupboards as well as the lighting fixtures. The living room, under and over everything, including behind light switch and electric plug outlet covers. The phone, of course, and all the electronic equipment Matt had so reluctantly purchased in the last couple of months.

Then the French doors to the patio, the patio, and back to the living room and bedroom for a second check.

It took thirty-five minutes.

When Kinsella came to sit on the Kagan sofa, he spoke at ordinary volume.

"A good thing you have such a spare design for living. Hard to bug. And no one has. *Yet*, I take it. You should check the phones, though, like I did, after I go, and every day. If you know what's supposed to be in there, you recognize what isn't. So what's going on?"

"I wouldn't have bothered you—"

"You have never bothered me." Kinsella's smile was so slight it was anorexic.

His face was angular and arresting, rather than handsome, but Matt guessed that women didn't notice the difference.

"You wouldn't call on me unless something was drastically wrong," Kinsella went on. "What?"

Matt pointed to the snake ring.

Kinsella's long, spidery fingers plucked it like a grape, then held it up to the light as if his fingertips were a bezel for a jewel.

"Good quality. Craftsman made. Perhaps not in this country. Not very valuable. A few hundred dollars maybe. The worm Ouroboros, of course. It symbolizes eternity."

"Is that all?"

"Probably not. More would take research." He held the ring toward Matt.

Matt couldn't help it; he drew back as from a live snake.

"Speak," said Kinsella, as if addressing a trained dog.

"I thought it came in the mail when I got back from out of town. But I dumped all the mail on that table." He pointed to the matching cube still covered in unopened letters. "I now think this was 'delivered' earlier. When I was gone."

"Someone surreptitiously entered your unit, that's why you suspected bugging. But who? Who'd want to bug you?"

"An acquaintance of yours."

Max's gaze shifted to Matt's midriff. "Kitty the Cutter. Temple does have a way with words, doesn't she?"

"Yes, she does, and this Kitty woman is your auld acquaintance not-to-be-forgot, not mine. She's . . . attached herself to me, I don't know why, but she's getting dangerous."

"Not 'getting,' my lad. She always was."

"Drop that phony brogue. This is not Ireland, north or south. This is not twenty years ago, and this is not my problem."

"Why would Kitty O'Connor send you a worm Ouroboros?"

Matt picked up the Post-it note and handed it to Kinsella.

"Don't you have tweezers?"

"No."

"Pliers?"

"No."

"Sugar tongs?"

"For the love of God, no! What has that to do with anything?"

"Only that we shouldn't be handling these artifacts. Pieces of physical evidence, in fact. In case we need the police to take fingerprints."

"I don't have any pincerlike devices. You saw the place."

"Then get on the phone, call Temple, and ask her to bring up some tweezers."

"Do we have to involve Temple?"

"You called her in the first place."

"I don't want her to know about this."

"All right. Go down, come up with whatever story it takes to get them, and borrow some tweezers."

Matt rose, left the apartment door open, took the stairs beside the elevator a floor down, then headed for the small private hallway to Temple's apartment.

Before he rang the bell, he put his palm on the door, like a medium reading the scene of a haunting. This was the scene of a haunting, all right, his own haunting.

He rang the bell, waiting on pins and needles for her to answer.

"I need a pair of tweezers," he blurted out on sight.

Temple blinked, signifying polite mystification that he should be eager to dispel. She knew something was up. He didn't dispel anything. She was more suspicious than ever.

"Tweezers? Has Max—?

"I've got a . . . domestic emergency. Have you got some tweezers or not? Quick!"

Still blinking, Temple disappeared. She reappeared a moment later with tweezers rampant in a raised, closed right hand. A fist, as it were.

"Will these work?"

"Thanks." Matt snatched them before he had to look into her soft steel blue eyes too long. He was bound to start saying more than he should. "I'll bring 'em back . . . tomorrow or sometime."

He raced down the little hall, around the big circular hall, and up the stairs again.

In his apartment, Kinsella was bending over the cube table staring at the Post-it note.

He looked up to say, "Plastic baggie?"

"That I've got." Matt went to the kitchen to fetch a big one.

Taking Temple's tweezers, Kinsella placed the manila envelop and

the Post-it note in the baggie. "A present for Molina. She'll do anything for you, right? It would be best not to mention the suspected
source. Tell her a demented female fan is stalking you."

"It's the truth."

Kinsella cocked his head. "Sit down and tell me about it."

Matt sat, but he couldn't bring himself to speak for a moment. He
still felt like a body double for the real actor in this instance.

"I don't get it," he exploded finally to Kinsella. "She's a demon
from your past. What's she doing in my present?"

"Bad luck, I guess. What does this phrase mean, 'Wear me'?"

"I think the snake is a ring. She's approached me a couple of times
again recently."

"To maim again?"

"No. She knows I'd never let her get that close again." Matt felt
his hand go to his scarred side, despite himself. "This TitaniCon I
took Mariah Molina to—"

"And how did that happen, I wonder?"

"That has nothing to do with this. Temple showed up there, and a
woman I used to work with at the volunteer hotline, ConTact. And
all three . . . females were somehow attacked during the convention,
including Mariah."

Kinsella became very intent. "I didn't know that."

"You don't know everything, after all, I guess."

He smiled. "No, I just act like I do. Part of the magician's code of
behavior. I know you hate coming to me with this, but it's better than
Temple, isn't it? Why?"

"Because this Kathleen threatened Temple. And Sheila, the Con-
Tact employee, and Mariah, and even poor Janice."

"Janice?"

"You don't know her. I hope. She's an artist, does sketches for the
police sometimes."

"*Hmmm.* The talented portraitist of Miss Kitty. I did see that piece
of work."

"The fact is, this woman has threatened everybody. And now she
sends me this . . . token. Like she's daring me to not do as she says, or
she'll take it out on the people around me."

"Why you?"

"Because you're not available, right? You're Mr. Invisible. You're
her real target, you have to be. But you're holing up somewhere no

one can find you, except Temple probably, so the rest of us have been turned into targets. She *is* your old girlfriend, after all."

"Besides my professional services, what do you want?"

"I want you to tell me everything about her and your relationship with her."

"Sorry, Father, I'm not about to confess my youthful sins to you."

"I'm not a priest anymore, and you're not a kid anymore. Whatever happened in Northern Ireland twenty years ago triggered what's happening here and now. I've got to figure out what's driving her. Don't you understand? Temple is in danger. We're all in danger. Except you."

Kinsella smiled and turned the Ouroboros ring in his fingers.

"No, I'm in danger too. It's just not obvious yet." He glanced at Matt. "I suppose she's targeting you because you're the equivalent of the seventeen-year-old boy I was all those years ago. You're a virgin, right? Don't bother denying or claiming it. I don't care about your sex life, or lack of it, as long as Temple isn't involved. You're *me* seventeen years ago. An overeager innocent trying to right global wrongs in a single summer. You don't come across greenhorns like that every day, or at least Miss Kitty doesn't, not with the role she's played for the IRA all these years, seducing rich old men for gun money. Guns and roses, that's been her specialty. Fortunately, she's spent most of her time in Central and South America. Until now.

"But I doubt the rich old guys have done anything for her ego. It's poor young men she really likes to prey on. I don't doubt that she's been trying to track me down, and she wouldn't have if I hadn't settled with Temple here in Vegas for a few months. So you're right; it's my fault she found us all.

"That's all I can tell you. She seems to want to replay that deadly summer in Londonderry, when my cousin Sean was blown up in a pub bombing by the IRA. I lived to tell the tale only because I was losing my innocence to Kathleen O'Connor at the very moment he died."

"You realize," Matt said, "that if she's repeating a pattern, and if I'm right in suspecting that she sent your cousin into that pub bombing deliberately, that she'll need to kill one of us . . . again?"

"Will she? What does she want now? Right now? From you. Best guess."

"To torment me." Matt thought that was obvious. "To force me to do what she says by threatening the people around me."

"But not me."

"She's never mentioned you to me."

"Hmmm."

Matt hesitated. He couldn't tell Kinsella Kitty's stated price: Matt's body and soul, i.e., his body would do because the soul went with it. Kinsella would probably laugh, and say, "Screw her, then, and save us all." Kinsella would probably just laugh.

He wouldn't understand the price Matt had paid, that his soul did ride on his priestly purity, even now that he was no longer a priest.

Especially, he couldn't tell Kinsella that emotionally, spiritually, he was utterly married to Temple. That she was the only woman he could see sharing his first sexual moments with, that in his heart, reality aside, he was still saving himself for Temple.

He remembered teaching virginity to preteens, using Saint Maria Goretti, the forgiving rape victim, as a model. That was going too far; that was woman as eternal victim. But the violation of rape or molestation was real, for a child, and for an adult. For a woman, and for a man.

Matt still had innocence to lose, long beyond the age most people are permitted to be innocent.

If Kitty O'Connor coerced that hope and dream from him, she had done something worse to him than Cliff Effinger had managed in years of daily domestic tyranny. He couldn't let her do it and still be whole.

And, of course, she knew that.

Max Kinsella could never understand that. Except possibly Matt's hopeless devotion to Temple. That he would understand only too well, and too personally.

Where could Matt go, who could help him, who would understand what he was up against?

Which was a devil in human guise.

He looked at the serpentine ring.

Beware of beautiful women bearing gifts.

And old grudges.

And golden chains.

Chapter 29

Damage Control

As soon as Max left Devine's apartment he ducked into another unit's cul-de-sac hallway and pulled a small folding cell phone from his jacket pocket.

The unit was small enough to be overlooked in a cursory search, and certainly small enough to cause no unseemly lumps in his Italian tailoring.

Before he did anything else, though, he slumped against the wall and closed his eyes. He felt as drained as if he had just done his second two-hour show of the night at the Goliath.

"Master of Mystery" had been one of his billing sobriquets, but the Mystifying Max had never believed his own hype. The mysteries of life mastered us, we the people, the eternal actors and audience at one and the same time.

Right now he felt the exhaustion of a spy who had been in the camp of the enemy for too long.

The word "enemy" made his lips spasm in the impulse of a smile.

Matt Devine would be astounded that anyone might regard him that way, but it wasn't personal, at least not between Max and Devine.

It was just that Max knew quite well that whatever had happened between Temple and Devine during Max's enforced absence—or whatever had almost happened—had not been trivial. Even a master of illusion couldn't compete with substance.

And not that his and Temple's relationship didn't have substance, but circumstances kept forcing it to indulge the surfaces rather than get lost in the depths below.

So Max, who had lived and worked all over Europe in his twenties and knew the attractions and evils (and that sometimes they were the same) of many worlds, found himself momentarily KOed by his recent tour of one ex-priest's apartment. Mentally knocked off his own self-certain foundation.

Maybe it was just the intimate glimpse into someone he had to regard as a rival.

As residences went, the place was pathetic: more unfurnished than not, with an air of undergraduate impermanence. Except for the slashing grin of the red suede couch in the living room—it reminded Max of some surreal Marilyn-mouth of a loveseat designed by some artist or other whose name he couldn't remember—everything was strictly brick-and-board and borrowed looking.

The bedroom especially, with its tiny TV on a cheesy cart, the kind of setup you'd find in a low-rent nursing home, with the childish island of a single bed, a fact Max found sad and a woman like Temple would probably find in need of fixing, with that shelf of paperback heavy reading, philosophy and sociology in broken-spine and dog-eared array . . . and then between Thomas Merton and Thomas Mann, the oddity of a single bestseller here and there. He found the presence of *The Joy of Sex* sinister. And only one popular fiction work . . . *Surrender* by Sulah Savage . . . Now, what was that about?

Max suddenly recalled that Temple's engaging aunt in Manhattan, the one who owned that terrific Village condo, wrote historical romances. Maybe *Surrender* was one of hers. Temple had given it to Devine for some reason, and he had felt obligated to set it out. It hadn't been read, certainly.

Manhattan. A flood of familiar emotions replaced the uneasy feelings Max was indulging now. Finally, finally, he had overcome the deep breach he had driven between himself and Temple by vanishing without word for almost a year. Even though she understood better than anybody his urge to protect her from the deadly forces on his trail, the wound of abandonment within was raw and oozing.

It was only on the alien ground of Manhattan and during the magic of the Christmas holiday, the little-kid-wanting-the-impossible time, that Max had been able to break through her hurt to the trust of a physical relationship again. It had taken every bit of the considerable charisma he possessed, and the accommodating aunt. He never made the mistake of taking Temple for granted, nor of assuming their current situation would satisfy her forever.

And, then, to spend time touring the premises of the next most likely candidate . . . and to end up feeling a pang of sympathy at the impermanent, solitary, on-the-run lifestyle Max himself knew far too well, half postadolescent rootlessness, half monkish withdrawal.

And those sudden, obviously new acquisitions blooming like high-tech bouquets amid the arid landscape: gadgets in the kitchen, the video and audio equipment in the living room, the answering machine in the second and even emptier bedroom, all of them with curled-cover instruction booklets sitting next to them . . . it was laughable, poignant.

For Matt Devine, Max wondered, was Temple a mysterious new gadget in his brave new world, and did he wish that she came with an instruction booklet?

Max laughed quietly to himself, then sobered as he considered the reason he had been called in as a debugging expert. He supposed Devine had hated his intrusion as much as Max had. Max remembered the man's startled expression on seeing him outside the door, even though Devine was expecting him.

The feeling was mutual, bub.

Most men were too homophobic to much notice the looks of other men, but every time Max saw Devine he was stunned by the matinee-idol handsomeness. It wasn't just a photogenic face. Real matinee idols knocked other people out: gender or age had nothing to do with it, just some genetic combination of features that stunned everyone.

Max suspected this unasked-for gift was more a barrier than anything. In Devine it was combined with an unconsciousness—no, a disregard—that made the good looks all the more compelling.

Max had met only one other person in his life with that kind of visual impact: Kathleen O'Connor. He laughed again, seeing Sean and himself acting like clumsy clowns, tangling their tongues, their overgrown feet, trying to compete for a colleen like Kathleen.

She was as dewy as the fabled island that spawned her, moist and fecund and lush and intriguingly cloudy, elusive. She made even boys understand why the Cavalier poets had written reams to their mistresses' ivory white skin, rose-petal lips, and "brunette beauty."

Max had long since learned to get past beauty, but he wondered what would happen to that if he saw Kathleen, or Kitty as she called herself to Devine, again after all these years. From the sketch Devine had commissioned of her, age had not withered a scintilla of it.

And, yes, he took the threat she posed seriously, though he hadn't let on to Devine. Max was used to keeping his own counsel, to directing the show of his life and his life's work. Only part of it, the least important, had been onstage.

So. He leaned against the wall, partly indulging his ego with a paranoid sense of personal competition, partly putting off confronting the ugly certainty that lives he cared about were in danger, and only he could do something to stop it.

In the years between Sean's death in Northern Ireland, he had atoned for surviving the IRA bombing, for the sin of not being there, by saving strangers' lives. Now it had come full circle. The lives he needed to save were those as close to him as he allowed these days, Temple principally, of course, but he had to save Temple the loss of those she cared for to save her completely, and that was a wider circle.

And it included Matt Devine, ironically.

And even Kitty O'Connor was not an island. Max had other enemies from his undercover days, and had made new ones during his uncustomary long stay in Vegas. Molina, for one. She worked for the law, and she regarded him as the epitome of lawlessness. No quarter there.

And Devine was right: Max's past had brought the danger into their own living rooms. His now, Temple's . . . when?

Damn, but Devine was too good-looking for any woman's good! Temple or Molina, maybe even. Or even Kitty O'Connor? Did she have a vulnerable spot she was hiding with her implacable persecution of Matt Devine?

Beauty. Yeats had described the truth and terrible cost of the Irish freedom movement as "a terrible beauty" being born. And beauty *was* born, not made. It wasn't an option.

Maybe that was what drew Kathleen to Devine, for worse or for better, the one thing they had in common that infuriated her. And she was infuriated. She had already acted on it by her first, shockingly physical surprise attack on Devine. Where would her fury strike next? And at whom? If she couldn't find him, and was taking it out on others, could he find her first? Take her out. One way or the other.

Meanwhile . . . the current show must go on.

Max pushed himself off the wall, straightened his slumping backbone into onstage steel again. Enough wallowing. Back to being the Mystifying Max Kinsella, able to defy gravity and create illusions out of insubstantial air.

He was going to have a busy night of it.

First, he called the private backstage number for the Cloaked Conjuror.

It was well before showtime, but CC would be in. Magicians always came early to triple-check the arrangements for their shows. One slip-up could cause career-terminating embarrassment.

CC sounded very glad to hear from Max, and even gladder to hear that his missing leopard had been found.

"No, you can't have Osiris back anytime soon," Max told him. "He's . . . quarantined. No, not sick. Only . . . suspected."

Max quickly laid out the murder and the leopard's presence at the death scene. "The Animal Oasis has taken charge of Osiris. The other big cats and the herds remain in place, with their usual tenders. There's nothing you can do except visit Osiris, which I don't recommend. The police don't know whose animal he was, and you don't want to step forward, because Osiris's owner would be a prime suspect in the murder. Who else could control the animal?"

"I never even heard of this Van Burkleo guy and his head-hunting ranch," CC objected in an odd voice: his own, unmasked by a vocal synthesizer. Contrary to his muscular onstage image, his pleasant tenor would serve a bingo caller well.

"Say you. I do wonder why you never got any ransom demand for Osiris. Also about a couple other things involving his abduction. Stay out of it. The Animal Oasis people will take princely care of him. If you want to do something, give the AO a big donation. Having an exotic animal dumped into their facility with no notice puts a huge strain on the staff, the accommodations, and the budget. It's a non-profit."

"Listen, that's a 'ransom' I'm happy to pay. You'll let me know as soon as Osiris is cleared? I mean, it's ridiculous that a leopard would be suspected of murder."

"I agree." Max didn't mention his biggest worry: not that the leopard would be charged with murder but that community outrage at any "wild" animal attacking a human might mean a hasty putting down. "All you need to worry about is staying away until the real killer is caught."

"How can you be sure that he will be?"

"Or *she*. I guess I'll just have to see to it myself."

"My God. You don't mess around when you set out to do something, do you?"

"Nope. And when it *is* safe to get Osiris back, we'll have to abduct him. You really can't risk claiming him publicly, ever, for a number of reasons."

"You mean the Synth as well as the police?"

"Yes, and probably the Girl Scouts are involved too."

"What!"

"Never mind. A bad joke. I have a lot of bases to cover tonight and I'm getting a little slap-happy. I'll call again when you can do something for me."

Max punched off the phone and snapped it shut.

Next he had to tackle Temple without telling her too much. That would be difficult, and against his wishes, if not his better judgment.

Maybe he could sic her onto Molina. That would clear his operating field of two complications at once.

She responded to his knock on her door with surprised but rewarding pleasure.

"Max! You're knocking like a real boy. Your nose doesn't even look too long from recent prevarications. In a good cause, of course. Come in. I get to be a real hostess. Sit down. Would you like a shot of scotch and a petit four?"

He laughed and let her lead him into her lair.

"I can't stay." Max sat gingerly on the sofa cushion edge. "Listen,

Temple. Did you ever look into that strange geometric figure we found etched on the floor at the professor's death scene?"

"Um, no. It hasn't been a priority."

She sat on the coffee table opposite him, a red-headed sprite in aqua leggings and matching big fuzzy sweater whom he wanted to pull onto his lap. Her bare feet were thrust into black patent-leather high-heeled mules that would go fetchingly astray if he made any sudden moves, but he had two murderers to hunt and no time for intermission.

"Maybe you can coax some information on that out of Molina."

While her eyebrows shot up in disbelief at that revolting idea, he added, "Or your New Age acquaintances. Have you seen anything like this?" He pulled an artsy, mostly blank newspaper ad page toward him, drew his fountain pen and sketched the worm Ouroboros.

Temple got up to lean over his shoulder, smelling faintly of lavender something. Just faintly enough to be interesting. "No. Is it made of metal? Is it a bracelet?"

"Possibly. I don't want to prejudice you. See if you can track down this symbol, however it's used."

"I'm sorry, I've been so busy at the Phoenix. I didn't have a chance to follow up on this Synth stuff."

"No hurry." Max stood and then kissed her, because if he kissed her sitting down it might not end. "It's very important. I hate to leave, but I have to."

"All right."

"Lock your door after I leave."

"Always."

In the hallway he waited for her dead bolt to snap to, while he planned his next calls.

Standing there, he realized that Devine's apartment was directly above hers. No wonder they had become friends, or something more than.

Max grimaced. He supposed he owed Kathleen O'Connor a smidge of gratitude for occupying Devine thoroughly enough to make interaction with Temple unlikely, and even a threat to her well-being.

It wasn't often a mortal enemy did him a favor.

Everything was acting up at once. Molina was personally investigating Cher Smith's death. Kitty O'Connor was turning the screws on Matt Devine. Rafi Nadir was butting his nose into everybody's business, maybe because he had something to hide, like murder one. And the Synth had possibly set up the Cloaked Conjuror's leopard as a murder suspect.

Where next?

He checked his discreetly talented watch. It was getting late. Time to put Vince into long-term storage and to get out his long-lost soul brother. Who? Time would tell.

Baby Doll's was three tiers down from Secrets as strip clubs go.

Max had decided on an off-the-wall approach, partly motivated by that mother of invention, necessity. He went in as an Elvis wannabe, cannibalizing bits of the Elvis impersonator outfit he had put together a few weeks earlier.

Shades, sideburns, poufed and sprayed black hair. Who could see beyond the cartoon to the face beneath the icon's mask?

He would get a lot of attention, yes, but it wouldn't be hard to talk to people.

He slouched into the joint as if he were used to going everywhere in this weird getup. Bell bottoms, boots, and mod-pattern shirt.

"Got a gig down the Strip yet tonight, Elvis?" the bartender asked.

"Naw, I did a couple of the fringe casinos. That's it. Tourist stuff mostly." He grabbed a fistful of peanuts and stuffed his craw. "Came here to meet a girl."

"We got 'em."

"Not that way. Friend of mine. Good little peeler. Sometimes goes by Delilah."

"Had 'em, seen 'em, not any here now."

"Or . . . Mandy."

The bartender stiffened, then shook his shaggy head. He looked about two weeks off of Wine Bottle Row himself, and now he looked scared. "I only been working here a couple of weeks."

Max laughed at his own accuracy. "Anybody here who might have seen her a couple weeks ago?"

"You're not the only one who's asking. Maybe you two should get together."

Max turned in the direction the guy's single eye that focused was looking.

Maybe . . . not.

If he had gone for the over-obvious, Molina had settled for same old, same old. Worn jeans, weathered jean jacket, black turtleneck sweater, suede red, white, and blue shoulder bag big enough to tote a revolver. He spotted, and admired, the chipped polish on her fingernails. A nice touch. More makeup than the usual nil, but applied slap-dash.

She looked like a weary, low-rent PI who was used to trailing unfaithful husbands to motels roaches wouldn't rent.

Right now she was talking to a blowsy stripper who should have retired two decades ago, making notes with a stubby pencil on a cocktail napkin while nursing a Bloody Mary.

Max wished he had a camera.

"You ever take on freelance muscle?" he asked Wino Willie over his shoulder while he watched Molina shout her questions over the noise of the taped music. He could just about read her lips.

"Yeah. The bouncers come and go as much as the girls do. Guess they're all bouncers." He cackled.

"Guy named Raf."

"Yeah. I seen him."

Max spun around, engaged at once. "Yeah? Big guy. Well, thick guy anyway."

Willie was nodding his head on his stringy neck. "Now that you mention it, this Raf first showed up the night of the Incident."

"Incident?"

Willie shrugged as he swabbed a filthy wet rag over the cigarette-blistered Formica bar top. "I guess you're askin' made me remember. Mandy. Second night I was on. Girl got herself killed in the parking lot."

"They don't 'get' themselves killed. Someone does it for them."

"You know what I mean. Didn't catch her name, but this Raf guy ducked out before the police came. Forgot about him. Round this place you remember the girls and forget the guys."

"I guess." Max/Elvis leered toward the stage where the black overhead spotlight was painting somebody fluorescent purple-white in all the right places.

Molina had moved on and was talking to a burly young bouncer with a pool-cue scar on his upper lip.

The music was as loud and even fuzzier than the sound system at

Secrets. The strippers here all moved in a dream, matching the sparse clientele.

A bit of energy burst through the door, and several sets of eyes flicked its way, Max's among them.

He almost dropped the prop cigarette he had been twirling through his fingers like a baton.

Rafi Nadir.

Max panned to Molina. She wasn't wearing sunglasses after dark, naturally.

Elvis was.

He swiveled off the barstool and ambled in her direction. This would be the greatest magic trick of his career. Nothing to do but head her off, get rid of her, and keep Nadir to himself.

"Hi, uh, ma'am?" Sound like a rube.

She turned to find him slouched behind her, sticking a fresh cigarette behind his ear like a '50s hood.

"Yeah?"

"Guy at the bar says you was askin' 'bout Mandy?"

"Yeah."

"I had some words with her. Guess she was the girl who got killed. Guess you're one of these PIs?"

"Yeah."

Max looked around, shifted his engineer-booted feet. "Don't wanna talk here, you know? You got a car?"

"Yeah."

"We kin go there?"

"Why should I? I don't know you know anything."

"I knew Mandy. Sort of. That's more'n most here. She was new, like me. Guess I lasted and she didn't."

Molina looked impatiently around the place. She had a plan that didn't include a hick Elvis who wanted to croon in a car.

Nadir was leaning over the bar, cadging a genuine drink from Willie.

"I sing real purty," Elvis promised, with a wink.

"Get real. Or is that against your religion?"

"Hey, the King was real. He was jest misunderstood."

"Aren't we all."

She was turning away, toward Rafi Nadir.

Nadir was turning away from the bar, smudged glass in fist, ready to survey the scene.

Elvis caught her arm, spun her back to face him, feeling an instant tightening of bicep under the denim jacket. Not big, but hard. She worked out.

"No, listen," he said. "I feel real bad about Mandy. Dyin' and all that." Max had never sounded more sincere, maybe because it was easier to say the truth in another guise. "Mandy . . . she loved Elvis. Like a kid, you know. That's why she talked to me, told me what she was afraid of."

"Afraid of?"

Molina jumped on the bone he threw her like a cop on a clue.

Rafi had his drink in hand was swaggering toward mid-room. Toward them.

"Can't we talk here?" she wanted to know.

"No!" Elvis's edge of hysteria overlaid an air of Kingly command. "It's gotta be outside. Mandy was afraid of something inside."

"All right." Frowning, Molina started for the door, her trademark laser blue eyes refracting the reflected rays from the lurid black light.

Nadir was looking their way, attracted by the motion.

Elvis swooped his extradark aviator shades from his face. Max braced for Molina to recognize him in the second before he pushed the glasses onto her nose. But she was distracted by the unwanted shades.

"What are you doing?" Her arm went up out of reflex, hard.

He blocked it with his forearm, a careless bump. "It's bright out there, ma'am. Those big parking-lot lights. You wear Elvis's shades. They're a protection. He had bad eyes, you know. Too many bright lights. You don't wanta let 'em bright lights get you. I'm a performer, I know. You ever see me do the King over at the Alhambra Inn?"

He had her out the door before she ripped the glasses from her face, her own authoritative persona coming through the cover loud and clear.

"No! And I don't need these stupid props. Now have you got something to tell me, or what?"

Max donned the glasses she thrust at him and shrugged. "Jest trying to help, ma'am. Like we do in Tennessee. You ever been to Tennessee?"

"No. And we can talk here. What about Mandy? What was she afraid of inside there. Who?"

Max leaned against the building to disguise his height and tamped his boot toe bashfully into the littered asphalt. "She was a real nice girl. New to town, like me. Maybe jest new to this place. She seemed . . . kinda nervous, though. A nice girl. I like to come to see the nice girls, not those hard city women."

"Really." Molina was gritting her teeth at the hick act, so annoyed she couldn't see straight. He hoped. "So you remember the date you saw Mandy?"

"Yes, ma'am. It was a Sunday, couple weeks ago. And then a couple days later, they said she'd been killed, so I remembered. But I'll never forget that girl." Something in his tone, maybe the truth, riveted her for the first time. "She didn't want to be here, but it was all she knew to do. I was new, too, so we talked a little. She said some guy had hassled her at Secrets, that's why she was over here at Baby Doll's. It wasn't as classy a joint, but someone told her it would be safer here."

"But it was just the same. What'd she expect? Never mind. Okay, who hassled her at Secrets?"

"I dunno. Some guy. Another guy named . . . Vince? Yeah, Vince scared him off. I never saw any Vince here, though." *Might as well give yourself an alibi while you're at it.*

"You're sure? Seventies sleaze disco kind of guy? Gold chains, greasy hair?"

"Ma'am, we don't have anybody like that in Tennessee, 'ceptin' Elvis, of course, and he *was* seventies."

"I guess you'd know." She gave him a disgusted once-over so speedy that she failed to recognize even Vince beneath the Elvis getup.

He'd told Temple the truth: naked was the best disguise, especially if you were a naked embarrassment.

"Like I said, I bought her a drink, she seemed to like to drink more'n dance, and we talked and she told me she didn't feel safe here. Then she left sometime after her number. Never saw her go. Wish I had. I woulda seen her home."

"And held her hand, no doubt." Molina snorted. She pulled out her notebook. "What's your name and where can I reach you?"

"Bobby Rae. Bobby Rae Dixon. You can reach me at the Alhambra Inn most nights. I do two shows, seven and eleven, but the eleven o'clock's the one that really rocks."

"Oh, joy." Molina finished jotting down the lies he had told her, then looked back at Baby's Doll's vacant, graffiti-smudged exterior.

The parking-lot lights were bright and it was almost one in the morning. She probably had a full twelve-hour day of real work to put in ahead of her.

Would she give up with the shreds he had given her, and leave Nadir to him?

"Kin I see you to your car, ma'am?"

She looked at him as if he was crazy. "Take my advice. You need to run for the boonies. I'll find my car myself."

She stalked off, deflected by relentless southern redneck courtesy.

He waited politely by the building, on watch until she got in her car and drove off. Not her real car, of course, without her license plates.

He wondered where she had dug up the beater. She didn't have a convenient network to tap into, as he did, because the last thing she'd want would be for anyone in her department to know she was out freelancing.

"Razor's edge, Lieutenant, ma'am," he murmured in farewell. "Listen to Elvis. He knows that stuff."

Straightening, Max turned back to Baby Doll's. Time to find out what Rafi Nadir was doing at the scene of the crime. Again.

Chapter 30

Ringed In

Matt's ringing phone dredged him up from the first deep sleep he had fallen into for a week.

His bedside clock read 2:00 A.M.

At first he heard only the blare of music and a vague party sort of clatter and chatter. It sounded like a TV movie frat-house scene.

"Did you get my present?" a husky voice asked on a tone of unwelcome intimacy.

"The worm." He tried to make it sound like what he'd call her face to face if he had a chance.

"For I am a worm," she said, laughing, repeating the Good Friday antiphon.

"No, just a very sick woman."

"Oh? Then you'll do as I say. Let me ask you, what are you wearing?"

He also recognized the obscene phone-call ploy so often used by men against women that it had become a cliché.

"I guess I'll hang up, or just whistle into the phone."

"Oh, don't hang up. Whistle, just whistle, and I'll come to you, my lad."

It was the second time tonight someone he had reason to loathe had called Matt their lad, and he was getting sick of it.

"Listen, there's a point where you push someone too far."

A pause. "Shall I tell you what Miss Temple Barr is wearing tonight?"

A chill climbed his spine like ghostly fingers with long nails. Another thing to tell Kinsella: don't drop in on Temple without expecting to be seen by your worst enemy. Kinsella wouldn't like that, Matt warning him away from Temple. Matt didn't mind.

"Not necessary," Matt said as coolly as he could manage. "I'll wear your hellish ring, but not the way you think."

"Oh, really? Now you're making this interesting. I *will* check up on you. Somewhere, sometime, some way. Thanks for making it interesting. But, then, you always do."

She hung up.

He wiped a thin dew of sweat from his upper lip and remembered—tasted—a fresh burst of the corroding hatred he had once felt for his former stepfather.

Matt had thought himself over such negative emotions.

He had been wrong. Dead wrong. He should ask God for forgiveness, but he didn't want to drag God into this. It might cramp his style.

Chapter 31

Elvis Leaves the Building

Max leaned against the filthy exterior of Baby Doll's and actually smoked one of his prop cigarettes.

This was getting way too complicated. How could he get Molina off the night beat and back into her office where she belonged?

Nail Cher's killer, that's how. And nail Van Burkleo's killer while he was at it. This was getting to be too big a job even for Superman.

A flare of smoke and music spat into the clean night air, the burst as shocking as the spray of a machine gun.

When the single front door to Baby Doll's slammed shut, Rafi Nadir was out in the darkness with Max.

He stalked over.

"You the PI who was bothering the customers and girls in there?"

"Me? Man, I'm PE. Presley, Elvis, suh! Yes, suh, Colonel." Max ran up a mock salute.

"You sure are a moth-eaten Elvis, man, now that I look at you.

Sorry. I'm the house police, and I heard some private dick was hassling the customers. You got another coffin nail?"

"Shore." Max tapped out a cigarette and provided a match for it, watching Nadir's bloated features swell into focus while the match flame and the cigarette's terminal ember flared. "Naw, I'm jest a country boy tryin' to make a buck in the Big City. Quite some place."

Nadir leaned against the building, took a deep drag. "Yeah. Cheesy town. Nothing like L.A. In L.A. you got your black and your yellow and your Mexican side of town. Big-time. Not the so-called 'hoods they have around here. It's an industry there, man. This place is like a studio back lot. All show and no go. All front and no real action behind it. Like, even the Mob's gone corporate. Trading stocks instead of bullets. There's no real action anywhere here anymore."

Max nodded. "I get yah."

"Well, I'll be outa this penny-ante bouncer stuff soon. There's still something goin' on I can latch onto. Maybe make a big buck or two while I still know how to spend it. Aw, whata I care whether some PI is nosing around, asking about some hopeless stripper who got herself throttled?"

"Throttled, huh? How'd you know that?"

"Word's all over the strip clubs. The stupid whores are wearing dog collars to deter the Strip-joint Strangler, can you believe it? Nobody's more superstitious than strippers and whores. They all think luck is what's gonna save 'em. You see that rotten PI around here, *son*"— Rafi Nadir thumped Max several times on the chest with a stiff forefinger—"you send 'im to Rafi Nadir for a talking-to. But only tonight. I'm gone after tonight. I got a brand-new gig. With a classy outfit. I'm on my way back up. That'll show . . . whoever. When next you see me, I'll be a customer with bucks to burn. I'll be able to buy this place and use the profits to light my cigar.

"Here."

Nadir stuffed a twenty-dollar bill in Max's cigarette-cupping hand. "Here's some money to burn, Elvis. You remember Rafi. You're gonna hear about him again."

Chapter 32

Animal Wrongs

"You look tired, Lieutenant."

Morey Alch's voice floated over Molina's head like a dampened volcano of rumbling concern.

"What are you, my mother?" she growled back. He didn't retreat.

He stood at her office door, knowing enough to keep his distance. He usually knew better than to get her back up by suggesting she was doing too much. Today he was right: she was too pooped to overreact.

"We've got a lot of cold cases to solve," she went on mildly. "And then this nutso leopard killing—"

"Definitely nutso. You eyeball that woman?"

"I think it's a woman."

Alch had poured two mugs of coffee—overbrewed sludge—at the big urn near the door. Now he nodded and transversed the long, narrow office walking like a man on a tightrope. He set one mug down at her place before settling at the other side of her desk. His own white mug was artfully decorated with dried-coffee drips of various lengths and intensity. He tossed her packets of creamer and sugar and ripped into his own duo.

Molina sighed. "You and Su getting anywhere on the likely suspects in that case?"

"Besides the leopard, you mean." He looked up quizzically from his coffee ritual.

She laughed, as he had intended. "Right. The Leopard Man did it. You ever see those old black-and-white movies when you were a kid? You know, the African cult that dressed up in leopardskins and clawed their victims? Am I hallucinating, or does this Van Burkleo case smack of jungle drums, my friend?"

"*The White Zombie,*" Morey declaimed. "Movies like that. Great stuff. The leopardmen in those movies wore these, uh, you know, gloves, with claws in the fingertips. Reminds me of my trip to England. Me and the wife, before . . . well, before. Anyway, I got into the Black Museum at Scotland Yard. Only me. Only pros. Don't let spouses in, which was just as well. Anyway, they got Jack's letters there. The Ripper. And they had all these confiscated weapons, and I'll never forget, a Freddy Krueger glove."

"*Freddy Krueger Goes to Blighty?*"

Alch sipped and nodded. "This crude canvas glove with razors for fingernails. Thing is, the Brit coppers found blood on the blades. Human blood. Never found who it came from, though, or who wore the gloves. Said it was time a little censorship got put into play."

"That's the trouble." Molina sipped, shook her head. "There is no such thing as 'a little' censorship. So what did you find out about Maison Van Burkleo, overlooking the animal-rights activists for now?"

Molina stopped him before he could answer by looking steadfastly over his shoulder. "Come in, Su. We're comparing notes."

Merry Su paused at the coffee urn, shook her head and minced past it on high chunky heels, those Minnie Mouse oversized Mary Janes so popular with the young and kicky set. Temple Barr would look ludicrous in those gunboats, but somehow the equally petite Su didn't. She dragged a side chair next to Alch's.

"That stuff'll kill you," she pronounced, drawing a bottled water from the low-slung bag at her side with as much slow satisfaction as if it were a gun. "You'd be better off drinking straight whipping cream and cyanide, given the chemicals in those innocuous packets. Corporate murder."

"Alch was just about to run through the Van Burkleo suspects," Molina said.

"Before Morey does his old professor act," Su said, "I'd like to raise an issue. We all know that the animal people are right and Van Burkleo was probably running a high-dollar hunt club there."

Nods. "That's not our jurisdiction," Molina pointed out.

"I know. But . . . if the leopard *didn't* do it, like animal-amok stuff, what about who used to own the leopard? Maybe somebody found out and didn't like where it had ended up, playing pincushion for some would-be he-man bow-and-arrow hunter. If my Bichon ever ended up like that, I'd go hunt some two-legged game myself."

Alch, taking notes, stopped on a pen point. "Your what? A bison?"

"Bichon. Bee-*shown* B-i-c-h-o-n. My Bichon Frise." Bee-*shown* freeze-*ay*.

Alch was awe-stricken. "My God, it's a hairstyle as weird as her eyebrows," he told Molina.

"It's a dog, dummy."

"That's verbal abuse," he noted with both tongue and pen.

"Children." Molina leaned her head on her hand. "Su makes an interesting point. But, as I understand it from the animal-rights people, and I believe they know the chapter and verse on this, the animals that Van Burkleo offered to target shooters—okay, target *mis*-shooters—were either raised for it, like the hooved animals, or the big cats were obtained from private owners who couldn't handle them or caring for them anymore, or zoos who had old or excess animals they needed to get rid of."

"Zoos?" Su was steaming now. "*Zoos* would sell their animals to outfits like Van Burkleo's?"

"Why do you think the protesters were out there in the desert?" Alch pointed out. "They had something legit to protest."

"I'm told," Molina put in, "that in some parts of the country some zoo board members actually own canned-hunt ranches. Cozy, huh?"

"That does it." Su was surefooted now. "The killer could even be a zoo employee who learned that an animal he, or she, tended had ended up there. That leopard is a beautiful animal. Did you see it before they took it away?" She looked at Alch. "Shooting it would have been a sin."

Molina was surprised. "I hadn't thought about the condition of the leopard. Su, since you're a *bee-shown freeze-ay* expert, call the guy over at Animal Oasis, what's his name?"

"Kirby Granger."

"Granger. Right. Call him and get a statement on the leopard's age, state of health, probable source, that kind of thing. Maybe Van Burkleo planned to keep it as a personal trophy, if it was that fine a specimen."

"Specimen!" Su huffed.

"I had no idea you were a cat lover," Alch put in slyly, "from your attitude to certain black members of that species."

"I'm not. I'm a dog lover. But a beautiful animal is a beautiful animal, especially if it's an endangered species."

"Passions would run high," Molina agreed. "Alch, you seem to have an affinity for the widow. See if you can get the leopard's provenance out of her."

Molina felt pleased with herself. Su was a good choice to handle the gruff Animal Oasis founder, and Alch had a way with women that wasn't obvious, but was effective. Precisely because it wasn't obvious.

He was even now twinkling at her, aware of how she was dividing and conquering the sources.

"I expect you to make some real headway with Leonora Leopard-Lady, Morey."

Alch promptly pulled out a narrow notebook and flipped through with the satisfaction of a thorough man.

"Okay. The wife. The widow now. I'm sure you've been wondering about—"

"I heard. The wife-turned-widow." The obvious always made Su impatient, and nothing was more obvious than Leonora Van Burkleo. "You don't need to go far to run her down. What a freak!"

"Oh, I don't know." Alch did a patented old duffer act of riffling his notebook pages and looking out from under his shaggy eyebrows. "I'd say that gals who pluck their eyebrows to resemble a pair of broken chopsticks are, uh, a *hair* on the freakish side themselves."

Su's exotically shaped brows lifted, lowered, and took flight, simultaneously. "Lieutenant, we have sexual and ethnic harassment here, all at once."

"Go after the perps, not each other," Molina advised. "You know

Alch wouldn't say a word about your eyebrows if he didn't love you like a paternalistic sexist pig."

"Oink," Alch contributed.

Su laughed. "It's a fashion thing, Morey. How can a mere man get it?"

Molina had to admit that Su's eyebrows were the most elaborate and striking she had ever seen . . . with the odd exception of the brows drawn on the forehead of that vanishing lady magician, Shangri-La. Who had nicked an opal-and-diamond ring Max Kinsella had given to Temple Barr, in Manhattan, no less. Which very same ring Molina had found a couple weeks later at the church parking-lot death scene of a former magician's assistant . . . another unsolved case. Not to mention the dead professor at UNLV and a third man falling dead at the New Millennium Hotel to match the earlier ceiling deaths at the Goliath and the Crystal Phoenix Hotels, one almost a year ago.

"Did I say something, wrong, Lieutenant?" Su's face sobered.

"No. I'm just thinking about our case load. So, Morey. You were about the enlighten us about the widow Van Burkleo."

"Like I said, inquiring minds want to know, is it nature or is it human error? Since Leonora Van Burkleo's appearance is so noteworthy, I tried to find out if she had it done to her. On purpose." He waited, trying not to look at Su's on-purpose eyebrows. "The answer is a resounding, if puzzling, yes."

"Plastic surgery." Molina nodded. "How'd you find out?"

"Used the phone records. A lot to a local doctor. Some were out of the area code. The L.A. and Manhattan ones were fancy-shmancy plastic surgeons. These guys do movie stars. Their minions weren't about to say much to a homicide detective, except to confirm that the way she looks is the way she wanted to look."

"How long have the surgeries been going on?"

"Three years."

"Interesting. She was married to Van Burkleo for six."

"So," said Su. "The lady aimed to please. Maybe she was being coerced into this freaky remodeling job and decided to kill him. Involving the leopard was a way to make a statement at the same time: he made her into a cat-faced woman, a cat would bring him down."

"Perhaps." Molina sipped her coffee and made her usual face on first tasting it. "I don't see this woman as the type to alter herself to anyone's specifications, though. If anything, she's the control freak."

"Affirmative," said Su. "I like my Leopard Lady theory, but it's pretty out there. The plastic surgery is probably just an extreme expression of that tendency to control nature. The word I got nosing around the ranch was that she was the one who really ran things, and with an iron fist. Van Burkleo was the client back-slapper."

"He got his back more than slapped by that antelope horn," Alch observed.

"The scenario we're being asked to buy," Molina said, "is that the leopard got loose in the house, scared Van Burkleo, and he ran himself through trying to get away from it." Molina leaned back in her chair. "The introduction of the leopard brings our attention out of the house and onto the grounds. At the least it implies an outside accomplice to handle the leopard and let it indoors."

"The place is crawling with keepers," Su said, "and private security types."

"Any of them recent hires?" Alch asked.

Su consulted her own narrow notebook. "Three. Two animal guys and one security guy."

"I'm sure you ran all the names through records." Molina looked at Alch.

He nodded. "Nothing major. One had a hobby of collecting traffic tickets. One had a couple altercations at a club, but he was a bouncer, you'd expect that. Cost of doing business. The other was as clean as a dinosaur's tooth."

"Dinosaur's tooth," Su jeered in retaliation for the eyebrow crack. "Your age is showing, Morey."

"Let's see the list." Molina held out a palm.

"My notes are kinda scrawled."

"I know your notes. If anything happened to you we'd need an Egyptologist to translate them. . . ."

"See something, Lieutenant?" Alch asked hopefully.

Molina didn't answer right away.

Because even in Morey's scrambled handwriting she could translate the recognizable letters, Rfff Ndr. The letters "alt" followed the name. Short for altercations. This was the strip club bouncer.

Talk about turning-point moments. How far did she go to protect Nadir from official inquiry while she ran her own half-assed unofficial inquiry? If he was more than suspect, even a real live perp, at what point did her personal interest add up to endangering the public while protecting her daughter and herself? Now? Sic 'em on Rafi? Alch and Su to the manhunt? Kinsella hadn't panned out, that was for sure. Molina cleared her throat, swallowed duty one more time. She simply didn't believe Nadir had done it, not for personal reasons, but in her professional judgment. Now Alch wanted to know what had given her pause, something plausible, besides conscience.

"Just your execrable penmanship," she told him affectionately. "You need to have these things translated, Morey."

"I can read 'em better than I can type. You should see my typing, you want hieroglyphs."

"It could cause trouble in court," she said. "You can have the captain's secretary type them up."

"Captain wouldn't like that."

"You mean you can't sweet-talk Arletta into doing you a favor? Just show her these pathetic notes. Her sense of order will put her at your disposal."

"You overestimate his charms, Lieutenant," Su told her. "Morey's bashful act doesn't go over with uptown women like Arletta."

"Then you type 'em up for him, Su. You *are* partners," Molina told her with a frigid smile that meant business. "You're supposed to compensate for each other's weaknesses. But do it after this case is over. We have a lot of folks already involved at Rancho Exotica. And we haven't even looked into the upscale clientele."

"You mean the sick weekend hunters," Su said.

"You think the animal-rights people have a cause?"

"Darn right they do. Saw a feature on one of those TV news magazines. Had some kind of wild ram pinned against a fence. Shot so many arrows into his body he looked like a pincushion. Poor thing was panting and heaving, just lying there, waiting for the macho incompetent to kill him inch by inch in order to spare the head and chest for mounting. I'm a homicide cop and it made my stomach turn. I was ready to off the hunter myself."

No one wanted to break the silence. Then Alch shifted to look at the scowling Su. "That cute little fuzzy jacket you wear when the temp dips below sixty, what's that made of?"

"The magenta one? I guess, well, maybe, fur. Something they raise on farms. It's not the same thing."

"They don't waste time with arrows, I bet, but I also bet that Peter Cottontail didn't want to die for your fashion sense, either."

Molina raised her hands to head off a serious spat in the detective team. Morey was right, a lot of things were easy to swallow if you didn't know, or think, or see too much about them.

"That part of the case is not our jurisdiction," she reminded them both. "We're here to get people-killers. We don't even have proof that Van Burkleo's place was a hunting ranch, and we're not about to waste man, or woman, power on that. It's only relevant as a motivation for the animal-rights protesters, and I have a hard time buying a group kill. That only happens in Agatha Christie mysteries."

"Maybe not a group kill," Alch said. "Maybe one did it and the others are protecting him, or her. Or just don't know. *Somebody* let that leopard into the house."

"How about Van Burkleo himself?" Su asked, engaged again. "Maybe he liked to live dangerously. According to his wife, he was alone in the house that night because she stayed over in town."

"Accidental death?"

Su shrugged. "We've seen some pretty incriminating death scenes that turned out to be accidents. Remember the alcoholic woman who went into a fit and tore up her living room? The place looked like an interrupted break-in, with attempted rape and successful murder."

Molina nodded. Anything was possible. The medical examiner had reported head and body blows and bruises, but those could have happened while V. B. was running from the leopard.

"And then, for another theory—" said Su. And stopped.

"Yes?"

"There was the usual black cat on the premises."

"What 'usual black cat'?"

"The usual black house cat we keep running into on crime scenes lately."

"If it's showing up at crime scenes, it can't be a house cat," Molina said.

"Big, shorthaired male?" Alch asked Su with interest, ignoring the boss.

Molina kept a dangerous silence.

Su made a point of consulting her notebook, just for show. "Not so big. Not so shorthaired. Maybe not so male. The description sounds female."

"Oh," said Alch. "The other one, then."

"Sorry." Molina slapped her palms on the desktop for attention. "I refuse to believe that Las Vegas domestic cats could get out into the desert like that. Must be a stray attracted by the big-cat food."

Su shrugged. "Some of the attendants spotted it, earlier the same day that Van Burkleo was killed. Said it was hanging around the leopard's cage. A little too coincidental, Lieutenant?"

"It'll be a little too coincidental if I catch you wearing a jacket that looks suspiciously like cat fur, that's when I'll concede coincidence. Forget the house cat. What could a house cat have to do with a murder? We have enough big cats mixed into this case to make even Siegfried and Roy suddenly allergic to the species."

After they left, Molina finished her too-strong, too-cold coffee, then headed for the women's rest room, brooding.

The ethical line she was walking was fishing-line thin. If Raf was at the scene of another murder . . . he should be brought in and questioned. She could let Team Su-Alch do it. He didn't have to see her at all. She could warn them not to mention her name . . . no, that would be out of character.

The door whooshed shut behind her the way rest room doors always do. She was alone in here, which wasn't odd. Not that many women in a police facility even now.

Normally she didn't check herself out in mirrors, but she glanced up while washing her hands. Granted even the brutal overhead fluorescent lighting, she looked haggard. Not good. Looking frazzled would generate questions, and questions would generate evasions, and then she was down the slippery slope and heading face-first into a tree. . . .

A sound from one of the three cubicles interrupted her self-reflection. She hadn't felt another presence. Sounded suspiciously like a sniffle. Someone with a cold, or one of the secretaries with a bum personal life.

While she considered how to graciously retreat, she realized that she had been frozen in silence for some time, first while studying her unlovely face, then while thinking . . .

A cubicle door swung open and Su emerged, stopping when she saw Molina.

Her eyes looked red.

"Merry?" Molina asked.

"Nothing." Su stomped to the other sink and ran both taps full force, washing her hands with the furious energy of Lady Macbeth.

"Merry—"

"Never mind, I said!"

"It's not, not Alch's crack about the coat, the jacket, is it?"

"I just spotted it and tried it on." Su lifted her hands and shook them, spraying Molina with ice-cold drops. She jerked a fistful of tan paper towels from the wall dispenser. "I didn't even look at anything besides the price tag. I didn't think."

"That was Morey's point, I guess."

"Damn!" Su jerked another unneeded wad of paper towels from the wall. "I loved that jacket. Now what'll I do with it?"

"Donate it to the homeless? They'll wear it out using it for the right reasons, to keep warm, like the cave people, right?"

Su suddenly laughed. "Yeah, it'd look great on Crazy Clementine, wouldn't it? She's sure no size two on the streets!"

Molina smiled at the mention of one of the chief characters along the Strip. "It's done. Move on."

"Right. No one is going to wear a bunny in my presence scot-free from now on. Unless it's Bugs."

Su headed for the door, then stopped. She didn't look at Molina.

"I hope it isn't one of the animal people."

It was almost seven by the time Carmen Molina slogged from the attached garage into the kitchen.

Something about the silence in the house alerted her.

She charged into the living room, alarmed, to find Mariah making like a hammock on the comfortable old couch, a book propped on her awkwardly swelling chest. A *Buffy the Vampire Slayer* book. Oh, well, it could be worse.

"Where's Dolores?" Carmen asked, carefully.

"I told her to go home. She's got dinner to fix for her family."

"Dinner." Carmen sat on the nearest chair.

They had none.

Mariah's head lifted from the sofa pillow. "You've been out all the time lately, even nights."

"The workload—"

"Okay." She shut the paperback book and sat up. "I'll make dinner."

"You'll make dinner?"

"You don't think I can?"

"S-sure, but—"

"It's okay. You've been up late a lot."

Carmen sat there, stunned. Her twelve-year-old daughter taking on a domestic chore? It would probably be Hamburger Helper and frozen pizza, but at this point . . .

She kicked off her low-heeled shoes. How did Temple Barr wear those spikes of hers? Carmen's feet were killing her and she'd spent most of her day on her behind. Maybe it was all psychological. She flinched as she heard banging and rattling in the kitchen. *Let the kid do her thing. Don't be a control freak, you might end up looking like the MGM lion.*

Leo.

That was the name of the MGM lion.

Mrs. Van Burkleo's given name was Leo-nora. Or an assumed name? To match the face. *Stop! Stop thinking about the case. Stop thinking about Rafi Nadir.* Carmen only calmed down after mentally urging herself to do just that for a few seconds.

She was at home now. Time to restore the frayed synapses. Relax. Spend some quality time with her kid, who was starting to act like a responsive adult, hallelujah. Not like a *responsible* adult, mind you, just a responsive one. That was something. Dinner was something.

She sighed, pushed her hair off her face, which she didn't need to do because she wore it in a functional blunt out.

Mariah had even fetched in the mail. Amazing!

A small padded manila envelop lay on the cluttered coffee table facing the sofa.

A surprise. She hated surprises. Not healthy. Okay, we are all kids at heart. I love a parade. . . .

Carmen froze to hear a kitchen appliance whirring. *It's okay. Give the kid space. You can fix anything that can go wrong except chopped-off fingers . . .* She'd been in homicide too long.

She looked at her name on the typed—computer-generated, these days—label. C. R. Molina. Odd. These promo packages usually came addressed to "Resident."

Still, maybe the day, and the nights before it, had been too wearing, but she felt the slightly giddy curiosity of a child with a surprise present. She didn't get many of those nowadays. Certainly not at home.

She ripped open the adhesive flap at one end. Who had the energy to stagger into the kitchen—Mariah's domain of the evening now—to look up a steak knife?

A small boxy item was inside. She practically had to squeeze it out, like a newborn.

Then she stared at what lay in the palm of her hand. A pair of white minibinoculars, something alien with two round sides. It didn't look like an America Online CD, much too small, but who knew what innovation lurks in the heart of today's technology? . . .

She groped in the empty package and pulled out a plum: a piece of memo paper folded in half.

"Not for correction," the typed capital letters read, "except in color."

Weirder and weirder. Carmen twisted one plastic screwtop. Too small to be plastic explosive . . . would she quit thinking like a cop for one single minute—? No.

Floating in a viscous fluid was a bit of colored Saran Wrap. Huh?

"Mom, I need some advice," a voice piped over her shoulder. It dropped a register. "Mom! What are you doing with a contact lens?"

So that's what this was. A set of contact lenses. *Not for correction, except in color.*

The abrupt, one-word signature below the cryptic phrase suddenly registered.

Chameleon.

"Oh, my God . . ."

"I haven't even made anything yet," Mariah complained defensively.

"Oh, not you!" Carmen turned and smiled encouragingly, like all mothers everywhere. "Go to it, *niña*. If you make it, I'll eat it." She would regret this promise.

The manila envelope was still pregnant with possibility, another lump. She midwifed out another sibling: some solution in a bottle.

A whole kit and kabottle. Soft contact lenses. A change of eye color. Boring brown, she noted.

Somewhere, sometime in her nightly undercover rambles she had crossed paths with him. He was sending her a message: if you play at undercover work, dress the part. Do as I do, do as I did, and hide your lying eyes.

She pushed the hair she didn't need to brush aside back from her face anyway, remembering her image in the mirror, the mirror she so seldom consulted. Vanity was not a vice.

She had worried that a haggard face might betray her to a friend.

She had been on the right side of the law for too long to think like a perp. Moving onto dangerous ground, she had counted on her altered getup and her cop's instincts to see her enemies first, before her vivid eyes gave her away like a blue-light special at Kmart. Gave her away . . .

To Max Kinsella.

And to Rafi Nadir, should she be caught off guard and meet him face-to-face. According to this packet of joy and admonition from Kinsella, she had come too damn close to meeting Rafi for any of their goods.

Would she heed the warning?

Of course.

Did she appreciate it?

Hell, no.

"Dinner's ready," Mariah caroled from the kitchen.

It was much too soon for anything edible.

Carmen put on a happy face, if not contact lenses, and went into the kitchen.

She smelled burning cardboard.

Chapter 33

Track of the Cat

The desert sky looks like one of those Strip hotel dioramas: big bowl of dark sky, twinkling lights for stars, a nice crescent moon tilted artistically low on a horizon tinted a smoky indigo color from the distant aurora borealis of Las Vegas.

Except that this sky is real, and dark, and deep.

The dark in the building behind us is even more impenetrable.

"I smell something bad, Mr. Midnight," Groucho pipes up.

And I do mean "pipes." The pipsqueak sounds like a soprano cricket.

"So do I," is my response. "And do you know what it is? I smell a rat."

"We are not afraid of rats," Golda puts in.

"I mean the human kind," I start to respond, just working up a really withering retort, when someone else decides to do it for me. A roar rends the night like it is a silk curtain.

All of our ears flatten in joint pain and consternation. A lion's roar in the wilderness is a primal thing. It sounds fiercer than the volcano in front of the Mirage at eruption time. Worse than a jetliner taking off from McCarran. Probably worse than a tornado coming to take you away to Oz.

While we all wince in common pain, my two henchthings whimper.

Sounds of an ominous nature occur behind our backs: the scrape of claw on concrete, a soft growl that never ends, heavy breathing. I feel hot breath on my spine.

I turn, resigned to laying down my life in defense of the wimpy.

Although I have also been resigned to the fact that the canine species, no matter how ridiculous, is gifted with superior sniffing power, I discover that my prime sense is the most useful now. By the all-seeing eyes of Bastet I observe that the impenetrable darkness is not quite impenetrable.

As my legendary night vision adapts to the situation, I discern a life-saving fact: bars.

Then I discern the nature of the awesome feline muscle behind those sweet bars: a Big Cat whose silhouette is a negative of the night. A mirror image of myself magnified about twenty times.

Finally the gent gives up the growling and shows his teeth. I survey the Rocky Mountains of feline dentures and cannot help noticing that both Midnight Louise and I would fit fine in there, along with the Yorkshire constabulary.

A paw the size of a dinner plate thrusts through the bars.

I am afraid the dinner plate is out here, and we are sitting on it.

"Back! Back!" comes a falsetto cry.

Golda has leaped to my side and our defense with an ear-splitting yap.

"Back, back!" seconds Groucho, now pressing against my other side.

Half-pint courage is all well and good, but not when you are facing about forty quarts of snarling predator power.

Our opponent's jaws spread wider.

I expect to hear a *Fee, fie, foe, fum* any second now, as this giant gets ready to grind the bones of whoever is dumb enough to stand up to it.

Then I hear something crack, and close my eyes. Bye-bye, bitty dog!

But the fluffballs bracketing me have not been snagged by the exploring mitt, and my eyes widen as I see the grin of death before me turn into a . . . yawn.

Another impressive jawbone crack, and superfeline smacks his fangs. "You. The runt cub in the middle. I saw you in my cage the other day, making off with part of my lunch."

"Me? No, sire. I mean, sir. I was in Las Vegas doing my nails at the time. This is my first visit to Rancho Exotica. I swear it on my mother's vibrissae."

A growl again, but it sounds like a chuckle. "You do not look big enough to have whiskers, Cub, but maybe your mother might." The huge eyes blink at my bodyguard. "Usually visitors bring rodents along only if a snake is in residence, and there is none on the premises now."

"Snake." I have visions of a boa constrictor big enough to swallow the Ritz Hotel. "Rodents. Oh, you mean my, uh, muscle. These are not rodents; they are miniature dogs."

"Dogs." The big dude yawns again. "They are lucky they feed us well here." The broad brow furrows. "All except the theatrical guy from the New Millennium Hotel. Him they did not feed well. But he did not stay very long. Our population keeps coming and going, I am not sure why."

I am not about to tell this dude the facts of life at Rancho Exotica. No use upsetting the natives when they might develop a nervous appetite in response.

"Yeah, well, I am a private investigator operating out of Vegas, and I am here to find out why some of our best cats are disappearing."

"Vegas?" The big guy almost grins. "I hear that town is filled with disappearing cats. I am from Provo myself. I was a roadside attraction at a reptile ranch until the authorities confiscated me. Then I did time at an animal rehabilitation ranch until the management had a big spat over the donation money. We

ended up being shipped hither and yon. And this is my hither."
He yawns again. "It is not a bad life, no worse than any other
place I remember, but somewhat boring."

I hate to tell him it will go from boring to fatal in short order.

"They call me Midnight Louie," I introduce myself. "I would
appreciate your not eating my bodyguards in a reflex motion.
They are small but occasionally useful."

"What a coincidence," the big guy answers. "They call me
Midnight. And Ebony. And Inkspot. It depends on where I land
and how much imagination the two-legs have. But you can call
me Butch."

"So how long have you been doing time here, Butch?"

"I am a senior resident. About as long as it takes a fat moon
to get skinny and back again."

"And Osiris, how long was he here?"

"You know the theatrical dude! Why did you not say so at
first? He was a little peeved and a lot panicked when he was
here, but I cannot say that I blame him. They had him on
rations so short they were invisible."

"So you said. For how long?"

"Several suns. Then they took him away one dark time, and
he never came back. That happens, though, like the waning of
the moon and the swelling of the sun each day. We are always
being brought and taken away."

There is something so sad about such a big bruiser being
caged and subjected to the whims of an inferior and weaker
species that for a moment I am lost for words. These big guys
in the Big House have not got the free will of the smallest alley
cat.

In the silence, Groucho yaps out, "Sounds like the panther
could use a good lawyer."

Amen.

"Come to think of it," Butch goes on, "I remember you tres-
passing on my territory twice. You brought back the picked-
clean bone. What weird behavior. Must come of living and
working in Las Vegas. Say, I get it! Were you bringing your
compadre Osiris a secret snack?"

I wish I could say that I keep silent from modesty, or unwill-
ingness to credit Midnight Louise with the life-saving operation,

but I am mostly loath to let the big guy think that I stole his lunch for any reason whatsoever, in case he expects me to make it up to him personally.

"That was a good deed, little fellah," he rumbles on.

I blink. He likes me. He actually likes me. "It was nothing that I would not not-do again."

While he is trying to decipher that phrase, I press on. "In fact, we are here to find out where Osiris has gone. These here are my personal noses, which is why I would be grateful if you big dudes can refrain from munching them while we conduct our investigation."

"Investigate away. We have always been curious about where our compatriots go."

I hear a couple of short growls of agreement from near and far, and realize that we have been eavesdropped on by some mighty big ears.

"No one ever bothers to tell us," Butch rumbles on. "It is like they think we are deaf and dumb."

"Can I take it that the entire compound will give us carte blanche?"

"We do not have any carte blanche that I know of, but we will answer your questions if we can. We are more than a little bored anyway."

So I make the rounds, in the course of my investigations meeting one toothless lion, two ocelots, and a puma in a dead tree.

They all confirm the panther's story. Osiris was not fed while here and was taken away, never to be seen again.

We end up at the empty cage that housed the kidnapped leopard.

"Any scents worth trailing?" I ask the Yorkies.

They zip through the bars like floor mops, not even ruffling their trailing coats. I see their shadowy little forms, nose to concrete, vacuuming up the residue on the cage floor. At times like these I am glad that dogs, like the French, are more renowned for their "nose" than my breed.

"Ooh," says Golda. "More Big Cat." She sneezes so hard her ears lift horizontal to the ground. "Why do I not smell any dog out here?"

"They do not hunt dog for trophy heads," I point out. "No value in it."

Groucho growls at me, all four tiny feet braced. "We are more valuable as hunting partners than prey. What has your kind ever done to make itself useful to mankind?"

"We have inspired innumerable art objects, from the Sphinx to the MGM Grand lion."

"Exactly nothing, then." Groucho wheezes with laughter while Golda sneezes again.

I feel like the Cowardly Lion being berated by Munchkins, or toy windup Totos. If I did not need these noses at the moment, I would hand these two over to Butch and his ilk for between-meal palette cleansers. All that hair would make pretty good dental floss for those saber-tooth-size fangs, I bet.

But I control my savage side and play the urbane drawing-room detective.

"I hope, my little furry friends, that 'exactly nothing,' is not what your noses have come up with."

While Groucho and I have been debating, Golda has been running around the cage floor in imitation of the Energizer battery ad bunny.

"Water, water everywhere," she complains, taking another swab around the floor like an industrious mophead.

"Then all traces of who has come and gone here have been washed away," I say.

Golda sniffs indignantly. "Not all. Not to the connoisseur." I notice that Groucho is sitting back and letting her do all the down and dirty nose work.

She finally comes over to us and sticks her hairy little head through the bars.

"I smell the track of the cat, of course. He is much too big and earthy to miss. His trail goes that way." She jerks her bow to the left. "I smell many, many man feet. They have walked in enough excrement of all kinds to make the cage floor into a lit-ter box of sorts."

"Then it is hopeless," I cannot resist predicting. I have never been one to put all my faith in dog noses anyway.

Golda sits on what would be her tail, were one discernible

under that fountain of hair. "Perhaps not. I detect a random pattern to all the manfeet scents but two,"

Groucho leans forward, interested. "And how do these trails differ?"

"They go in opposite directions," she says promptly, "the only two trails that do but one thing: enter the cage area, and leave."

"Which directions?" I ask.

She jerks her bow left again.

"Ah, with Osiris. This must be the person that removed him from his cage to the scene of the crime. And the other direction?"

She jerks her head in the opposite direction.

Groucho stares into the darkness, sniffing. "But there is nothing that way but empty desert for miles and miles."

You can guess which trail we end up following.

Chapter 34

Calling on Agatha

"What we need," Temple said, "is an Agatha Christie moment."

"You mean," Max said, "an Agatha Christie climax."

"Really, Max! Agatha Christie didn't put those sorts of things in her books. Although . . ."

"What?"

"Her husband's first name was Max. One of them, anyway."

"How did you learn so much about Agatha Christie?"

"Read a few of her books, ages ago." Temple eyed him seriously. "Do you know what I mean by an Agatha Christie moment?"

"You want to call all the suspects together."

"I dream big."

"And then finger a murderer."

"No, I'd be happy with just a little more insight."

"That's dreaming big?"

"A little insight that would point toward a murderer."

"Let me think." Max thought, rather as theatrically as Hamlet did.

He finally glanced at Temple with an expression both amused and promising a dramatic solution. "Do I look like someone who needs to shoot animals to you? A weekend game hunter?" Max's expression grew craven. "Moneyed, maybe."

" 'Moneyed' may be all we need to 'open sesame' at the Rancho Exotica," Temple agreed. "Okay. Here's the setup. You're a client. A Phoenix high roller. I want to impress you with the very special services the Phoenix has to offer." Temple made a face at the iffy ethics of her own scenario, nothing she'd do in a million years for real. "But why would I be there with Mr. High Roller?"

"Maybe you put a lot of yourself into your job."

"Hey! I'm no floozie. I'm a PR professional."

"You haven't had me for a client yet."

"Well, I guess if I can covet chain-mail bikinis from Macedonia Jones, I could pretend to be impressed with a client's special customer."

"Especially if he bought you a bauble from Fred Leighton's at the Bellagio."

She made another face, this one stronger. "I've heard PR people called corporate prostitutes before. I just never thought I'd be living up to the lowest level of the profession so soon. I don't think I need a bauble as a cover."

"No, but you're missing a ring." Max's expression was even more masked than usual. Temple couldn't tell if the emotion behind the mask was anger or sorrow, but it was something much darker than his deliberately whimsical tone. She wished he and Louie didn't share a certain catlike inscrutability. "I can provide another," Max said a trifle wistfully.

"You've given up on getting the other one back?" She found herself talking around a sudden lump in her throat, as if they were discussing replacing a dead pet.

"I never give up on getting anything back."

"Are you just talking about the opal ring? Or about me, or even your preundercover, fancy-free lifestyle?"

"How about all of the above?"

"You dream big."

He took her hand, her bare left hand. "I know nothing will replace the ring Shangri-La stole onstage at the Opium Den in front of God, Lieutenant Molina, and everybody. I promise you, I'll find her and I'll get it back."

"It's all right, Max. Really. Rings like that are only worth what they mean. You've got more important things to worry about."

His grip tightened. If she'd been wearing a ring, it would have pinched her finger. "No. I don't."

Who could look away from the Mystifying Max when he was being this intense, and this truthful? Not Temple.

She smiled around the lump that still hadn't gone away. "I know you don't, and I know you will. Get it all back." His grip eased as he smiled and gave her hand a small shake. "So, about the stage prop. From Fred Leighton's? Really?"

"Just as a cover, of course," Max amended, careful not to crowd her. But was it a cover for something more than the current charade? Was Max still insecure about her?

"I'd need a pretty convincing cover," Temple said airily, moving onto less serious ground. "And you'd have to look like a pretty convincing high roller."

"Absolutely."

"It's returnable, of course."

"Absolutely."

That was how Temple reentered the Van Burkleo household wearing a ten-carat vintage emerald ring surrounded by diamond baguettes. Temple always found it intriguing that bread—a slang term for money, like dough—also came in baguettes. French bread, of course. From Paris.

Even Leonora Van Burkleo's mascara-smudged, mourning eyes widened to do a quick mental computation.

"I'm so terribly sorry," Temple began.

It wasn't clear if she was apologizing for the ostentation of her ring or for an intrusion on a house of mourning.

Leonora Van Burkleo spread beringed, inarticulate hands.

It wasn't clear if she was acceding to or expressing the callous fact that the universe must go on. As the heart must go on. *Après le Titanic, le déluge, c'est commerce.*

"Mr. Maximilian"—Temple gazed moistly at her escort—"has

most-favored-nation status at the Crystal Phoenix. Perhaps you can guess why."

"I can indeed." Leonora prowled within scratching distance of Max, who was dressed more expensively, and thus more quietly, than ever. "I am sure we can offer him something worth . . . bagging."

"Actually," Max said, taking a hasty spin around the two-story hall with the long-horned antelope heads mounted high like once-living chandeliers, resembling a man casket hunting at a cut-rate funeral parlor, "I'm interested in buying the total operation."

"Really?" Leonora's lean, mean eyes paid tribute in exact turn to the Patek Philippe watch (no mere Rolex for Daddy Maxbucks), the Roman ring, the Zegna suit worn with . . . gasp! . . . a Gap turtleneck.

Where did he dig up these things? Temple wondered. Was there a Wardrobe Anonymous Warehouse somewhere for undercover operatives? The same place where rotating cars were stored? Someplace where it can be easily done. Perhaps out on Highway 375 near Area 51.

"My condolences," Max said with scintillating sincerity, taking Leonora's paw. Hand. The golden menagerie of charms on her wrist jingled like spurs. "Perhaps it's too soon to discuss business."

Leonora's long, lacquered nails curved possessively around his fingers. "Business?" she purred. And she did purr. Temple wondered if all her plastic surgeries had damaged her vocal cords somehow, had given her that contralto rumble. Or was it another affectation, like her new face?

Temple restrained a warning growl.

"I'm sorry, madame," Max continued, not sounding it at all, "to intrude at such a time, but an enterprise like this needs a guiding hand"—her lethal nails curled harder into his fingers—"or at least a front man with international connections." Max was suddenly all brisk business. "I'm in this country only a short while. I was interested in seeing the facilities, if you don't object."

"Not at all. But I'm afraid that the assets will be tied up for some time. Cyrus was not one to share his financial dealings."

Max reclaimed his hand and stuck them both in his blazer pockets as he strolled around the vast, southwestern-style entry area.

"Quite an impressive layout. I understand from . . . Miss Barr that you have an equally impressive, ah, head shop, so to speak, here also?"

"How quaintly you put it."

At that moment another woman entered the huge hall, moving more like its mistress than an employee.

Temple sensed Max's immediate interest as Courtney Fisher, as tall and tan as the girl from Ipanema, came swaying into their charmed circle.

"Is there anything your guests need, Leonora?" Courtney asked. "Refreshments? I've finished copying all the computer files."

Leonora lifted a languid wrist and opened her mouth to perform hostess duties, striking Temple as a trained animal warming up for a familiar act. She spared her the effort.

"I met Mr. Van Berkleo's assistant on my earlier visit. Maxi, this is Courtney Fisher."

"Charmed." Max took her hand, bowing so low over it in a European fashion that his face gazed at the vee of her maize linen suit and any presumable décolletage anyone so slender might be expected to have.

That's when Temple tumbled to the fact that Courtney probably *had* been a mistress here: Van Burkleo's.

Max had sensed it instantly, in the way the two women prowled at just too much social distance around each other, like nervous tigers in a too-small-for-territoriality cage.

"I don't care for anything, do you, darling?" Temple responded to the recent beverage offer.

Max hesitated just long enough to flatter both women. "No. We are here to see the animals."

"Then you must start here, which is, oddly enough, the ending point." Leonora's strangely immobile face managed the tiniest moue. "For the animals as well as poor Cyrus."

"You needn't show us." Max sounded amazingly sincere for someone who meant the opposite.

"It is nothing." Leonora's face grew smug. "Cyrus died among his beloved beasts. If he could still be here with them, I'm sure he would be. In fact, I'm having him cremated so he can remain with them. You would have no objection to agreeing to his eternal residence, Mr. Maximilian, if you purchase the ranch?"

"Ah . . . no. Of course not. Highly fitting."

Highly freaky, Temple thought.

She heard Courtney Fisher jingle away behind them as they moved toward the den, aka the scene of the crime.

Leonora also jangled and glided away, but toward the lair in which Temple had met Cyrus Van Burkleo. She still wore the colors of the Serengeti Plain. Her widow's sackcloth and ashes were spots and stripes. She resembled some Bob Mackie edition of a Camouflage Barbie doll, small golden trophies of animal likenesses surrounding her person like clanging temple bells.

Temple glanced at her new ring as she followed Max and Leonora into Van Burkleo's office. It had the opal ring from New York beat by about fifty thou, but she wished she had that one back.

She remembered how the friendly clerk at the estate jewelry shop had blinked not an eyelash when Max had whipped out cash to pay for the ring. "This is the fastest and flashiest way to establish credibility," he had whispered to Temple as they left with the ring on her finger. "Like it, darling?" he asked loudly on the threshold.

"Love it," Temple confessed, just as loudly, with smarm, as they swept into the concourse crowded with people.

And she did. Not the ring so much as feeling like she was starring in a Noël Coward play. She was much too short to star in a Noël Coward play.

But that was then. This was now. Now she was reduced to a supporting role in an Agatha Christie play, as the pampered wife took command of the handsome stranger, leaving the feisty ingenue in the wings with one hell of a winking emerald ring. Temple was beginning to feel like a traffic semaphore, giving the green light to other people's comings and goings.

She trailed the pair into the loathsome office, amusing herself by picturing Leonora's clumsy face and feral eyes in the place of the noble visages that actually occupied the walls.

Not one, she noticed, was a leopard. Was that why the leopard in question had been brought into the house? To be stalked on its owner's own home ground? She wouldn't put anything past people who made a living from dead animals.

Anyone that could tolerate old, confused and semidomesticated animals to be gunned down from a few feet away by men who had paid ten or twenty thousand dollars a head for the privilege . . . well, such a person deserved to be represented for eternity by a headstone.

She had not seen the animal-rights protesters, so she couldn't gauge their ability to kill in defense of taking life. She'd think not, but on the other hand, nothing enraged her as much as the deliberate death of the helpless: a child, a prisoner, an animal.

If someone threatened Midnight Louie in her sight . . . although it was usually the other way around: someone threatened her in Midnight Louie's sight, and on a couple of occasions he had taken most effective action for a house cat.

Her imagination had sometimes magnified Midnight Louie to big-cat size and pictured him patrolling her fifteen-hundred-square-foot domain at the Circle Ritz, trolling for prey.

Eight hundred pounds of snarling feline fury.

Somehow she never imagined him snoozing on his back with all four paws splayed to the four corners of the room like the king of the beasts on his African savanna. Well, to the four corners of the earth. Actually, given the round shape of the Circle Ritz and the globe, none of that four corners stuff made sense. Who came up with those figures of speech? Mapmakers? A pope before Galileo, or long after him?

Galileo. Leo. How the English pronounced the name Leo in a Noël Coward play. Lay-oh. As in Lay-oh-nar-do Dee-Creep-io. Odd how many "leos" there were in this case. The leopard itself. Leonora. Leo the lion on Van Burk*leo*'s wall. Next thing she knew *Leo*ntyne Price would show up as a suspect. Or No*ël* (Leon *backward*!) Coward himself. No, he was dead.

All they needed now was a suspect named Ole, but that was a name you only ran into in Minnesota. . . .

"Temple," Max said for what sounded like the third time from the emphasis he put on it.

"Yes?" She had been mentally leo-gathering, she admitted to herself. Maybe because a female was always superfluous around Leonora, the prototypical predatory woman.

"Would you like to see the outdoor facilities? Leonora has kindly offered to guide us. And your emerald could use some fresh air."

Any daydream to avoid facing the nightmare of dead animal heads on walls.

"Of course," she said, waving her ring-bearing hand in a very Noël Coward leading-actress way.

Max came to take proprietary possession of the ring. Of her hand, that is, and they both beamed with nauseating expectancy at Leonora.

"I really don't know why you'd care to take on a game operation in Las Vegas, Mr. Maximilian. It's a low-profile enterprise, best suited to those with a passion for wildlife."

"Oh, Maxi has a passion for wildlife," Temple said, linking her arm possessively through his, "although he has a quite subtle dislike of the obvious."

The woman's leonine face lifted at the muzzle—upper lip to those used to human anatomy—at Temple's implication. Temple thought she spied a sprinkling of hairs on that strangely elongated upper lip. At the least Leonora needed a good waxer, if not a wax museum.

"The grounds," Leonora added, eyeing Temple's strappy high-heeled sandals, "might be hard on those shoes."

She herself wore sporty, cork-soled wedgies with enough rope ties to form a slingshot.

"These shoes," Temple said stoutly, "are usually harder on the ground than vice versa." She turned an ankle to display a claw-sharp spike.

"Ladies," Max intervened. "I doubt that the animals will care much about footwear."

"Unless they're in need of something old and smelly to chew on," Leonora added with a pointed look at Temple's feet.

She clattered out of the room ahead of them and led them via a long, circuitous route to the house's huge institutional kitchen and finally out to the yard that faced into the foothills.

At first one saw only the pool and waterfall, the plantings and rock gardens.

As they walked farther, the desert reasserted itself, and the vast acres of land alongside the house grew apparent.

Although it was still spring in Las Vegas, there was no shade on the desert, only a sense of the sun warming every stone and grain of sand, creating a tanning-booth intensity of light.

Despite her redhead's pale, freckle-prone skin, Temple could understand why cats basked.

No cats lounged amid the sand and scrub, though.

A long, low structure proved to be a suite of barred cages, like those you see in a circus, under a common roof, accessed by a security-number pad that opened a sliding metal gate. Behind the cage bars within lay, sat, slept, and paced an assortment of big cats.

A smell of sun-warmed fur, dung, and raw meat radiated from the area. The concrete surrounding the cages was streaked with rivulets of water that trickled into the ground-level cages themselves.

Temple was offended by these mean, utilitarian living conditions for the huge creatures, especially after passing through the luxurious house. No wonder Letty the Leopard had wanted in. Or Lennie.

"It's not a zoo," Leonora said as if reading Temple's mind. Or face. "It's an animal compound. None of them stay here that long. We have quite a demand."

"All hunters?" Max asked.

She turned quickly, as if liking the question.

"Many. But we resell a few to those requiring exotic animals for business, or pleasure."

"They don't look old." Max had wandered up to a cage holding a black leopard, better known as a panther.

"Some are mere zoo excess," Leonora said, watching him like a cat.

The panther came to rub against the bars, stopping to sniff Max's hand.

He uncurled the fingers slowly, like a petal opening. The huge cat pushed its blunt face forward as if to brush against the palm.

"Be careful!" Leonora spoke sharply, her voice a rasp of caution and shock.

Max was concentrating on the cat, not moving.

The two stood there for a few moments, as if communicating in a silent language.

Then the big cat moved on, began pacing against the opposite set of bars.

"Do you know where all your animals come from?" Max asked.

"No. Don't looked surprised. We have suppliers. Sometimes it's best not to know too much."

Max moved on to an empty cage. "It's always best not to know too much. Is this the cage that the . . . rogue leopard occupied?"

She came to stand beside Max. From the rear her artfully teased and streaked long hair looked amazingly like a mane.

Her voice was gruff. "Yes."

"Any idea how the leopard got out, got into the house? Someone had to know the keypad number sequence."

A silence.

Temple, ignored (and glad that Max and not she was the focus of this strange woman) studied Leonora's body language as she answered.

Her posture shifted from the weight on one leg and hip, like a model, to an equal-weight stance, like a pugilist. Her shoulders lowered and squared. The mane brushing the tiger-print silk blouse twitched, ever so slightly, like a tail.

Leonora Van Burkleo was not pleased with questions about the how-tos of her husband's death.

"How did the leopard get out?" she answered the query with another question. "It did not let itself out. Someone had to have released it, admitted it into the house."

"How is that possible?" Max continued, ignoring her mad-cat signals. He was the same way with Louie. "Even if you knew the code, how would you handle the loose leopard? Granted, you get semi-domesticated animals here, but they don't just trot after people like a dog, into houses. Was it confined and then released inside, do you think? Was it led along, on a leash? Was it a particularly domesticated cat?"

"I don't know! We never ask these things. They're not here that long anyway, and if the exotic-pet fanciers don't select them quickly, we pass them along to the hunt staff." She paused, shifted her weight back to one leg, leaned inward to Max.

"A leopard is not a particularly large big cat. The hunters prefer lions and tigers."

Max lifted his hands, framed the pacing panther in them like a film director planning a shot. He nodded. "Big is everything these days. Could your husband have let the animal into the house?"

Leonora's weight dropped back to both feet, her knees sagging.

"Cyrus? But why? He'd never done such a thing before. These animals are . . . doomed, most of them. Cyrus was not a sentimental man, but he knew better than to personalize any of the creatures. And you're suggesting he would 'let' one in, like a dog? Why?"

"I merely offer suppositions," Max said. "The vague circumstance of his death might leave a taint about the place. You know, the ranch where the hunters become the hunted. Not too popular a concept with flabby weekend warriors looking for wall candy. But I agree. I see no reason that your husband would let a big cat into the house like a dog. Unless, of course, it behaved like a dog."

At that she laughed, and took his arm.

"Believe me, Mr. Maximilian. Nothing behaves less like a dog than a big cat, no matter how many zoo habitats it has lounged in, or how many backyard cages it has languished in. A cat is wild, through and through. No one owns one. No one tells it where to go or what to do."

"You're right," Max agreed, turning to Temple at last. "Want to see the hunting grounds next, darling?"

"Dying to," Temple responded with feeling.

And she knew just what kind of mythical beast she'd like to hunt there. Catwoman.

The Jeep jolted back to the cage area. Temple supposed that was part of the Rancho Exotica "experience." A sense of "roughing it" in everything—desert landscape, rugged ride over rough terrain, emptiness, and then sniping at some confused, fenced-in animal until it was cornered and could be killed by a blind man.

Temple, who sat up front with the taciturn driver, tried to relax her jaws but they remain clenched.

It didn't help that she was covered in dust from eyelash to ankle, and that some muscular guy in safari-suit khaki was advancing to help her out of the high-seated Jeep Laredo like a great white hunter dealing with the client's spoiled daughter. Even her emerald-and-diamond ring was clouded.

It also didn't help that she sensed a cloud of cold fury enveloping Max behind her as the GWH took hold of her waist and lifted her down to the ground.

"Thank you," Temple muttered into her assistant's dark and brooding face.

This was beginning to feel like *Mogambo*. From Noël Coward to Clark Cable and Ava Gardner. That's what you got from watching too many old movies.

She turned quickly to reassure Max with a look and discovered that it wasn't fury he was radiating but fear. It was a fleeting expression, but Temple was stunned to find Max visibly anxious.

She turned to study her unasked-for escort.

"One of our security guards," Leonora said. "His name is Rafi."

Temple nodded at Rafi—odd name—and was about to introduce herself when Max interjected himself into the scenario like a leading man treading on the lines of an extra who had stepped out of place.

"Call me Maximilian." He stepped in front of Temple. "Terrific layout. I'd really like to discuss it with you from a security viewpoint."

"Rafi is a new hire," Leonora began.

"Excellent. A fresh point of view is what I want. Care to stroll around the grounds for a moment, if you can spare one?"

Rafi, a sullen type who was immediately suspicious of Max's enthusiasm, glanced carefully at Leonora.

She shrugged. "Mr. Maximilian is interested in buying the property."

"You'd sell?" the security man asked incredulously.

Rafi seemed a bit belligerent for a hired gun, Temple thought. And Leonora's feline face took on an edgy, guilty look that surprised her.

"Don't worry, my man," Max said quickly. "I'd keep on the staff. That's all right, isn't it, Mrs. Van Berkleo?"

"Of course. If they want to stay. You may want to hire Miss Barr away from the Crystal Phoenix, if you require an assistant," she added cattily.

"What about—?" Temple began.

"Courtney has decided to leave for greener pastures," Leonora said demurely. That blunt face did not do demure well.

Max's attention had wandered, as if bored by discussion of people when a miniempire was before him. He gave the man called Rafi a man-to-man grin.

"Now, about those peripheral fences. Barbed wire? Do you really think they'd keep out interlopers?"

"What kind of interlopers?" Leonora demanded, overriding Rafi's answer.

Max looked startled. "Every enterprise has its enemies. What about . . . say, those ethical-treatment-of-animals people. Vegetarians. You know what I mean," he directed toward the security man.

He was walking Rafi away from the two women, off into the bush, so to speak.

"Quite . . . commanding," Leonora commented.

Temple wasn't sure which man she was referring to: Rafi, who had hauled Temple out of the Jeep like a delinquent twelve-year-old, or Max who had commandeered the security man like he was recruiting for the IRA.

"Yes." Temple joined her hostess in looking after them. "Do you have enemies? It might explain your husband's death."

"You mean—?" Leonora examined Temple carefully, as if seeing her for the first time. Perhaps she was. This was the sole occasion that the distraction of men wasn't around, and Leonora seemed to concentrate solely on men. Temple wasn't sure if it was because she was one of those dependent yet manipulative women who loved to coax things out of men (she was still covertly eyeing Temple's ring every ninety seconds or so), or because she watched them in a purely predatory sense.

One interpretation made her a greedy widow. The other made her a greedy murderess.

Murderess, the old-fashioned form, seemed to fit her to a T-shirt. Animal patterned, of course.

"What did you think of this Rafi character?" Max asked as they drove away.

"Calling him a 'Rafi character' predisposes me to not think much of him. Also your hauling him away like he had the plague."

Max had recovered his equanimity and grinned at her as the car bucked over the rutted desert road. "I'll rephrase that. What did you think of that guy?"

"I thought of him as the great white hunter from a forties movie."

"Central Casting is you. So what does that mean?"

Temple had to interpret her own reaction. "He's one of those apparently smug men in what should be the prime of his life who's seen it all go sour and is living out on the fringes, recapturing his virility by controlling the uncontrollable. How's that?"

"Awesome." Max spoke seriously. "Villain or victim?"

"How about a little bit of both?"

"Dangerous or posing at it?"

"Potential or pose, they're both dangerous, aren't they? I didn't need as much help dismounting the Jeep as I got. There's a kind of contempt for women that poses as gallantry."

Max nodded. The dusty drive in the open car had ground sand

into the fine lines radiating from his eyes, giving him a steely, early-Clint look Temple hadn't seen before. But then she hadn't seen Max in any but an urban environment.

He seemed to get grittier in the desert: more suspicious, like someone out of his element. Temple had never seen Max out of his element before.

"Why are you so interested in the Rafi character?" she asked. "Leonora said he's a new hire. I doubt he could be involved in the death."

Max's hands tightened on the steering wheel, for no particular reason.

"That's what we came out here for, to study the scene for suspects. Maybe he was hired to move a leopard indoors. Did you notice something odd about the empty leopard cage?"

"It had been washed down today."

"Right. The leopard's been gone for three days. Looks like somebody wants to make doubly sure there's no trace evidence."

"Of what?"

"Of whatever happened that moved a leopard from a cage outside into a living room."

As the car jolted off the private road onto the highway, Temple immediately noticed that Max turned north, not south.

"Where are we going now?"

"To visit the only Ranch Exotica suspect we haven't interviewed."

"Suspect, singular? Aren't you forgetting the animal-rights activists? I haven't seen hide nor hair of them, excuse the expression, under the circumstances."

"No need. I've kept pretty good tabs on them."

"Oh. So I get to see the indoor suspects and you get an exclusive on the outdoor suspects. Smacks of great white hunter, if you ask me."

"I can't think of a good excuse to introduce you to the activists, who are a paranoid lot at best. But this last suspect is an outdoor/indoor variety, and there's already a precedent for you paying a visit there."

"So who is it?"

"The leopard, of course."

Chapter 35

Tiger Paws

The sun comes up like a Pop-Tart, sudden and sweet and hot.

It smacks our trio of hikers in the rear like a Jedi light-sword. We leap forward, knowing that the gentle cloak of night is lifting from the sand and that soon every grain will be burning into our tender, sore pads.

The Yorkshire constabulary have their twin noses glued to that very sand, lifting them only at the usual patches of cacti.

"Are you sure," I ask again. Panting. Still. "Are you sure you are following the same scent trail that you found in the leopard's ex-cage at Rancho Exotica?"

They lift heads and once-shiny black noses, now desert-dried to matte black. Their high, squeaky voices are almost inaudible from thirst, but they are still game.

"Yes, Mr. Midnight," says one, nodding until the wilted satin bow on its head is a blur.

"Yes, sir!" says the other. "We follow the man-steps, as always."

"That is interesting." I pause to sit under a spreading, er, Joshua tree, which, frankly, offers about as much shade as an upright crochet needle. "You have been telling me all night that a human has walked into the Rancho Exotica, and out, without benefit of wheels. Most unusual. We must have trekked for miles."

The silver-gray heads nod, less vigorously than usual. "Indeed, honored *Capitan*," says Golda with a sharp salute.

(I have encouraged the pair to adopt a French Foreign Legion approach to rank and discipline on this trek, that being the only desert model I am familiar with. I have never failed to watch old black-and-white reruns of '50s TV's *Captain Gallant of the Foreign Legion*. When it comes to situational etiquette, I would be lost without reruns.)

"*Mon Capitan*," I correct her sharply.

I claw my way up a small dune to survey the terrain ahead of us. More sand, sweat, and tears. Luckily, neither of our breeds sweats or cries, although we certainly can suffer.

"I see civilization ahead," I announce, farsighted leader that I am.

The Yorkies pitter-patter up the dune, pocking sand with birdlike tracks as they go. I am not sure that they are not really a species of kangaroo rats, so well have they adapted to desert warfare.

Their desiccated noses scent the arid air, still effective despite the lack of lubrication.

"The prey awaits ahead, *mon Capitan*," Groucho announces in a sandpapered voice.

"Good," croak I. "And water?"

"Nothing near," Golda says with a forlorn headshake. "I could use a bath and an air-dry and a comb-out in the worst way."

"Be of good cheer," I counsel the troops. "Once we return to civilization you can return to all the comforts of home."

I am lying through my dehydrated teeth, of course. It is called keeping up morale.

We resume our course, the Yorkies in the lead, noses to ground unless an impoliticly placed cactus has caused a deviation.

The morning shadows have shortened like clock hands before we are within sight of the distant buildings.

We pause to pant again, aware that water must await in the oasis before us.

I so tell the troops. "Water must await in the oasis before us."

"It is an oasis, all right," Golda agrees, sitting on her tiny haunches with her forelegs in the air, sniffing. "An animal oasis."

"What gives you that idea? Your overeducated nose?"

She shakes her bow in a southeasterly direction. "The sign says so."

I blink and look.

Indeed.

The little bowhead still has sharp eyesight as well as nostril power. A huge sign sits near a gravel road, and it reads "Animal Oasis."

"Another hunt club?" I wonder aloud.

Groucho sniffs the wind. "I smell lions and tigers and bears. And antelope, deer, and rams."

I shake the sand out of my claws for the umpteenth time, and point to the sign. "Furward!"

In no time flat, or flat-footed, we are slinking around the smells and signs of civilization again.

The diminutive dogs are sniffing circles, confused by the profusion of animal life, and the overwhelming scent of fresh water.

I give up and let them lead us to the water bowls first.

In minutes our three lips and tongues are plunged nostril-deep in an ample pond of fresh water.

In only another minute, we sense a large engulfing cloud that has shadowed our private pond. I look up.

Amazing how clouds will take on the shape of earthly beings. I could swear the Lion King himself is looming over us. Oh.

"Hello, *Mon Majesté*." I salute. "We are weary travelers from afar and athirst, seeking succor at your royal claws. Er, paws."

Leo lays himself down, almost crushing the Yorkshire constabulary. They yip and dance away, their whiskers dripping purloined water.

Leo yawns, displaying a feline Himalayas of dental peaks. "Are these sand fleas?" he asks me.

"Compared to Your Royalness, yes."

"And you are—?"

"The name is Louie. Midnight Louie. I am an investigator out of Vegas."

Leo laps lazily at the pond that has been our salvation, almost licking up the Yorkies in the backwash.

"What can I do for you?" the lion asks politely.

Well. The Yorkies flutter to my side while I sit down, wring my whiskers free of excess water and make my presentation.

"We are on the trail of a dude who has something to do with the murder at the hunt club over yonder."

"Hunt club?" Leo looks cross-eyed at a fly on his majestic nose, frowns, and swats it to Kingdome come. His flyswatter is the size of a pizza pan.

I decide right then and there not to tell him too many of the nefarious goings-on next door, so to speak. Might agitate the local wildlife.

"Murder?" Leo repeats again, yawning while the dislodged fly darts into his maw by mistake. "What is murder?"

I forget that these big guys, however domesticated, are serious predators without my fine-tuned and human-oriented sense of right and wrong. Leo would probably consider a dead big-game hunter a case of anything but murder.

"A human was killed and no one can tell who or what did it."

Leo nods sagaciously. How could one not look sagacious with a head that big, wearing a wig reminiscent of an English judge with a blond dye job?

"You hunt the hunter," he says.

We nod agreement for once.

"You are a little small for the job," Leo notes.

I shrug. I refrain from pointing out that I am big enough to get by without needing an "Animal Oasis."

Groucho is emboldened to squeak. "We are looking for a feline party, name of Osiris."

"Oh, the little guy." Leo nods again. With his head of flowing blond hair, he reminds me of a somber Fabio, the romance-novel cover dude. "I wondered why he was set apart. He does not look like a man-eater, but then it does not always show, does it?"

We nod. Truer words were never growled.

"I have never seen a man-eater," Leo goes on, grooming a foreleg the size and shape of Florida. "I begin to think it is a mythical beast. I do not like stringy limbs and haunches myself, and I have not had to fend for myself, so cannot say much about this type."

"Well," I say, glancing at the pond, "thanks for the drink. We will mosey on down the line and have a chat with Osiris in person."

"Be my guest." Leo yawns and rolls over on his back, all four paws in the air.

The Yorkies have had to move briskly to avoid becoming mini–bath mats. Talk about a matting problem!

"That was a waste of time," Groucho growls as we mush on through the sand like the Three Musketeers.

"Not at all," I say. "We have checked in with the head honcho. That never hurts. That smell still doing it for you, Golda?"

"Oh, yes, *mon Capitan!*" She responds to authority as well as any individual of this feisty breed can. "In fact, I see a leopard pattern dead ahead, and the scent trail leads directly to his compound."

Osiris is lounging in the shade of some sort of imported plant, digging his claws into a huge felt toy of some kind.

We sneak around to the rear of his area, where more imported greenery shades us as well.

When he spots me, his long, lean, measle-spotted body leaps up and bounds to the fence.

We shrink back, but it seems that Osiris is as happy as a hound dog to see us. Or rather, me.

His huge pink tongue laves the airy fence wires, missing my puss by only about three inches as I jump back as fast as he leaped forward. Nobody washes Midnight Louie's face since I left my mama's supervision.

"Thank you!" Osiris purrs, rubbing his decorator-approved side back and forth on the wires separating me and the tiny duo from his hyperactive four hundred pounds.

"For what?" I naturally ask.

"Lunch!" He pauses to regard the Yorkshire constabulary.

They rush in where pit bulls would fear to tread, hurling themselves yapping against the fence and incidentally a good portion of the pacing Osiris.

"Idiot feline!" they screech. "We are highly trained tracking animals here to clear you of a murder one charge." They bounce off the wires and lunge forward again, rather like attacking Ping-Pong balls with very long fungus.

Osiris backs off, blinking, and sits on his lean haunches. He still looks like he could use some lunch, but I see that his idea of edibles is not the Yorkies.

"I meant," he says, lying down to wash his face and much resembling a faux leopardskin rug. "Thanks for lunch the other day, at the other place. The two-legs had given me nothing for several dark-times and I was almost ready to eat the mats between my toes, which you two in some ways resemble, no offense."

He is eyeing the Yorkies askance, which is the only way to regard such an uppity breed of sand-hugging dog.

I realize with chagrin that the big rug has mistaken me for Midnight Louise.

Much as I like to take any undeserved credit I can, I cannot let this notion go unchallenged, so explain that his benefactor was a friend of mine, not me.

"Ah." Osiris nods sagely while cleaning behind his cauliflower ear. (The big boys have these round, blunt ears that look as if they had been in the ring for years, not the svelte, pointed numbers we smaller cats do.) "I did detect a whiff of female that is distinctly lacking now." He gazes benignly on the Yorkies. "And are these your and the lovely little black Miss's cubs?"

I do not know whether I am more insulted to be taken for sharing the state of parenthood with Midnight Louise, or to be mistaken for contributing to the production of the Yorkie twins.

"No relation. Despite appearances, these are dogs."

"I am not familiar with the breed," Osiris admits.

Imagine that! What a sheltered upbringing. "Now that we know who's who we need to find out what's what," I go on. "Meanwhile"—I turn to Golda and Groucho—"you two track down the human scent you have been following. I want to know who from here hiked all the way out there and back again."

They scamper off, happy to be of use, I suppose (dogs are like that) and happier to be away from Osiris's big white teeth.

I settle down, my mitts tucked under me for a long summer's siesta.

In no time Osiris is pouring out his life story. Now it is my turn to yawn. Basically, he has had a pretty soft time of it until now. He was born into a performing family, but separated at an early age by an animal trainer. He did some commercial film work—we chat about the ups and downs of that profession—and caught the attention of his recent master thanks to an ad for spandex animal-print pants from something called "The Yap."

"I would stretch like this"—Osiris curves himself into a long, lean arc—"and they would superimpose an image of Cindy Crawford stretching in her leopardskin-print capri pants. I got a lot of fan mail from that one, but not as much as Cindy Crawford."

"Yeah, the humans hog the limelight. Did it not bother you to advertise a product based on your hide, so to speak?"

"No, we are all protected now, and a guy has to make a living somehow. I figure if the humans are happy with faux, we are all better off for it. Besides, Cindy Crawford gets asked that all the time too."

"About making a living from selling her hide?"

"Right. Some of us are just too beautiful to hide our light under a barrel."

"That's basket."

"Whatever."

"So how did you get out to the Rancho Exotica?"

"The what?"

"That is where the head human was killed. You know, the guy you were found dancing the cha-cha with, only he was dead?"

"Oh, him. I thought he was a stuffed decorator item. The place was filled with the kind of props I was used to seeing on a film set. Also, inside the new boss's house. He is a good guy. He lets me indoors, which is why I was not completely lost when I woke up inside that place, although all the shapes and scents were new, and I did stumble around for a while, which is when I accidently sharpened my nails on the . . . on the—"

"Corpus delicti is what we call it in my trade. If Burkleo was already dead. Was he?"

"Oh, yes. Had a nasty smell about him already. I was quite upset I had mistaken him for a scratching post at first. But I was not quite myself from the stinging fly."

"Tranquilizer dart," I explained.

"Tranquilizer?"

"It puts you to sleep so the humans can move you without damaging you . . . or them. Surely they used such a device on you before."

"No. I am trained. It is not necessary."

"So. You would have been pretty unhappy to be ripped untimely from your new position with the Cloaked Conjurer?"

"My new boss, you mean. He was not my trainer, but he would visit to play and pet and feed."

"And you were happy with him?"

"Oh, yes. He is a strange human. He has a face like mine in some ways, and a deep, buzzing, purring voice. I have never had such an agreeable boss."

"So you want to go back to him?"

"Of course. I have not finished my training."

"And you do not think he had anything to do with your abduction?"

"Why should he?"

I say one word, that even a naive leopard like Osiris can understand. "Publicity."

He rubs his big blunt nose on a forepaw. "My new boss has too much publicity. I figure he likes to avoid it. He seems a bit litter-lonely. He would come out after dark and talk to me, as if we were the same breed. Performers, he said, are prisoners of the public. I had not thought of it that way. He said I was a good listener."

Well, yeah. Like who can talk back?

Still, I do not wish to get between a boy and his human, so I only grunt what can be taken for agreement, then I restate the case:

"You were darted, woke up in a cage at Rancho Exotica, were watered but not fed for several days. Then you were darted again and woke up in the ranch house, alone except for what turned out to be the corpse of Cyrus Van Burkleo. You bumbled around, sharpened your claws on some handy portions of Burkleo's body, then panicked and ran through the house, overturning furniture. Who caught you?"

Osiris frowns, an expression that lends a leonine dignity to his already formidable presence.

"I am not sure. I remember rushing outside somehow. Butch was awake and pacing in his cage. Our eyes met. Then . . . I cannot remember."

"Someone must have caged you again, so the animal control people could handle you."

"I am not difficult to handle," Osiris says a bit huffily. "I am trained."

"Exactly my point. And perhaps you were being trained for the role of murderer."

"What do you mean?"

The Big Cats may be bigger but they are not always brighter.

"I mean that you were not fed for a reason. And your claws were allowed to grow for the same reason. Had not one of my ilk illegally obtained a forbidden snack for you from one of the other cages, and you had been released in the house ravenous and reverted to your savage state, you might well have mauled Cyrus Van Burkleo beyond all recognition—and destroyed the evidence of human battering, instead of merely puncturing him a bit."

"They were 'training' me to kill him?"

"They were training you to look like you had killed him, only it backfired."

"This is terrible! My professional reputation would have been ruined. My reliability is all I have."

"Your professional reliability would have been moot. If you had been found with bloody claws over a mutilated human body, you would be dead by now. As it is, you rest under a cloud."

"You mean I am still suspected of being a rogue animal?"

"And the people who set this up might want you permanently off the planet."

Osiris's yellow eyes gleam with the light of recognizing danger. His claws flex. "Who must I watch out for?"

"It could be anyone, and the best service you can do yourself is forget that I told you someone might want to kill you. If you jump the gun and attack an innocent Oasis worker, your career and your life are down the drain."

"So I must wait to be attacked?"

"I am afraid so. Frankly, my dear Osiris, it is nothing different from what would have happened to you at Rancho Exotica if they had sold your hide to one of their weekend hunters."

Chapter 36

Synth You Went Away . . .

Temple tried to imagine Midnight Louie covered in spots, leopard spots.

Then she looked again at the real leopard.

No, a domestic cat was not just a big cat. The leopard's head was smaller in proportion to its long, lithe body. (Long was a suitable adjective for Louie, but lithe was not.)

Its ears were smaller and rounder than a house cat's.

And its face was heavier and blunter.

It so much reminded her of Leonora Van Burkleo's surgically altered features that Temple would never be able to look at another big cat without thinking of that strange woman.

The leopard was contentedly gnawing a piece of raw meat, which Temple chose to regard as a vague blur of some unknown species.

"He was hungry," Kirby Grange commented. "Those damn people didn't feed him properly."

Max nodded, staring at the leopard as he had stared at the panther.

It finally rose, stretched, and came toward the fencing to view its three visitors.

No cages at the Animal Oasis, but outdoor areas set up for each animal.

Max put his hand to the fence. The leopard came over. Max unfolded his fingers, as if producing an invisible illusion. The leopard nudged its huge blunt nose into his palm.

Temple winced.

"He's been trained," Max said.

Grange shrugged and folded hairy forearms over his formidable beer belly. "A lot of the big cats that damned ranch gets are ex–roadside attractions, ex–circus animals, ex–zoo exhibitions, ex-pets. I knew what they were up to, but I didn't figure on 'em abusing the animals before they sent them out to be killed."

"Would hungry animals show more spirit during the hunt?" Temple wondered.

Grange's sharp look softened with pity for her amazing ignorance as he considered her question. "They don't need the animals to show what you call 'spirit.' The poor-spirited trophy collectors who come out to shoot them don't need any illusions. Just herd 'em out there where they can't hurt the shooter, but close enough to take a few bullets or arrows in the body and die sooner or later. More often later. Then hand the proud hunters the head and hide in a salt-packed box and ship 'em to wherever for immortality on the home or office wall. If every person in America who saw a mounted animal head in someone's place said, "Oh, are you one of those yellow-bellied canned hunters?" it might take the fun out of it and they wouldn't come back for more and drop their ten or thirty grand for one less of an endangered species. 'Course, I don't hold with shooting unendangered species like that either."

"There are," Max said contemplatively, still engaged in his odd eye contact with the leopard, "legitimate hunters."

"No, Max, there are not." Granger's voice was as firm as three-day-old concrete. "There are hunters who get licenses and hunt in season and who follow strict codes of ethics, like not endangering other hunters and fair chase and all that. And I still have no time for them. Nature's hard enough on wildlife as it is, why does humanity have to persecute it with all our high technology, especially now when we don't need that to survive?"

"Bow hunters aren't high tech," Max pointed out.

"No. And they're the worst of all, because they can maul and wound worse than any rifleman. Caveman mentality." He spat into the dust five feet away, startling a dirt-colored lizard into running to escape the acid rain.

"So," said Temple, "if you know about the ranch and what goes on there, why can't it be stopped?"

"Proof. Pull. Nobody wanting to stir up controversy."

"At least we got this guy out," she said, nodding at the leopard.

"At least he laid a claw on that Van Burkleo guy, but I don't believe he did more than paw at the body. I doubt I could keep myself from stopping there, and I'm a civilized human." Granger laughed bitterly. "As long as he's kept secure here, and they can't blame him directly for the death, they can't order him killed."

"They'd execute a leopard?"

"Yes, Miss Barr. When a wild animal we higher beings have under lock and key acts like it's supposed to, we kill it because we say it's become 'unreliable.' Even if it's just suspected of harming a human."

"Some people will never change their spots, Kirby," Max said wryly. "You know anything about those protesters that were out on the ranch land before Van Burkleo died?"

Granger shifted from booted foot to foot. "Might," he said.

"They were after more than disrupting a hunt or two, weren't they? Photos?"

"Yeah, maybe. But Van Burkleo had a big enough security force to keep anyone too far away to get evidence. You'd think the place was Area Fifty-one."

"You could have asked me," Max said. "I would have been able to get some photographic evidence."

"You're a magician, Max. Or were. When are you going to amaze the town again, anyway?"

Max waved his hands, dismissing the question of his future.

The leopard's muzzle and ears lifted at the gesture. It stalked over to the fence edge to confront Max again.

Temple was startled to hear the sound of a faint but large lawnmower.

The leopard was purring. He liked Max.

Midnight Louie he was not.

But then again, Max wasn't sleeping in the leopard's bed.

Max stroked the huge head as it rubbed by.

Granger opened his mouth in warning, but said nothing.

"I can get photos," Max said. "Just let me know when a hunt's planned."

"I don't know that stuff. I jest hear about it from the animal-rights folks after it's over. 'Sides, where can a fellah reach the Magnifying Max these days anyway?"

Max smiled. "The Mystifying Max. That is a problem. Temple can give you her card."

Granger suddenly relaxed into his usual good-ole-boy charm. "You sure you want to take that risk, partner? I might be tempted to call her number jest to hear that nice growly little voice of hers. Sounds like a tiger cub."

Temple cleared her throat and presented a card.

"Acts like it sometimes too," Max said. "So I wouldn't bother her unnecessarily."

"You're jest like that leopard there, Max. Territorial."

Max shrugged this time. "Only way to be, in this wicked world."

"Well, this here's my territory." Granger squinted into the monotonous distance. "And no animal that gets here gets hurt. Unless it's a man with a gun."

As they drove away, Temple shook her feet out of the sandals and planted her bare soles on the car's cool carpeting.

"*Ummm.* I've inhaled enough dust today to pass for an air cleaner. What is it with you and that panther and leopard? This is the man Midnight Louie won't honor with a passing glance, and you practically have leopards and panthers eating out of your bare hand. What are you, Dr. Dolittle?"

"No trick. They've both been trained to work with humans."

"Both?"

Max glanced at her just before he was occupied with turning onto the highway and merging with traffic.

"Both. That's what I found so interesting.

"Wait a minute! *This* is the Cloaked Conjuror's leopard, but you said the Synth may have kidnapped it."

"May have."

"And then . . . sold it to the hunting ranch? Why?"

"The Synth is angry with the Cloaked Conjuror. I wondered why he hadn't gotten a ransom demand. Obviously, the leopard was worth a lot to him, professionally. And you don't work with an animal without getting attached to it. I wonder if, after it had been killed, he would have been sent the head."

Temple made a noise of revulsion. "Why didn't you just tell Mr. Granger who the leopard belongs to and get him home?"

"For one thing, I don't want to alert whoever abducted the leopard that anyone knows where it is. That might be dangerous for the leopard. For another, Kirby has become less liberal since the days when he provided my cockatoos. He no longer approves of performing animals, no matter how well they're cared for."

"What about Siegfried and Roy and their breeding program for rare white tigers?"

"I don't know. Kirby's more of a hard-liner now than when I worked with him before."

"Maybe having a canned-hunt club for a neighbor has something to do with it."

Max nodded, looking abstracted.

Temple amused herself by trying to dust off her diamonds using the soft inside of her knit top.

"You can take custody of this," she said after a minute.

"You don't like masquerading as the rich and famous?"

"And as the mugged? I don't think so. Did you see how Leonora couldn't take her eyes off of it? And that Rafi guy, when he first spotted it, the look he had."

"What?"

"Angry. And hungry."

"Interesting. What did you think of him?"

"I already told you."

"As a woman."

"As a woman. You mean if I met him in a singles club, which I wouldn't because I don't go there."

"Glad to hear it."

Temple thought back. "He must be forty . . ."

"Age is the first thing you notice about a man?"

"That's the problem. I really wouldn't have noticed him if you weren't asking me to make observations. He's one of those older guys—"

"Older? At forty. Remind me to not have any birthdays for the next few years."

"He seems more like fifty, really. I get a sense he's been through the mill, that he's down and out and has been for a long time, but he used to be something once. There's an air of authority. Granted, it comes out as arrogance, but there's something unconscious about it. Oh, and my opinion as a woman, by which I assume you mean how sexy I find him: I don't, because I'm not looking for sexy, at least not outside the neighborhood, but he has a certain appeal in a noir kind of way. He's pretty good-looking, or would be if he didn't look so dissolute. You think he and Leonora have a thing going?"

"Now, that's an idea. Husband dies, he shows up."

"Now I get to ask you what you thought of Leonora."

"Why? Tit for tat?"

"I've seen her before and you haven't."

"Something to see, all right. What would possess a normal woman to systemically rearrange her face into something out of *Cats!*?"

"Fashion, I suppose. And a weird kind of tribute to her husband's business? But what did you think of her, as a man?"

"She comes across as sexually predatory, but I sense no heart in it. It's automatic. If anything, I'd suspect she's frigid."

"That eliminates a hot affair with Rafi."

"She might be able to fake it to get what she wants."

"Which is . . . was . . . hubby dead?"

"I charged in there like the Ugly American in Tunisia, ready to buy the place up from the get-go. And she was perfectly willing to entertain my offer. He's dead. She sells, takes the money, and runs before the authorities close the whole shebang down."

After a pause, Max glanced at Temple. "How do you read the perfect secretary?"

"Courtney? Oddly like Leonora. I mean, wearing all that gold big-game jewelry—They could be clones."

"All big-game hunters' women wear that stuff. You see it at big-game conventions. The men buy traps and guns, the women gold trophies in jewelry."

"You've been at a big-game hunter's convention?"

Max shrugged modestly. "In the performance of my duty. That's why I recognize the charm bracelets."

"Clones. But not in the face." A rough patch of terrain jolted some new ideas into her head.

"You think in the bedroom?" Max sometimes read her mind.

"Well . . . Courtney did strike me as the mistress type. But I sense that she's out in the cold, so what would she gain from killing Cyrus? Nothing, except a loss of position."

"If that's her only position."

"There's more than horizontal for mistresses?"

"There is if she's got another agenda."

"What? Max! Don't gloat. What did I miss?"

"I don't think you missed it, I just think you didn't draw the proper conclusion."

"Oooh! It's the jewelry, right?"

He nodded.

"So what's so special about ostentatious"—here she waggled her ring finger at him—"expensive baubles? Theirs are all animal-based designs. Heavy. Obviously eighteen-karat gold. Crude trophies when you think of the creatures that are killed by the men in their lives." Temple thought and jolted and stared at Sahara-style sand.

"Wait. Courtney wore one piece that wasn't clunky and ostentatious and representative of big game. That wiry pendant, really thin. Delicate."

Max's profile was grinning.

"*That's* why you did that salaam over her hand with your nose in her cleavage!"

"She doesn't have any cleavage. Believe me, I know."

"Neither do I, but I don't get those big-time bows. You were checking out the pendant."

"And—?"

"And it didn't look like anything, just some lines joined together." Temple pictured the oddly subtle charm in question. Her mind suddenly inflated it from two inches square to two feet square.

"Max! It's the . . . thingie drawn on the floor where Professor Jeff was killed. At the University of Nevada campus. The out-of-skew house shape a kid would draw. Courtney is with the Synth?"

"The Synth is apparently behind the CC's leopard being kid-napped. Maybe she's the reason it ended up at the Rancho Exotica."

"And who is the reason the leopard ended up alone together with a dead Cyrus Van Burkleo?"

Max lifted his profile to the horizon, dreaming as he drove. Why not, there was nothing out here but rattlesnakes and cactus and ruts?

"Cyrus. It almost sounds like Osiris."

"If a leopard could be Irish."

Max winced. "Don't remind me of that. The Synth seems fond of the arcane. Maybe there's a cosmic balance in a leopard named Osiris being on the death scene of a man named Cyrus. A balance, do you think?"

"The Synth is against trophy hunting?"

"The Synth may do its own form of trophy hunting, but I sus-pect—what would you call a gang of rogue prestidigitators . . . a sleight of magicians?—would be protective of the big cats they have traditionally worked with. Maybe the Synth was killing two birds with one stone: stopping Van Burkleo, and inconveniencing the Cloaked Conjuror."

"Then the Synth never meant to harm the leopard."

"No. I think the Synth is strictly interested in interspecies may-hem. Interprofession actually."

"It's much more likely that the women in his life killed Van Burkleo. He wasn't a rogue magician. He was just a greedy egoist."

"Then whatever the Synth's peripheral games, we're back to the women in the case."

They rode in silence for a while. Cyrus Van Burkleo, the big-game hunter, seemed to have met his match and ended up dead. Leopard Lady and Synth Woman.

"I can't really understand the woman," Max said.

"Leonora?"

"Yes. Unless I learn why she had turned herself into a plastic sur-geon's playground. Could a smooth PR woman weasel her surgeon's name out of her?"

"Maybe. But it could be somebody out of the country. I wonder how many U.S. surgeons would be willing to do that to a human face?"

"With enough money," Max said, "you'd be surprised."

* * *

"Was it a good Agatha Christie foreplay?" Max asked with a grin as he dropped Temple off in the Circle Ritz parking lot.

She grimaced as she got out, reacting to both her ride on the jolting Jeep and his lame joke.

"It sure wasn't a climax," she said, "but it was a good A.G. moment: an isolated camp in the desert, a cast of privileged and power-hungry people, the roar of the beasts in the distance, killing outside and in—"

He took off with a wave, the emerald ring safe in his breast pocket. Temple slogged toward the building, wishing the old pool had a new hot tub. She'd have to mention that potential improvement to Electra.

In fact, she saw the landlady's pink Probe pulling in right now . . . only it was white.

Huh?

Only the driver wasn't Electra, but Matt.

Double *huh?*

She stopped cold. "Am I seeing things?" she asked as he got out and headed toward the side door without noticing her.

Matt whirled as if she had shot at him. "What?"

"Your Elvismobile is parked over there. What are you doing driving Electra's car? And when did it turn white? Curiouser and curiouser."

Matt eyed the lot, nervously. "We'd better get in." He trotted for the door and stood holding it open for her like a parking valet.

She looked at the sky. No rain coming. And she couldn't hurry at this point. She trudged toward the door. "I don't get it."

The minute she put a foot on one small step into the building, he was pushing behind her and shutting the door.

He practically pushed her right into the wall.

"Matt! What's the matter?"

"Nothing. I've been awfully busy lately, that's all. I'd better get upstairs and check my answering machine."

"What? No lobby chitchat?"

"Sorry. It's been frantic."

He preceded her down the hall to the building's small black marble-lined lobby so quickly that she couldn't keep up with him.

When she got there, the space was empty. Both elevators were on the main floor, doors open, so he couldn't have taken one. He was using the stairs?

Curious, she went to the stair door and opened it, listening for footsteps above.

Nothing.

Either he had run up the stairs already, or . . . he had simply vanished.

Or . . . The opposite door to the hall leading to the wedding chapel caught her eye.

Maybe . . .

She was never too tired to solve a puzzle. Besides, she had a deep personal dislike of men disappearing on her.

Temple opened the door, listened to the silence beyond, then penetrated it.

Electra's drive-by wedding business was booming, but the big hotels with their fancy chapels had stolen the wedding bells from the tiny, quaint Lover's Knot.

The room with its corny bower wreathed in plastic flowers and white pews crowded with Electra's soft-sculpture people was dim and empty.

Maybe because it was dim and empty and neglected, it had the solemn silence of a real church. Temple hadn't been in one in years, except for a couple services at Our Lady of Guadalupe with Matt. Masses, that's what they were.

She noticed a familiar silhouette among the fabric people and started. Oh. Only Elvis.

Smiling, she sat down beside the King.

She had seen more than a few versions of Elvis at the Kingdome recently, but this one had snow-white hair.

"Hello, Izzy," she said softly. "Is real? Not this time."

If Matt was driving Electra's car, then Electra must be driving the new silver VW a supposed Elvis had left for him at the radio station.

Why would they switch cars? Why would Matt give up a perfectly nice new car for an old one? Why would he give up Elvis's last gift car?

Of course it hadn't been left by Elvis, but by a delusional fan. Or something like that.

Temple sat in the quiet, brooding.

She knew Matt was busy, that he had speaking engagements and media and all that stuff to deal with. But it didn't mean he should stop dealing with her.

And that's what she had felt like just now. Snubbed. Brushed off. Run out on.

Just like when Max had vanished without an encouraging word. She hadn't been so shocked in ages, and was not again until he came back like a clap of thunder echoing out of a clear blue sky.

Max on her second-story patio, back.

She supposed that incident might make her a little oversensitive to newer perceived desertions.

Still, it hurt to feel not wanted, especially by somebody she had flattered herself to think would always want her. Maybe Matt had found someone else. As well he should. But that didn't mean their friendship had to end.

Max, of course, would disagree. And maybe he was right. He usually was.

Temple took a long shower as soon as she got to her unit, then decided to face the mazurka, and called Leonora.

"Temple Barr. I can't tell you how impressed Mr. Maximilian was with your layout. Couldn't stop talking about the ranch house and the facilities."

Leonora purred her thanks.

"And as for myself, there's something terribly personal I'd like to ask you. I might as well just jump right in. Maxi was raving about your magnificent cheekbones. I'd noticed them on my first visit."

"Everybody does," Leonora interrupted, sounding pleased.

"May I ask—? It's terribly rude of me, but I wondered."

"Everybody does. I loved your ring, by the way. Wherever did he get it?"

Okay, reciprocating girl talk. "Fred Leighton's."

"Of course!"

"And your cheekbones? You see, I'd like to get some myself."

"Yes, you are a little flat-faced."

Flat-faced! That freak! . . . "I know. It's been the bane of my life. If you can recommend a good plastic surgeon, one that might be able to do something major with my . . . flat . . . cheekbones?"

"I'm sure Doctor Mendel can help you out. He has offices on Charleston."

"You recommend him? Personally?"

"But of course."

"Come to think of it, I've heard he does Savannah Ashleigh."

"Who?"

"Never mind."

"Well, good luck. I would certainly do anything I could to keep your Mr. Maximilian happy."

You did it yourself for Mr. Van Burkleo, Temple thought, *and look what it got you both.*

"My face is my work of art," Leonora added.

Cubist period, Temple added mentally. Hamlet was right, much as she despised the line: *Vanity! Thy name is woman.*

"I'll look right into it," Temple promised.

As soon as she hung up, she opened the Yellow Pages. Dr. Mendel, huh? She already knew him. She'd buffaloed him before, so she probably could flog some information about Leonora and her surgeries from him.

She dialed the office and asked for a consultation, soon. The matter, she said, was urgent.

Chapter 37

Human Error

Although I am the first to assert that my Miss Temple is a pretty sharp cookie you wouldn't want to try snacking on without a lip guard, I must admit that she does have her unguarded moments. Usually when Mr. Max or Mr. Matt is around.

These moments also occur when she is in the act of entering or exiting a motor vehicle, which I find a most convenient failing. Especially if Mr. Max or Mr. Matt is also in the car.

In this case, it has been a real lifesaver for me and my partners in crime solving.

Thus it is that we three—me and the Terrierable Twos, Groucho and Golda—are safely sheltering under the oleander bushes bordering the Circle Ritz parking lot by the time she accosts Mr. Matt shortly after Mr. Max has driven off.

I say "accost" because Mr. Matt Devine is behaving as I have never seen him do before. Instead of suffering from an inability to take his eyes off Miss Temple, he is darting them around the parking lot as if aware that I and the Dustball Twins are under the oleanders. He is, in fact, looking like a minor character in a bad detective novel. Were I in such a production, I would be forced to describe him as looking shifty.

Fortunately, I am not and can instead say that he is moving his gaze around the parking lot perimeter as if worrying that even the bushes have eyes and ears.

Which they do at this time, thanks to my stage-managing a discreet exit from the backseat floor while Miss Temple has the passenger door open and one dainty foot brushing the pavement while she is arranging an exchange of diamonds and emerald with Mr. Max Kinsella.

Handing off fifty thou or so in vintage jewels is sufficiently novel that they keep their eyes firmly on the ring and each other, and not on any side issues escaping out the ajar door.

The G-forces have been admirably obedient during our escape from Rancho Exotica via the Animal Oasis.

Thanks to their keeping their yaps glued tighter than a showgirl's false eyelashes, we have all been as silent and surreptitious as ninjas.

Wrrowwww-wrrowww-wow-wow-wow, goes Golda, ruining my self-congratulatory soliloquy.

Wrrowwww-wrrowww-wow-wow-wow, goes Groucho, doubling the odds of our attracting unwanted attention.

I need not have worried, Miss Temple has sped into the building, and Mr. Matt, with one last shifty glance around, has hastened to follow her. Would that the Yorkies were as consistent with me.

I sigh deeply as their *Wrrowwww-wrrowww-wow-wow-wow* duet falls on the slam of the Circle Ritz door.

Safe at home.

Then I see what they have been *Wrrowwwww-wrrowwwing* at.

Not so safe at home.

Miss Midnight Louise is sitting not two feet away, tapping the tip of her tail into the dry soil and raising, not Cain, but desert dust.

I sneeze, but get not so much as a "Bast bless you."

"You drove off without me," she finally says.

She is so mad that the sound comes out the side of her mouth, like spit.

"I could not help it. I could not get the interior latch open in time."

"You? The city's primo cat burglar, to hear you tell it? I think you could. I think you just decided to ditch me when the action got interesting."

"Ditch you! If I had wanted to do that, I could have done it long before then. You know how heavy-duty those meat-locker latches are."

"Yeah. They got to keep the meat from running away." She is being sarcastic.

I nod sagely. "Sometimes, depending on the quality of the establishment for which the shipment is destined."

She shakes out her ruff in disbelief and begins sweeping her rear member from side to side, raising a small dust devil.

"That leopard is *mine*," she says.

I am staggered. I have never seen Miss Midnight Louise so incensed, and, believe me, I have seen her incensed. With my deep understanding of psychology, human or feline, I suddenly realize that by feeding the starving leopard, Miss Louise has developed a maternal attachment to it. There is nothing so fierce in the females of my species as the maternal instinct. Unfortunately. True, Miss Louise was made politically correct at an early age. So call her a single mom, an adoptive mom. Obviously, her assignment with the leopard has tapped deep inner needs.

"Osiris is fine, and being fed plenty at the Animal Oasis. We just saw for ourselves."

Beside me, the thankfully mum Yorkie duo nod until the tiny bows on their heads seem to be seen through a strobe light. They remind me of those old-time kewpie dolls with springs for necks. Only these things also stick their tongues out from time to time. Dogs! Yuck.

However, Miss Midnight Louise is not being repulsed by Golda and Groucho at the moment. She is being repulsed by me.

"I am sorry," I say humbly. "The very next time it is necessary to take a long, uncertain arduous trek out to the desert, I will make sure that you and no one else accompanies me."

"I bet," she jeers. She shifts her weight from one slim black foreleg to the other, and deigns to curl her train around her toes. "So what did you learn?"

I sit down and fold my mitts into each other.

"The Yorkshire constabulary were actually useful. When we arrived at the ranch, we discovered Osiris had been moved."

"Moved?"

"But luckily, I had a pair of noses along that can cling to the desert floor like twin Hoovers. And where they led me was most interesting."

Chapter 38

Murder Wears a New Face

The outer office tabletops were buried by *Paris Vogue*, *Elle*, and *Vanity Fair*. Also with discreetly faceless bound folders filled with disgusting before and glorious after photos.

Temple spent ten minutes filling out a clipboard with her medical history. Then she was invited into an inner office for an interview with a nurse.

The walls were filled with photos of women who had been transformed by surgery into plastic perfection. Although all were admirably slender, smooth, and gorgeous, none were as extreme as Leonora.

The nurse was a brusquely blowsy woman, so unlike an advertisement for Dr. Mendel's procedures that you instinctively trusted her. She must be good to look like this and work here without undergoing continual reconstruction. Forty unneeded pounds pushed the buttons on her bodice to the breaking point. Her hair was a strawberry blond frizzle too undisciplined to be anything but natural, and good humor radiated from her unperfected features.

"How did you hear about us?" she asked.

This was better than a Broadway opening. Temple walked right through and to center stage.

"Leonora. Leonora Van Burkleo recommended you. Well, she recommended Dr. Mendel. Very, very highly."

The nurse's warm expression did not so much chill as grow sober.

"Her cheekbones," Temple explained, pointing at her undistinguished pair. "I would die to have cheekbones like that."

"She almost did," the nurse muttered as she jotted something down on Temple's information sheet.

"I beg your pardon? Oh. You mean she was in an accident and had to be reconstructed?"

"Yeah. Household accident." Her mouth twisted.

"How terrible! Well, she didn't mention anything to me. Is that why her new look is so exotic? She needed a lot of reconstructive work?"

"Dr. Mendel reconstructed her whole face."

"And she didn't specifically ask for the, ah, feline look?"

The nurse laughed bitterly. "Old Van Burkleo might say she asked for it." Her at-first friendly eyes were blinking nervously. Her entire plump figure radiated throttled fury.

Temple, bewildered, stumbled on conversationally. "It must have been a very serious fall."

"Several." The woman's haystack of hair hid her face as she bent over the papers.

What was she implying? Leonora had fallen down, repeatedly. Drugs? A drinking problem? One or the other so severe that she required full-face plastic surgery? Had asked for it?

"Look, honey." The nurse looked up, her eyes glaring. "I don't want you breathing a word of this to Mrs. Van Burkleo or Dr. Mendel. It's none of our business. But I can't have you . . . Listen. Your cheekbones are fine. You don't need implants. You don't need anything. Get out of here. And just be glad you're not that poor, poor woman."

"Leonora? But she's rich and, and—"

"You don't want to look like her, hon, even just in the cheekbones. Everything that's there today is the only thing modern surgery could do to repair years of battering. If she wants to make a fashion state-ment out of mutilation, I guess it reasserts some sense of pride, but I can't let innocents come in here wanting to copycat a tragedy. Young people today. Be happy with who and how you are!"

The woman handed Temple's info sheet back to her and walked out of the consultation room.

Temple sat there stunned.

Staggered.

Domestic abuse. She remembered suddenly another face, one that had been on the TV news when she was a kid: Heidi . . . no, Hedda. Nussbaum. That terrible case where that demented abusive lawyer had killed an adopted little girl. Hedda Nussbaum was the woman who had lived with him. Temple's mind still carried the before-and-after news photos of Hedda, how over the years her features had been pounded like veal scallopini until they were blunter and more swollen than any old-time prizefighter's mug. Just like Leonora's ersatz big-cat look.

This put a whole new complexion on the case.

Leonora Van Burkleo had motive one for murder, even if you were tempted to call it justifiable homicide.

Chapter 39

Collusion Course

For the first time in her life, Carmen lived up to her name in the mirror.

For the first time in her life, C. R. Molina really looked at herself in the mirror. She hadn't realized until now that she'd avoided that for as long as she could remember. The only thing she ever saw were her father's blue eyes.

Never had seen the father, just the eyes.

Damn his eyes.

But now his eyes were gone. For the first time in her life she was a brown-haired, brown-eyed Latina. With this one, fresh glance she had seen reflected an entirely different life for herself.

So a glance had become a stare, the stare a plunge into the past. Always standing out, bearing the Anglo brand from her earliest play days in the barrio. "*Gringa*," the others had called her. Later when they got older, their taunts grew more sophisticated. And then the boys had begun. "*Putona*," they'd called her then. Whore, like her mother must be to have produced a blue-eyed child.

Only her. The seven children of her mother's second marriage were all brown/brown, as the driver's licenses read. Only she was brown/blue. Sometimes black and blue from defending herself and her mother's honor.

Everything she was had been shaped by those damn blue eyes.

She eyed her new image with envy in the mirror. Finally she looked consistent. Even her father's height, a second birth-curse bestowed on the daughter he'd never lived to see, seemed acceptable when her eyes were brown.

Amazing what a difference that one color correction made, culturally, psychologically.

And to think she owed it all to Max Kinsella.

In the mirror, her upper lip curled at the thought. She began to see and feel the downside of her disguise. Calling these contact lenses "soft" seemed an understatement. She'd had to cram the viscous floppy shapes into each eye, which went against every admonition to avoid touching and injuring an eye she'd heard in childhood.

She didn't feel them, though. She blinked. Brown. She looked so *different*. Why hadn't she thought of color-changing contact lenses long ago? Maybe because she'd never needed glasses, never thought about it.

She turned away from the mirror. Turned back. She wondered how hard it had been to get brown contact lenses. Most people who used contact lenses to change or enhance their eye color went for exotic shades. Like violet. Or like Max Kinsella's magician green.

When she had gotten older and entered a non-Hispanic world, every now and then a stranger would comment on her vivid blue eyes. They considered it a compliment, but by then she'd been conditioned to disown her own eye color, or discount it. *Don't it make your blue eyes brown*, she mentally paraphrased the title of a song made popular by Linda Ronstadt. Latina Linda, despite the last name. Unlike any other woman in the country, she had always wished she could make her blue eyes brown. Now she had.

She finally examined her entire image in the mirror.

Her clothes were the same standard-issue, nondescript private-eye getup that she'd worn to Reno's apartment and to Secrets.

But the eyes made all the difference.

That was how Kinsella could eel in and out of one persona and another. One right touch could totally skew an identity.

She gathered her bag, pregnant with the Beretta in its portable black leather paddle holster. Dolores was in the living room watching TV. Mariah was in her bedroom playing makeup with her friend Yolanda.

Carmen made it to the kitchen without Dolores looking at her. Two adolescent tiger-striped cats skidded across the countertop, stopping to sniff the foreign scent of contact lens solution on her fingers.

They regarded her with wide yellow eyes, oblivious to the revolution in her appearance.

She gave them each a chuck on the chin and called good-bye to Dolores. "Yolie's parents will come for her at nine P.M. I'll be back . . . late."

"Fine." Dolores was used to late-night duty at the Molina household. She was happy to get away from her own teenage houseful, Carmen thought.

What was next on her agenda? A strip club called Kitty City, chasing a lead she had unearthed at Secrets. Not just strippers moved from club to club. Or bouncers. A nervous little itch jigged in the pit of her stomach, one she hadn't felt for a long time: knowing she was on the trail of a murderer, sensing she was getting closer, knowing that she might encounter Rafi Nadir and would have to fool him with her Hispanic eyes. Undercover, and hunting. Funny that Rafi Nadir hitting town had forced her to remember what homicide detail was all about.

Max was tempted to bring the Elvis impersonator out of the closet again tonight, but having been seen in that guise by Molina once, he didn't care to pull off a repeat performance.

And Molina would be out there somewhere. Hopefully trying out her brand-new eyes in another direction.

He smiled at Rafi Nadir's twenty-dollar bill, flashed at ersatz Elvis in a moment of braggadocio. It lay on his bureau top in a plastic baggie, ready to be dusted for fingerprints or checked for suspect serial numbers, if necessary.

Max doubted that would ever be necessary. Nadir was the stripper killer and would go down for that, not theft or counterfeiting or any lesser offense. Molina would owe him big-time for that, and then maybe she'd cooperate with him instead of blocking his every move.

He had decided to dress conservatively tonight: suits went to strip clubs too. Not many, and not to the fringe ones. More to the upscale clubs called New Orleans Nights that fronted billboards picturing James-Bond-level ladies in designer evening gowns. Guys from those places could slum.

So he put on a gray sharkskin suit. He didn't like gray. Liked black and white. Or rainbows.

Fascinating, Nadir working part-time at Rancho Exotica. More than that. Strange. Or not so strange. They hunted helpless animals at Rancho Exotica. Nadir hunted helpless women at the strip clubs.

For a moment, in the small mirror on the bureau-top accessory chest that had belonged to Gandolph, Cher's naked, defiantly frightened eyes peered at him through black holes of heavy eyeliner and mascara. A drunken deer in the spotlight. She'd been as easy to run down and throttle in the parking lot of that strip club as an aging, domesticated lion was to shoot at thirty feet in the dusty, fenced arena of a canned-hunt ranch.

Max found himself savagely knotting the conventional tie around his own throat. He hadn't worn a tie in years, but doing a double Windsor was like riding a bicycle . . . or a Hesketh Vampire. You never forgot how. He had slicked back his hair into a Wall Street sheen and donned tiny rimless glasses like a stockbroker. He looked like a comfortably-off nerd who needed help with women.

A pigeon.

That was the way to go into strip clubs if you were a man and wanted to learn something.

The woman at the bar was using the mirror behind it to check out the crowd, but her eyes kept pausing on herself.

Stop it! Molina told herself. This was not amateur night, even though she was posing as a PI, and even though she considered most of them amateurs.

She had to get past the oddity of her own appearance. It'd been too long since she'd done undercover work. Donning a micro-miniskirt and a bustier hadn't thrown her on the last case. Maybe because she'd done the standup trashy tart role in L.A. vice years ago. Maybe because it was such a far cry from her daily administrative civvies these days. Totally out of character. But this, this brown-eyed woman in the mirror was too close for comfort.

For concentration.

No doubt Kinsella had wanted to throw her off her stride, get her out of his hair. There. That thought had got her adrenaline flowing. Whatever he wanted, he would get the opposite.

She swept her eyes over the mirror from left to right, ignoring the naked ladies, concentrating on the men. This place attracted tourists in short-sleeved shirts, a few businessmen in light-colored, light-weight suits, sans ties, punk kids just past twenty-one in sports clothes. No truckers, few jeans.

No one here looked like Rafi Nadir.

She'd tied a narrow scarf around her forehead to pull her hair back, just in case.

She really did look different, dammit.

Eyes back on the suspects.

One in particular. Nobody had zeroed in on this candidate, because the profile was all wrong. This one wasn't obvious, like Rafi. But sometimes obvious wasn't right.

Then, a dark head came cruising into view behind her. It was like sighting a shark fin in the water. She tensed, willed herself invisible.

Instead of this shark going for the gaudy, subtropical fish schooling at Kitty City, they headed for him: blondes, redheads, black women in platinum-white wigs.

Molina glimpsed green dollar bills waving as Kitty City's strippers converged on the bait. "Chum," they called it in the ocean fish-baiting game. At a strip joint, any guy with cash to wave around attracted an attractive crowd.

This guy was pushing through the tide to the bar, promising drinks all round.

She breathed out. He was just another celebrating good-time Charlie, not a bouncer coming on the job. He wasn't who she'd thought he might be. . . .

The girls surrounding him sank to seats along the almost empty bar, putting him into high relief, like an outcropping of rock marooned by the ebbing tide.

Her eyes wanted to bug out past the veiling contact lenses.

It *was* Rafi Nadir.

Molina's eyes darted to her own reflection in the mirror, this time not transfixed by how different she looked to herself.

This time they were objective, keen, nervous. How different did she really look, to Rafi Nadir? Enough?

"Scotty," Max said. "Just call me Scotty."

"As in 'Beam me up'?" she asked through the smoke she breathed into a kind of holographic lace veil in front of her face.

"As in Hartford the Third."

She raised wire-thin-plucked eyebrows.

She was exactly the kind of woman you expected to meet in a strip joint. Not a stripper, but some kind of hanger-on. Probably an ex-stripper. Her smoky contralto voice vibrated through a buxom, inverted-triangle frame. She wore a glitzy jogging suit that hid most of her skin. She had found his slumming Yuppie persona unusual enough to merit personal attention.

"I bet they don't call you Scotty," she said, eyes narrowed to filter out her own smog. "I bet they call you Scott."

Max shrugged with what he hoped looked like embarrassment. He had lost the art of embarrassment a long time ago. As long as he looked like a babe in Toyland, women would talk to him. Strippers had a maternal streak, and when they talked, they bared more information about themselves than they did skin on stage.

She tapped her cigarette ash, as long as a mandarin's fingernail, into one of those black plastic bar ashtrays with jagged edges to hold cigarettes. They look like dead roaches with legs in the air.

"I have a son about your age," she said, surprising him. She looked like she'd been around, but not that old. "Name's Lindy."

'Your son's?"

"Hell, no! Skip the 'y' endings, kid, after twenty. You'll get taken a lot more seriously. My name's Lindy."

"Oh. Well, you certainly look like you know your way around this . . . scene."

"Shouldn't I?"

"I just meant—" Max stirred the skinny striped plastic straw around in his water-and-hint-of-scotch. "I'm kinda here looking for someone."

"Look, Scotty." She was violating her own rule and leaned near to put her hand on his arm and her smoky, raspy voice in his ear. "You don't belong here. Whatever you're looking for, or looking to forget, go on to some hotel on the Strip."

"Do you belong here?" he returned.

Her eyes widened with a touch of flattered youthfulness. "Oh, God. Sure I do. Not here, precisely. I'm just visiting the scene of the crime." She glanced at the stage, nostalgically, even a bit coquettishly. "Used to dance up there myself."

Max tried not to smile; he'd figured as much.

"But now I run my own club. Les Girls."

That he hadn't figured.

"No sense letting the guys get all the dough when we girls show all the go."

He laughed, but made it apologetic.

She patted his arm. "Now, who you lookin' for? Some girl you got a crush on?"

"No. Some guy who got a crush on some girl. A bouncer named Rafe. Something like that. This, uh, girl I met at one of the Strip hotels you were advising me to go back to, she said he'd been . . . stalking her, I guess."

"And you're going to put a stop to it, huh?"

"No." He shrugged, apologetically again. "I thought I'd offer him some money to leave her alone."

"You got it with you?"

"No, ma'am. I'm a fish out of the water, but I'm not shark bait."

Lindy rolled her eyes, displaying bloodshot whites. "Young man." She sighed again. "That girl isn't worth getting your face pushed in for."

"I can do some pushing back."

"Maybe. Only guy I know who bounces, and he bounces around from club to club, is Rafi. Like Rafe. That sound right?"

Max nodded slowly. "Where would he be bounced to now?"

"Don't know, hon. I heard he was quitting this racket. No loss, from what I also heard. You might check with my ex, Ike. He runs Kitty City. He's the type who'd like Raf's style."

"And what is Raf's style?"

Lindy made a fist and moved it toward Max's face. "To the moon, Alice. To the moon."

"That was all bluff," Max objected. "Ralph Kramden never hit Alice."

"Hey! You know *The Honeymooooners?* I thought only us old folks did."

"Everything old is new again. Cable TV."

"Not everything. Watch yourself around Raf. That guy was always trying to get something back. Those kind are dangerous."

"What was he trying to get back?"

"Money? A woman? Something."

Max nodded. He didn't see Molina as the kind of woman a man would auger into the ground for. Or over. Must have been money. Nadir seemed very hung up on money.

"Take care of yourself." She patted his arm again, then bore down as she propelled her weight off the barstool and into the smoky, sound-soaked distance that makes such hot, sweaty, crowded places into a negative image of reality.

Max felt touched. Nobody had patted his arm since Miss Rosenblatt in fourth grade. The return to innocence was refreshing, especially in a strip club.

Miss Rosenblatt would have fainted dead away if she had seen Max walk into Kitty City. Luckily, a dead faint was probably all that she was up to nowadays, as she would be confined to coffin and only rolling over in her grave in protest.

Kitty City enjoyed being a strip club: dim, loud, crowded and filled with milling almost-naked girls. Several mirrored balls turned overhead, strafing the clientele with bullets of bright, glancing light.

Its clients took the mental barrage like a Fifth Avenue mob would take ticker tape during a parade, with festive disregard. The place had a Mardi Gras look and feel. The girls (strippers were always "girls" no matter their age) and the men mixed it up like old, bawdy friends. The clients were as loud and disorderly as the taped raunchy rock music, and seemed to enjoy competing with it. Even the deejay guy in the glassed-in soundproof booth seemed to be having a good time.

And . . . so did Rafi Nadir.

Max bellied up to another sopping-wet bar and ordered another watered-down drink as costly as a pound-can of R-12 Freon. He was glad this place was crammed with customers, and probably always was. People tended not to bother remembering faces in joints like this until they'd seen you for the ninth or tenth time.

Rafi Nadir was the center of a bouquet of centerfold girls, obviously a visiting ex-worker, not on the job.

He wore a loose white shirt with sleeves rolled up and buttoned at the elbow over khaki pants. Something about his demeanor, the pale shirt, his dark, overblown good looks, the way he accepted the strippers' attention as his due reminded Max of Libya's Khadafy, one of the more sinister international figures, and that was going some these days.

Face it: to brush shoulders with Rafi Nadir was to loathe Rafi Nadir. He gave the word "lowlife" a new definition. No wonder Molina was having nightmares about this creep showing up in her life. No wonder she wanted him as far away from their daughter as a serial killer.

If Max managed to get enough on him for a murder rap, he'd be bailing Molina out of a pretty rough corner. She'd hate it, and he'd love it.

And Max was close. Nadir was out of control, not drunk, but high on some apparent good fortune. The twenties were diving into the surrounding G-strings like South Sea Islanders seeking pearls.

Men drunk on their own importance are only a half-step away from walking off a cliff. Max just had to watch Nadir, follow him, and he'd catch him deciding to force another stripper in a parking lot into early retirement . . . He might even be the one who had killed Gloria, Gandolph's old assistant. No telling how many stripper murders they could wrap him up in.

While Max was weaving happy endings, just as he was ready for a fadeout on Cher's smiling transparent face on high in the best black-and-white Hollywood tradition, he saw something unpleasant in the mirror.

She was tall, she was dressed like an aging flower child, she was talking to a guy at the other end of the bar who looked as much like a regular as anyone here tonight. And she glanced in the mirror at herself as if noticing a stranger, then her eyes ran down its length as fast and smooth as fingers whisking a run off a piano keyboard.

Max hunched over his drink, turned to the guy on his left, put his right hand with the clumsy college ring on it in front of his face, almost knocking his phony glasses off.

They made a perfect triangle: He and Molina at opposite ends of the bar and Rafi Nadir at the apex in the middle of the room, holding forth amid his harem, perfectly placed to spot either one of them, should the fates permit. Rafi Nadir on top of the world, which in this instance was a pyramid. A pyramid scheme, so to speak.

Molina's ears, feet, and—now that she had sat down at the bar—butt were killing her. But the eyes felt fine, except for the burning irritant of secondhand smoke.

But that was Las Vegas. No way would smoking be banned.

"You related to any of the girls?" Don, the regular, was asking.

She was relieved that she wasn't being mistaken for one of the girls, but miffed that he thought she might be somebody's mother. Or big sister maybe.

"No. I'm a PI, just following up some leads."

"Oh." He was a stocky blond in JT10: jeans/T-shirt/tennies. Roofer, but harmless enough. Roofing was your number-one occupation for transients with crime in mind.

"You're not kidding?" he asked. "About the PI part?"

"Who'd kid about that?" She glanced in the mirror again. This guy was dry; time to sink another well, but no good candidates presented themselves.

Then she noticed that Rafi was gone.

She stood up, scanning the mob. "Look, Don, I'm slowing down your action by sitting here. Thanks for the info."

"I didn't tell you much—"

"More than you think." Bystanders always did.

She knew from five minutes with Don that Kitty City girls tended to stay put here, that it was always this busy, that Rafi was a familiar figure around the place, and now—that he was gone.

She rose and headed for the strippers' dressing room.

Nobody noticed her as she beat her way through the heavy black velvet curtains at the side of the stage, then went down the hall, through the women's john, and into the long, ugly, bare room behind it.

The usual three or four girls waiting to go on were busy peeling off their street clothes and pulling on what amounted more to accessories than clothes: boots, spike heels, thigh-high hose, garter belts,

G-strings, body stockings the size and shape of intertwined rubber bands.

"Say, I missed talking to Rafi," Molina said. "He leave with anyone?"

They looked blank and shrugged and questioned her in turn.

"Can you help me with this hook?"

"This new thong look all right?"

It was girls' dorm, only the dorm backed onto a strip joint.

Molina hooked, nodded, and beat her way out of there.

"Rafi never plays favorites with the girls," one voice singsonged after her as she left.

Never plays favorites. So what was his angle?

Reentering the club area was like walking into a sonic boom. Her ears, eyes, nose, and throat burned from acrid smoke and one foul, gasoline-slick vodka tonic she had nursed for far too long.

Her watch said it was long past coach-turning-into-pumpkin time, but the kid in the sound booth was still nodding and shaking to the music only he could hear at normal volume.

Molina eyed the entire scene one last time, and gave up.

If just seeing Rafi (and him not seeing her) was an achievement, then the night was not a waste. But she needed much more than that. It might be time to delegate, let her own people follow up her suspicions, which had not one shred of evidence behind them but instinct.

She moved under the irritating mirrored ball that raked her face with spinning spitballs of light. Looking away, she glimpsed herself streaking past the end of the mirror behind the bar. Brown eyes. So different. Such a good disguise. At least she'd learned that tonight.

Pushing the superheavy door open—why did they always make it so hard to get in and out of these places? Never mind. Pushing the door open with all her weight, she moved out into the untainted air, still slightly chilly before spring abruptly became summer and the air was always as warm as bathwater, and more often hot-tub water.

No smoke to breathe in, just air. She took a deep, singer's breath, expanding her lung capacity to its fullest, drawing in from her diaphragm. As she exhaled, slowly, with control, a woman's scream hit a high note and sustained it until abruptly ending.

The sound came from . . . behind the building, which gave her three sides to choose from.

She raced around to the left, digging the gun from the paddle holster in her purse. The scene of the scream: parking lot on three sides, jammed with cars but deserted of people, who were all inside deaf as posts to any ugly noises outside.

That's why he struck in strip-joint parking lots, alone in a crowd. She had to be here to see it, hear it. A perfect setup if the timing was just right for everybody to be inside yet, whooping it up.

He had to know the pulse and timing that made strip clubs predictable in their own erratic way, Molina thought as she moved cautiously through the lot, scanning parked cars, hunting for a wrong motion, a glint of reflected streetlight on something, someone in the wrong place. . . .

The streetlights were few and far between, of course. Strip club visitors were as cagey as gamblers about not wanting to be seen coming and going.

The abrupt cutoff of the scream echoed in Molina's mind. Not good. A killer could be doing anything now, down on the warm asphalt between the cars . . . raping, strangling.

She moved unheard on the well-used moccasins she had found at the Goodwill, but she could hear no one else moving either, not even a distant blast of noise as Kitty City's door opened and closed. It remained shut.

The neon from the sign up front cast pink and blue images on the roofs and hoods of the trucks and vans and cars filling the lot.

Then . . . something scraped. A shoe.

Someone moaned.

Over there.

Suddenly footsteps, running.

From *two* directions.

She paused at the building's rear corner.

The parked vehicles had thinned back here.

She peered around the building's sharp concrete-block edge, then broke into the open, weapon lifted, feet and hands braced.

A man was bending over something on the unpaved sandy soil surrounding the rear Dumpsters.

Something thumped sand. Footsteps. Another man was rounding the opposite edge of the rear wall, almost like a partner forming a pincer action.

Except that she had no partners here, just suspects.

The man on the ground jerked his head around and up into a sliver of blinking neon.

Rafi Nadir.

The man who'd rounded the corner was heading right for him.

"Stop. Police."

She didn't shout it, but her low, deep tone had such a shocking note of parental, paternal authority that both men paused, one in rising from the ground, one in heading toward him to keep him on the ground.

"Stop. Both of you."

The gun was held two-handed, by-the-book style, ready to fire.

Both men recognized that. They stared at her.

Then Rafi continued rising, turned and ran, heading for the cars.

"Stop!"

The second man pursued Rafi, crossing her direct path of fire.

She bellowed, "Stop, or I'll shoot."

He glanced her way, saw the gun was pointed dead-on at him. "He's getting away."

She nodded, not taking her eyes from him. "Stop," she repeated, almost whispered. "Or I'll shoot."

Max Kinsella stood poised in midstep, staring like a deer in the headlights, not stricken, merely astonished into inaction. "That was Nadir!"

"I know."

"He's your killer."

"It's more important to check the person who's down. You do it."

"I can catch him. You handle the scene."

"No."

"You're letting him get away."

"Maybe. But I've got the gun, and you don't." She realized he might be armed, moved toward him.

Without even straightening from his running crouch, he put out an empty hand. "You don't want to come within range, or it'll really get serious."

She hesitated. The police professional couldn't afford to do anything a suspect under control suggested. Kinsella wasn't ever under control, which he'd just reminded her. "Check her."

He turned and did as she said, crouching over the fallen form as Rafi Nadir had only moments before.

An almost undetectable patter of running feet died into silence as she listened.

Kinsella had his fingers on the carotid artery. "Unconscious, but a pulse."

Molina dug in her bag for her cell phone. "Call nine-one-one for an ambulance."

"You're crazy!" he said, even as he dialed. "We had him—uh, yeah. A woman unconscious at Kitty City, Paradise and Flamingo, rear parking lot. Assault. Lieutenant Molina, LVMPD on the scene. Right." He looked up at her again. It was just bright enough to see that the look was bitter and accusing.

"Punch in oh-one," she said, "but don't hit talk."

He did.

"Now. Put the phone on the ground and kick it, gently, toward me."

He muttered something.

"What was that?"

" 'To the moon, Alice, to the moon.' "

"Never happen." She bent as the phone slid toward her, keeping the gun pointed at him. She picked up the phone, hit talk, and connected to the dispatcher, asked for assistance.

"I get it," he said suddenly. "You're going to pin this on me."

"Interesting idea. You *were* on the scene. The only witness to the running man, whoever he might be, is . . . me. And you, who nobody would believe. Worked for *The Fugitive*, TV series and movie."

He snorted with disgust.

She sighed. "I love it. A really great scenario. But not practical. What's her pulse?"

"Sixty-four."

A distant whine announced the ambulance.

"Not bad. She'll live. I think we'll let the EMTs handle this. Time to say good night, George."

He stood, slowly, as if every joint hurt. "It's not over."

"Of course not."

"I never thought you were crooked."

"Funny, I always thought you were."

"He's dead meat."

"I better not find your fingerprints on it."

He moved away from the fallen girl, who was beginning to moan like someone coming out of anesthetic. Molina didn't want any confusing memories on the victim's part.

"Go on. Get out of here, or I'll have to arrest you. Or shoot you. Take your pick."

He moved, slowly, deliberately.

By the time the ambulance squealed to a stop and the emergency technicians spilled out to tend to the victim, Kinsella was just disappearing between two vans and Molina was just finishing returning her unfired gun to its holster.

A patrol car and then another screeched up. She had deliberately called them second. Uniforms were fanning out, flashlights poised, ready to search the parking lot.

It was suddenly a crime scene, overlit, crowded, filled with milling people trying to save the victim and preserve evidence. The sounds and fury weren't too different from that inside Kitty City.

Molina gave what directions she had to, then accompanied the victim to the ambulance. A young woman, stripper going off duty, like any nurse or convenience-store clerk going into the dark to find her car and finding instead a man with a plan.

She was almost fully conscious.

"You'll be fine," Molina told her, bending down before the ambulance crew whisked her to the bright fluorescent lights of the emergency room.

Not exactly the spotlight the young woman had craved.

Molina watched the ambulance maneuver to turn around, saw it start off, the siren escalating into its usual ear-piercing yodel.

"Handy you were here, Lieutenant," a uniform commented, trying not to sound curious.

"Handy," she repeated blandly. "I'll leave it to you. Doesn't look like anybody died here this time."

"No, ma'am."

"I'd like a copy of the full report, though, first thing in the morning. This might be part of an ongoing."

"Yes, ma'am."

Too bad Max Kinsella wasn't one scintilla as respectful of rank.

Chapter 40

Calling the Cops

"Molina," the phone barked.

Matt felt a moment's qualm. She sounded pretty disgruntled. He was making a big mistake. But what else could he do? Everything he did nowadays could be a mistake, a fatal mistake.

"This is Matt Devine. It's vital that I talk to you."

"Go ahead."

"No. In person."

She sighed pointedly. "My desk is covered with case files up to my chin. This about one of them?"

"Not really."

"It's personal?"

"Partly."

"Do you have any idea of what I'm up against? All right. Come in at, um, six o'clock then. I'll buy you a cup of coffee dregs to celebrate Thank God It's Friday."

He hesitated.

"Yes, no, maybe?" she demanded.

"I'd rather not see you on the job."

"Who knows when I'll be home? I could call you when that sweet hour arrives. You're free nights up to eleven or so, right?"

"Right. But—"

"I don't have time for this."

"I don't think it's safe to go to your house."

"Safe? what's going on here?"

"That's what I want to talk to you about. Where can we meet where no one is likely to know about it?"

"Oh, God." He heard voices jousting for her attention in the background.

"That's it! A church," he said, inspired.

"Is this a scheme to up church attendance in America? Or just mine?"

"How about early mass at Our Lady of Guadalupe?"

"The old folks' mass at six A.M.?" She groaned.

"All right. Saturday evening mass, then. You must get some time off on Saturday."

"I suppose five P.M. Saturday is better than six A.M. Saturday."

"We could talk afterwards in the sacristy. Father Hernandez is an understanding pastor. He wouldn't mind. Or . . . I know! The confessionals. They've never been removed at OLG because the old folks would be lost without them."

"Just what I want to look forward to on a Saturday night after a monthlong workweek: an assignation in a confessional after Sunday late-snoozers' mass with an ex-priest. Do I have to kneel?"

"You can take the priest's seat. I'll kneel."

"Damn it, Devine, this had better be good."

"No. It's bad. Very bad."

He hung up before she could question him further.

Always leave them wanting to know more. That's what Temple said.

Matt's next call was to arrange cover. He made a date with Sister Seraphina and the nuns at the OLG convent for Saturday night mass.

Kitty O'Connor, he thought, would be pleased that she had made such a dent in his social life that he could only date old nuns.

Surely they would be safe from her obsessive, possessive insanity. Or were they?

Chapter 41

Hunt Club

"Temple!"

She turned, midway across the massive, sparkling, tinkling lobby of the Crystal Phoenix, flabbergasted.

Not that she was surprised to hear her name called here. Every time she visited to check on final touches for the new entertainment areas people expecting instant answers were hollering her name right and left.

Only they weren't Max Kinsella, doing it right out loud in public.

This one-of-a-kind event would not only scare the horses, it would stop Temple in midhurtle.

She spun in her tracks. He was almost on top of her. "What on earth—?"

Caught up, he grabbed her elbow and hustled her toward the indoor wall of greenery fencing the Crystal Court lounge. There was a look of strain on his face that she'd never seen before, except in jugglers who have six ax blades up in the air at once.

"I couldn't reach you on your cell phone," he fretted.

Temple began groping in her tote bag. "I have it right here. Somewhere right here. Or maybe there. Can we sit down while I dig it out?"

Max was looking around like he expected an attack by tsetse fly. "No. Where, why doesn't matter. I've heard from the hunt breakers."

She blinked at the term, finally diverting her mind from Jersey Joe Jackson and his mine ride to Max's recent high-desert adventure.

"Hunt-breakers? Oh, those protesters who put themselves between hunters and their prey."

"I promised to help them document the action at Rancho Exotica. They just told me a hunt is scheduled this evening."

"That's . . . nuts! Why would the ranch do business now that Cyrus Van Burkleo is dead? With all the attention his killing is getting, they risk exposing their illegal operation. The protesters must be wrong."

"They ought to know. They're out there, watching. I need someone inside the ranch watching too."

"Me? Why would I go there again?"

Max grinned down at her. "Because you're so good at plausible pretexts."

"Pardon me, but why can't *you* be the inside man?"

"Because I have to be the outside man." He lifted his thumbs and fingers, fanned to form a frame. "Home movies, remember? I need someone inside to stop the hunt before anything is killed."

"Anything? Or any*one?*"

Max shook his head. "This has nothing to do with the murder. This is purely because of a promise I made. Look, the least I can do right now is help these people out. They're liable to get hurt if they come between an amateur hunter and his target. If I'm out there documenting it on film, it'll keep them from doing anything foolish."

"What about *me* getting between an amateur hunter and his target?"

"I don't expect you to be as confrontational, or foolish, as that protester crowd. Just . . . distract the hunter. Scream or faint or something."

"Max, I don't think feminine wiles are going to work out there, not that I've got many of them."

"This might." He hefted a small matte-black gun from a pocket.

Temple took a deep breath. "What would I do with that? Throw it?"

"We never did get to a shooting range. You could always shoot it into the air."

"What's to keep some trigger-happy hunter from shooting me into the air?"

"They want trophies, not felony arrests. But I don't think you'll need this. Still, if it would make you feel better—"

"I'd feel better without it, using my wits for bullets, thank you. I guess if Leonora and Courtney Fisher are going to be there, I can stomach it. I do hate having to see Leonora again . . . after what I found out." She had called Max about the news from the plastic surgeon's office once she was home.

"It's nasty knowing other people's secrets, isn't it?" Max said sympathetically. "But abused people rarely turn on anyone, not even their abuser. Even if this case is an exception, I doubt she'd bother you."

"I'm not afraid that she might be a killer. That's not what's bothering me. It's just that I'll never be able to look at her bizarre face without picturing that awful man hitting her, crushing bones and cartilage. I suppose helping to stop a hunt before another animal is killed is one way to get back at Van Burkleo, even if he is dead. Don't worry about me. I'll think of something."

"Once I've got the vital footage, I can step in." Max frowned, as if remembering something. Or somebody. "Hopefully without being seen. Vintage Mystifying Max, hand quicker than eye. That's what I expect to happen."

Temple shook her head. "Imagine one good deed requiring so much forethought. What made you volunteer to film a canned hunt?"

Max shrugged. "These protestors! Babes in the woods on the Mojave. Well intentioned, but way too clumsy to pull off a useful surveillance operation. One mistake could turn fatal."

"That's really a nice favor," Temple began. "Aha!"

She pulled the cell phone from her bag, where she had been rummaging all during their conversation. She flipped it open while Max eyed her askance. "*Oooh*, Battery's dead. Guess I forgot to recharge it."

"Maybe you're best off without armaments," he said, watching her drop the phone back into the bottomless maw of her tote bag.

"What time is this hunt supposed to happen?"

"Five P.M."

"I suppose that's so all concerned can have a civilized dinner at eight. Except the prey." She checked her watch—1:00 P.M.—and looked around. The bustling lobby thronged with people who showed no interest in them whatsoever. "Can I take you on a quick tour of the innovations? I'm sure we can get to anywhere we're *not* expected in time."

Max looked around rather more thoroughly than she had. When his glance came back to her—the natural, blue-eyed one she had gotten so used to that she'd forgotten he'd ever hidden behind green contact lenses—his Irish eyes were smiling.

"Why not?"

"You seem a bit more chipper than you were a few days ago."

"Maybe I've decided that I'm no more bad for you than the next guy."

Temple decided not to ask if he had any particular "next guy" in mind.

Max offered her his arm and the tour began.

Chapter 42

Secret Witness,
Silent Witness

"Hey, kit," I whisper from the large-leaved shade of a towering canna lily.

I feel something like a dirty old man, to tell the truth.

But the kit in question has made claims to being mine—though I deny it up one side of my whiskers and down the other—so I am not about to get arrested on lurking charges.

Midnight Louise elaborately sniffs the air just to let me know she has other places to go and people to see. Then she sashays over to my canna lily plant and rubs against the lower leaves as if pausing for a moment's rest on her rounds.

I must admit that I am still shaken from just seeing my Miss Temple consorting—cavorting?—in public with Mr. Max Kinsella inside the Crystal Phoenix Hotel. One of the big advantages to Mr. Max Kinsella, in fact the only advantage that I can see to the man, is that his duck-and-cover past has kept him more low-profile than a straightedge razor. At least when it comes to intruding into my and my Miss Temple's lifestyle.

So it is disturbing to see this undercover pair conspiring in the shade of a wall of parlor palms. It is almost as disturbing as if I were to be seen associating with Miss Midnight Louise in broad daylight.

Which I will not be doing if I can get her to join me in the canna-lily shade.

She hisses a greeting and informs me that I had better not have any designs on Chef Song's koi, as they are her special wards now. It would go against her grain were anything to happen to any of them. She would then be forced to go against my grain, which she assures me I will not like.

"I am not here on any trifling errand," I say loftily. "I was merely doing you the courtesy of checking in before I head out to Rancho Exotica again. I would not wish to be accused of denying you the opportunity for a long ride in a Mob meatwagon. I know how you yearn to associate with the more upscale elements in town."

"Can the sarcasm," she advises me. "You still have those two nose jobs with you?"

"Alas, no. Their assignment is over. I now have a witness to the crime and it is merely a matter of returning to the ranch to take a deposition. Dull work, really. I could not blame you for staying someplace safe and luxe like the Phoenix and letting your elders do the dirty work."

"There is more than *one* of you? Say it is not so!"

"I was using 'elders' in the general sense."

"You are being very good-natured about leaving me out of this," she says suspiciously.

By now she is more leery of my wishing her to stay home than my possibly wanting her to come along.

I play her like a two-pound carp. "It is only that I know how unhappy you were last time to miss the bus, so to speak. I wish to give you every opportunity to learn from your elders."

"Ha! You probably are not sure you can cop a ride on the meatwagon without me to distract the muscle at the wheel. No go, Pops. This time *you* will have to play decoy. I will try not to let those heavy doors slam shut on anything of yours that you might miss."

She strikes a tough deal, but getting into the meat wagon solo is a delicate operation.

"So who is this witness?" she prods. (I mean she literally prods . . . her claw into my paw. *Ouch!*)

"A secret witness is not a secret witness anymore if I tell anyone who asks." I also do not tell her that she may be of assistance in wringing the story out of said witness. No sense letting the kit think she is more important than she already thinks she is.

Not half an hour later we are in line behind a Dumpster ready to take the afternoon stage to Rancho Exotica.

"Shhhh!" my darling not-daughter admonishes me.

"That is not me growling. That is my stomach. I neglected to have lunch."

"You can gnaw on a horse hock once we are aboard." She casts a baleful yellow glance my way. (A pity she did not inherit my soulful, lettuce-green eyes, not that we are related, of course.)

"Horse! I have interrogated horses. I would never eat them. Is that what they feed the Big Cats?"

"Among other things." Midnight Louise is squinting at the sides of beef milling around the van . . . not the frozen meat hunks, the hunks on legs, i.e., the ham-handed human dudes who are manhandling the meat into the rear compartment.

"Those are exceptionally beefy individuals," I mention.

"Minions of the Mob usually are."

"Strange that the experts say that there is no more Mob in Las Vegas."

"Please. You have been out of the hotel business too long, Pops. They still have a good grasp on the wholesale meat business, that is for sure. Were you a drinking dude and prone to hanging out in bars, you would be having guys offering you steaks by the slab at a very good price. The hotels lose their weight in purloined meat every year."

"Indeed. So these dudes mean business."

"I would not want to let one of them catch me by the hairs of my chinny chin-chin." She eyes me. "So you think you can distract them while I slip into the van?"

"Uh. Sure." I am not as nimble—or do I mean nubile? I suspect both words are somewhat the same—as Miss Midnight Louise, but I certainly know my way around the criminal elements, even when they are packing lamb chops instead of revolvers.

Not that they might not be packing revolvers too.

While the dudes return to the warehouse to load up another cart of cartilage, I dash from the Dumpster to the front of the vehicle. I figure Miss Louise's trick of yowling has gotten old by now, so I bound up on some piled boxes to the van's roof and bide my time.

Ooooh. That refrigeration unit is blowing hot air onto the hot metal roof, making it into a steel stovetop. If I do not watch it, my toes will sear and I will be worthless in a five-yard dash.

In fact, my best move would be to jump down the back right into the van, but first I must distract the boys from Syracuse so that Louise can sneak into the meat locker.

I give a low moan.

"Yo, Vinnie," one guy says. "You getting frostbite? Do not leave any fingerprints on the merchandise."

"Hey, Manny. You got indigestion or something? Must have sampled the goods."

I moan again. You would be surprised what eerie vocalizations we furred dudes can produce . . . unless you had been at one of our community sings or love-ins, and then you would not be surprised at all.

I hear Vinnie clomp around to Manny on the side of the van. "You do not think that some of this meat is still alive?"

"It is fresh," Manny says, "but I am sure it is also fresh dead. You do not think some of this meat is haunted?"

"Haunted? You mean tainted. Naw, it is all primo stuff."

I lean over the back roof of the van just in time to see a pennant of black fur whisk out of sight into the cool dark below.

I leap down to the metal floor—an iron iceberg—and nip behind a few haunches of what I hope is beef. It is odd how we become accustomed to certain incivilities of life. Or death. I would never be hungry enough to eat a horse, despite the saying, but I would have a cow.

I almost have a cow right there when a sharp-featured appendage curls into my shoulder.

"Get behind the prime rib, Daddio. The meatheads are coming to see if the standing rack of lamb has the heebie-jeebies."

I hunker down, toes curled against the cold, biting down hard to keep my fangs from chattering. If I had to claw my way out of here for some reason, my shivs would probably snap off like icicles.

We arrive at our desert destination during the apex of the day's heat, but must wait many icy minutes while our chauffeurs wrestle frozen meat onto carts and out of our way.

Finally, sensing a lull in the action, I stumble to the open van door and drop down to blessed, and solar-heated, terra firma.

A moment later Louise lands beside me. We cold-foot it farther under the vehicle, obnoxious as the shade is to our chilled bodies.

"It was warmer when I was with the Yorkies," I mention.

"Overheated, hyperactive canines."

I roll . . . er, swagger to the raw edge where shadow and sunlight meet. As soon as my toes defrost, we can make a run for the big cat compound.

Meanwhile, Manny and Vinnie tromp back and forth, slinging hash, so to speak.

My stomach unfortunately objects audibly to the downloaded edibles disappearing from sight.

Manny's engineer boots pause but a foot from my nose. "Vinnie, you will have to have that looked into."

"Maybe one of the tires is losing air," Vinnie says.

I hear knees creaking and scramble to hide behind an opposite wheel.

"Nope," says Vinnie. "Tires are all pumped up."

Midnight Louise lets out a hiss of exasperation as the boots thump away. "You and your Ghost of indigestion act. A plain old yowl would have been less intriguing to these mutton-heads.

Okay. Tootsies toasty? Let us head for some cover that matches the air temperature."

She is gone like an eightball caroming across a sand beige pool table. I streak after her, expecting toes to snap off, and am pleasantly surprised when they do not.

By an ever-handy Dumpster we catch our breaths.

"So where is this secret witness of yours?" Louise asks. "Are we heading for the house or the hills?"

It is so tempting to mislead the little snip, but my toes, frankly, are not up to laying false trails.

"The compound."

Stalking like shadows on ice, we pad over the hot sandy dirt toward the now-familiar row of cages in the outbuilding.

"Looks like you have been busy," Louise concedes. "You seem to know your way around this place."

"I have hoofed this terrain from here to the Animal Oasis."

"Animal Oasis. What is that?"

Before I can answer her, I stop to stare in shock.

It is the same old, same old, all right. Lions and tigers and . . . and bare cages.

Two of them.

Not just Osiris's but the one that contained my secret witness.

Even Midnight Louise is frowning at the lineup, counting noses and coming up one too few.

"Looks like another Big Boy is AWOL," she notes. Then she looks over and sees my expression. "Oh, no, Daddio Darnedest! Is the missing person your secret witness?"

I nod glumly.

The witness is definitely not here to see us.

I can only hope that is not a permanent condition.

Chapter 43

The Black and Blue Max

Four-thirty.

Max had been watching the world through the view screen of a video camera for so long that he felt like he was looking through the Cloaked Conjuror's mask.

At the moment he was basking snakelike atop the artificial rocks forming the skeleton for a simulated waterfall, his black clothing so dust covered it had gone gray.

He had managed to procure a Jeep Laredo the color of mud. Driving a security-force vehicle look-alike got him fairly close to the compound. The Laredo was parked in a thicket of palo verde trees. His circuitous way to the ranch house area had been booby-trapped by so many fellow prowlers that it was almost laughable, like a scene in a *Pink Panther* film farce.

The three earnest hunt breakers were out there, armed with binoculars and flare guns. They too had managed to come very close, despite the patrolling security guards. That made Max more nervous than the pairs of guards that rode or walked both near and far from the ranch house. The protesters were as unpredictable as lizards, and in their safari khakis, as easy to overlook.

Once ensconced where he was least likely to be expected, on a perch well greased with bird droppings, he had recorded various wheeled arrivals. A white van proved to be a meat delivery truck and left after unloading. A bronze Ford Expedition, that held the title for biggest dinosaur in the outsize SUV world, was the second arrival. It had disgorged a man in an Aussie-style hat, not pinned up on one side, so that Max couldn't see his face. Obviously the hunter. Shortly after that had come Temple's aqua Storm, now parked by the house's soaring entry door in front of the bulbous behemoth that was the Expedition, looking like a mislaid turquoise chip in this dun-colored setting.

Meanwhile . . . Max switched the camera for a pair of binoculars that were both surprisingly powerful and incredibly petite. Kind of like Temple.

His vulture's-eye view of the scene showed the trio of hunt protesters hunkered down sixty yards away in the desert and creeping ever closer.

Not thirty yards away one of the rifle-bearing security guards scanned the terrain like a point man.

Max raked the magnifying lenses over the compound and spotted a cluster of feminine hair colors by the ranch's soaring entrance doors: Temple's cocklike comb of red, the tawny mane of the widow Van Burkleo, the assistant Courtney's slick yellow poll.

He lowered the binocs, disturbed to see the guards stationed all around the area, like beaters. Now that he had inventoried the forces assembling, he was sorry he had asked Temple to be on hand. He was even sorrier that she didn't have the Colt pocketlite he had offered her. Although in a crisis she was more likely to draw her cell phone than a gun.

He swooped the binocs back to the hunt breakers: more unarmed innocents in a nest of vipers.

A movement in the desert between the compound and the nothingness that stretched to the horizon caught his eye. Something black like him, but smaller.

Wait a minute. He swept the binocs over the empty horizon again. Not quite empty. Max saw something else he didn't like. Something he never would have noticed had he not taken the high ground to look around. Odd how earthbound people thought, in terms of miles and roads and fences. Not as the crow flies, though . . . or the vulture. The vulture was a far more appropriate image for this situation, with so many human vultures gathering around for what human vultures crave . . . not dead flesh, but the material remains of the dead flesh.

His heartbeat accelerated. In disbelief? Or disappointment? Or did he just not want to tangle with this particular opponent? Damn! He was less interested in finding a murderer than a missing leopard, but now he'd managed to do both. Just this minute, just when he was trapped in this perch, watching and recording.

But was there any new danger? The worst was over, wasn't it? Van Burkleo was dead. That's what everyone had wanted, each in his own way. Van Burkleo dead. The hunts were over. The beatings ended. The ranch was about to be sold. The money made and taken away. The animals dead or dispersed . . .

Then why one last hunt?

Was there one last victim?

Chapter 44

Pretty Please Don't!

"*I can't have the panther?*"

Temple managed to sound both astounded and indignant. Your typical disgruntled customer.

She had been pretty pleased with herself for using the panther as an excuse for her latest visit to Rancho Exotica. She didn't have another pretext to hand or in brain. She would have to ride that panther until it dropped.

And it was warm out here. Temple blew upward to lift her curls from her damp forehead. She hated being the only curly-haired woman in the girl group.

Leonora and Courtney exchanged pointed looks.

"My heart was set on the panther," Temple said.

"I thought your heart was set on Mr. Maximilian." Leonora glanced pointedly at Temple's ring finger.

Oh-oh. She had been much too rash in throwing the trinket back.

"Sapphires," Temple said.

"I beg your pardon?"

"We decided I looked better in sapphires. A new ring is on order. Now. About that panther—"

"I'm sorry, but we had scheduled one final hunter and he chose the panther."

"You're shooting it?"

Leonora stiffened. "Not personally."

"When? Where?"

The two women turned to look at the Expedition parked behind Temple's Storm in the driveway like Godzilla poised over Mighty Mouse.

"Now?"

Temple had never pictured *her* panther, her Midnight Louie in an extra-large cat suit, as the object of the hunt Max wanted to stop. Where was that nasty little gun when she needed it?

"What is the swine who's doing the shooting paying for the privilege?" she asked.

"Really, Miss Barr, this is our business and your *friend* was willing and eager to buy it—"

"I'll double the fee."

"I don't see how—"

"Is it easier to let them take potshots at poor dumb animals, instead of you?" Temple asked, goaded beyond empathy. "Is that why you don't care about these helpless animals being gunned down without even a fighting chance? Your husband is dead. You don't have to live like you did. You're not just another hunted-down trophy. You can stop it now."

Leonora went white, her bizarre feline face a ghost of itself, like the white lions that Siegfried and Roy trained. "You . . . you—"

"I'm out of this." Courtney turned on her Anne Klein heels and stamped away.

Leonora's narrow catlike nostrils flared as her breath huffed out of her body like a noxious exhalation. "What do you know? What do you want?"

"I want that panther. Alive. Let's hope he still is. Take me there."

"You're crazy. It's out on the desert. We can't walk there." She looked down at their strappy, high-heeled sandals.

By some bizarre stroke of fate, Temple realized, they were both wearing the same model of Onyx sandals. Talk about walking in someone else's shoes. . . . The realization almost knocked her off her feet, which the desert would do later if shock failed now.

Max was counting on her to improvise.

"Then we'll drive." Temple grabbed Leonora's stringy arm and shoved her into the passenger side of the Storm. It was like maneuvering a puppet.

Luckily, she had left her keys in the ignition, so was saved the time of dredging her tote bag for them. "Which way?"

"Left at the fork." Leonora pointed, her taloned hand shaking. She glanced at Temple quickly, aslant, like a feral animal. "What do you know?"

Temple jerked the steering wheel and set the Storm rocking down a rutted trail made for four-wheel-drive vehicles painted desert-rat-chic camouflage.

"I know why you've had your face remade. It had to be, to hide the damage. Not hide, camouflage. You don't have to buy into Cyrus's violence and obsessions anymore. He's gone. You can start doing things your way now."

"I have no way," Leonora said bitterly. "No way but his."

"You have the money."

She shook her mane as if dislodging flies. "Money. I suppose so, but I don't care. Isn't it odd that a leopard named Osiris did Cyrus in?" she asked dreamily. "Maybe it was karma."

"It was coincidence," Temple said. "And maybe the leopard is innocent."

Leonora was suddenly quiet.

"I just don't get why you stayed, put up with it." Temple had to watch the— "road" was too good a term—ruts. "How far do we go? Is the panther still alive?"

"I haven't heard shots," Leonora said in a monotonous voice. "You usually hear shots. Unless the client is a bow hunter."

Temple gunned the motor, making the Storm buck like a turquoise-painted pony. "Just get me to where it's happening. That's all I ask."

"I don't know. This is a big place. It may be fenced, but the animals have room to roam. I don't know where they're doing it this time. Besides, what can you do about it?"

"Something. Buy the panther back from the hunter."

Leonora's slitted amber eyes slid Temple's way again, wary, challenging. "You don't know hunters, or you wouldn't say that. You wouldn't ask why I stayed."

"So why?"

"Because he would have tracked me down if I left. Hunters never stop hunting. And it's a rule of the chase. If you wound something, you follow it until you can finally kill it."

Her toneless words made Temple shiver despite the heat. She had never heard such an apt description of domestic abuse in her life. The analogy of the hunter and prey fit the situation like a throttling glove. About now *she* was ready to kill Cyrus Van Burkleo.

"There." Leonora was pointing to a line of squat, scraggly trees.

One of the dusty little Jeep Laredos the security staff drove was parked nose-first in the shade the brush provided.

Parked and empty. It meant the riders were on foot, and had become stalkers.

Chapter 45

The Most Dangerous Dame

I sit down in the dust.

"Now I wish I had those two little beetle-noses."

"Beetle-noses?" Midnight Louise inquires.

"They are shiny and black, are they not? The Yorkies' noses."

"Ours are shiny and black as well," she says.

"Ours are matte and black. Much more elegant. But ours do not smell as well."

"What kind of smelling do you require?"

"The Gees and I trailed our way all night, for miles and miles, all the way to the Animal Oasis, where I then interviewed the suspect in the Van Burkleo murder, Osiris the leopard."

"And while you were off doing that, someone absconded with your secret witness. Now that the witness is missing, perhaps you will tell me what or who it is."

I paw disconsolately at a cage bar. "It is Butch."

"Butch? I am glad you are on a first-name basis with one and all, and thankful that you are not so with me. But who the Devon Rex is Butch?"

"Your lunch pal."

This gives the kit pause. She frowns prettily, but I dare not tell her so.

"My lunch pal . . . oh, you mean the panther from between whose paws I nipped the treat for Osiris."

I nod, not enthusiastically. I am not about to tell her of the high regard in which she is held by both victim and beneficiary of her meal-exchange scheme. Nor am I about to tell her about a new worry of mine: I have spotted my Miss Temple's small aqua car in the driveway as we were working our way to the compound. Apparently she arrived here after us. Why, I cannot imagine.

"Well, if we cannot track him like the Yorkies," she says briskly, "we will have to use our superior feline brains and deduce where he has gone. Do you notice a significant absence around this cage area, Pops?"

"Besides the Yorkie noses?" I snap.

She dodges my flashing teeth, and my sarcasm. "People. I do not see one keeper or guard. Which tells me they are off doing something else. Something more important than watching the stock."

"And I know better than you on how many thousand acres they might be off doing that more important something."

She has already turned and started trotting around the sprawling ranch house. "We will start with the nearest acres, then."

I do not like following Miss Midnight Louise, so I manage to catch up and sprint past her by the time she reaches the front of the house.

But I stop cold, frozen by another inexplicable absence.

"My Miss Temple's Storm," I squall, dismayed. "It is gone! This was supposed to be a simple deposition mission. Now I have her to look after too."

Miss Louise's eyes narrow to mean-business dimensions. "I

presume that 'too' means that you feel obligated to 'look after' me as well."

"Not at all. I would not look after you if you came by carrying the queen of England's train in your teeth."

"Good," she says. "What is that vehicle still squatting on the driveway?"

"Big?" I suggest.

A withering glance. Dames have no sense of humor.

"It is an in-town off-road model of SUV, which I suppose means Suburban Uppity Vehicle."

"Hmmm." Miss Louise goes to sniff the giant tires, doing a pretty good imitation of a scent hound. Her matte-black beetle-nose wrinkles. "Creosote bushes, sagebrush, and prickly pear. I suspect that there is where we will have to head."

"The bush, you mean." I am ahead of her. I am already heading that way.

She scampers to catch up.

"It is a hunt," she suggests a bit breathlessly.

I enjoy making the kit hustle to keep up with the mature operative, and pedal faster.

"Yes, it is a hunt. But I suspect that there is more dangerous game and more hunters out there than the driver of that Suburban Uppity Vehicle has dreamed of." Why else were Mr. Max Kinsella and my Miss Temple conspiring at the Crystal Phoenix not four hours ago?

Now I know what must be done, and I am just the dude for the job . . . once I have managed to stow Miss Temple Barr and Miss Midnight Louise out of harm's way.

That is the real most dangerous game.

Chapter 46

Stalemate

"We'll have to hoof it from here," Temple said, eyeing desert and brush untracked by tires.

Speaking of hoofing it, a doe-eyed eland gazed at her through the palo verde thicket before vanishing. Not only hunters might cross their paths out here, she realized, but prey. Some of it pretty big prey.

"We can't," Leonora said when Temple came around to jerk the passenger car door open, eyeing her fashionably clad feet in dismay.

"Heck, we can navigate on these pitons better than anybody. Haven't you waltzed down the flight of stairs from the art museum at the Bellagio a few dozen times, with not one misstep? What's a little desert?"

Leonora allowed herself to be coaxed out. "Doing PR for the Crystal Phoenix makes you very pushy."

"Doing PR makes anyone very pushy. You can't afford to be a fading violet."

"I've never been out here," Leonora said, gazing around as nervously as the vanished eland. "I have no idea where they might be."

"We'll have a better idea when we look. Come on! We've got to try."

Temple didn't mention that Max was counting on her.

Together they minced over the sand and gravel and into the shade of the palo verdes.

"Isn't this area pretty bushy for desert?" Temple commented.

"We're still fairly close to the ranch house compound. It was planted with more tree-type growth so that the hunting would be more like . . . hunting. There are underground sprinklers to keep the trees growing."

"No expense spared," Temple muttered.

"I get the impression you disapprove of our hunt ranch."

"Me? Oh, no, I'm just a crass PR flack looking for a hot attraction for my client. Why should I care if a bunch of confused, helpless animals are slowly slaughtered in the name of macho decorating schemes?"

Leonora stopped. "You loathe it. You loathe me."

"Does it matter?"

Leonora couldn't make up her mind, but stood there teetering, her remade face bluntly ugly in the broad daylight.

"Look." Temple stepped closer. "I think you loathe it too, only you've never had the luxury of thinking about anything beside your own situation. Let's worry about all that later. Right now, let's just find and save one panther. Okay?"

Leonora nodded and started forward, toward the break in the bushes where the eland had peered through.

A voice put a period to her progress. A deep, annoyed, authoritative male voice.

"Just where the hell do you ladies think you're going?"

They spun to face the man who had come up behind them as silent as a cat.

He wore the short-sleeved safari-shorts uniform of the security force, mirror shades, and the usual bush hat. A rifle lay in the crook of one swarthy arm like a big stick, pointed at the ground. Despite the uniform, Temple recognized him right away: the man who had lifted her out of the Jeep just a couple days ago. Who had put a flash of fear into Max's eyes.

"It's all right, Raf," Leonora was saying with some of her old, synthetic confidence. "We just want to go to the hunt area. This lady has offered to pay a prince's ransom for the panther. We can't let it be killed."

"Sorry." He shook his head, but he didn't look or sound sorry. "I can't let you go any farther for anything. They're stalking the cat just beyond those bushes. You could get killed, and I'd be held responsible."

"We're responsible for ourselves," Temple said. "And Mrs. Van Burkleo is in full authority here."

His shook his head. Temple wished she could have seen—read— his eyes. He sounded as hard-nosed as a highway patrolman who had caught you doing eighty-five in a sixty-five-mile zone.

"Sorry, ma'am. No can do. Now you two ladies just get back in that car and turn around and go wait at the ranch house until it's over."

"But when it's over the panther will be *dead!*" Temple exploded.

"Better it than you, ma'am."

Chapter 47

Dead Ahead

"Good," I say, ducking back under some sagebrush.

"It is good that the great white hunter has your roommate and her companion at rifle point?"

"That is the only thing that will keep them safe. This is called a paradox. I will explain it to you later, when the worst is over instead of yet to come."

I turn to continue my trot toward the danger ahead.

Miss Midnight Louise does not move a muscle. Not even a whisker. "You mean you are going to walk away and leave your significant other in that appalling situation?"

Ah. Little Miss Midnight has just shown me how to kill two birds with one very sneaky stone.

"Of course not," I say indignantly. "I am going to leave you here to deal with the armed man. Obviously, my Miss Temple, competent as she is, has her hands tied at the moment. Not only does she have that extremely large and heavy tote bag to lug around but she must also consider the safety of the, uh"—I look carefully at Miss Temple's companion, and then look again—"catwoman. It is up to you, Miss Louise, to watch the situation and take action if required to save the ladies' lives. I imagine that you can handle one mighty hunter with a rifle?"

"Of course," she spits back without thinking.

By then I have turned tail and am running through the brush before she can gather her wits and argue with me, or worse, follow me. I have neatly put her between the devil and the deep blue sea, as they say. The man with the gun is the devil, and if she leaves her post to follow me, she will feel guilty. The deep blue sea is me; if she follows her instinct to interfere with my plans for the sake of it, she risks harm to the helpless humans.

I am practically chuckling at the fiendish cleverness of my move as I run, except that I cannot chuckle. But I can think about it.

For the presence of the rifle-toting guard makes one thing clear: If they have posted a guard here, the real action must be pretty near.

Dead ahead, in fact.

Chapter 48

Men in Beige

Max watched the hunt breakers edge closer like animated mushrooms.

Their clothing and movements were properly stealthy, but they were pushing nearer their human prey. Too close for Max's comfort.

He eyed the two huntsmen in beige below, who faced a sand-scoured shack open to the sky and wind about twenty-five yards in front of them.

The client carried a rifle. But so did the Rancho Exotica guide/security man.

The desert wind skittered across the sand, creating a constant microdermabrasion tattoo on any exposed skin surfaces. Max had been suffering that soft scouring for over an hour now, and it was getting on his nerves.

No, that wasn't what was getting on his nerves. It was the sleek 9-mm gun on the rock beside him.

Max hated guns. He hated bombs even more, but he hated guns

too. He'd taken perverse pride in rarely carrying them during a decade-plus of serious undercover work, and never using them.

Now he might have no choice. He would never have suggested that Temple come to this scene without having the backup of a loaded gun in his pocket. The Colt he had offered her weighed down his jacket pocket, but it was superfluous, not suitable to this distance and this situation.

Against rifles, of course, either weapon was useless, the movies aside. Amazing how many film heroes held off whole armies of heavy artillery with endlessly firing pistols.

Max was a fine magician, but he wasn't that good.

A basso growl gritted across the sands with the wind.

The guide pointed with his left arm, the rifle still cradled in his right.

The client was a taller man, wearing the same style khaki clothing, except his shirtsleeves and pants were full-length. Despite his amateur status—and he certainly seemed awkward holding the rifle—he was the more sinister figure. The security boyos in Bermuda shorts always struck Max, like Las Vegas's similarly attired bicycle police, as overgrown Boy Scouts.

Both men wore short boots and new bush hats, the guide's rakishly snapped up on the right. The client's hat still shaded his face all around, as did a pair of wraparound sunglasses. The guide scorned sunglasses, and squinted professionally at the shack.

Suddenly he lifted his rifle and shot to the right of the structure. The sharp report, the shooter's body jerking at the recoil, the ping of a bullet hitting stone, startled Max despite himself.

It also startled something hiding inside the shack. A low black form streaked out of the shade and the shelter.

Max felt his gut tighten as he saw it: a panther, black as midnight, but its coat shining slightly rusty in the glaring sunlight. It could be Kahlúa, the panther he had borrowed once for a stunt. This was a beautiful, bright animal, sculpted like an art deco onyx, crouched and vigilant, knowing something was *wrong*. But also knowing only rewards and kindness from the hand of mankind so far. Until today.

Max scowled at the "client." At least the bastard wasn't a bow hunter. Not that a "hunter" who needed fenced and tamed prey could be expected to kill with one well-placed shot.

Max filmed the cat, still crouching, but now exposed. Filmed the two men conferring, moving closer.

The client lifted the rifle, placed it awkwardly against his right shoulder.

Max found his hand on the 9-mm Glock on the stone beside him, itching to touch the trigger. Shoot into the air, scare the panther off. And give away his own position.

He looked for the protesters. They were belly-crawling along a wash behind the fence, nearing the shack and the panther, inching into the rifleman's shaky range.

And Temple?

His binoculars found no flash of red. Good. Something had delayed her, thank God. At least *she* was safe.

All these actions, thoughts, took scant seconds, as they always do in a crisis.

The guide nudged the client's rifle barrel a shade to the left, lifting it a trifle too.

Paint-by-numbers shooting.

The panther, panting, eyed the two men, perhaps hoping for food or water, not death.

Max gritted his teeth, not knowing whether to lift his video camera or binoculars or gun.

Suddenly the crouching panther backed up, snarling, staring to the side as if stung.

A small black banshee came screeching out of the bushes, charging the big cat's face, swiping at the long, thick muzzle whiskers.

The panther, more shocked than angered, backed up farther, growling.

The small animal leaped to harry its rear, dashing in, then away, spitting and screeching, sparring at the creature's huge haunches.

Before Max could blink, the tiny spitfire had herded the panther back into the shack like a lion tamer maneuvering the king of the jungle onto a one-foot-diameter circus pedestal.

Max glanced at hunter and guide. Their rifle barrels drooped toward the ground in their slack grasps like agape jaws.

Before the impotency image could harden, the guide rallied, lifted his rifle, and shot into the shack. Wood splintered from a Big Bang that reverberated across the desert and drilled into Max's ears.

Apparently the staff of Rancho Exotica aimed to please.

The guide stalked toward the shack, ratcheting another bullet into the chamber, determined to drive the animals from their shelter.

He came right up to the shack, rifle raised and pointed, ready to fire again.

This time the black banshee fell from the sky . . . fell from the branches of a palo verde tree leaning over what was left of the shack's roof. The plunge knocked the guide's jaunty bush hat to the ground, exposing his face to a whirlwind attack of slugging claws. The man went down on one knee, but the rifle hit the ground and discharged. . . .

Directly into the shack, at just-above-ground level.

A roar seemed to explode the rotten wood structure, then the black panther itself exploded snarling into the sunlight, muzzle drawn back to expose stalactites and stalagmites of teeth gleaming ice white in the sunshine.

Thirty feet away, the hunter lifted his rifle again, walking toward his distracted target, who was posed like a '50s porcelain panther, muscular and frozen, a sitting duck. . . .

The protesters, seeing the inevitable, wailed as one and lurched up from the cover of the wash, charging and climbing the fence until it broke under their weight.

To Max in his observation post, it was like watching diverse blips on a radar screen converging for a spectacular, fatal meeting in the middle.

There was no humanly possible way he could intervene. Disaster on a converging course. The determined hunter with his rifle bearing down on the panther, the guide rolling and screaming and nursing his blood-blinded face, the bloody-fool protesters surging to put themselves between hunter and prey . . . good God, Max thought in slow motion, this was not just a showdown between hunter and prey but between murderer and . . . and *witness!*

He gathered himself for the most spectacular athletic vault of his career, down into the middle of it all he would plunge . . .

And was beaten to the punch by the same black banshee that had corralled the panther and savaged the guide.

The black cat ran out from the shadows in which he had circled behind the hunter. He leaped up to land on his neck like a vampire leech, a nightmare even Edgar Allen Poe couldn't have dreamed of in his most fevered hallucinations.

The man dropped to the ground just as Max landed in front of him—knees bent to absorb the punishing shock, hands out to wrest the rifle barrel from his grasp and smash the butt into the man's suddenly exposed jaw, the bush hat and sunglasses flying away to reveal . . .

Max had no time to linger.

He looked around. The guide's face was a road map of claw marks. He was out of it.

The protesters had circled the still-crouching, growling panther, singing "We Shall Overcome" off-key.

Max spotted an oncoming flash of red through the palo verdes. He grabbed the hunter by the khaki lapels, looked into the dazed face.

"Why?" Max asked.

The bleary eyes focused on his, then went AWOL.

Max looked up. Temple was almost here. He would have to get the answer to that question later.

Best he be gone now.

He looked around for the black cat.

Midnight Louie had made the same, split-second decision.

Great minds and all that . . .

He was thinking of Louie, of course.

Chapter 49

Bless Me, Mother

There was no way Matt was going to join three nuns in attending 5:00 P.M. mass without committing to 6:00 P.M. supper afterward.

Or so Sister Seraphina had told him on the phone.

"We're used to six A.M. mass, you know, Matt, dear. But we understand that with your late-night radio show that's early for you. So let's make an occasion of it. It will be such a treat to see you."

"Can we make it supper at seven? I want to visit with Father Hernandez after mass." How many Hail Marys, Matt wondered, did it take to wash away lying to a nun? To an old nun. That was worse than taking candy from a kindergartener.

Kitty the Cutter was pushing him down the slippery slope to deception and sin already.

But Sister Seraphina had accepted the lie as only logical, and Matt prepared to put in twenty-four hours of fretting before his meeting with Molina.

He had almost been tempted to poll callers on his radio show on whether he was doing the right thing to involve Molina, but people stressed out by their own problems made impenetrable Wailing Walls for the woes of others.

He got through the day by rote, avoiding everyone, seeing phantoms everywhere. Now he understood the power of paranoia.

The poetic justice of it all hung over him like a looming guillotine of conscience. Once he had tracked Cliff Effinger. Now he was tracked.

Except Effinger had probably been too mean, and too dumb, to worry about a stalker as Matt did.

And Kathleen O'Connor was a lot more demonstrably dangerous than Matt ever had been.

At four-thirty Saturday night, Matt's new old Probe joined the streams of cars heading somewhere to have fun in Las Vegas.

He headed south, away from the city, then circled back toward North Las Vegas. He watched his rearview mirror as if some hood had hidden in the backseat to hold a knife on him. A stalker was only a rear-seat hood, one car-length removed.

No vehicle seemed to stay near him long.

When he finally pulled into the old-fashioned alley behind Our Lady of Guadalupe convent, not a car was in sight. He parked in the deep shade of an ancient pine tree anyway. Pine and palm trees, only one more signpost of how schizophrenic a city Las Vegas was, an oasis in the desert, a theme-park town with a variegated bouquet of socially acceptable sin and churches of every sect known to religion.

A knock at the convent's back door produced Sister Mary Monica, beaming like a frail apple-faced doll. She swept him into the large, spare kitchen like a prodigal son.

"How wonderful to see you!" Sister Seraphina O'Donnell just swept him into a wholehearted hug. "We know you're so busy nowadays, but we do miss your visits."

"Busy is no excuse," Matt said, seeing that they had already set out the supper plates in the plain dining room with its cluster of small, separate tables. He felt like a worm for using them as a cover.

The six nuns chatted happily as they all walked to the nearby church in the warm afternoon sun. Las Vegas didn't offer the tree-shaded streets of the Midwest, but the climate's sun-scoured, healthy openness was always an upper. Our Lady of Guadalupe's spire, capped with red tile, simmered in the last blaze of undiluted afternoon sunlight.

The nuns' short black veils seemed more like linen mantillas than a last vestige of more formal habits. Matt almost felt himself transported back to the heyday of California's Hispanic-Catholic culture. Young and middle-aged people were also converging on the old-fashioned adobe church. Their half-Latino, half-Anglo greetings and banter gave the forthcoming ritual a preface of celebration.

Matt could literally feel and see a community assembling, and for a moment he was homesick for his past at the center of so much goodwill.

But when his party passed into the shade inside the church and dipped their fingertips in the tepid holy water of the entrance fonts, when the sign of the cross replaced chatter and the only sounds in the interior stillness were the scrape of soles on floor tile and the thump of kneelers being lowered to the floor, he felt he was back a hundred years, or maybe only thirty, and about to hear a Latin mass.

Illusion, of course. The nuns led the way to a pew near the front and bracketed him in their midst. He managed to study the confessionals as they entered.

Darn! They were on *both* sides of the church. He'd forgotten to tell Molina which side to meet at.

The choice was simple: on one side St. Joseph ruled at the tiny side altar. On the other, Mary. There was an assignment for the amateur operative: which would Molina choose?

It was bad enough to arrange to slink into one of the unused little rooms; playing musical confessional would attract certain attention.

He glanced around as the congregation stood for the entrance of the celebrant and two altar boys . . . one altar boy and one altar girl, what do you know? Molina was about as tall as he was, and he didn't spot her anywhere in this traditionally short crowd.

So even as the familiar prayers and responses of the mass settled on him like a warm, familiar blanket of sound and motion, Matt found himself fidgeting, fretting. Turning slightly to check out the pews. Studying the confessionals: three doors with a tiny arched window covered with pleated white linen.

At communion time, he was so distracted that he was mostly

thinking about how he'd have such a good view of both confessionals on the way back to his seat. Then was the time to spot Molina, or make a choice. And he should also be on the lookout for Miss Kitty. It'd be just like her to show up where least expected. Imagine sliding behind one wooden door and finding her in the confessor's seat!

Worry, Matt realized, was a great distraction from prayer, so he settled down and asked God to help him find the right confessional, please.

Not a very noble request, but all he could muster.

Someone tugged at his sleeve. He had stood automatically with everyone else for Father Hernandez's exit. "We'll see you back at the convent later," Sister Seraphina whispered.

Matt nodded, kneeling again quickly and burying his face in his hands as if in private prayer. Why had he decided to go with the nuns? They had chosen a pew far too close to the altar. There was no way to turn around discreetly to figure out if everyone had left, or Molina had arrived. If she would come. Maybe something had come up, an emergency.

The church was still and growing dark except for the eternal red light near the altar, signifying the presence of the Eucharist. Maybe this meeting mocked the place and its purpose. What had he been thinking of? Desperately consulting Molina, that's what. Kinsella was not much help. Matt needed comfort as well as aid, and Molina was the only person besides Kinsella he figured was strong enough to go near and not risk her life.

So she might aid him. Comfort? That was a foolish, reflexive need. Nobody got comfort anymore, except the dying in a hospice.

He sat on the pew and bent to lift the kneeler out of the way. The sound of it resting against the pew back ahead echoed like a single knock on a big wooden door.

Matt stood, tossed a mental coin, and opted for St. Joseph. A lot of women reared Catholic had overdosed on the Virgin Mary by age twenty. Molina would choose Joseph, because he was a missing person as far as the Scriptures went. He was a mystery and she was a cop.

Matt opened the nearest confessional door and slid in, checking the church. Utterly vacant, except for the Eucharist.

He had forgotten how dark these old confessionals were, although St. Stanislaus in Chicago had kept sinners lined up for confessionals long after the ritual, renamed and repositioned as the sacrament of reconciliation and practiced face-to-face in well-lit rooms, had become commonplace.

He felt his way to the vague white square of pleated linen, the priest's porthole, so to speak, on the ocean of self-proclaimed sinners that would come in wave after wave on both sides of his claustrophic box. Matt had been there.

Matt knelt. This kneeler wasn't even padded—*ouch!* Nothing like the Spanish for blending religion and pain. Guess sinners didn't merit padding.

He heard a wooden panel sliding open, a soft stiletto of sound, like honing a knife. Or a razor. For a moment he imagined Kitty the Cutter lying in wait, a gray silhouette seen through a linen curtain pleated thickly.

"This is the kinkiest meet with a snitch I've ever had," Molina's voice whispered through the material instead. "I used to have to go with my grandmother to these guilt boxes when I was a very young kid. She took forever too! What took those old people so long in confession?"

Matt smiled. That one he could answer. "What children and the old confess is remarkably similar. In both cases, innumerable venial sins. Many of those old people were overscrupulous to the point of obsessive-compulsive disorder. Many priests committed sins of impatience listening to them; it was usually a double absolution in those cases."

"Hmmm. Actually, I kind of like sitting here in the control booth. Sin Central. No women allowed."

"I thought you would."

"How'd you know which side I'd be in."

"I figured you'd pick the St. Joseph side. He's a mystery."

"Right pick, wrong reason. The other side has that gruesome twelfth station of the cross with Christ crucified on the wall next to it. I see enough gore in my day job."

"Which station is outside these confessionals?"

"Jesus before Pilate."

"Always the cop, wanting everybody in custody."

"Not everybody. So what's the crisis? I can only take feeling silly so much longer."

Matt gathered himself. "I wish I could just feel silly. In fact, I probably should, but I'm too scared to."

"Scared?"

He was flattered that she was surprised. "That woman I told you about? The one who—"

"The razor-wielding priest hater. That's what this is about?"

"She's stalking me. More than me. Anybody I associate with."

"I told you back then it was a hate crime. You should have let me have a real go at her then."

"How? She appears when she wants to." His knees were starting to kill him and he shifted position.

"What's she done? Specifics."

"She confronted me again. Made demands. She sent me an object. Made demands. She, uh, she was at TitaniCon, and I think she attacked Temple, and Sheila, a friend of mine from my ConTact hotline days. And . . . Mariah."

"What!"

He had her attention now. "Mariah's the one who noticed the pattern. They were all silly mishaps, but there was malice behind them. Then, as I was leaving, someone jabbed me in the kidneys when I was going down an escalator. Felt like a gun. Felt like a warning that she could do anything she liked to me, anywhere, anytime."

"And? Did you confront her?"

"Couldn't. It was a mob scene. She vanished into the crowd. But she left her 'weapon' behind. Dropped it. Mariah retrieved it."

"Oh, my God."

"I know. It could have been an explosive. But it was an aspergillum."

Silence held inside the confessional rooms as well as outside them.

"Father, forgive me," Molina intoned laconically at last. "You were right to be so cautious."

"An aspergillum is—"

"I know what it is. I've had my catechism lessons. I've seen it used at my grandmother's funeral. Little metal implement for the dispensing of holy water. Scary thing, she could have had it wired into a bomb. An instrument of blessing made into an instrument of death. So. What does she want?"

Matt took a deep breath.

"No one toys with anyone," Molina prodded, "including the police, unless he or she wants something: publicity, fear, revenge."

"She wants souls. Specifically mine."

"A soul is an immaterial thing."

"She wants my soul in a very material form. She's . . . demonic is the word I'd use."

"We've run into religious nuts," Molina mused, thinking as a police officer. "Usually they're men. I don't get this woman. I don't get her nuisance attacks on these innocent bystanders at TitaniCon."

"Not all nuisance attacks. When Temple, Mariah, and I were seeing Sheila to her car in the parking garage, a vehicle came right at us, followed us across the bridge to the hotel and crashed right through the glass doors."

"I heard about that! Stolen car. It was pursuing *you*? And Mariah?"

"And Temple."

"I am furious that no one told me about this. I'm the child's mother. I have a right to know."

"We weren't sure what that was about, some nutso driver who couldn't find a parking place, or a drunk gambler with a gripe against the hotel . . . I hadn't put it together yet. I wasn't really sure until she approached me a few days ago and told me what the price of peace and quiet for all involved was."

"A soul? That's demented."

"You still don't understand."

"Maybe I'm a little more concerned about my daughter's life and limb than I am about your soul. So what was this woman doing at TitaniCon anyway?"

"Stalking me is all I can figure out."

"Oh, I doubt you're that intriguing. There's got to be another reason."

She was right, but Matt wasn't ready to tell her that. Kinsella's past was his to keep, and Temple would feel betrayed if Matt gave it away to Molina, even if it put some of Max's actions in a better light.

"I'm afraid her prime objective is just me and my soul."

"You can't extort a soul from someone."

"I didn't think so either, but I underestimated her. It's really simple, Carmen. What has been my core belief for most of my life?"

"The Church."

"How have I honored it?"

"By being a priest, until lately."

She still was oddly obtuse. He had never confessed a true sin that made him feel as slimy and ashamed as Kathleen O'Connor's method of extracting, extorting his soul. He was glad they were both in the dark, locked in a ritual room from their common past.

"Yes?" Molina demanded.

"I suppose it's a simple thing to most people. No big deal. But she knew how to find the one thing . . . What's the hallmark of a Roman Catholic priest, laicized, as I have been, or not?"

"Religion. The collar, bingo night? . . ." Her joke found no response and he could hear her squirming on her side of the linen curtain. Funny, confessees usually squirmed, not confessors.

"Oh. That," she said at last, absolving him of putting it into words. A long silence.

"It *is* fiendish," she whispered, almost thinking aloud. "Isolating. Abusive. Like something out of a melodrama, only with a role reversal. This woman is mad."

"I asked Kinsella for help. He checked out my place for bugs. There was nothing. Yet. But she left a package there while I was out of town."

"Right. It could have been a bomb."

"I don't think she wants to hurt me. At least not physically. Not anymore. She's made her mark. It's just others. I didn't tell him what her price was. I was afraid he'd tell me to pay it."

"You can't." Molina's voice was crisp. Certain. "You know what I'd do if someone was putting Mariah in that position?"

"I'm not a child. I'm not helpless."

"Yes, you are, which is why you wouldn't let the Mystifying Max in on your ugly secret. We're all helpless, Matt, if someone wants to destroy us badly enough. This is fiendish. You can hardly dare go to anyone for help, you can't associate with friends. . . . Has she targeted Temple Barr?"

"I don't know. She said something about watching her, but it was more to prove that she was watching me. I think she knows who my friends are, but she doesn't know—"

"Who you really care about. That's good. Keep it that way. She seems to be aiming at the women around you, like the jealous bitch she probably is."

"Carmen!"

"Sorry. I forgot where we were. Where I am. You know how hard it is to stop a stalker. Legally."

"I know. And she's too smart to attack me physically again, although if I hurt her back, a man against a woman, who'd support me?"

"Fiendish."

"I wonder," he began, then stopped.

"What?"

"Oh, speaking of role reversal. I hunted Cliff Effinger down. Probably drew the wrong people's attention to him and got him killed. I wonder if this isn't a case of just deserts."

"Forget it! Effinger brought on his own death by associating with a crooked crowd. Besides, this woman . . . what does she look like anyway?"

"Great. Beautiful. A late-twenties Elizabeth Taylor. And don't say—"

" 'Just relax and enjoy it?' No, I won't. Heard that about too many rape victims to think any age or gender welcomes abuse. Looks have nothing to do with the crime, but they might have something to do with the criminal. With looks like that, she could get almost any man she wanted. Why fixate on the one man who doesn't want her, won't succumb. It's a power thing, as usual. All about me, me, me, even as they fixate on you, you, you. Can you get me an image of her?"

"Yes."

"Yes?"

"I had Janice do one."

"Oh, Janice. You've been busy. Do I sense a wee hesitation there?"

"I was trying to see Janice lately."

"Trying? Guess this woman fixed that."

"And I have the note and envelope the ring came in. Kinsella suggested you might want prints."

" 'Kinsella suggested.' Who is he? Mr. Police Expert now? I'll take it. And what ring is this?"

"What she sent me. She demanded I wear it."

"I begin to get her MO. What kind of ring?"

"A gold image of a serpent eating its own tail."

"Seen something like that."

"It's called the worm Ouroboros. Ancient infinity symbol going back to the Greeks."

"So. You wearing it?"

"Just what she called to ask. I told her yes."

"Must stick in your craw."

"No. On my keychain."

Matt had seldom heard laughter from the confessor's side, but he did now.

"That's right. Fight her with the letter of her own law. She can't think of everything, Matt. She's not supernatural. She's just ahead of the average person because she's spending all her time and energy on tormenting you. You know what you have to do?"

"Concentrate on finding and stopping her just as hard. I'm a stalker again."

"Bingo. Okay, hand over the physical evidence. You've got it with you, I assume. Just leave it in your cubicle when you go. Mail me that sketch Janice did. Follow your regular work and travel routine. See only who you have to, and very briefly. Visit the library and look up books on surveillance, bugging, police and covert techniques. Don't check them out, just read them there and make notes if you have to. Web-crawl the law enforcement sites."

"Web-crawl! I have to buy a computer too?"

"The wail of an immaterial man being made flesh."

"You're saying I have to *become* her to overcome her."

"I'm saying you've got a new full-time job. I'll look into what I can, but it won't turn up much. She sounds like she's been doing this for a while. If she's done this before, if she's left a trail, if she insists on breaking in and getting caught, you could maybe have her put away for a few months."

"What's her ultimate goal? What does she really want?"

"There's only one way to find out, and you don't want that route."

"What's that."

"Sleep with her and see what she does after."

"I doubt anyone has ever gotten that advice from a confessor before."

"It's not advice. It's reality, but, hey, you don't have to give in to reality. It's not a law."

He was going to protest when he heard something else he'd never heard in a confessional before.

The yodel of a cell phone.

"Is there no sanctuary anywhere?" Molina growled to herself and her phone. "Yeah? Yeah. At the ranch? Shooting? Right away. This is one denouement I don't want to miss."

Matt heard her rise. "Come on. Let's give your stalker something to chase. Some friends of yours are in mucho hot water out in the desert."

Chapter 50

Action Traction

Temple came running into the clearing, using her high heels like the pitons she had claimed they were, driving her forward faster than even she believed possible, the security man and his ponderous boots tamping sand behind her.

Leonora had stayed behind in the front seat of the Storm, the door open, her delicate shoes planted on the desert sand, quivering.

But she had ordered—ordered—the man to go with Temple and do what she said.

The scene in front of them wasn't chaotic, but it was like a stage with three spotlit acts, a three-ring circus: you didn't know where to look first.

The three dusty wayfaring strangers trilling like a Salvation Army chorus in front of a loose panther was the most riveting vignette.

They were singing, she thought, the song about the lion sleeps tonight. The panther had obviously not been sleeping today.

The lone man on the right, on his knees holding a bleeding face in two blood-gloved hands, caught her attention next, and held it.

Behind her, Rafi's footsteps veered away and toward his fallen fellow guard.

And then there was the third scene stage right: Max coated in sand dust, beside another fallen man.

Temple couldn't tell whether he was helping the man, or holding him in custody, or both.

Max's eyes flicked across Temple, their expression changing from something dark and unreadable to relief, then to wariness as they moved on to Rafi, helping up the stricken guard across the clearing.

Max looked around farther, then focused back on her.

Her eyes questioned him, so he nodded toward the guard's bleeding face. "Louie's work."

"My Louie?"

"You know another?"

She stared at the man in Max's grasp. He was bleeding from the mouth and his head was turned away. "Your work?"

"His own." Max kicked the rifle toward Temple, then unlatched his belt and pulled it through its loops like a whip.

Temple thought for a moment he was going to take it to the man, but instead he crouched and bound the guy's wrists behind his back.

"This might hold him, it might not. So if I were you I'd pick up the rifle and make like a guard."

A rifle? It was to laugh. But Temple squatted beside it, picked up the stock, being careful not to get near the trigger, and stood, pointing the lethal barrel at the ground. That was where she intended to leave it.

"I take it," Max said, "that you've called for reinforcements."

"I left my cell phone with Leonora. Don't worry, I used a spare battery for it, and gave her Molina's personal number. Several times."

Max, oddly indifferent to his prisoner, instead watched Rafi.

Temple could see calculations moving across his mobile face. Not all of them were pretty. Were anyone else other than she watching, he wouldn't let even that much show.

"It's up to you," Max said abruptly. "You need to get that Rafi guy the hell out of here. Tell him . . . the cops are coming and this is a mess and he's best out of it."

Max turned to go.

"And this is—?" Temple gestured gingerly with the rifle.

Max nodded. "The killer. In more ways than one." His voice was drenched in disgust. "God have mercy on his soul. I certainly wouldn't."

He turned and scaled the rocks, disappearing into their dun-colored contours and then over their crest like a lizard.

Temple looked from vignette to vignette. The panther, burnished red-black by the westering sun, had settled on its belly, licking a paw. Apparently the singing had quieted it.

Raf had ripped a sleeve off his shirt and dabbed at the other man's face until the scratches beneath the blood were revealed, nasty but not serious.

The bound man on the ground stayed still, knees tented, head bowed into them, face obscured.

Rafi, his fellow worker tended to, suddenly saw Temple with the rifle.

"Hey! Little lady, you can't do that! Just stand there and let me take that thing off your hands."

Temple would have been happy to relinquish the weapon. It was darn heavy, for one thing, but she remembered Max's instructions. He had given them brusquely, against his druthers, she could tell. She had a feeling he was being more merciful to Rafi than to the killer, for some reason of his own.

"Thanks." Temple lowered her voice as Rafi neared. "The police are coming. In force. You've been so helpful, I wouldn't want to get you into trouble. I think this guy killed Mr. Van Burkleo."

Rafi's features sharpened like a hunt dog's. He swept the rifle out of her grip anyway.

"Killed him, huh? Who belted his wrists behind him? Not you?"

Temple blinked. "I don't know—" She meant she hadn't thought up a good story yet. "A masked man?"

"It's not a joking matter. Murder."

"Neither are the police, if there's some reason you'd prefer not to get involved with them."

It was odd, but Temple saw the same indecision and calculations crossing Rafi's face that she had seen on Max's only moments before.

Both men were torn, she suspected, between considerations not quite visible to anyone around them.

Rafi suddenly gave Temple a, well . . . raffish grin. "Yeah. Never good to let the minions of the law get too hard a grip on you." He looked over at the threesome still making a human fence in front of the panther. "Hey! Peaceniks. Any one of you fur freaks know how to handle a rifle? We got a human hunter needs watching until the authorities come."

They stopped singing, stunned. Finally the lone woman stepped forward.

"You mean cover the lowlife who tried to shoot the panther? I can do it in a New York minute."

Raf eyed her lean, mean, sixtyish form. "I bet you can, Iron Grandma. Here."

He held out the rifle. The woman marched forward and took it, aiming it at the sitting man.

Raf turned to Temple. "Thanks, Red. I do like to keep a low pro-file."

He turned and headed back on a long, circling-around arc that would keep him safely on the fringes until out of sight.

Temple wondered if he and Max would cross paths in their joint but separate surreptitious getaways. No, too surreal.

In the distance, a scream of sirens wailed their intention to get up close and personal.

Temple braced herself for explanations of the inexplicable.

She looked around one last time at the animal fair.

The panther and the killer were there.

By the light of the sun,

The panther was the one,

Who was combing his auburn hair.

Chapter 51

Cops in Khaki

Matt's penance had been one of the most strenuous ever assigned.

First he'd used Molina's cell phone on the run to call the convent and call off dinner. Something urgent (it was) but not serious (not for him, anyway) had come up, he'd said truthfully, and he'd explain later.

Then he'd been a door-clutching passenger in some junker stick-shift heap that Molina manhandled to within a block from the police parking ramp. A cell phone had hugged her ear all the way, though Matt had thought that there were laws against driving while doing that sort of thing.

He had trailed her, running, into the ramp, where she had claimed a Crown Victoria and gunned it down the exit spiral. Now she was interacting intensely with the onboard computer screen and mobile police radio.

If the police drove like this, he didn't want to know what they arrested ordinary citizens for driving like.

By the time they turned off the highway onto the darkening desert road, three police cars all boasting blinking headache bands up top and an unmarked car with a portable blinking cherry stylishly off-center on its roof joined the procession.

Matt's head was beginning to throb from the jolting and the constant squawk of radio traffic and the piercing sound effects.

They converged on . . . oh, Lord! Temple's car. The little aqua Storm, marooned in the desert.

A woman with a monstrous face sat on the passenger side, hysterical. When swarmed by Molina and company, she pointed ahead.

A uniformed officer stayed behind while the others forged forward on foot. Molina looked over her shoulder at him. "Come on!"

Matt did, feeling like a spaniel trotting behind bloodhounds.

Temple? his mind protested. Why would she be here? On what was obviously a major crime scene.

Then, again, why wouldn't she be here?

Matt trotted into a clearing crowded with police personnel.

He could barely pick Temple out of the milling mess, much less Molina. For once he had forgotten Kitty O'Connor. No way could she be here, or could she have followed this circuitous trail. In an unexpected way, he was momentarily free.

It felt wonderful, despite the chaos, and despite seeing a man in a khaki bike-police-type outfit being led away with a raw, scratched face.

More men in khaki were coaxing a handsome black panther into a cage.

Matt glanced around, anxious. Where was Temple?

There, being loomed over by Lieutenant Molina.

That was a fate he wouldn't wish on anyone, particularly Temple, who was sensitive about her lack of height.

He hurried over, just in time to catch Molina's "Who is this guy again?"

Temple was shaking her little red head like the little red hen.

"I just can't believe it. The last person in the world you'd suspect. Maybe it's a mistake. But why else would he be trying to kill the panther. You're going to need to talk to animal trainers on this one."

"I *am* an animal trainer," Molina retorted in a harassed tone. "*This* is a zoo. Okay, we've got the guy in custody. Now you give us a reason why. Shooting at a panther on a canned-hunt ranch isn't reason enough."

Matt joined the pair and Molina frowned at him. "This is an official interview, Devine. Butt out."

"I haven't said a word."

"Keep it that way." She let him stay and focused again on Temple. "Just tell me the facts."

Ma'am.

"His name is Kirby Granger. He runs the Animal Oasis for confiscated, lost, and abused animals of all kinds, domestic or exotic. That's why I can't believe—"

"The hunt breakers have already said they saw him aiming at the panther."

"But that's . . . heresy for someone like him. He wasn't even working with performing animals anymore, like he used to just a couple of years ago when . . ."

"When?" Molina asked.

Temple glanced at Matt.

"No side consultations," Molina said. "You distract the witness again, Devine, and you're walking home."

"Oh." Temple was very interested. "Matt came with you?"

Molina's blue eyes flashed with wicked humor. "I take the Fifth on that, Miss Barr. Now. Answer my questions. You can ask your own later. Why would an animal-rights advocate shoot at a virtually helpless animal?"

"I don't know," Temple admitted. "I can see why he might kill Cyrus Van Burkleo—"

"I am so glad that you can. Because I can't. And if I can't, I can't arrest him, much as whoever wrapped him in Armani and left him here to dry might wish. You know anybody with a size thirty-two Armani waist, hmmm? Can't be a bleeding-heart animal lover. It was a *leather* belt."

"You'll just have to ask the suspect, Lieutenant."

"He isn't a suspect on your say-so. I'll have to let him go."

"Don't."

They turned at the interjection of a fresh voice. A husky, shaky voice.

Leonora Van Burkleo stood on wobbly heels by herself, having hiked in from Temple's car.

"I . . . I found them."

"Found?" Molina asked.

"Them?" Temple asked.

Molina gave Temple a quelling glance. "Found where?" Molina asked more gently, sensing Leonora's fragile state.

Leonora shrugged, looked to the side as if envisioning a scene from a movie. "In Cyrus's office. That man had . . . pushed Cyrus. The . . . horn was sticking out of his chest. A big dark point like a thorn. Giant thorn. It looked like the oryx had done it. So odd. After seeing all those horns on the wall, seeing one . . . going through Cyrus like a rifle barrel." She shivered, though the day was at its hottest.

"She's not a well woman," Temple said. Cautioned.

Molina gave her a look that could kill. She made cases on not-well women and men. Murder revolved around not-well men and women.

Temple glanced at Matt, who grimaced his sympathy. The law on the trail of a vulnerable witness was not a pretty sight.

"So," Molina said with satisfaction. "The leopard was set dressing. I thought so."

"I thought of it," Leonora said, lifting her mishapen face, tossing her leonine mane.

"You?" Molina hesitated, no doubt thinking of Miranda warnings. "You could be an accessory to murder," she said, spewing the ritual faster than a TV huckster.

Leonora, having abandoned fear, was unstoppable. "I don't care. I let him into the animal area, punched in the security code. He did the rest. Brought the leopard along, brought it inside. Didn't need anything but his voice. And then he left. That's a crime? Letting a man release a leopard?"

Molina looked at Leonora for a long moment.

"There are extenuating circumstances," Temple blurted.

Molina did not look at her. "Call a lawyer," she advised Leonora softly. "Meanwhile, I'm taking you all in."

"All?" Temple asked.

Molina still did not look at her. "I assume you can drive Mr. Devine home, Miss Barr."

When Matt made a move in protest, Molina answered it, edging near so Temple couldn't hear. "I'll give you a police-car escort. That ought to keep the bogeywoman away. Now." Her voice escalated to public level for Temple's benefit. "Off with you. I want to do my job."

Temple gave Leonora a thumbs-up as she edged over to Matt.

He put an arm around her. Her bare arm was cold and goose-pimpled.

It was getting dark. No self-respecting stalker, he was willing to bet, was hanging around this headache-bar-lit crime scene.

"Are you okay?" he asked.

"No. And I don't understand any of it, except poor Leonora."

"What happened to her?"

"What didn't? If Molina—"

"I think she gets the message. She'll treat her with kid gloves."

"Since when has she treated *anyone* with kid gloves?"

"How about her own kid?"

"You think so?" Temple glared at him, an aftershock of the evening, then her expression softened. "Matt, what on earth were you doing with Mother Macabre anyway?"

"I had a confession to make."

"Oh! Joke your way out of it! All right, I give up. Take me home."

"I'll have to stop to pick up the Vampire at Our Lady of Guadalupe."

"You weren't kidding about the confession," Temple said.

"I never kid."

She paused in stomping off the overlit scene to smile at him. "I wish you did. Sometimes."

Two officers in summer khaki examined their IDs before they were allowed to get in the Storm and drive away.

Chapter 52

AnticliMax

"I hope it's not too late," Matt said.

"For you, never."

Sister Seraphina swung the convent door wide, but Matt still checked his watch as the hall light fell on the dial. Ten-thirty. He'd been taught not to inconvenience the good sisters since he was six years old.

Old nuns had placid, plain faces, most of them, and Sister Seraphina's was as honest and perceptive as ever.

"Want a snack?" was all she said though, leading him toward the building's rear kitchen.

"I'm terribly sorry about standing you up for dinner. It was . . . well, a police emergency."

She stopped and spun to face him, the small gold crucifix at her breastbone glinting spanglelike for a moment. "Police emergency?"

"Not mine," he reassured her. "I just happened to be along for the ride. I don't suppose I can explain too much."

"Of course not. Police business. Besides, mystery becomes you. You always were too honest."

She turned and led him on.

Too honest? Funny thing for a nun to say. Maybe she meant people who seemed to live in broad daylight all the time were less interesting than people with hints of shadow, as in Janice's sketches. Janice always sketched shadows behind her portraits of perps. A shadow that put their faces in the spotlight and made them look more substantial, if sinister.

The deserted kitchen, brightly lit by an overhead oval of milk glass, felt as utterly functional as a school cafeteria. Maybe it was the blond Formica table-and-four-chairs units dotting the floor like bastard Swedish modern flotsam on a vinyl-tile sea.

Sister gestured him to an empty table and had whisked cotton place mats and sets of plain stainless steel silverware onto the bland Formica before he could sit down.

"Can't I—?"

"No. We take turns at kitchen duty and today's mine." She grinned over her shoulder as she headed for the stove. "So you just sit there like Father and get waited on as usual."

"Ouch."

In half a minute she had set a bowl of stew in front of him and sat down with her own at the place opposite. "Just my little joke."

"How did you happen to be up?"

"Happen nothing. I knew you'd come by."

"Why?"

"Guilt. A Catholic grade school teacher, retired or not, has a nose for guilt that would make Pinocchio's longest lying nose look like a toothpick."

"I really regret the change in plans."

"Yes, but that's not what you're guilty about."

He was flabbergasted, and showed it.

"You're guilty about whatever you were up to when you invited us to mass in the first place." She waved a hand before his stupefied face. "But don't worry about it. You don't have to tell me a thing. Eat your stew."

Matt picked up the soup spoon, then set it down. "There are some things I just can't tell you. Shouldn't tell you."

"I should hope so." She took several gusty swallows of the thick medley of vegetables and beef cubes.

Matt suddenly realized he was ravenous, and decided it was better to obey than to equivocate.

"Water?" she asked after a while. "Or the bishop's brandy?"

"The bishop can keep his brandy," he said, laughing. "Water's fine. This is great stew."

"You're hungry." She got up and bustled. "I bet you have three cartons of yogurt and some frozen dinners at your apartment."

Matt didn't bother disagreeing. She brought big plastic water glasses to the table. He discovered he was thirsty too. Must be a salty stew.

"So," she said, seated again. "I never see that darling redheaded girl you brought to mass."

"She's thirty."

"She's still a darling girl."

"Yeah." No point in debating the truth. "I think so too."

Molina drove home, the streetlights stroking across the Toyota's hood and windshield like slow-motion strobes.

The light, motion, and rhythm were hypnotic, an environmental sleeping pill acting on her exhaustion. Even keeping the windows open didn't help. Street noise came muted and rhythmic too. Everything conspired to lull her into numb complacency.

She drove deliberately, with extreme caution, trying not to think of the events behind her at work, or farther behind her at Rancho Exotica. She finally spotted the lit spire of Our Lady of Guadalupe, and let her tense muscles relax. Only a couple of blocks more to go. Here she was back where she had started—what? Only six hours ago.

The sound of the motor turning off after she'd pulled into the driveway was sweeter than hearing "Summertime" sung by Lady Day.

She sat in the car, hands still on the wheel, and envisioned the scene at headquarters.

Thanks to cell phones, more lawyers had descended on the place than cops and suspected killers.

The animal-rights people had called in the big-time lawyers to defend the Animal Oasis and Kirby Granger. An operation like his had its celebrity supporters, but this was ridiculous. The final straw had been when Johnnie Cochran had shown up, representing the Cloaked Conjuror.

Molina lowered her head until her forehead rested on the top of the steering wheel. What a comedy of counsels for the defense. All she needed was another secretive magician meddling with her cases.

Of course Leonora had her legions too, not only a high-priced attorney but some sister members of a domestic violence therapy group. Molina had not been surprised, thanks to Temple Barr tipping her off to the reason behind Leonora's plastic surgery before they left the ranch: not vanity but violence.

The only suspect in the case who wasn't up to his neck in defense attorneys was Osiris the leopard, who remained in custody at the Animal Oasis, and who was, like every other detainee, definitely not talking.

Molina had left the circus, the zoo, the human tragedy to her detectives. She could see the outcome now: Leonora Burkleo would get a suspended sentence; no prosecuting attorney would let a jury see that face and the reasons behind it and expect to get a conviction.

Granger was a goner. He had cared so much about his animal haven that he had ceased to care about himself. The Animal Oasis would go on, he had seen to that, but he would serve a long sentence in a compound for dangerous and displaced and often ill-served humans.

As for Rancho Exotica, from the buzz she was hearing among Leonora Burkleo, the animal-rights activists, and assorted attorneys, it would probably and ironically end up acquiring the canned-hunt property and animals.

She shook her head to jar out the ironies and went into the house.

Dolores was waiting at the door with an accusation. "You're later than you thought."

"No interrogations. I've had enough of that downtown."

Molina marched for the kitchen, taking her paddle holster from the back of her belt and laying it on the counter while she opened cupboards scrounging something, some food, crackers, cookies, she didn't know.

"Mariah went to bed at ten?"

368 • Carole Nelson Douglas

Dolores shrugged. "She went into her room at ten."

Molina's hand patted the shelf and found the envelope of tens and fives she kept ready for Dolores. "A long evening. I'm sorry. What is it, eight and a half hours?"

Dolores nodded, skeptical and watching, as Molina counted out bills, then hissed in aggravation and counted them out again.

"You work too hard," Dolores said.

"Yes. But tomorrow I can sleep in until noon. And I will."

"Tomorrow is Sunday. Last mass is at eleven."

"I didn't forget," Molina said, though she did add, "I went to mass already this evening."

Disappointed at failing to catch Molina skipping church, Dolores took her money and sniffed, "Drunkard's mass."

"Not in my case. Unless you count"—she waved the open packet of cookies her questing hand had found in the cupboard—"an Oreo cookie addiction."

Dolores shrugged again. "We always go to nine o'clock mass."

"Then you'd better head home and get some rest yourself," Molina suggested, seeing her out.

Dolores was a traditional Latina mother, herding her household to church and to distraction. Still, the method had worked for a long time, and most of Our Lady of Guadalupe's parishioners were honest, hardworking people. The neighborhood gangs fought their wars away from home.

When she shut the door on Dolores, the house's silence settled on her like a pall of dust.

She sat on the comfortably lived-on sofa and carefully peeled the chocolate cookie top off an Oreo.

A meow in the dining area drew her attention to Catarina, or was it Tabitha, stalking on gangly adolescent legs to the sofa to inspect the kill?

The young cat leaped up to sniff long and hard at the uncapped Oreo. With a patented feline look of disinterest, it moved down the sofa and began grooming its face and feet.

Carmen began licking off the cream filling in catlike bites.

The usually forbidden pure sugar fix was as potent as brandy.

The Rancho Exotica case would sort itself out over the next few days, but Osiris was off the hook. The leopard sleeps tonight.

Soon the lieutenant sleeps tonight. No night-crawling on the trail of the stripper killer. Not tonight at least. Not until she had figured out what to do about Rafi Nadir. And Max Kinsella.

The victim at the Kitty City parking lot had been too shaken to identify her attacker, who had come up behind her. She thought he was a dark-haired man.

He could have been Nadir. He could have been Kinsella.

Carmen opened another Oreo and began on another circle of icing, pale as a communion host but not tasting of paste.

Not a bad theory: Kinsella attacks her, she gets off a scream, he runs. Nadir, leaving the club, hears the scream as he's about to drive away, runs to investigate (he is a professional security man, after all), and a watching Kinsella decides to come out of cover and pretend to discover the problem *after* Nadir.

Who did the guy think he was, anyway, acting like a cop? He had always been a suspect in her book, and he was still one. For the fact was, every time and every place that Rafi Nadir had been on the scene and easily capable of doing the crime, Max Kinsella had been there too, whether he was got up as "Vince" or as some self-appointed vigilante.

No, the suspect list for the death of Cher Smith wasn't narrowing down. It was getting longer.

Carmen eyed her icing-free cookie and tossed it toward the waste-basket at the end of the kitchen/living room divider.

She made a basket.

"Max! I expected you to call hours ago."

"I had some thinking to do."

"Kirby, you mean."

"I worked with him, Temple. He was my Birdman of the Mojave when I was doing my act. I had to figure out why he did it."

"Killed Van Burkleo?"

"Hell, no! That's understandable. It's even more understandable when you realize that the Animal Oasis and Rancho Exotica touch borders. I haven't finished looking into it, but I've uncovered a money trail. Cyrus had bought into a consortium that held the mort-gage on the Oasis land and wanted to add it to the hunt ranch. I've discovered that Granger couldn't stop a foreclosure. He owed a lot of money, especially since he stopped working with trained animals.

High principles often mean no profit. Apparently, he had trouble with it philosophically. Even with my innocent cockatoo illusion. You know, animals that are trainable thrive on challenge, but more recently Kirb saw it all as exploitation. That's what I've been able to figure out so far."

"So . . . he killed Van Burkleo to stop the brutal acquisition of his peaceable animal kingdom for a murderous purpose."

"I don't think he meant to kill Van Burkleo. He went over there in a rage when he discovered what was up. I think the death was accidental. Then he began figuring out how to cover it up."

"To save his skin."

"No. It was always the animals' skins he wanted to save. That's what got him off the rails in the first place."

"Then what haven't you figured out? You've unraveled how and why."

"Shooting at the panther was so out of character. He'd killed to protect the animals. Why kill an animal?"

"So. You tell me."

"The panther was trained, I told you that."

"Like the leopard. Who, by the way, is cleared of all charges, right?"

"I don't see Molina bringing even a second-degree murder charge against a leopard. Not even Molina."

"Your favorite long arm of the law."

"Yeah. And not often long enough away. My theory is that the panther was trained by Kirby, long ago. It was a witness when he took the leopard inside. He got the leopard back. The panther was out there. It must have preyed on Kirby's mind. What if the panther was sent to his facility because the ranch was sold or shut down on Van Burkleo's death? What if his relationship with the panther was observed by somebody who could put leopard and panther together? And then him as trainer of them both?"

"Somebody like you, Max. You coming around, with me. Asking questions. Looking at files."

"Don't say it! Don't say that I precipitated it. I think what happened to Van Burkleo unhinged Kirby. He was so . . . antiviolence, and here he'd become an example for the other side. He never underestimated animals, how smart they were, what they knew and how they showed their emotions, their perceptions. He respected them enough to panic, talked himself into believing he had to kill the panther to protect the Animal Oasis. He killed, and he became what he most hated."

"Max, everybody who murders kills the thing he or she hates the most. When I think about it, there's usually a noble reason underneath it all. Every killer is a wronged person in his or her own mind. Every victim is wrong. Somehow."

"Somehow. Anyway, you say that Molina took Granger into custody. And Raf?"

"I told him to run, and he did. I don't understand why you wanted him out of it."

Max chuckled bitterly over the phone. "I don't understand it either, Temple. Were you able to handle him all right?"

"Fine. He . . . it was funny, he had this weird pull to stay and be in charge of things, like he was responsible somehow. But he also had this instinct to run. Is he . . . someone to worry about?"

"Oh, yes. But not for you, I think. Not for you."

" 'Not for you.' Isn't that a line from a song? 'But not for you.' I can't quite place it."

"Don't try, darling Temple. I'm just glad you're safe at home, even if Molina made you get there with Devine."

"How did you know?"

"I always know what's important to me. Don't you know you've got someone to watch over you?"

"Another song, another line. You are full of lines, Max Kinsella."

"And you are worthy of every one."

"Why, thank you."

"Good night, Temple."

"Good night, Max."

Chapter 53

Cat Burglar

"This is the first time I've ever literally been a cat burglar," the first man in black whispered to the second man in black.

"I don't know why I let you talk me into this stunt," the second man in black said, "but I have to admit I'm enjoying it."

Their voices came soft and distorted, like the buzzing of insects more than human syllables.

But they understood each other.

Like twins, they both wore tiger-striped cat faces that resembled camouflage paint. It was hard to see the human features beneath the feline.

They crouched together, catlike, in obscuring foliage as dark as the night itself, watching a dappled big cat lying in the moonlight.

"You'll have to lose the gloves when you handle him," the first man warned. "He needs to recognize your scent immediately."

"And what are you going to do to handle yours?"

"Hope he remembers me. Get yours first."

The man rose, tall as a Joshua tree it seemed, and approached the fence. He stripped off his black gloves and thrust them through his broad black belt, then held his fingers to the wires and made a scratching noise with his bare fingers against the metal-studded leather of his belt.

The leopard rose, darted to him, and sniffed his hand. It rubbed its side against the fence as the man bent and began snipping thick wires with the heavy-duty cutter he removed from his boot.

When he pulled the torn section away, he bent to put a collar almost as big as his belt around the leopard's neck. "Hello, Osiris," the odd mechanical voice whispered. "I've come to take you home." A lead clicked onto the collar ring as Osiris stepped through the gaping wires like an obedience-school dog.

The second man in black edged nearer, cautiously extending his bare hand to Osiris. After the big cat had sniffed his fill, the man straightened and took the wire cutters from his partner in crime.

"That other cat doesn't know you," Osiris's master warned. "It might be a lot harder to bring along."

"That's why you'll take Osiris to the van first. I'll come along after you've got him caged again."

The man nodded, and led the leopard off into the moonlit desert landscape.

Max prowled past some other containment areas, evoking a guttural noise from a majestically maned lion.

His prey was in the next enclosure, and harder than the leopard to spot: black as any shadow. Max tried the same trick of scraping his nails on fabric, but nothing happened. He bent to begin cutting the fence. Though the sound snapped at the night's quiet no one came. This visit had been timed to avoid the guard's nightly rounds.

The snipping sounds did what fingernails didn't.

In an instant, Max was face-to-face with a huge black fanged head.

He froze, still crouched in place. Opened a bare hand and hoped the scent would waft into the massive black nostrils only inches from his own masked nostrils.

The panther snuffled noisily at his hand, at his hidden face. Max stood as slowly as he could, inch by inch.

The panther rubbed absently on one stiffening leg. Max stroked his head. He unfastened the huge leather collar and leash he carried coiled around his neck—his cat burglar garb didn't have the secret pockets that the Cloaked Conjuror's did. He slipped it as softly as a wish around the beast's neck, took a deep breath, and was rewarded with a short purr.

He began walking, and the panther, reacting to previous training, walked with him.

The sixty yards to the palo verde thicket that concealed the black van seemed the longest of his life. There was not only the panther stalking beside him, who might balk at any moment, but the open desert where he and it made such obvious targets.

The guard would be coming by here soon, but Max didn't dare run, or look back.

They passed as if on parade, man and cat, until the stunted trees, gathered like an inkblot, were close enough to absorb them into their safety and shadow.

CC stood at the gaping van doors, patting the carpeted floor of a cage. "Up," his mechanical voice rasped.

As the panther leaped into the cage, CC swung the door shut and Max closed the van doors as softly as he could.

It was not softly enough.

"Hey!" a distant voice objected.

They scrambled for the front of the van, CC's cape flying around his figure.

A powerful flashlight beam caught Max's mask full on, just before he leaped into the van's driver's seat where the keys were still in the ignition.

The engine growled into life, generating an echo of growls from the enclosures behind them.

"Stop!" the guard was shouting, his voice vibrating from his sand-pounding pursuit.

Max gunned the motor, spraying gravel, and drove back into the desert, soon leaving everything behind him but sagebrush.

Behind his ever-present mask, CC laughed. "This was a kick. I don't get out much. I'm glad you forced me to come along. But why did you want to take the panther as well? It complicated everything."

"It was a performing animal too. It craves more of a life than retirement, no matter how cushy. I figure you can always use a good cat."

"But did you ever figure out who took Osiris and why?"

Max stared into the desert vistas passing through the stabbing spotlights of the van's headlamps. "The Synth was sending you a message all right. It was a spite crime. You would never have seen Osiris again. They sold the animal to Van Burkleo for a few hundred, no questions asked, expecting it to be dead meat in days."

CC growled through his mask, a sound of disgust that was echoed by one of the big cats. "Why wasn't he?"

"The Synth didn't reckon on Van Burkleo's vanity. I checked up on him and his widow. Van Burkleo was born in July. He was a Leo, astrologically. His wife's birth name was Linda. She reinvented herself as Leonora after she married him. Like a lot of hunters, Cyrus Van Burkleo identified with his prey; even the women of big-game hunters drip with pricey gold charms of lions and tigers and bears. Then along comes a leopard named Osiris, an unintentional tribute to the mighty hunter's first name. He probably intended to keep it as a mascot."

"That didn't suit the purpose of the Synth."

"No, and I suspect they had an agent here at the ranch to see to that, but Granger charged in and changed everything."

"If the big-game people identify with their prey, why kill it?"

"Some people need to conquer any creatures big enough to kill them. I've always thought they're out to find, track, and silence the fear inside themselves. Or maybe it's the eternal independence of the Other they're out to kill. They're like the worm Ouroboros, swallowing their own mortality."

"Whew. That's way too philosophical for me. I'm just glad to get Osiris back."

CC looked over his shoulder. "Those two are nosing each other through the bars like a couple of small-town gossips over a fence. They make a handsome pair. I wonder what they're communicating."

"At least they get along. I'm wondering something else: what the guard will make of his glimpse of my face wearing your mask."

"Shoot! Do you think I'll be fingered for this kidnapping?"

"I doubt he got a good enough look to be sure what he saw, but maybe we'll start some leopardmen rumors. I'd like to shake up the Synth."

"Fine. You do that. I'll get back to business as usual. Osiris will be happy to get back to his usual digs. We'll have to rig a separate setup for, for . . . what should I call the black one?"

Pulling off the mask, Max smiled and thought of Midnight Louie.

"Call him Lucky."

Midnight Louie Enjoys Being a Pussycat

There was a time when I dreamed of being a Lord of the Jungle. Or the Plain. Or whatever.

I pictured myself away from the Big V, this urban Neon Jungle in the desert, and out where the Wildlife commences, where the lion and the wildebeest play. (In the lion's case, it is probably playing with its food, which is a wildebeest.)

I contemplated lolling about the veldt under a spreading baobab tree while Midnight Louise prowled docilely off to round up some food on the hoof for my royal appetite.

My claws, the size of jumbo shrimp, would pulse in and out of their gigantic sheaths.

A few worshipful cubs would gambol about the edges of my magnificent eight-hundred-pound frame stretched out to its full twelve or thirteen feet. A flick of my powerful aft appendage would drive clouds of flies into retreat, too insignificant and frightened to come to rest upon my handsome hide.

Oops. My handsome hide.

Maybe a handsome hide is not a biological advantage in this modern world.

Now that I have seen the lives of Jungle Lords up close and personal, I understand why they are such an endangered species and why my subcompact version of lordliness is mostly endangered by overbreeding. From what I have seen, Beauty and the Beast are a combination that results in imprisonment and premature death.

Even those lordly ones with glamor jobs in the show ring or onstage are in danger of being downsized in their old age and thrown into the brutal arena for the amusement of a bunch of feeble humans whose IQ is about the caliber of the firearms they carry.

Although we pocket-size domestic varieties also suffer neglect and abuse, at least we are too small to make into rugs! And our mugs would look pretty ridiculous on some Great White Hunter's wall.

Thank Bast for small favors, of which I guess I am one.

I will never wish to be King of the Beasts again.

I have just come to this momentous resolve when my Miss Temple wanders into our bedroom and finds me sprawled catty-corner across the comforter. (Little does she know that I have barely beaten her back to domicile, sweet domicile. Thanks to the hysterical Miss Leonora leaving the Storm door wide open for any footsore souls in need of a discreet ride, Louise and I slipped into the backseat and hid on the floor.)

I expect to be gently moved aside, but instead she sits on the end of the bed and regards me with what I can only describe as wistful fondness.

"Oh, Louie." She sighs. (The dames are always sighing around me, and do not doubt that I take full credit for it.)

"Apparently," she begins in a confessional tone—you would think that I was Matt Devine—"apparently I have not been a responsible pet owner." (She has a pet? News to me. This I must look into. I do not like interlopers.)

"Apparently I am supposed to keep you safe at home. I

should nail shut your bathroom window escape route, and see that you nevermore shall roam." Here she frowns. "But you roamed all the way out to the Rancho Exotica. And you prevented a panther from being cruelly hunted down and shot. And your presence unmasked a murderer. So you ended up saving, in the long run, lions and tigers and bears. Oh, my. And you have in the short run, and on more than one occasion, saved *me*. What is a mother to do?"

(Here she fondly smooths the hair on my brow.)

"Obviously, Louie, you are not an ordinary cat."

This she intones as if it were a revelation.

"Obviously, you are especially trustworthy, loyal, helpful, friendly, courteous, kind, obedient, cheerful, thrifty, brave, clean, and irreverent. Well, maybe not 'obedient,' but I would not put that word into a wedding vow anyway. Obviously, dispensations have to be made in your case, and your case alone. Since you are now reproductively responsible, I suppose I will have to let you be about your business, no matter what the world at large will think.

"The others just do not understand. Rather than *you* having anything to fear from the world at large, the world at large has much to fear from *you*. You can take care of creatures great and small, including me. This is your mission, Louie, and I will not stand in your way, despite my puny fears."

She bends down and kisses me tenderly on the right ear. *Ummmm.*

"Just promise me one thing, big boy. Take care of yourself too."

Not to worry, Miss Temple. Is the Dalai Lama Tibetan?

Okay, she did not say it all *exactly* like that.

But it was close enough.

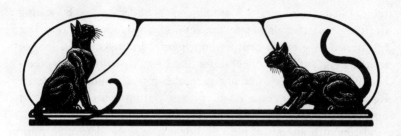

Carole Nelson Douglas Considers Louie's Future

It's hard to accept that Midnight Louie has actually learned a lesson from his latest case.

I thought he was far too feline to admit that he had anything left to learn.

Perhaps the lesson we could all learn is not to envy creatures apparently greater than we are. Often they face greater stresses as well. This goes for people as well cats.

I should mention that canned hunts are illegal in Nevada, although not in other states, so the Rancho Exotica is a totally fictional enterprise. But a state that boasts Area 51 and legalized prostitution ranches could very well spawn an illegal animal-hunting outfit aiming to satisfy monied clients. Those as appalled as Temple and I by the notion should look up "canned hunts" on the Web to find and support organizations that are working to ban the practice.

And real-life hunt breakers are more cautious about where, when, and how they disrupt a hunt, usually keeping a safe distance from their armed opponents, such as foiling mass bird shootings by scaring the prey into the air before the hunters are ready to shoot. I've researched nineteenth-century hunt parties in England and France for the Irene Adler historical series that I resume writing in September 2001, with *Chapel Noir*, about another infamous hunter, Jack the Ripper. These aristocratic country-house outings with their aura of upper-class civility destroyed an obscene number of animals: thousands upon thousands of birds and deer in a single day, often hundreds by a single shooter.

So given the assertion that many big cats who end up on canned-hunt ranches are less able to protect themselves than the average alley cat, it was only appropriate to let a decidedly "unaverage" alley cat take on the bully boys with the guns personally. Louie really dug into his assignment.

Some readers have fretted that Louie will not be giving (and getting) comeuppance far enough into the future to suit them. I hasten to reassure: Midnight Louie and company are launched on a twenty-seven-entry meganovel, and are less than halfway there.

That means that unsolved murders from past books and the characters' ongoing personal quests are all part of an overarching background plotline that will be tied up by the series' end.

For those who fear the Z book ending Midnight Louie's many lives too soon, I can only remind them that Louie appeared in a miniseries of four romances-with-mystery before he launched this mystery-with-relationships sequence, so he's unlikely to curl up his toes and say die at the drop of an arbitrary letter like Z.